The Right Kind of War

The Right Kind of War

John McCormick

Naval Institute Press
Annapolis, Maryland

LIBRARY OF CONGRESS CATALOGING-IN-PUBLICATION DATA
McCormick, John
The right kind of war / John McCormick.
p.   cm.
ISBN 1-55750-574-8
1. World War, 1939–1945—Campaigns—Pacific Area—Fiction.
I. Title.
PS3563.C34456R54   1992   92-19546
813′.54—dc20   CIP

Printed in the United States of America on acid-free paper ∞

3   5   7   9   8   6   4   2

First printing

For the strawberry blonde

The Right Kind of War

At the Point

We took turns at the point. In the jungles of the northern Solomons, the underbrush was so dense, the vines and creepers and lianas and bamboo thickets so unyielding, that the Marine Raider in the lead, the man at the point, slashing his way with a machete, was soon worn down. Every five or ten minutes, as we shoved through the thick jungle single file at three-yard intervals, the second man in line moved forward to relieve the point man of his place and his machete; and, already breathing a little easier, the first man dropped back to the end of the file.

There was a second, more compelling reason to take turns at the point. In those occasional murderous sparring matches that erupted in the jungle, the Japanese—if they spotted us before we spotted them—would invariably shoot our point man first. It was a grim business, a Marine Raider game of Russian roulette. Yet it was a duty from which no man in a patrol excused himself. When it came to taking risks, all Raiders, officers or enlisted, were equal. Whether resolute or fearful, energetic or weary, each Raider, when his turn came, moved up to take the point.

In battle too, we shared the burden. For the 4th Raider Battalion that burden began in July 1943, when we wiped out the Japanese on the island of Vangunu, two hundred miles north of Guadalcanal. We then moved on to eliminate the enemy's small garrison at Viru Harbor. Convinced that we had done well in our first combat experience, our leaders sent a flotilla of destroyers to

1

ferry us to a rest camp on Guadalcanal. But only a few days later we were back in action. The 1st Raider Battalion, under strength because of heavy losses the year before in the fighting on Tulagi and Guadalcanal, had been stopped by the enemy during an attack near Bairoko Harbor in northern New Georgia. Sent north to help them out, we hurried to a ridge a few miles south of Bairoko and bivouacked several days while waiting for a battalion from the Army's 37th Division to join us. While we waited we sent out patrols each day, in every direction. Some patrols encountered the Japanese, and we lost more point men.

As a tommy gunner in the 3d Squad, 3d Platoon, of Dog Company, I was frequently invited to volunteer for jungle patrols and had frequent opportunities to take the point. My luck had been good. But there were men in our platoon whose luck had run out. Swede Meyer, late one afternoon, had just taken the point when he blundered into an unexpected clearing and caught three slugs in the chest from a Nambu machine gun. We lost Jerry Cramden at the point the next day to a Jap sniper and a .25-caliber bullet through the head. Other platoons had their losses too, light losses, perhaps, in the larger scheme of things. But the prospect of taking the point each day, even for just a few minutes several times during a patrol, became so nerve-racking that we looked forward to the time when we could make a frontal assault on Bairoko and get the whole deadly business over with.

Not only were the patrols deadly, they were a source of considerable irritation as well. Why, we asked each other, did the Japs insist on shooting the point man first? The proper and practical way for them to conduct an ambush, to kill the most Marines, was to let the point man pass by along with perhaps a half dozen others before attacking. But when the Japs shot the point man first, the rest of the men in the patrol scattered, formed a skirmish line, and fired back with rifles and machine guns. All that firepower whining and crackling and ricocheting through the underbrush gave the enemy something to think hard about; and very often they retreated in a hurry.

The fourth morning of the battalion's wearisome wait near Bairoko, Captain McNail, our company commander, sent the 3d Squad on a dawn patrol into the mangrove swamps below the ridge where, the afternoon before, a C Company patrol had traded shots with a platoon or so of Japanese. If the Japs were still down there, we were to surprise them and treat them, as McNail put it, "to a breakfast of hot lead."

Not as enthusiastic about the assignment as Captain McNail, we pushed through three or four tension-filled miles of jungle and swamp without running into anything more dangerous than the usual mosquitoes, land crabs, and flies. By late morning, safe, sound, and much relieved, we were back at the bivouac. While most of the guys in the patrol dug out what rations were left in their packs, I went off to ask our corpsman what could be done about the jungle rot on my legs. In a half dozen places on my ankles and shins, deep, ugly, and painful abscesses had developed, each about the diameter of a quarter. The worst one was on my right ankle, just where the top of my shoe made contact. After swabbing the affected areas with something that looked, smelled, and stung like iodine, the corpsman pronounced me in excellent health and fit to return to immediate duty.

As I slung my tommy gun and drifted back toward the 3d Squad foxholes, I ran into Bill Werden, a friend from boot-camp days. The only men in our sixty-man boot-camp platoon to volunteer for the Raiders, he and I had gone up to Camp Pendleton together and had been good friends ever since. Not long after becoming a Raider, Werden had joined the Scouts and Snipers Platoon and had adapted so readily that he was now considered the most skillful reconnaissance man in the battalion.

"Moe!" he said. "Just the guy I'm looking for. I need one more tommy gunner for a ten-man patrol Colonel Maxim wants me to take out."

"What?" I said. "Goddamn, Bill, why me? There're seven hundred other Raiders been sitting on their asses around here all morning."

3

"Two reasons," said Werden. "You can shoot straight, and you ain't ever had malaria."

I understood the first reason. I could shoot so straight that the Marine Corps, in what was for it an unusually generous policy, paid me, and all other expert riflemen, an extra five dollars a month.

"What's this shit about malaria?" I asked. Although 90 percent of the 4th Raiders were either suffering from malaria or, their bones aching with fever and their ears ringing from quinine, were just recovering from it, I was apparently immune, and so was Werden.

"We ain't taking any malaria people on this trip," he said. "They'd fall out before we got two miles."

I jerked up my dungarees and revealed the jungle rot. "I ain't got malaria," I said, "but look at these beauties."

Werden gave the ugly ulcers a scornful glance. "Hell, Moe," he said. "That ain't nothing. The sting will only make you run faster."

I tried one more time. "I just got off patrol," I said. "Been out since first light."

Werden laughed. "That's good news. You'll be all wound up and ready to run." He paused a minute. "Your tommy gun will give us five submachine guns, three BARs, and two M-1s. With all that firepower, we can take on the whole Jap army."

I wasn't so sure we could take on the Jap army or even a Jap platoon, but I had used up all my arguments.

"Where're we running?"

"Not far," he said. "A few miles along the ridge."

The crude maps that had been issued to our battalion showed that the ridge where we were camped rose about two hundred feet above the surrounding mangrove swamps and ran straight east for two or three miles before curving south toward the big Japanese base at Munda.

"Yesterday afternoon I found a native trail a couple of miles east," Werden went on. "Colonel Maxim wants us to follow it toward Munda for maybe ten miles. The Japs down there are supposed to be getting ready to move toward Bairoko. They've probably already discovered the south end of the trail." He paused and looked at my tommy gun.

"You got ammunition for that thing?"

"Eleven clips," I said. "Two hundred twenty rounds."

"Grenades?"

"Two in my pack."

"Get your ass in gear and find six more. We leave here in ten minutes."

The ulcers on my ankles forgotten, I hurried off to borrow six grenades and to tell Don Floyd, our platoon leader, that I had been shanghaied for a combat patrol. Then I trotted back to the big banyan at the south side of camp where Werden and the rest of his volunteers were gathering.

"OK," Werden was saying, "single file, three-yard intervals. I'll take the point."

No one said anything. It was understood that when Bill Werden led a patrol, he took the point and kept it. Even in the trackless rain forests, Werden seemed to know instinctively the path of least resistance. And whether in deep jungle or on a narrow trail, he could smell out a Jap ambush. In fact, Werden had been put ashore from a submarine weeks before either the 1st or 4th Raider battalions landed on the island and had scouted the entire area from Segi Point to Munda and north to Bairoko.

Now he glanced at his GI watch. "Colonel Maxim said to take off at high noon. We got five minutes."

As we milled around waiting for the last few minutes to tick by, I noticed for the first time that Werden had a sheathed samurai sword fastened to his pack. I pointed to it. "Where'd that blade spring from, Bill?"

Werden grinned. "Borrowed it from a Jap major at Enogai," he said. "He ain't going to need it no more." He looked at his watch again. "Let's go," he said, "before Colonel Maxim gets itchy and calls off the game."

Off we went through the light undergrowth along the ridge until, about two miles east, we hit a narrow trail. On that trail we

5

moved fast: a hundred yards at a rapid trot Marines call double time; the second hundred at a fast-paced walk; the third hundred at double time again; the fourth at that quick walk; and so on for mile after mile. It was the way of the Raiders, a pace that required much stamina but ate up the miles.

At times only a trace through the trees, at others perhaps a yard wide, the trail held to the ridge line, curving here and there with the natural contours of that rough land but heading generally east until, about five miles out, the ridge took a sudden swing to the south. Here we stopped for a short breather. So far, of the Japs, we had seen and heard nothing.

As we rested, Werden scouted ahead before returning in a few minutes with a brief admonition. "Cut the pace to a steady walk," he said. "I'm going on alone for a couple of miles. No need to worry about an ambush. If there's one up ahead, I'll know it before they see me. Give me ten minutes and then come on." He gave us a half wave and took off up the trail on the run. An hour later, still moving steadily south, we rounded a turn in the trail, and there stood Bill Werden.

"Whoa," he said in a low voice. "Company's coming. Jap patrol. They'll be here in about twenty minutes. We got to get ready for them in a hurry."

"Damn!" said Jim Akers, who in Werden's absence had taken the point. "How many?"

"Fifteen, maybe twenty," said Werden. "We'll stop them right here." He pointed to the jungle on one side of the trail. "Good cover in that stuff. Get in there and spread out about three yards apart. Moe, you stick with me."

As our eight comrades eased into the jungle, I followed Werden for a few yards back up the trail, the way we had come, to the spot where it made its sudden turn left.

"There's got to be a way to make their point man stop right here," said Werden. "Right here at this turn in the trail."

I knew what was going through Werden's mind. If the leader of the Jap patrol stopped, the entire patrol would also stop, and,

6

waiting in our ambush, we would be provided with fixed, not moving targets.

Werden stood there puzzling it out for just a few seconds and suddenly smiled. "Moe," he said, "pull that samurai sword out of there."

Beginning to guess his plan, I seized the hilt and pulled it free of its sheath. For a moment I held that sword and admired it—the long, razor-sharp, shining blade, the slight, artistic curve, the perfect balance.

"Let's have it," said Werden. He took it, held and admired it also a few seconds, and then, just beyond the turn of the trail, plunged its point into the ground. It quivered there, three feet long, a shaft of sunlight streaming through the high jungle canopy flickering off the naked blade.

"There!" said Werden. "That will stop any man in the Jap army. The bastards love those blades more than they love their mothers."

He went quickly back down the trail, peering into the jungle where our men were hidden.

"Good," he said in a voice just loud enough for all to hear. "They won't see you till it's too late. Get those safeties off your weapons. When I whistle, spray the bastards in front of you. Give 'em the whole clip. Don't stop shooting just because they go down. Put in another clip and blast 'em again."

He turned and came rapidly toward me. I had already backed into a thicket of canes and vines. He shoved in a yard or two to my left. "I'll take the lead man, Moe," he said softly, "and the two right behind him. You spray on down the line."

In silence we waited, hearing for a long ten minutes only the rustle of leaves and the steady buzzing of flies. Then, from some distance down the trail, the sound of approaching footsteps— heavy, rapid, emphatic—until, like some pack of jungle animals, the Japs were there.

They were moving fast, those men of that Japanese patrol—not running but walking rapidly and purposefully, close together and single file. These were not the usual run of Japanese troops we had

7

met and disposed of at Vangunu and Viru. These men were different. They were older, their uniforms a kind of dirty khaki, their leggings old-fashioned and wrapped. Their shoes were not the rubber-soled, split-toed kind, but heavy and hobnailed. Their helmets, more like those of Japanese paratroopers than those of the regular Army rank and file, were clamped tightly on their heads.

They were heavily armed. Three of them carried Nambu light machine guns, each man holding the long, black, ring-grooved barrel in one hand, the butts balanced on their right shoulders. Three men, in addition to their rifles, carried the small but deadly knee mortars; two, right behind the leader, were armed with short-barreled submachine guns of a type I had not seen among Japanese troops before. Every man had, stuck in his belt, three or four grenades that looked like German potato mashers.

They were, all of them, hard-faced, tough, disciplined, determined. It was evident in the way each rifleman carried his weapon, not loosely and carelessly slung, but gripped tightly in one hand and with a long bayonet fixed in place. These men were veterans, professionals, warriors—the samurai. They had bunched up a little there on that narrow trail, hastening to keep up with their grim leader.

That leader: stocky, powerful, heavy-featured—pistol ready in his right hand, samurai sword swinging at his side. Wearing a look of perpetual anger and pride and hate, he pounded along looking neither right nor left, rounded the bend in the trail, and halted as abruptly as if he had run into an impenetrable wall.

"Ka!" His involuntary shout was a loud, husky guttural.

Behind him the whole patrol crashed to a stop, piling into and overrunning one another, the man immediately in front of me nearly driving his bayonet into his comrade just ahead.

Into that momentary chaos on the trail came the sound of Werden's whistle. It was not the whistle of a man whose throat and lips are dry with fear. It was loud, clear, intense. As one man, we reacted—a sudden crash of sound and fury: one hundred rounds of .45-caliber slugs from the tommy guns, sixty rounds of .30-

8

caliber bullets from the three BARs, sixteen rounds of .30-caliber bullets from the two M-1s. The men of the Jap patrol were slammed on back and side by the force of our lethal blast, nearly all of them dead before they fell, the others catching extra bullets as they crumpled beside the trail.

Our ambush had been a near perfect one. Not quite. A second or so after Werden's whistle, as we fired full bore into the doomed patrol, one more Jap had slid onto the scene. The last man in the patrol, he had apparently gotten a few yards behind and had been running to catch up. Just as we opened fire his momentum took him into the edge of the action. Someone among us had staggered him with a quick shot, but, limping badly, he had dived into the jungle across the trail and disappeared.

Quickly we released our empty clips, rammed new clips into place, and, as the smoke cleared away, examined the bodies on the trail. They were all lifeless, their leader still with that look of hate and anger impressed on his features.

"One got away, Bill," said Jim Akers.

"I saw," said Werden, "I'll get him. You guys search these bastards. Moe, take a look at their point man. He's got a map case." He headed off into the jungle.

Before I tore open the Jap leader's map case, I removed the pistol from the limp fingers of his right hand. It was a beauty. About a .32-caliber, it had a serrated wooden grip and a fine balance. The half loop of the trigger guard was extra large up front, apparently to accommodate a gloved finger. This pistol had been produced for men who fought in colder climes. I held it only a second or two, then put the safety on, released the clip, and stuck clip and pistol into my pack. If we ever got back to Guadalcanal, it would make great trade bait.

About the time I finished searching the leader's map case, I heard off in the jungle the quick rattle of a tommy gun. Werden had finished off the straggler. By then I had also relieved the patrol leader of his samurai sword. He would need it no longer. In a few minutes Werden was back.

He and I and the others in our patrol walked along the line of shattered men making certain that no wounded Jap was left to die alone. Among that first half dozen lying there, where the .45-caliber slugs from the tommy guns had done their deadly work, there was not much blood, not much torn flesh. Along the middle of the line, however, where six or eight men had been hit by the .30-caliber bullets from our three automatic rifles—the BARs—the bodies were badly torn and the trail was slippery with blood. I was already wondering if our old teacher, Gunner Townsend, had not been right all along about the superiority of the BAR.

Now, satisfied that all of the Japs were thoroughly dead, Werden spoke up. "Pull these bastards off into the jungle," he said. "Maybe the Japs will never find them. All they'll know is that they've lost a twenty-man patrol." As we dragged the dead Japanese a few yards off the trail and covered their bodies with branches and leaves, Werden and a couple of others gathered their weapons. Each of us would haul a heavy load on the way back.

When the cleanup job was done and we made ready to head back along the trail, Werden came up to me as I stood beside the samurai sword, still in the fateful spot where he had plunged its point a half hour earlier.

"OK, Moe," he said. "Stick it back in its scabbard. It's done its job." I pulled the sword out of the ground, once again admiring it for a second, and then shoved it into the scabbard hanging from Werden's pack.

"Take the point on the way back, Moe," he said. "I'll scout around to the rear."

I had taken a couple of steps up the trail when there came a sudden command from behind me.

"Wait a minute!" It was Werden. I stopped. He came up to me. "What the hell happened to that Nambu pistol?"

"Hell, I don't know, Bill," I said. "Somebody must have made off with it."

"You bastard, Moe!" Werden was starting to laugh. "I know goddamned well who made off with it." He gave me a sharp rap on the helmet. "All right. Keep it then! But when you trade it and that sword off to some damned flyboy back on the Canal, I get half the liquor."

Darkness, the total darkness of a jungle night, engulfed us before we were halfway back to the bivouac. We spent the night spread out in the tangled underbrush twenty yards off the trail. Although it was extremely unlikely that the Japanese would surprise us there, we split the watch, half of us always awake, an hour on and an hour off, throughout the long night.

As I sat there cross-legged in the darkness on first watch recalling the events of that violent afternoon, I saw again that Japanese patrol pushing hard along the narrow trail—their grim, fearless leader; their looks of tough, determined, professional pride; their worn weapons and the way they carried them as if each man's rifle or Nambu or knee mortar had become as much a part of him as his leg or his arm.

These men were surely veterans of battle after battle in Manchuria and China, Malaya and Singapore—veterans of hard experience in the business of killing. And an unwelcome, almost annoying thought crept into my mind. Whatever their murderous histories, whatever their killer's intent, they were professionals. It was almost a shame to destroy such men.

Months later I would tell Werden of the fleeting thought that had come to me that night along the Munda trail. He would consider a moment. "The trouble with veterans is they get too sure of themselves. They get to thinking they'll never die. They're setups for surprise."

Next morning we moved out warily with Bill Werden bringing up the rear once again, and since there was now the possibility that we might run into a Jap combat patrol heading our way from Bairoko, the rest of us took turns at the point. By late morning we were back at the bivouac reporting to Colonel Maxim and showing off the weapons we had taken.

We were pleased with ourselves. Especially in those early days and early jungle battles, the Raiders considered themselves the men at the point for the whole Marine Corps, just as we considered the Marine Corps itself at the point of the great American counter-attack up through the central Pacific. For the 4th Raider Battalion, that place at the point had begun in the hills of Camp Pendleton in the fall of 1942.

Werden

Most of the Marines who taught the 4th Raiders the fine art of hand-to-hand combat had trained with the British Commandos well before Pearl Harbor and had even gone on some Commando raids. Later, quite a few of them were in the early fighting on Guadalcanal and Makin. During our months of intensive training at Camp Pendleton in the fall of 1942, those of us in Dog Company drew three of these experts as our tutors.

One was a wiry sergeant named Jackson. I never knew his first name. No matter. We gave him two: Loose Screw and the Spinner. Loose Screw because he occasionally seemed to tilt toward madness; Spinner because he could make a 360-degree turn quicker and oftener than any other man alive. Spinner Jackson labored to instruct us in jujitsu.

The second expert in liquidation techniques, Corporal Batsu Cribbs, explained and demonstrated the nimble art of knife fighting. And the third, Gunner Gut-the-Bastards Townsend, taught us how to fix a bayonet and direct it at the proper angle toward the enemy. The Gunner, who informed us from time to time that, as a tender sixteen-year-old, he had fought the Germans in Belleau Wood during World War I, emphasized again and again and twenty times again that if your bayonet sticks in your target, just pull the trigger of your rifle. The blast and recoil will loosen the bayonet, and you can jerk it right out. What we failed to understand, although we were too timid to challenge the Gunner, was why anyone

13

who still had a cartridge in his rifle would stick a bayonet into a Jap anyway.

In the first months of our Raider indoctrination at Camp Pendleton, we were in the violent presence of Spinner Jackson, Batsu Cribbs, Gunner Townsend—one or all of them—every afternoon. First came Spinner Jackson and jujitsu.

"What I need," the Spinner would announce as soon as he had a platoon-size group of us in front of him, "is a few live demonstration dummies." He would beckon pleasantly to several of the biggest men in the group and, when they stepped reluctantly forward, arrange them in a three- or four-man file in front of him.

"Well now, here are my volunteers," he would say. "All set for some lively exercise." He would reach forward to the first of his so-called dummies, a giant with arms like tree trunks and legs to match. "Relax! I most devoutly wish for you to relax. Assume the attitude of an old coon dog. Relaxation is the key to survival in this game. Nobody's going to get hurt. This is not a hurting game like square dancing or crap shooting. It might sting a little once in a while, but it ain't gonna hurt nobody none."

Satisfied that his live dummies had begun to relax, he would turn his attention to the spectators. "What I'm going to show all you slopeheads," he would shout, "is a harmless throw I call the Commando whip!" And suddenly he would seize his large volunteer by hand or arm, make what appeared to be a lazy shoulder turn, and send his victim rolling in a cloud of dust several yards away.

"Be sure to get all of your weight set on the balls of your feet," he would shout, "and get that shoulder in under the poor bastard you're planning to slam. He'll go sailing away as you have just witnessed." Spinner would turn then toward the unfortunate demonstration dummy, just now emerging from the dust, and chuckle. "When you hit, try to roll through the landing zone. It ain't gonna sting as much if you do." Then, swinging his attention back to his audience once more, he would shake his head sorrowfully. "Don't get the idea that it makes me happy to bounce you people around,"

14

he would say, his tone indicating clearly that he was delighted with every forceful minute of his day. "I'm only trying to keep you from getting your nuts kicked out by the damned Japs. It's what I get paid for." He would then reach out and pitch another live dummy into what fighter pilots have long known as a half roll.

Although day after furious day Spinner Jackson slammed us around and encouraged us to slam each other around on the rocky soil of southern California, D Company had only one serious injury in the jujitsu instruction pit. It occurred when Powder River, one of the larger guys in the 1st Platoon, got a little leverage on Ed Derning one day and tossed him into a playful slam. The slam itself did Derning no serious damage. He was well adjusted to being slammer one minute, slammee the next. The damage was done by the six-inch blade of Ed's stiletto, which had slipped out of its scabbard, preceded him to the ground, and landed so that the point was perfectly positioned to enter the small of his back when he arrived.

Ed was still conscious when the medicos hauled him off to the nearest Navy hospital, his most serious concern being that Platoon Sergeant Floyd might let some other guy in the 1st Squad have his tommy gun. In six weeks he was back, none the worse for his unexpected experience with the stiletto, and Floyd had saved his tommy gun for his return.

This incident, although somewhat bloody and painful for Ed Derning, in no way diminished the intensity of our training program in jujitsu or anything else. We went right on honing our executioner's skills, as a result of which we were for weeks in succession decorated from crown to toe with bruises, cuts, and abrasions.

An early afternoon jujitsu experience with Spinner Jackson usually lasted about an hour. Then when Spinner tired of his play, he would, without granting us so much as a five-minute break, hand us over to Batsu Cribbs. In a trice, Batsu would be dancing around in front of us, wild eyes rolling, demonstrating this or that way of slashing throats or cutting guts.

15

"When you cut the bastard's throat, for Christ's sake, cut it! Cut it deep! You're not giving the son of a bitch a Saturday shave. You're making him a new mouth. Don't, for Christ's sake, be gentle. He won't thank you for it anyway." Then he would stand there for a moment, as if awed by his rhetoric, before suddenly launching into a demonstration-lecture that taught us how to maneuver around until you could ram your stiletto into a Jap's temple.

"I'll double guaran-damn-tee you that will make him spit out his teeth and say thank you!" It was Batsu's daily joke, and it invariably propelled him into a fit of glee.

Batsu's lectures and demonstrations were usually brief. Afterward he would pair us off and sic us onto one another, cautioning us that since this was only practice, we must keep our tempers hobbled and our blades sheathed. We'd get all the carving we wanted, he told us, as soon as we caught up with the damned Japs. After we were thoroughly worn out with all our dancing, arm wrestling, and thrusting, Batsu would give us to the Gunner, but not before offering a final admonition: "Don't just kill Japs! Kill the bastards dead!" Then he would shout, "Take these stoneheads away, Gunner!"

Gunner Townsend was forty-two years old. A powerful man in excellent physical condition, he was as light on his feet as a man fifteen or twenty years younger. He had a full head of dark red hair, crew-cut into a stiff, inch-thick brush. Nevertheless, he seemed to us to be an old man. It was as if one of our fathers had stepped into a pair of Marine Corps dungarees and arrived to teach us all about bayonets. Even so, nobody ever called Gunner Townsend "Pop."

The Gunner liked especially to have us fix bayonets and charge through or over some diabolically constructed barbed-wire entanglements to a row of straw-filled dummies beyond. After letting out a howl that was supposed to freeze our enemies with terror, we could puncture them with our bayonets at leisure. The dummies neither screamed back nor dodged nor ran away. It was the sort of cooperation a novice in bayonet fighting was thankful for.

16

The barbed wire was not so amiable, even though Gunner Townsend assured us that it would do us no harm. "Concertinas are easy," he would announce, and gaze appreciatively at the extended roll of wire and long, sharp barbs. "Each platoon sends three men about three yards ahead of the rest. When these three leaders hit the wire, all they have to do is extend their arms, left hand on forward grip of the rifle, right hand on butt, and then throw themselves face down right on the top of the wire. That flattens it. Then the rest of the guys in the platoon use the first three as a bridge." He would drag three victims out of the crowd, pat them on the back, and announce that he had found three brave volunteers willing to build a bridge with their tough little bodies.

"Now when I yell charge," he would say, "you three run like you got a bobcat on your ass and throw yourself on the wire. The rest of you follow as hard as you can go right behind them. Just use these three as your bridge." He would pause and pat his quaking volunteers. "When you hit the bridge, try to step on their packs. That will be like a springboard to take you clean over the wire."

Meantime, the three victims would be taking on the expressions of poor souls who have been asked to cooperate in their own execution by tying knots in the hangman's noose. The first time the Gunner grabbed three volunteers and outlined the bridging technique, one of them dared to ask a hesitant question. "What about the barbed wire, Gunner? Ain't that gonna cut us up some?"

"What about the barbed wire?" the Gunner repeated. "Well, what *about* the barbed wire?" He paused for a second as if he simply could not comprehend what he had just heard from a strong, brave, youthful Marine. Then there was a definite click as the Gunner snapped his teeth together.

"For Christ's sake, man!" His indignation was building. "What's a few yards of barbed wire compared to a machine gun slug in the guts? Anyway, for Christ's sake, barbed wire is made to ram through the hides of steers. It ain't made for humans. Now when I yell charge, you charge."

17

The Gunner's logic was so compelling that even the chosen three relaxed. At that moment the Gunner bellowed "Charge!" in a voice that carried all the way to San Clemente, and, led by our three bridging devices, we charged.

On the few occasions when I was recognized and honored as a beam in a Gunner Townsend bridge, half the guys in the platoon missed my pack as they went over, and their heavy shoes—we called them boondockers—caught me on the back of my neck or the small of my back. Meantime, the barbed wire I rested on dug numerous holes across my middle. But in a few days my headache went away, my back stopped hurting, and the wounds across my abdomen healed. When I suggested to Gunner Townsend that some of the guys I had unintentionally roughed up during jujitsu practice were maybe getting even, he laughed and recommended that I step on their heads the next time I caught *them* on the wire.

Except for the fact that all our work and practice in the hand-to-hand arts had provided us with some good, healthy exercise, the training was wasted. Although we all thought jujitsu might prove useful in barroom brawls, we never had much of an opportunity to use it in any such practical applications. In the first place, we were seldom given leave to visit the watering holes of Oceanside and San Diego. In the second, the swab jockeys and dogfaces we met the few times we wandered into a bar were mostly peaceful creatures. On the rare occasions when a brawl began, we forgot our training and swung our fists.

We never did develop either enthusiasm or finesse as knife fighters. Although our stilettos were pretty blades, we never used them to stab a Japanese sentry. Our K-bar knives we found especially useful for sharpening tent pegs and opening C-ration cans. But none of us really wanted to get close enough to a live Jap to cut him. And our bayonets? BAR men and tommy gunners were not issued bayonets anyway, and those Raiders armed with M-1 rifles almost never went into action with bayonets fixed. We preferred to shoot, to throw grenades, or to blow the Japs out of hole or cave with our favorite high explosive, nitrostarch. We had ample fire-

18

power. Why risk running up to an enemy soldier if you could shoot him down with a rifle or a machine gun from a hundred yards away?

There were exceptions. The most notable in the 4th Raider Battalion was Bill Werden. Back in boot camp, he'd marched at my side during close order drill, moved immediately ahead of me in the chow line, and occupied the bunk next to mine in the Quonset hut that for eight weeks our platoon called home.

Side by side on the rifle range, we'd practiced for six days and on the seventh fired for record. "Firing for record" means that on a certain day, individual members of the boot-camp platoon fired one hundred rounds each at targets set at ranges of one hundred, two hundred, and three hundred yards. A man's performance on that day established the rating he retained throughout his tour of duty in the Corps. Expert is the highest rating; then comes sharpshooter. All Marines who score below the level of sharpshooter are called marksmen.

At the end of the day on which we fired for record, Werden and I were pleased to find that the two of us and one other man in the platoon had qualified as experts. Our accidental close association for the previous seven weeks had made us mere acquaintances; now we began to regard each other as belonging to a small fraternity of Marine Corps specialists in the most important specialization of all—aiming a rifle and hitting a target.

For a Raider, Werden was not especially big—about six feet two, 185 pounds—and no stronger than many other Marines. But he had a genius for managing that strength in the quickest and most productive way.

Werden had extraordinary blue-ice eyes and, when he spoke to you, he always looked exactly into your own. This habit made some men uneasy, because they realized intuitively that behind those eyes was a force, a presence, an inflexible will. Most of the guys in the boot-camp platoon and later some of the men in the 4th Raiders thought Werden odd.

I liked Werden. I didn't find him odd. I thought of him as one of a rare species: a fearless practitioner of uncompromising logic. If a fifteen-hour-a-day boot-camp routine converted raw recruits into potential Marines, then Werden was willing to put in a fifteen-hour day. If the way to get the war over with was to kill Japs, then he dedicated himself to killing Japs, efficiently and without mercy.

Werden was a bit impatient with tough guys, who could be illogical and unreasonable. Every boot-camp platoon had a few men who thought they were tough. One of these, a large guy named Maven, marched directly behind Werden in our boot-camp platoon. One day Maven accidentally stepped on Werden's heel. Werden stumbled, picked up the step again, and marched on. A few strides later Maven stepped on Werden's heel again, this time with intent. Werden stumbled slightly once more. A minute later Maven stepped on Werden's heel again. This time when Werden stumbled, our drill instructor—our DI—called a halt, ordered Werden out of the ranks, and made him do thirty quick push-ups while the platoon looked on. Later during a brief break, Werden walked up to Maven and asked him to be more careful where he put his feet.

"You dumb, cat-eyed bastard," Maven said. "Keep your goddamned feet out of my way or I'll spread your ass all over this parade ground."

With a movement so graceful that it appeared to be in slow motion, Werden smashed the butt of his rifle into Maven's right shin. Maven let out a howl and went down. While Maven writhed, Werden bent over him and said in a calm, almost comradely tone, "Friend, next time I'll smash your kneecap."

Maven looked at Werden in disbelief before the truth slowly soaked in. Werden meant business. He did not play by the rules that tough guys try to impose on the world around them. So when our DI walked up and asked what the hell was going on, Maven said that he had accidentally tripped over Werden's rifle.

"Keep your damned rifle under control, Werden," the DI said and walked away. He had seen the whole thing and had probably

20

been expecting it. Maven, even with a slight limp that lasted a week, became the daintiest, most precise marcher in the 696th Platoon.

Although he had no more trouble with Maven, Werden's method of dealing with the problem did attract the attention of one of Maven's friends. This mean-looking giant muscled his way between Werden and me in the chow line the next morning.

"I want to tell you, you smart bastard," he muttered to Werden, "that as soon as we get liberty from this place, I'm going to catch up with you and smash your face."

"You might want to change your mind about that, friend," Werden said. "Save yourself a lot of pain."

"I'd smash you up right now," the guy said in a low, mean voice, "if that damned DI friend of yours wasn't watching."

"You got the right idea," Werden said. "Keep thinking with those ifs. Save yourself a lot of pain."

I thought for a second that the guy was going to tear into Werden, but at that moment our watchful DI headed over and ordered the tough guy back to his place in line.

"If you need any help with that jerk, Bill, just holler," I said, although I was not sure that Werden and I together could handle him.

"He won't do anything," Werden said. "He's probably a nice guy who's hopped up because I had to give his friend some helpful guidance. He only needs to learn to be a cut more reasonable."

I wasn't so sure the guy wouldn't cause trouble. He was, after all, a good bit bigger and about fifty pounds heavier than Werden, and he looked as if he had been in more than one roughhouse over the years.

Fortunately, fate stepped in. The next morning the guy was found unconscious on the concrete floor of the Quonset hut where we showered each day. Sometime during the night someone had rammed a medium-size screwdriver into his right kidney. A couple of days later our DI told us that the guy was going to survive. There was an investigation, but the victim claimed he had never seen his assailant, so it was hard to pin the blame on anyone.

Werden took the news philosophically. "It'll be a couple of months before he gets out of boot camp now," he said. "The extra time to think about things will do him a lot of good."

"Yeah," I said, "he'll probably get religion and wind up a chaplain's runner."

Werden laughed. "Anyway he won't be able to beat up on us for a while." I was pleased that he had said "us." Werden was a good man to have on your side.

As Werden and I gradually became friends, he told me a few things about himself. His parents, he confided one evening, had been killed in an accident when he was fourteen, and he had lived with relatives for a few months. Then, when the Roosevelt Administration started the Civilian Conservation Corps, he had lied about his age and joined up. A couple of years later he left the CCC and bummed around the country until the summer of 1942, when he joined the Marine Corps. These things he told me privately. With other listeners he was vague.

But he never refused to answer a question, no matter how direct. If an inquisitive Marine asked him the name of his hometown, Werden would say Logan, Utah. Was he married? Yes. Children? Two. Wife's name? Sarah Bea. What did he do for a living before the war? Drove a truck.

That was on Monday. On Tuesday he came from Ajo, Arizona, where he had left a sweetheart, an eighteen-year-old Mexican girl; and he had worked in a copper mine. On Wednesday he came from Laramie, Wyoming; on Thursday he moved east to Hannibal, Missouri. Fridays he'd spent his early years in Palatka, Florida; Saturdays in Cut and Shoot, Texas; Sundays in Pawnee, Nebraska, or Pawnee, Oklahoma.

His Tuesday sweetheart became a redheaded Irish miss on Wednesday; Thursday she changed to a widow who had picked him up when he was hitchhiking east of Denver. As for jobs, he had worked in so many places that he must have been able to separate himself into fours whenever he needed to be several places at once.

Now and then someone would call Werden to account for his inconsistencies. A skeptical guy in our boot-camp platoon was especially persistent one day.

"Now hold on a minute, Werden. What the hell's going on here?"

"You asked me and I told you," said Werden. "What more can I do?"

"Well, what the hell," said the bewildered boot, and he walked off shaking his head.

"You're going to drive that kid into the nut ward, Bill," I said.

"He'll be all right," said Werden. "He needs to learn to relax. He needs to be more careful about the way he handles his M-1, too. He's going to catch his thumb in the receiver during rifle inspection one of these days."

The next thing I knew, Werden had caught up with the kid and was giving him some instruction on keeping his thumb from getting smashed by the rifle's powerful bolt.

As the last days of boot camp approached, we all wondered what Marine outfit we would be assigned to. All of us naturally supposed we would be sent where men were most needed—into the combat zones. We were surprised then to discover that we could ask to be sent to this or that regiment or division or special service. Right away several men in the platoon, alarmed by stories of the vicious fighting on Guadalcanal, put in for cooks and bakers school. Werden and I and the others just waited.

The night before the final parade-ground inspection— Graduation Day, the Marines called it—our DI sent word for Werden and me and the third man who had qualified as expert to come to the cubbyhole he considered his office. He was waiting with two Marine officers, the first officers we had ever seen up close. One introduced himself as Major Bank, the other as Captain Walker. They were recruiting for the Marine Raiders, who at that time had the authority to recruit men directly from boot camp or from anywhere else in the Marine Corps. They were, they said, looking for expert riflemen, and we had qualified. Did we want to volunteer?

We had heard of the Raiders, a hit-and-run outfit that had made the Makin Island raid and held the line during the most critical fighting on Guadalcanal. Flattered, Werden and I volunteered right away. The third expert, a much wiser man, muttered something about suicide, declined, and departed.

Two days later Werden and I were at Camp Pendleton, fifty miles north of San Diego, where the 4th Raider Battalion was being formed. For a week after we arrived, we were the only privates in the outfit. Major James Roosevelt, our battalion-commander-to-be, was there, along with a handful of officers and NCOs. But for the time being, Werden and I were pretty much left alone. Each morning began with calisthenics and chow; then we organized our own routine of hiking through the hills to keep fit.

In a few weeks men began arriving from every outfit in the Marine Corps, and the individual companies and platoons started to take shape. I was assigned to the 3d Squad, 3d Platoon, of Dog Company. Werden was handed over to a good-humored cutthroat named Captain Certin, who, in the fighting on Guadalcanal, had proved himself to be a master of jungle reconnaissance. Certin was forming a special platoon to be called Scouts and Snipers, and he welcomed Bill Werden with enthusiasm.

3d Squad, 3d Platoon

The men who made up the Marine Raiders had volunteered twice: first, for the Marine Corps itself; second, for one of the four Raider battalions. For the 1st and 2d Raiders, which were formed in the early days of World War II, the Corps had no trouble getting five times as many volunteers as it needed. Most Marine outfits were still Stateside then, and few of the men had had any experience in combat.

When the 4th Raider Battalion was organized in the autumn of 1942, however, the recruiting officers had a far tougher job. By then practically all Marines with any length of service were already in the Pacific, and many of these had been much sobered by combat on Guadalcanal. They were in no mood to succumb to the blandishments of men bearing promises of even more exciting adventures, such as paddling rubber boats through a pounding surf to a beach littered with land mines and defended by fanatic Japanese Marines.

Among the limited number of combat veterans who did volunteer were the usual heroic figures for whom danger has an irresistible appeal. Also among them were a handful of wise old hands who figured that by signing up for the 4th Raiders, they would return to the States for at least a few months. If during that brief period they were favored by fortune, their chronic malaria might progress into blackwater fever. Or they might get pinned under a truck or a jeep or perhaps snap a bone in a training exercise. They would then wind up in a Navy hospital, from which it would be only a short, quick step to the land of make-believe and afterward the psycho ward.

With the exception of these patriots, the men who came from every direction to join the 4th Raiders at Camp Pendleton had been in the Marine Corps only eight weeks to six months. When about six hundred of the one thousand men required for the battalion had arrived, we left the spartan comforts of the main base barracks and hiked twenty-five miles back into the hills to an area the Corps had christened Tent Camp 3. There were no tents and there was no camp, only a rocky creek bed angling along through dry, knee-high brush, cactus patches, and low, scraggly trees.

For a couple of days our camp was the creek bed, our canopy the heavens above. Around noon of the third day, a convoy of trucks roared up to the spot where we were getting some early jujitsu instruction, and a working party dumped out bulky bundles of heavy green canvas, ropes, and poles—all of this on a fairly straight line that stretched for 150 yards along the creek bed we already considered our new home.

Our pyramidal tents had arrived. Our instruction in jujitsu abruptly postponed, we gathered at the droppings of the trucks, each squad dragging off a canvas pile to an assigned place along the line that would become the battalion street. Then, pooling our muscles and ingenuity, we went to work to pitch our tents. But not one of us knew anything about pitching a pyramidal tent. We might be there still, pondering the paradox of long poles, short poles, pegs, guy ropes, and canvas, except for the providential arrival of a character who, throughout almost all my days in the Pacific War, would be my close friend, daily antagonist, cynical adviser, and frequent ally in unmilitary antics—Private Bernard B. Cole.

Private Bernie Cole, having volunteered for the 4th Raiders on the previous day, had been immediately assigned to the 3d Squad, 3d Platoon, the last man to join our ten-man squad. Cole marched up confidently to Ed Flecher, our squad leader, who was displaying his leadership by tiptoeing around the problem, occasionally stopping to kick the canvas bulk and utter profanities. Inspired by our leader's example, the rest of us were also circling, kicking, and uttering our own epithets.

"Which one is the ringmaster in this little circus?" Cole said in a loud, demanding voice that bystanders could hear fifty yards away. It was a sound we didn't expect, an implied rebuke we felt we did not deserve. As we turned to confront the speaker, we saw a boyish face and a bland, understanding smile.

There was loud, appreciative laughter from Marines in the other squads nearby. Startled, Ed Flecher jerked erect, his face reddening with embarrassment. Embarrassed for him, the rest of us reddened too. As we stood there considering this apparition in boot-camp khaki, the insinuation that we were a band of morons hung in the air on that golden California afternoon.

Flecher broke out of his trance. "Who the hell wants to know?"

"I, Bernie Cole, private, United States Marine Corps Reserve, just arrived at Tent Camp 3 from San Diego boot camp, and assigned ten minutes ago to the 3d Squad, 3d Platoon, of this battalion of amateur warriors—I, Bernie Cole, want to know."

"Well, hot horseshit!" Flecher said. "Drop your gear. You're just in time to put your goddamned genius to work."

Cole put down his seabag, shrugged off his pack and knapsack, and placed his rifle tenderly on top of the pile. He rubbed his hands together and gazed at the lot of us. "The first thing to do," he said loudly, "is to get this rabble organized." He pointed at Bob Faltynski and me. "You two there. Untangle those ropes." He turned to Kleck and Williamson and Cuth. "You three lay out the short poles and pegs so we can see what we've got. That long pole there has to be the one that holds up the peak." The instructions and orders went on at a rapid clip, and every man in the squad hopped to in response. Even Ed Flecher was soon helping Private Cole find a level spot for the tent.

Other squads began to gather. As they kibitzed, we scrambled to obey the stream of commands issued in an insistent tone. We thrust the long pole into place and raised the tent peak on high. We positioned the short poles at the four corners, pounded in the tent pegs with handy rocks, and fastened and tightened the guy ropes. The work completed, we stood there happily contemplating the product of our efforts while Private Cole, gifted architect, sat down on his seabag and looked around.

The first thing that caught his eye was a gaggle of officers who had edged to within thirty yards of us, apparently to gather some surreptitious knowledge about pitching a pyramidal tent. Cole turned to Ed Flecher, by now a jolly pal.

"Who," said Cole in a stage whisper, "are those fine, healthy gentlemen standing around with their hands on their ass while we do all the work? I thought all Raiders worked together. No exceptions. Gung ho, and all that crap."

Among the officer group there was an uncertain stir.

"Those are the battalion officers," said Flecher in a low voice. "And for Christ's sake, not so loud!"

"Officers?" said Cole loudly. "The first I've seen up this close. In boot camp the nearest I ever got to an officer was when a drunk one almost ran through our platoon with a weapons carrier." From his seat on the seabag, he gave the group a wave and a broad smile and turned his back.

A week later, after the officers knew their way around and had more confidence in their authority, Cole's performance would have resulted in disaster. He'd have been called down, cussed out, and perhaps dispatched to the brig. But, as we would see, Cole always knew how far he could push.

A lieutenant named Flake had arrived in camp that morning; for nearly a year, he would be our company commander. A large, muscular Marine, Lieutenant Flake was straightforward and fair, but he believed with a fierce determination in all the things he had learned in Officer Candidate School. Dealing sternly with insubordination in the ranks was one of the lessons he remembered.

Flake was scratching the ground like a Mogollan bull and had actually taken a couple of steps toward Cole when Cole leaped up, rushed over to the nearest group of tent pitchers, and began issuing loud suggestions on how they too might get things properly done. Within five minutes he had moved up the street, issuing additional orders. Flake, apparently deciding not to interfere with progress, let Cole go his way and came over to critique our handiwork.

After another string of trucks skidded to a stop along what was now beginning to look like a company street and dumped off our seabags and cots, we moved into our tents. We piled our seabags around the center pole and threw our packs and weapons on top of them. Then our family of six—Flecher, Bontadelli, Cannon, Faltynski, Cole, and me—set up our cots. We were home.

In the beginning, Bill Bontadelli did not quite fit in the 3d Squad. In fact, he didn't quite fit in the Marine Corps. He was as capable and strong as any Raider needed to be, and he did whatever he was ordered to do. But he constantly exasperated us by seeming to do things sullenly, grudgingly. Nor did he participate in the constant discussions, arguments, and banter that boiled along during the brief periods when we had a chance to relax in our canvas home. Instead, he sat withdrawn and grim in his cramped corner cleaning his rifle, folding and unfolding his extra pair of dungarees, or laboring over a letter home.

All this changed a few days after a special session with Batsu Cribbs. Batsu that afternoon had been trying to teach us how to use a compass. Although a gifted instructor when demonstrating the skills of stab and slash, Batsu was less certain of his ground in describing mechanical contraptions.

"This here gadget," he began, holding high a black object about the size and shape of a lady's compact, "is a compass, M16-A6-1936 model, provided to the U. S. Marine Corps by the procurement activities of the United States Navy. It is a circular-shaped, hand-held object intended—"

"Say what?" interrupted Private Cole in his most insolent tone.

Batsu Cribbs paused and shot Cole a look that would have vaporized a charging elephant. "Goddammit!" he shouted. "Knock it off and pay attention!"

Cole shut up, and Batsu went on. Magnetic north, the direction toward which the compass needle pointed, he proclaimed, was not true north. True north was exactly at the top of the world, whereas magnetic north was somewhere to the right or left of Newfoundland. What mattered was that we get our heads straight or by God he would have to take an entrenching tool and pound the lesson into our inch-thick skulls. Furthermore, we'd better by God remember something about an ass-muth and a backass-muth.

As Batsu paused for breath, our platoon runner, Duff Chapman, butted in. "Hey, Corporal Cribbs, why all this stuff about true north and magnetic north? Why don't they call magnetic north true north and let it go at that?"

"Jesus Christ, how the hell should I know!" shouted Batsu. "I didn't make the goddamned world! Now knock it off and pay attention!"

Duff asked no more questions; even Cole held his peace. Meantime, Batsu charged ahead, holding the small black object aloft again and snapping it open to reveal all of its inner mysteries.

"This here needle," he shouted, pointing toward something that could be seen by only those four or five Raiders standing nearest him, "is suspended on the pinnacle—or maybe it's the binnacle or barnacle—I ain't sure which." Whatever it was, it would, he assured us, always wiggle around close enough to true north to provide the guidance to keep anyone but a damned fool from wandering about lost in the jungle, the mountains, or on the open sea. There was some additional instruction about gimbals and declinations, but by that time my mind had dropped a solid curtain between a compass and any understanding of such a cheerless object. Rather than be a slave to a stupid instrument, I resolved to stay lost wherever I might wander on the face of the globe.

What amazed me was that everyone else in the squad understood all about compasses right away. Faltynski and Cannon each took a turn at explaining its workings to me, and so did Cole—to no avail. The next morning Flecher tried one more time to help me understand, but I became even more determined that, by the Al-

30

mighty, I would stay lost rather than learn the first damned thing about magnetic lines. Disgusted, Flecher finally handed me his compass and told me to figure it out for myself.

Back in the tent toward sundown that day, Bontadelli and I waited for the other guys. While Bontadelli grappled with his next letter home, sharpened pencils, broke points, and muttered, I pulled Flecher's compass out of my seabag and stood in the tent entrance, attempting to locate some logic in the mysteries of magnetic north.

"For Christ's sake you damned, dull-wit moje," Bontadelli said suddenly. "Haven't you figured out how to read that damned compass yet?"

I was too startled to make an indignant reply. "Do you?" I said. "Do you know how?"

"I do!" he said. "I learned how to use a compass when I was a Boy Scout."

"Well, maybe you can educate me, you smart-assed bastard!"

Bontadelli pushed himself to his feet, took the compass from my hand, pulled me out of the tent, and began to instruct. It was a noble effort, but it was all wasted on me. He began swearing, and he shouted that I was the most stupid moje he had ever met. Frustrated and desperate, he walked in a small circle round and round me. Then, as if hit by an inspiration, he suddenly stopped and scratched a line and then another in the track his footsteps had made in the dust.

"This circle is the compass," he said. "You're the needle. Stick out your arm toward this mark. That's magnetic north. This mark right next to it is true north."

He leaped across the circle and scratched another mark. "This is the back azimuth," he said. "Stick out your other arm this way."

Suddenly I saw.

Back from their jujitsu and barbed-wire entanglements, Flecher and Faltynski came toward us. I turned to Flecher and held out the compass. "Bill Bontadelli is a genius!" I hollered. "He showed me how to make some sense out of this damned thing!"

Faltynski gave Bontadelli a friendly slap on the back. "By damn, Bill, you must be a genius," he said. "Nobody but a genius could get through to this dim-bulb mick."

Bontadelli was smiling happily. "He was acting like a stubborn damned moje," he said.

"Moje?" said Faltynski. "A perfect name for the dumb jerk."

And so for a time I became Moje, which was soon shortened to Moe, a name I accepted without protest. From that day forward, Bontadelli and I were friends.

As the months went by, Bontadelli became more and more confident. In all the time we were in the same platoon, from Camp Pendleton to Japan, he never faltered, whether on a thirty-mile hike in the hills behind Tent Camp 3, a combat patrol on Vangunu, or an attack on a Japanese pillbox on Guam. Sadly, he never got the recognition he deserved. He was one of those men who are so taken for granted that if he had knocked out a Japanese tank with a slingshot and a peach pit, he would not have received as much as a pat on the back.

Bontadelli was cautious with Cole, who was far too unpredictable and made lighthearted comments about Bontadelli's nose. Bontadelli was civil to Cannon even though he was offended by Cannon's excesses, which included a fondness for swearing, things alcoholic, and vignettes about loose women he had known. Bontadelli admired Cannon's unabashed conviction that without his presence, the world would burn out its bearings or shatter an axle. Cannon was, after all, a tommy gunner in the 4th Raider Battalion, one of the two elitists in the squad.

Every man in the Raiders wanted a tommy gun. That was, of course, before we learned that the BAR was a surpassingly superior weapon. Between 1939 and 1942, all of us had studied many a photograph of dashing British Commandos cheering and waving Thompson subs as they prepared to wipe out Hitler's army. We had heard many a tale and seen numerous motion pictures in which gangsters like Dillinger or Capone used their tommy guns to discourage those who dared to interfere. And we had thrilled at the great FBI counterattack led by J. Edgar Hoover and Melvin Purvis, both armed with tommy guns that apparently fired much more rapidly and accurately than those fragile pieces toted by lesser men outside the law.

Each Raider squad was supposed to be armed with three tommy guns, three BARs, and four of the brand new M-1 rifles. In those early, formative days, however, the Marine Corps' bin of weaponry was just about bare, and we had been issued only two Thompsons and one BAR per squad. Cannon and I, the squad's chosen two, the men with the tommy guns, were conceded a degree of respect denied to other members of the great Marine warrior caste.

Gunner Townsend frequently proclaimed that in war tommy guns were children's toys and the BAR was the weapon for a Marine. The BAR, said Gunner Townsend, had been around since World War I, and even though the American Expeditionary Force had landed in France with fifty thousand of them, not one had ever been used in action against the Germans. That was because the BAR was so superior to any small arms the Germans possessed that General Pershing was fearful several might fall into enemy hands.

We scoffed. Gunner Townsend, we were certain, was old and, at forty-two, skidding toward senility. But the 3d Squad tommy-gunners, Cannon and Moe, were young and wise.

Daniel Eugene Cannon was blond and curly-headed and had a face much scarred by acne. From Fort Smith, Arkansas, he had been a meat cutter in civilian life. Even though he was only twenty-three, he had for a year or so successfully operated his own butcher shop. But Cannon had a temper and was quick to react to injury or insult. He had had to give up his meat-cutting business because of a violent misunderstanding with a large man who insulted a lady for whom Cannon was chopping five pounds of pork ribs. When Cannon stepped forward to chastise him, the man had produced a small pistol, and Cannon clouted him over the head with the sharp side of the cleaver.

If Cannon had seized his antagonist's pistol or even produced a pistol of his own and shot the fellow dead, the town would have reacted with satisfaction and good will. But the weapon he had used seemed to the Smithians a bit primitive; moreover, the lady the gentleman insulted had been splashed with blood. For these reasons, the local district attorney had suggested that Cannon might want to seek shelter in the Army or the Marines. So Cannon handed over his apron, meat block, scales, and cleaver to a brother-in-law and joined the Marine Corps.

Although Cannon had a ready grin that featured a gold front tooth, and he usually seemed delighted with the world, he would turn out to be an almost pathologically fearless combat Marine. He never did acquire much skill with things like knives and fists.

But Faltynski, whose spot in our tent was between Cannon and Flecher, fought well with both. The Marine Corps in a very short while had instructed him in the arts of weaponry; his father much earlier had taught him about throwing punches. Faltynski's father, a tough hombre who worked for the railroads, slung gravel with a large spade and drove railroad spikes with a sledge. Although not a cruel man, he did believe that rebellion should be dealt with sternly. And because the teenaged Faltynski was occasionally rebellious, the old man felt obliged to belt him around from time to time. For several years Faltynski rode with the punches, nursed his bruises, and bided his time. At sixteen, he figured one day that he was big enough to fight back. After that father and son got along warily but well, until at eighteen, just out of high school, Faltynski went down to the local Marine recruiting office and volunteered.

All that fatherly discipline had not made Faltynski bitter, humorless, and forever seeking revenge. He wished everyone well. He was probably the best-natured, best-liked guy in the company. After Cole began hiding Faltynski's cigarettes, Faltynski went around bumming them from every smoker in the outfit. Nobody ever turned him down, to the great frustration of Cole.

Ed Flecher, our squad leader, who had the corner to the right of the entrance, had gone into the Marines two years before the war.

34

Like many Marines, he had first done time in the CCC, so boot camp was easy for him. He was an ideal squad leader, and we were all displeased when at the end of six weeks he was moved off to the machine gun platoon.

The sixth man in our tent, Bernie Cole, would prove to be a good Marine. For one thing, he had stamina. Although he seemed to sleep only a few hours each night, he never appeared worn. A thirty-mile training hike through the hills of Camp Pendleton taxed him not at all. On those rare occasions when the battalion commander called a halt for a ten-minute break, most of us lay down on our backs to rest our legs and feet; not Cole. He trotted here and there along the company line making deals and intentionally stumbling over his buddies. He scolded me for having a sloppy looking pack, he warned Faltynski that smoking would shorten his breath and eventually ruin his lungs, he perceived a nonexistent spot of rust on Cannon's tommy gun and instructed him on the proper way to clean it off, he criticized Bontadelli for shuffling his feet, and in one way or another he antagonized every man in the squad. Then, if time remained, he would begin a random harassment of the whole platoon. When the word came down the line to saddle up, we were pleased to leap to our feet and light out if only to be free of our persistent gadfly for a few more miles.

Cole would also be a friend—a loyal and lasting friend. That is, if you didn't mind being driven to desperation at least once every day. Twenty times in our years together I raised my fist to smash him in the face. Forty times I watched as Faltynski or Cannon raised their fists to do the same. But sixty times we relented, and either dropped our hands in frustration or merely slammed a punch into the muscles of his arm or shoulder. We usually referred to this perpetual motion machine when he was absent as "that little bastard," an epithet that changed to "you little bastard" when he was close at hand.

A bastard Cole may have been, but little he was not. Just under six feet, he was so broad that he looked short. A two-hundred-pound block of energy, he had a weight lifter's arms and heavy legs.

He had pink cheeks, light blue eyes, and a habitual expression of injured innocence. All these characteristics combined to produce a Marine who, even when he had just beaten a buddy to the punch in a boxing match or was happily strangling a friend with a judo hold or a wet towel, always managed to look boyish and defenseless.

Perhaps we called Cole little because, for a while, he was the shortest man in the squad. This meant that any time we moved along single file, he was the last in line. "It's the safest place to be," he would say. "You big dumb bastards up front will get your ass shot off first, and I can pick your pockets and give you last rites as I go by."

Cole had been in the 4th Raiders only a few days when he accomplished an extraordinary feat: he made a close and lasting friend of our battalion cook, Move-the-Line Sledd, the most inept and terrible-tempered cook the Corps had produced since the Boxer Rebellion.

Because during those days of rough and tumble training we were fed and watered only twice a day, we were always on the ferocious edge of starvation. Although the chow was insufferably bad, we always managed to shovel it down. Even so, on those days after Sledd had been on one of his famous binges, heroic efforts were required.

At chow time as we slowly approached the paniers full of half-cooked potatoes, charred beef, pork, meat loaf, or Spam, and the gallons of watery peas or spinach or corn, we had to pass Sledd, who usually stood close to the pots and pans, watching the men on mess duty to see that they didn't dish up too generous a portion to any one man. He was always in a rage because he had had to roll out of the rack at four in the morning, or because some stupid Marine on mess duty had peeled the potatoes against the grain, or because someone had borrowed a fifth of gin Sledd had brought back to camp from San Clemente the night before.

"Move the line! Move it up! Move the line, you damned slopeheads! For Christ's sake, we'll be here until doomsday!"

While he was shouting he was also listening for any critical comments about his chow, to which he responded with a torrent of obscene abuse. The first day Cole approached this fount of fury, he waited until he was about three steps from Sledd and, during a lull in all the shouting and countershouting, said in the voice he used when he wanted people to hear him one hundred yards away, "Those are the best looking damned pork chops I've seen since I've been in the Corps. When pork chops have that fine curl around the edges, you know you are seeing the work of a master chef."

Sledd's mouth stuck in mid-epithet. His surprise was absolute and for a long moment he was unable to speak or move. He was still open-mouthed when Cole accepted the greasy, ugly chop an assistant cook slung onto his mess gear. Cole reached into the pan and pulled out another chop, an action almost certain to invite the wrath of any cook in the Corps.

"Hey!" said the assistant cook. "You can't do that! Put it back in the pan!" Cole moved on. "Too late now, buddy," he said. "It's contaminated."

The assistant cook, his heavy spoon raised, moved along the other side of the line. "Put it back, you smart bastard!" he shouted. "I'll whack you with this ladle!"

Sledd suddenly came to life. "Let it go!" he yelled at the assistant cook. "Get back to your place! You're holding up the line!"

Later as we sat around bolting our chow, we saw Cole speaking earnestly and most respectfully to Move-the-Line Sledd. Although we heard not a word of the conversation, we observed an incredible event: Move-the-Line Sledd suddenly seized Cole's hand and shook it warmly. Cole had made a friend only a shade less important than the battalion commander.

Cole cozied up to everyone in the outfit who counted for anything. In no time at all he and Sergeant-major Bleak were buddy-buddy, and he was in and out of headquarters tent so often that he was known to every officer in the battalion. He was on a first-name basis with the company top-sergeant, Jacko Brown. He was in solidly with the battalion armorer, the gunny, and the company clerk. And whenever his services were required, he acted as a sort of religious barker and unofficial runner for our new chaplain, Father Paul Redmond, who had been assigned to the 4th Raiders a few weeks after we'd set up shop at Tent Camp 3.

Fearless and athletic, Father Redmond had been an enlisted man in the Navy in World War I. Soon after that futile conflict, he decided to become a priest and eventually went back into the Navy, this time in the Chaplain's Corps.

On Sunday afternoons Father Redmond would drive a pickup from Pendleton's main base to Tent Camp 3 and prepare to celebrate Holy Mass from the back of the truck. Then the field music—the Marine term for *bugler*—would blow church call, and the faithful gathered to hear the word of God.

The initial response was meager—just three or four Raiders standing respectfully with heads bowed and caps in hand while Father Redmond rattled off the liturgy in Latin and threw in a short sermon in English. He did it all in about twenty minutes, while the remaining 996 of us loitered or dozed in our tents.

On those late Sunday afternoons, Father Redmond was competing against a powerful adversary: exhaustion. Our training program consisted of six eighteen-hour days. On Sunday we rested, after being blasted out of our sacks at five in the morning by our bugler boy, Russ Galvo, and chasing each other around the hills in one training exercise after another until four in the afternoon. After that we did get the remainder of the week off, although we were expected to use the time in constructive activities such as taking very cold showers; washing shorts, socks, and dungarees; and steeling ourselves for the week ahead.

Father Redmond contended against another powerful force: the belief among tough, healthy young men that they will never die. Father Redmond, an old-fashioned priest, had no doubt that the soul was immortal. But he had had enough experience in World War I and with wounded and dying men brought back from Pearl Harbor, Midway, and Guadalcanal to know that the human body is fragile. He therefore hoped fervently to get our souls into an acceptable condition before we moved on into the great beyond.

Distressed by the modest turnout for Mass that first Sunday, Father Redmond sought out the battalion commander. Major Roosevelt was off somewhere, but the battalion exec, Major Bank, was on hand and already chatting with Cole. "I would have been there at Mass myself, Father," said Major Bank, who had not knowingly been within a hundred yards of chapel, church, cathedral, or shrine in the twelve years he had been in the Marine Corps, "but I had to concentrate my attention on the battalion's material needs."

Father Redmond nodded. "Yes, yes. I'm sure of that. It's not you old hands I'm concerned about. You people are probably beyond redemption anyway. My concern is with these mad young men, especially the enlisted men."

A cool pragmatist, Major Bank did not appear disturbed at the prospect of going out of the world with a soul unredeemed. "There's not much we can do," he said. "We can't order the damned fools to go to church. Be a violation of their Constitutional rights. If I were you, Father, I'd just let them go their merry way to the Devil."

"Major Bank, I didn't volunteer for this job to let the Devil have his way. I've looked at the records. There are four hundred Catholics in this battalion and a whole churchful of other Christians. My duty is to bring them the word of God, and by God I'm going to do it."

Cole invited himself into the debate. "Tell you what I'll do, Father," he said. "As soon as you get here next Sunday, I'll drum up a few Christians for you."

The next Sunday afternoon, about a half hour before Mass, Private Cole, leading a group of four other renegades, swept through the camp, rousing the sluggards in tent after tent and announcing that Mass would begin at "1630 hours," and that "you Catholic sons o' bitches better get your asses out there, or you'll have to answer to Major Bank or Father Redmond. The rest of you goof-off Christians better get the hell out there too and hear the word of God." This pell-mell approach was met mostly with torrents of threats and blasphemies, but there were some positive reactions. Father Redmond's congregation swelled to maybe twenty-five souls.

When, hell-bent on his holy work, Cole came into our tent, we were stretched out on our cots trying to get back some of the sleep we had lost. "Everybody out!" he shouted. "Especially Moe and Faltynski!"

Faltynski and I were the two Catholics in the tent. We looked at each other, groaned, and dragged ourselves out of the tent and over toward the unenthusiastic group gathering around Father Redmond's pickup. Behind us we could hear Cole berating the other Christians in our tent about their disgusting paganism. In a minute or two Flecher and Bontadelli, unable to sleep because of Cole's religious fervor, headed our way. Determined not to be converted, Cannon jumped up, rushed out, and hid himself away in a spot safely out of Cole's range.

A half hour later, as we drifted back from Mass, Faltynski suddenly stopped. "Hey, Moe," he said, "that little bastard Cole didn't come to Mass, did he?"

It was true. After all his zealous proselytizing, Cole had not showed up at Mass himself. When we got back to the tent, there he was lying on his back, snoring contentedly. We did the only thing we could do: we turned his cot over and dumped him out on the gravel. He came up startled and indignant.

"Hey, wait a minute you little bastard," Faltynski interrupted. "You drive us off to church and then don't show yourself. How come?"

Cole smothered his indignation. He assumed one of his woebegone expressions and leaned down to put his cot back in its proper place. "Well," he said, "it's time I told you guys about my religion." He picked up his blanket and shelter half and threw them onto the cot. "I can't go to a Christian service. It wouldn't be kosher. I'm a member of the Hebrew persuasion."

Just as Cole made this amazing announcement, Cannon came in from where he had hidden during church services. The three of us stood there looking at Cole and the hurt expression he had assumed, and we burst out into one roaring chorus of glee. "You a Jew!" Faltynski said. "If you're a Jew, I'm a Sherman tank."

"You ain't got brains enough to be a Sherman tank, you damned Polack," said Cole. "Anyway if I'm not a Jew, what am I?"

It was a good question. We had never stopped to consider what Cole was. We thought of Flecher as German, Cannon as Irish, Bontadelli as Italian, and Faltynski as Polish. Everybody knew I was mostly Irish. But we had never classified Cole.

"You are a damned con man, that's your persuasion," said Faltynski.

Cole's hurt expression deepened. We knew the look. It was about number eight on a list of two dozen expressions he could adopt at will. And for those of us who had studied his ways for several weeks now, it was about as convincing as the grief-stricken attitude of a man who has just inherited three thousand acres of good bottom land from a fifth cousin he has never met.

"He's at it again," said Cannon. "Our chief con man is setting us up for another ride on the roller coaster."

"Say what you like," said Cole, "I know what I am."

"You're trouble. That's what you are," said Faltynski.

"Well," said Cole, "I'm walking out of here until you guys get a hell of a lot more respect for your buddies." He headed out of the tent in the direction of Move-the-Line Sledd's domain. We watched him walk stiffly away. But he hadn't taken a dozen steps before he was exuberantly calling to some fellow con man fifty yards down the company street.

"He's already forgotten he's a Jew," said Faltynski as he watched Cole. "Tomorrow he'll tell us he's a Zulu." He turned my way. "What do you think, Moe? Do you think that crazy bastard is really a Jew?"

If Faltynski was seeking an expert opinion, he had sought it from the wrong man. As far as I knew, there were no Jews in Tampico, Illinois, the nearest big town to my father's small farm where I had spent my first twelve years. The only Jew I had ever known was an ancient peddler named Rubin who sold pins, needles, thread, and other small items to farm wives. So Faltynski's question was wasted on me. There was no comparing the friendly, humble old man I had known to our Private Cole. I merely shook my head, shrugged, and let the question go skittering by.

If Cole actually was "of the Hebrew persuasion," as he had proclaimed, he was one of a small group. There were only a few men of Jewish extraction in the 4th Raiders. That was not considered significant. We simply assumed that all Jews our age would naturally be inclined to go into the Army and fight in the European theater against Adolf Hitler. Even so, there were several Raiders with names like Goldman or Rosenberg. One I knew well was Mel Blum, a friend of Cole's, who wandered our way from time to time.

A demolition man, Blum seemed happy in the Corps. He was best described as jolly, especially when he was practicing those explosive techniques that would come in handy when he would be called on to blow up pillboxes or toss packs of nitrostarch into Jap caves.

So it was something of a distinction to have in our squad, our ten-man melting pot, one who claimed to be of the Hebrew persuasion. We were already pleased with our mix of Polish, Irish, Italian, and German. This was much of America on a very small scale.

We wanted to believe Cole. If Flecher or Cuth or anyone else in the squad had announced that he was a Jew, we would have been pleased to accept the announcement as true. But Cole? Our battalion provocateur and con man? There had to be a reason. There had to be a trap or trick somewhere. We put it to a squad vote. How many of us believed that Cole was telling the truth? The tally was nine to one that he was not, Cole's vote representing the only affirmative.

We decided to consult the experts. We asked Goldman. He said he thought Cole was Scandinavian. We sought out Rosenberg, who said, "Cole is a screwball. He's from Screwball Land."

42

Next time Blum came by, we put the question to him. Blum said that one of Cole's ancestors might have once been a galley slave on the Sea of Galilee, but that was about as close as he was related by blood to the people Moses had led out of Egypt.

Sergeant-major Bleak wasn't so sure. "Cole might be telling the truth," he suggested. "He sometimes does. But the funny thing about Cole is that when he's telling the truth, you think he's lying, and when he's lying, you think he's telling the truth."

A few weeks later, the battalion doctor conducted a routine "short-arm" inspection. During this prolonged exercise, each platoon lined up and gradually approached a covey of corpsmen who had the unenviable job of peering at private parts in search of genital diseases. The men of the 4th Raiders were certainly among the healthiest specimens in the family of man; but once in a while, a few weeks after playtime in L.A. or Dago, certain unhappy symptoms might appear. Those afflicted were understandably reluctant to ask for medical help. Although this help was provided free and recovery was practically assured, painful procedures might have to be applied, and penalties were sure to follow.

During short-arm inspection, as Private Cole moved toward the waiting corpsmen—all the while making obscene remarks about how the Navy and its medicos seemed to take an unusual interest in studying male physical characteristics dangling below the waist—I noticed Faltynski following ever more closely behind him. Later, as we headed back toward our tent, he beckoned me to one side.

"I got one on our buddy, Cole," he whispered. "I was right next to him at short-arm inspection. He ain't no Jew. He ain't been circumcised. I'll spring it on him one of these days and see how he lies his way out of that."

Although Faltynski kept this evidence in reserve for the time being, he did harass Cole in the late afternoon chow line. "You still a Jew today, Cole?"

"Yes, sir," said Cole, "today, tomorrow, and always. My uncle is a rabbi in Indianapolis."

"Yeah," said Faltynski, "and my cousin is a drunkard in South Bend."

Loud laughter rolled up and down the line. Cole ignored it. "I've been talking to Father Redmond," he announced in his ringing tone. "He's authorized to hold Christian and Jewish services. He's going to conduct a special service for Blum and Goldman and Rosenberg and Bleak and me when Hanukkah time comes along."

Father Redmond, standing in the chow line thirty paces back with soon-to-be Colonel Roosevelt and Major Bank, looked as if that was the first he'd heard of these plans.

Cannon snorted. "Yeah, you'll get it all organized and then forget about it." Cannon was right. Cole did persuade Father Redmond to hold those special services right on schedule, badgered a reluctant Mel Blum and the others into attending, and then managed to miss the event himself. He had been shanghaied for a working party, he explained, and the sergeant in charge would not believe him when he argued that he should be excused for a religious holiday.

Whether Cole was Jewish, Christian, atheist, or heathen, our training program rolled on, but somehow amid all the frantic activity of every long day, Private Cole found time for personal activities designed to amuse and enrich. For amusement he put rocks under our sleeping pads and pebbles in our shoes, mixed up our weapons, tied knots in our shoestrings, loosened the slings on our rifles, hid Faltynski's cigarettes, and made obscene changes to pictures of girlfriends.

As one step toward enrichment, he manufactured Japanese battle flags. The flag factory began with a sergeant named Carrigan, a somewhat battered and shaken veteran of the 1st Raiders' battles on Guadalcanal. Carrigan, a gunny sergeant, had been sent back to instruct us on the things the Marine Corps had learned about the Japs. After telling us that it was a good idea to put a couple of extra bullets into every dead Jap, he usually completed the instruction period by entertaining us for a half hour or so by recounting a few of his personal experiences on places like Bloody Ridge. After that shoot-out, the 1st Raiders had picked up numerous Japanese battle flags and soon afterward learned that Army and Marine pilots, Seabees, engineers, and others who had not been up front were willing to pay good money or even trade high-grade whiskey for these otherwise worthless souvenirs.

"Did you ever make any of your own?" Cole suddenly interrupted one day.

"Make what of our own? You mean flags? Wasn't no need to. We picked up stacks of them. Every Jap bastard had a flag on him." He stopped, closed one eye, and rotated the thought. "It might not be a bad idea, though."

Private Cole was already converting it into a plan that promised early and easy returns. That very night by dim lantern light, he began converting the plan to action. Using a *Life* magazine photo as a model, he drew the likeness of a Japanese battle flag on a piece of light cardboard. Not for him the simple Japanese emblem of an orange sun against a white background. He created the more complex battle flag with crimson streamers flowing outward from a blood red sun. From this he cut a stencil.

We sat there as he lifted it and examined it critically against the flickering light. Apparently concluding that it still lacked the artistry only he could provide, he laid it out on his cot once again, trimming away a few rough edges here and there.

"You planning to start a flag factory, you wacky bastard?" Faltynski asked.

Cole held the stencil up in front of me. "Whaddaya think, Moe?" he said. "I'm asking you because you're the only guy in this squad who ain't a damned primitive."

I pretended to scrutinize it carefully. There were still plenty of rough edges. Cannon walked up behind me and eyed it over my shoulder.

"Tell him what you really think of it, Moe," he said. "A collector's item for the San Clemente garbage dump."

"Our expert on garbage has just spoken," said Cole. "Tells us he was a meat cutter in real life. All he's ever really done is rustle Arkansas hogs."

Cannon reached into his seabag, jerked out the meat axe he kept there, and gave the end of Cole's cot a whack. Unconcerned, Cole laid the stencil out for one last readjustment. Cannon gave the end of Cole's cot another whack. "Put that toy away, butcher boy," Cole said. "You're wrecking my concentration. One of these days you'll take a swing with that thing and castrate yourself."

Cannon was by now grinding his molars, but Cole seemed not to notice. "What do you think of it, Moe?" he said.

"It's as good a stencil as I've ever seen," I said.

Faltynski erupted with a cynic's snort. "It's the only one he's ever seen," he said. Cole ignored him and laid it out on top of our seabags. Then, with a happy sigh, he pulled off his shoes and stretched out on his cot for the night.

The next day he went to his friend Move-the-Line Sledd for his material requirements: artist's brushes, red paint, and parachute silk. The brushes and paint were obtained quickly. The silk took longer to procure, until a supply sergeant drinking buddy of Sledd's remembered that the 1st Marine Parachute Battalion had left some practice parachutes behind when they had shipped out for Guadalcanal earlier in the year. Working in the cook tent late on a Sunday afternoon, Cole and Sledd produced fifteen Japanese battle flags. The fact that the paint dried unevenly on the fragile silk and that the flag did not have the authentic number of crimson streamers did not deter Private Cole. During his first liberty in Los Angeles, he sold or traded off every one of the flags, most of them to servicemen who planned to send them home to gullible relatives and admiring girlfriends. And he gave one flag to the reservations manager at the Pershing Hotel. This last was a master stroke in an era when hotel rooms all over the United States were scarce, especially for United States Marines.

Cole's inside link with the Pershing Hotel was useful when, toward the end of November, Major Bank persuaded our keepers

46

to grant the battalion a rare forty-eight-hour leave. Because of his numerous contacts throughout the battalion, Cole knew all about this great event two days before the rest of us had even heard a rumor. With a field phone provided by Move-the-Line Sledd, he called his friend at the Pershing Hotel and rented the bridal suite.

On the Saturday that our surprise liberty was to begin, Major Bank addressed the battalion at morning roll call and made the happy announcement. Liberty would begin that day at twelve noon. A convoy of trucks would take us from Tent Camp 3 to the coast highway. From there we could easily hitch rides to L.A. or Dago.

Everyone except a few old-timers or those who had wives or girlfriends in San Diego planned to head for Los Angeles. That city was filled with what we called B-girls—generous young ladies who were fun-loving man chasers said to be characterized by a pleasing promiscuity.

While the rest of us rushed around preparing for our big week-end, Private Cole moved surreptitiously here and there privately buttonholing first one and then another of his numerous acquaintances. For five dollars each night, he informed them, they could share the luxury of Room 932, the bridal suite at the Pershing Hotel. "Just come to that room," he said as he collected ten dollars each from man after man. "The door will be open for you and yours. Big bunks and bouncing springs. Might even be a few drinks available."

Somehow each one of twenty-two Raiders who was delighted to part with ten dollars for the privilege of sharing Room 932 with Private Cole got the impression that only two people—he and Private Cole—and perhaps a young lady or two would occupy that promised paradise. By midnight that Saturday, eighteen of the twenty-two—eleven of them accompanied by sportive and expectant young females—had wandered in. There was some animated discussion of deputizing a posse to track down and deal harshly with Private Cole, who, with his usual wisdom, had taken himself off to Room 424 and was sleeping a sleep undoubtedly filled with happy dreams of financial success.

On Monday at noon, when Cole's twenty-two pigeons had returned from their less-than-ideal liberty, they tracked Cole down one by one or in agitated bands. Sadly and earnestly, he explained that the whole thing had been one big misunderstanding, that he had never intended for them to get the idea that Room 932 was to be anything more than a way station for his buddies to come to for a few refreshments or perhaps to recite romantic poetry to their female friends. Although some of his strong-willed victims were threatening to slam him on the crown with the butt of an M-1, no one did. Just before taps that night, I watched him as he lovingly counted his profits from bridal suite and flags.

In January of 1943, when the battalion shipped out for the Pacific, Cole was still insisting to all of us doubting Thomases that he was, in fact, a bona fide Jew. Meantime, Faltynski never mentioned his discovery that Cole was not circumcised.

To the Island of the Holy Spirit

While at Camp Pendleton I had not seen much of Bill Werden. The Scouts and Snipers Platoon had gone way back in the hills for some special instruction in stalk and kill. They had still not returned to the battalion when we began to break camp and load ship for our long journey into the South Pacific. The ship was a prewar, passenger-cargo liner, the *President Polk*. Steel platforms mounting 3-inch, 5-inch, and 40-millimeter cannon had been installed on the bow, stern, and at various points along the port and starboard sides. The guns were manned by swab jockeys who, if we could judge by the way they conducted themselves, seemed to know one end of a cannon from the other.

The November day we boarded the *Polk* was a chilly one in San Diego. Several thousand Army engineers and Seabees were already on board and had helped themselves to the best compartments below deck. The ship's captain was obviously impatient to get under way: as soon as our last company had clambered up the gangway, the ship's horn sounded and the Merchant Marine crew began scurrying around in preparation to cast off.

Just then, four more truckloads of Marines came tearing onto the dock. It was the Scouts and Snipers Platoon. As their last man, Captain Certin, stepped onto the main deck, the *Polk* began to slip away from its berth. Each platoon leader in the battalion conducted a last roll call.

Then the veterans in the outfit, those who had already made the trip to the Southern Hemisphere, began to spread an important word. Gunner Townsend passed the word to our company: "It's cold on deck today," he said, "but remember, you stoneheads, we're heading south. Down around the equator the sun gets hot. Below deck this ship will be hot as hell day and night. Before all these dumb-assed dogfaces and Seabees get wise, stake out a place on the deck wherever the overhang gives shade at least part of the day. It'll be a good place to sleep at night, too. After you stake out your spot, be ready to fight for it. Some of those stupid asses might get desperate when that sun begins to beat down on their square heads."

While he was talking, we were already setting our sights on the best places to seize. A few seconds after he dismissed us, Raiders scattered in every direction. Our squad headed for a 5-inch-gun platform located on the port side about halfway between bridge and bow and, before anyone beat us to it, grabbed the space on the side nearest the rail and threw our packs, blankets, shelter halves, and weapons there. For twenty-one days that spot was home. Morning, noon, and night, at least five of us were always there to discourage interlopers.

The *President Polk* was an old, unattractive tub, but it could move right along. With no convoy to delay it and not much time spent zigging and zagging, it probably averaged 350 to 400 miles in a twenty-four-hour day. After several days the sun became increasingly hot and the space below deck more and more uncomfortable night and day. When the Army engineers and Seabees began to prowl around the deck in search of shade, they discovered that a battalion of cocky Marines had squatter's rights on all the best locations. There was some discontent, nervous rumblings, and a few outright challenges.

On the fifth afternoon out of San Diego, a half dozen of us, including Bill Werden, were playing poker in the pleasant shade cast by the 5-inch-gun platform above us. Werden had just called an obvious bluff by Cannon when a group of four large dogfaces edged up. Their leader was a hard-looking, not-very-happy sergeant.

"Deal us in," he said.

We ignored him. Cannon doubled the bet.

"I said we want in," the dogface said, a whole lot louder this time.

"It's a private game," said Bill Drapp, the smallest member of our group.

The big dogface pushed closer and began to kick our packs and other gear out of his way. A life jacket skidded into the middle of the pot.

"Move your ass the hell out of here, Jack," said Bill Drapp. "This is private property."

"The hell you say, smart bastard," the big guy said. "You goddamn Marines don't own this ship. You can't hog all the shade."

"First come, first served," said Drapp. "We've been here going on five days. Now edge back."

"I'll edge your ass back," the big guy said. He reached down, got Drapp by the collar, and slung him toward the rail. Drapp only avoided going over the side by making a desperate grab at the lifeline. Together Cannon and I dived toward the rail and pulled him back on board.

Meantime the big dogface reached for Werden's collar with the idea of tossing him in the same direction. In an instant Werden had the guy's right elbow bent back, and the guy was yelling for help. By now three or four of our friends had arrived, and we began easing the dogface group back into the hot sunshine of the main deck. Werden was still applying enough pressure to the big guy's elbow to keep him tiptoeing along.

"I don't want to have to make you uncomfortable, buddy, but I sure would hate to see you throw anybody over the side," Werden said, letting go and giving him a slight shove. For a second the guy just stood there; then he began to curse and threaten.

"I'll get you, you bastard," he said. "You'll be swimming with the sharks before this trip ends."

"Go away, friend," said Werden. "Just go away. Save yourself a lot of pain." The guy backed off, still blustering. In five minutes we had returned to our poker game. Bill Drapp, shaken from his narrow escape, was digging around in his pack for his K-bar knife.

"If that son of a bitch comes at me again," he said, "I'm going to cut him with this K-bar."

"He won't be back," said Werden. "He's had his afternoon fun."

Even so, we decided to keep one man awake and on guard that night. Once again, though, fate stepped in. About mid-afternoon the next day Major Bank came by for a brief visit. During the night, he told us, the Army had lost a man, a sergeant. He had probably fallen overboard. Some of his friends had said he'd been in a shoving match near our gun platform the day before. Had we seen or heard anything during the night?

Of course we hadn't. We told Major Bank that one man or another in our group had been on watch all night long, and that if anything had happened along our side of the rail we would have known about it. The night had been unusually clear, with a full moon.

Major Bank went on his way, stopping to discuss the matter with other Raiders sitting or lying about under gun platforms, lifeboats, or overhangs.

When Werden came by for the afternoon poker game, he had already been told that yesterday's enemy would visit us no more. "It's too bad," said Werden. "Deep down he was probably a nice guy. Maybe I should have talked to him awhile longer." He sat for a long moment gazing pensively out across the limitless sea, then abruptly turned back. "Deal the cards," he said.

On the twenty-first day out of San Diego, the *President Polk* steamed into the French New Hebrides and dropped anchor near the island of Espiritu Santo. Our entrance to the channel between Espiritu and the long island called Pentecost across the way had been a very deliberate one, the captain of the *Polk* probably recalling that a sister ship, the *President Coolidge,* had hit a mine there some weeks before and had been lost. From along the rail we had our first view of the reptilian green of a jungle island. Although we were tired of the ship and eager to put land under our feet, what we now saw did not provoke pleasant expectations.

"I believe I'll stay aboard," said Cannon. "Maybe ask for a transfer to the Navy. You guys go ashore and play your jungle games."

"We'll probably stay aboard a few days while we unload ship," Faltynski said hopefully.

Gunner Townsend was standing at the rail nearby. "What the hell did you expect? Nobody said we were going to Frisco or Honolulu." He laughed cynically. "Wait till you slopeheads see Guadalcanal."

Bill Werden seemed pleased. "There's plenty of cover over there," he said. "Plenty of places to hide. No Jap could see you coming in that stuff."

Top-sergeant Jacko Brown arrived, ordered a quick roll call, and gave D Company the word. "We're supposed to start unloading ship right away," he announced. "There's one screwup. The Merchant Marine is on strike. Some crap about overtime pay in a combat zone. The Navy will run barges out here, but we can't get the Merchant Marine sons o' bitches to operate the winches and cranes."

There was an incredulous silence. In the middle of a desperate war, one we had been losing until very recently, a strike? How could the government allow such a thing? Men fighting on Guadalcanal were in critical need of food, ammunition, guns, planes. And the government was letting men in the rear areas go out on strike?

"Lend me three men with tommy guns, Top," Gunner Townsend said. "In five minutes I'll have those bastards unloading this ship, or they'll be floating face down." The company greeted this request with one loud cheer.

Jacko held up his hand until the yelling stopped. "I'd like to do it, Gunner. I'd like to shoot the sons o' bitches myself, but it's against the law."

Against the law? We were amazed. Were we going to sit here on this ship with a war going on in every corner of the Pacific while a few Merchant Marine bastards and the politicians in Washington dillydallied over an hourly wage?

Colonel Roosevelt came aboard. He had, he informed the battalion, been off conferring with the island commander. If we could unload the ship ourselves, the Navy would haul jeeps, trucks, ammunition, and all the rest of the battalion's paraphernalia ashore on barges. "Anyone in this battalion ever work on the docks?" he shouted. Eleven men stepped forward; a few Navy hands from the gun-platform crews stepped forward too, saying that they had had some experience offloading ships. We uncovered the hatch where most of our equipment and supplies were stored and went to work.

In about fifteen minutes a ten-man delegation from the Merchant Marine union marched up and informed Major Bank, who was in charge of offloading, that we were interfering with a legitimate strike and what we were doing was not going to be allowed. Major Bank turned his back. The leader of the delegation, obviously a Merchant Marine strong-arm man, leaped around to confront Bank and repeat his warning, this time at the top of his lungs. As he did he gave the major a brisk bump. That was the signal. Before the gentleman and his nine companions realized what was happening, they were being slung across the deck along a line of angry Raiders.

At the ship's rail stood Bill Werden. One by one he caught them as they came his way and pitched them over the side with so much emphasis that they sailed far out over the water before beginning a free-fall. Although the heavily loaded *Polk* squatted deep, the distance from rail to channel must have been twenty or thirty feet. From a few yards away, a cluster of the ship's crew had witnessed the whole thing. They scattered off toward the ship's stern and did not reappear.

Meantime, Major Bank had taken a leisurely stroll to the rail to view the swimmers below. "Throw a dozen life jackets down there, Werden," he ordered.

"Don't you want to let the sharks have them, Major?"

"No. It wouldn't be Christian," Major Bank said, and returned to his work station.

Somewhat unhurriedly, Werden and a couple of other Marines collected a dozen life jackets and tossed them to the swimmers below; a few minutes later, their friends on the stern threw them some lines. We saw no more of them.

Not much time was wasted in unloading; the Marine Raiders traveled light. For a few hours after our brief engagement with the American Merchant Marine, we were stimulated by the thought that we had won our first battle of the Pacific War. By nightfall we had laid out a campsite, and a detachment was already pitching tents. We were laboring so efficiently and industriously that we scarcely noticed the hordes of mosquitoes humming toward us for the first of their nightly assaults.

Shortly before daybreak, the twenty-five Raiders who were still on board the *President Polk* hoisted the last load of our supplies onto the barge below, and from there onto the pestilential island of Espiritu Santo.

The island of the Holy Spirit—surely one of the least healthful landfalls on Earth. The men of the 4th Raiders had been ashore only a few days before they began to refer to it as the Cesspool of the Universe. Dengue and malaria were common ills; elephantiasis, skin ulcers, and beriberi were available to one and all. A dip in an island stream left swimmers with a fungus that invaded their ear canals, to remain forever after.

The climate was barely tolerable. Rain poured each day, and the jungle steamed in the heat. Mosquitoes attacked in great squadrons. Regiments of flies assisted diners. At night, large black bats screamed like demented fanatics experiencing exquisite torments. Earthquakes shook the island's foundations at the most unexpected times.

We were cautioned that cannibals and headhunters roamed the deepest jungle, and that these people had never been pleased with the French who governed them. Sometimes, as we hacked our way through the rain forests on a training hike fifteen miles from camp, we encountered bands of large, resentful looking natives trotting along a jungle trail. They never smiled or held up a hand in greeting; they just clutched their machetes more firmly as they headed steadily along on some grim mission.

On Espiritu Santo Bill Werden's reputation spread throughout the battalion and beyond. Tales of his exploits had already circulated from squad to platoon to company, but on Espiritu his name was soon known to all. This was mainly because Captain Certin, leader of the Scouts and Snipers Platoon, had, a few weeks after we arrived, devised a fascinating night game. On one side were the scouts, on the other the company that had the guard. Each night, anytime between dusk and dawn, selected scouts would attempt to creep up on guard posts or patrols. A scout who could crawl within three yards of a guard without being seen would whistle a few bars of the "Marines' Hymn." But if the guard spotted the scout first, there would be shouts of "Halt! Hands up!" or "Get your ass out of here!"

The game was good for all hands. It guaranteed that the guards would be especially alert, and it gave the scouts practical experience. In a similar deadly game against the Japanese, there would of course be no "Marines' Hymn," merely a blow to the head or a slash across the throat.

It was a game at which Werden excelled. Even before Captain Certin had invented it, Werden had practiced on his own. In the evening we would be sitting around our tent writing letters or playing cards by dim lantern light, and suddenly Werden would be there in our midst. We never heard his approach; he would simply be there. He had powers of emanation a ghost or a banshee would have been proud of. He was almost always armed with knife, pistol, or tommy gun—or all three together.

Werden could sneak up and place a hand on or run a sheathed blade across the throat of the wariest guard. At one time or another, we all had to stand guard, and many of us had had this uncanny experience. Several times while on guard, peering into the darkness, I had suddenly felt his hand on my shoulder.

"You're a dead man, Moe," he would whisper and laugh and disappear to embarrass some other guard a half hour later, halfway across camp.

Once, I surprised him. I had the twelve-to-four guard shift on a particularly dark night. A storm had moved in, and the usual tropical downpour was under way. In a few minutes I'd had enough. My patrol area took me past a very large banyan tree. The roots at its base formed a canopy about six feet high. As I pushed up close to get at least some shelter from the rain, I discovered an opening. Shoving through it, I was suddenly in a dry, dark shelter. It was an ideal spot for one who watches, and I stayed there while the storm roared on.

Suddenly there was a flash of lightning just as the rain stopped. Highlighted in that flash was Werden, standing only a yard or two from my shelter.

"You're a dead man, Bill," I said into the darkness.

A few seconds went by and then, "Screw you too, Moe," Werden said. There was a pause. "One of these nights I'll steal your damned tommy gun while you're sleeping on it."

Werden knew that I and most other men in the battalion slept with our weapons under the thin pad the Marines referred to as a mattress. I was just about to give him some abusive response when there was another flash of lightning. He was no longer there.

One thing was certain. Werden would try to make good his promise—soon. He didn't much hold with lengthy delays. So the next night before I tucked in my mosquito net, I tied the trigger guard of my tommy gun to the side of the cot before shoving it under the edge of my mattress.

Next morning the tommy gun was still there, and the morning after that. On the third night when I dropped off, I had almost convinced myself that Werden's promise was intended to keep me from getting a good night's sleep. Nevertheless I tied the tommy gun securely in place. Sometime in the night I awoke with a start. Something—a stone or stick—had struck the side of the tent just above me. I sat up in a tangle of blanket and mosquito net and reached for my tommy gun. It was gone.

A voice came out of the darkness. "It's hanging on the tent pole, Moe," the voice said. "If I'd been a Jap, your ass would be mud."

"You bastard, Bill," I said.

"Yeah and you too, Moe," the voice said. "Now we're even." I untangled myself from net and blanket and leaped to my feet. My tommy gun was hanging where Werden had said it would be. He had slipped into that tent with its six sleeping occupants, untied the thong, pulled out the tommy gun, hung it on the pole, and slipped away. Although it was an incredible performance, I didn't tell the other guys about it and neither did he. It was our private game, and we both knew who had won.

Toward the middle of our fifth week on the Island of the Holy Spirit, Dr. Wilson, who had been our medicine man since Tent Camp 3, called Colonel Roosevelt's attention to a critical problem. The whole 4th Raider Battalion, he reported, was getting sick. An epidemic of dysentery was sweeping through camp; men were already suffering from malaria, dengue, and something called cat fever; and every man among us was plagued with skin ulcers. These were deep, ugly sores that started with a scratch or a mosquito bite and rotted clear to the bone. Even the new sulfa drug, which was supposed to cure everything, had no effect on these or any of the other tropical ills.

Dr. Wilson, usually quiet, reserved, and respectful to his superiors, was beginning to make such an emphatic case that those of us who were near battalion headquarters could clearly hear his impassioned plea.

"I'll tell you what we need to do!" He was getting louder. "What we need to do is stop this twenty-hour-a-day training crap and police up around here. We need to turn the whole battalion loose and clean up this damned rat's nest. We got to get rid of these mosquitoes and flies and dry up this swamp we're living in."

58

Colonel Roosevelt and Major Bank merely sat quietly and accepted this harangue. They knew Dr. Wilson was right. In their zeal to ready the battalion for the battles to the north, they had forgotten some of the elementary rules of sanitation. The company streets were muddy channels; the heads were filthy; the ground beneath the trees was covered with branches, coconut husks, and coconuts—ideal breeding ground for every kind of rodent, insect, and parasite.

So for three hard days the whole battalion attacked the enemy that Dr. Wilson had identified, an enemy that threatened to destroy us more effectively than the weapons of the waiting Japanese. We dug ditches; we filled in low spots; we piled and burned coconuts, husks, and dead branches; we dug new heads and nailed up screens to keep out the flies; we hauled in gravel and coral to cover the mud of the company streets and all the pathways to our tents; we cleared away underbrush and sprayed the ground with kerosene and oil. After three days we believed that we were winning the battle against filth and disease. Apparently, Colonel Roosevelt also believed. After a Saturday afternoon inspection of our newly resurrected area, he thanked the battalion and declared that except for the officers, whom he would ask to take over the guard duty for one day, the whole battalion would have Sunday off.

On Sunday, right after morning chow, Faltynski, Cole, Werden, and I set out to explore the north end of Espiritu, that part of the island where the jungle thinned out into a few open spaces. Several miles from our camp, the 2d Raiders, freshly returned from the guerrilla warfare they had fought behind the Jap lines on Guadalcanal, had pitched camp in one of those open spaces—a pleasant, grassy area not far from the ship's channel. There we paused for a while to visit a friend of Cole's from high school.

The legendary 2d Raiders! Many a man in the 4th Raiders had volunteered after hearing or reading accounts of the 2d's exploits during the Makin Island raid. And all of us had heard about the thorough beating they had given the Japanese on the Canal. What we expected to see was a collection of fierce creatures sharpening knives, practicing new ways to cut throats, or planning their next big bloodletting. What we saw was a group of ordinary looking guys, solemn and restrained, lounging about in the tents, reading, playing checkers, chess, or cards, and talking in low tones.

Cole's friend, who had received a bronze star for machine-gunning a platoon of Japanese on Makin, was completing a calculus test to be mailed off to the Marine Corps Institute. A bit let down by all this propriety, we gossiped a few minutes and then went on our way.

A mile or so beyond the 2d Raiders, Cole and Faltynski veered away to explore a nearby patrol plane base, the home of the PBYs. Out on the island road, Werden and I caught a jeep ride toward a Seabee camp a few miles farther north. The Seabees, we had been told, considered themselves older brothers to all Marines, and especially to the Marine Raiders. A hungry Raider who dropped in on the Seabees anytime would be treated to a steak dinner for the asking.

From our back seat in the jeep, we could see many of the ships in the channel between Espiritu and Pentecost. An aircraft carrier, probably the *Enterprise,* was anchored a few hundred yards out. Right amidships was a monster hole torn by a bomb or torpedo. Out in the channel we also saw the *President Polk,* riding at anchor just where we had left her nearly five weeks earlier.

"Well I'll be damned," said Werden. "Are those Merchant Marine sons o' bitches still on strike?"

In front of the Seabee camp the jeep driver stopped and pointed toward a building he was pretty sure was the mess hall. As we jumped out we saw, getting off a truck a few yards ahead of us, two guys in Merchant Marine outfits. Obviously planning to visit the Seabee camp themselves, they came strutting along toward us, examining our worn caps and dungarees with ill-concealed contempt.

We recognized them immediately. One, very large and tough looking, was the same union hood who had bumped Major Bank back on the *President Polk,* the same man Werden had pitched over the side. His partner, a weasel of a man, had also taken the plunge that day. I looked out once more at the ships jammed into the channel. From this high point in front of the Seabee camp I could clearly see the *President Polk*. Bill Werden was glancing that way too. We turned back as the two Merchant Marine characters came up.

"Are you bastards still on strike?" I said. They came to a sliding halt a few feet away and looked us over. As all the implications of my question began to sink in, the big guy's face flushed with indignation.

"What?" he said. "What the hell did you say, you goddamn Marine bastard?"

I was about to repeat my question, but Werden beat me to it. "Are you bastards still on strike?" His tone was calm, almost polite.

"Watch your mouth, you son of a bitch!" the big guy shouted. "You ain't surrounded by fifty Marines with tommy guns now."

"Easy on the bad words, mister Merchant Marine man," Werden said. "It's Sunday. We're going up to the Seabee mess hall for chow."

The big guy was working himself into a rage. "One more word out of you yellow chickenshit Marines, and I'll kick the shit out of both of you." He stuck his left hand into his pocket as if reaching for a knife or pistol.

Werden did not move. "Maybe you ought to stop a minute and think it over, friend," he said mildly. "I'll guarantee you, you'll save yourself a lot of pain."

The big guy, now certain that Werden was losing his nerve, pulled out a pair of brass knuckles and slid them over his fist. He was drawing back to smash Werden's face when Werden, quick as a panther, gave him a judo chop so powerful that the movement was a blur. The blow struck the big guy's right wrist just in back of the protruding bone. There was a sharp, sickening crack, and the guy's hand and fingers dangled useless at the end of his arm. The shock of the blow and the immediate intense pain showed on his face, and he let out a strangled, involuntary cry. Werden reached out gently, slid the brass knuckles off the dangling fingers, and thrust them into a pocket of his dungarees.

61

"You won't need these anytime soon, friend," he said sympathetically. Then he turned to the big guy's buddy, who was fixed in place. "Maybe you should take your buddy off and look for a doctor if you can find one that's not drunk by now."

He turned to me. "I guess the game's over, Moe," he said. "Let's go get that steak."

A half hour later as we sat in the Seabee mess hall eating a couple of huge steaks a friendly cook had fried up for us, I reflected that the union hood had been lucky. Werden had done him no permanent harm. If he had been a Jap, the blow would have been to the Adam's apple, a shattering experience that, when imposed by Bill Werden, would put a man in his grave.

The Sacrament of Killing

Several days later, a complaint from the captain of the *Polk* came through the island commander and along official channels to Colonel Roosevelt. A veteran crewman on the *Polk*, the report stated, had been severely injured by a drunken, demented Marine. The victim was certain that he could identify the offender. A similar complaint, we learned, had been sent to the acting commander of the 2d Raiders.

Nothing was done in response to either complaint, both commanders knowing that although their charges were frolicsome at times, they were basically respectful boys, and some of them even had hearts. The Scouts and Snipers Platoon was by now gone anyway; Bill Werden was on board a submarine heading toward New Georgia. There they would be making their first violent moves.

It was April 1943. On the island of New Georgia, 175 miles north of Guadalcanal, an Australian coast watcher named Kennedy believed that the Japanese were planning to attack him. Early in the war Kennedy had established a lookout station at Segi Point on New Georgia across the channel from an island called Vangunu. All during the fighting on Guadalcanal and into the early months of 1943, he had stayed at his post reporting to interested parties on Guadalcanal the southward passage of every Japanese formation of ships and planes.

Now the Japanese, who were constantly moving more men, equipment, and supplies into the area, were closing in on Kennedy.

He was respectfully requesting help. Admiral Halsey's first response was to ask the 4th Raiders to send in their Scouts and Snipers Platoon. In addition to giving Kennedy some limited protection, they could scout here and there on Vangunu and New Georgia where Halsey and his fellow strategists planned to attack in force very soon anyway. As soon as possible after the Scouts and Snipers had done their introductory work, the whole 4th Raider Battalion would follow with two companies to land at Segi and two more at Wickham Anchorage on Vangunu. They could thus bring additional protection to Kennedy as well as wipe out any Japs they might encounter. It would all be very simple: Raiders out to New Georgia and Vangunu and back to Espiritu in a few days, a kind of tropical vacation with pay.

When the Scouts and Snipers went ashore in rubber boats and landed near Segi Point during the night of 20 April, a couple of Jap patrols were wandering through the jungle only eight or so miles away, but they had suddenly turned back, one patrol heading for Munda airstrip, which the Japanese had established some months before, the other going off in the direction of Wickham Anchorage. This second patrol of about thirty men with a major in charge hiked north for a day and then turned about and headed toward Segi Point once more. It was this patrol that had the bad luck to run into Bill Werden.

Werden had been scouting alone north of Segi, he told us later, and had run across the familiar tracks left by split-toed, rubber-soled shoes. The trail was fresh and he followed, moving rapidly. The season of heavy rains would not begin until June or July, so the jungle floor was relatively clean and dry. In a few hours he heard in the near distance the voices of the Japanese.

In those early days of the American counterattack in the Pacific, Japanese admirals and generals experiencing the force of it were increasingly alarmed. Soldiers in the ranks, however, were not at all concerned, still apparently certain that they were far superior to the so-called fighting men of the western world. They had met the Americans in the Philippines and the British in Southeast Asia and had defeated them easily, the Americans surrendering in great clusters on Bataan and Corregidor; the British always retreating. Guadalcanal had been a different story, but few Japanese in the lower ranks were aware of the dimensions or the implications of this disaster. Most Japanese soldiers believed that the American Marines and soldiers had once again suffered a catastrophic defeat on that jungle island.

So contemptuous had they become that they had begun to neglect even the most basic security measures. They marched along those jungle trails with rifles held loosely or slung carelessly across their shoulders. They put no point men out ahead of the column, no guards at the rear. When they stopped for a break, they often did not post riflemen a few yards out on each flank. Nor did they spread out, instead gathering in groups for cigarettes and loud, boisterous chatter. Against a man like Bill Werden, they were not well prepared.

Just at dusk, Werden came up on the Jap patrol he was pursuing as they were making camp for the night at a wide spot on the trail. When he crept close enough to see them through the twisting vines, not one man among the thirty had a weapon in hand—only cigarettes and, here and there, a bottle of sake making the rounds.

Werden had three grenades. He had long ago learned a special technique on the practice grenade range, a technique that few men could imitate, even if they had the nerve to try. One by one, he pulled the pins from two grenades and, holding the spoons tightly in place, transferred each to his left hand. A third grenade hanging by the pin from his web gear he jerked loose with his right hand, leaving the pin behind. Now he had three grenades, one in his right hand, two in the left, all of them armed and ready to throw.

The Japs by this time had pretty much arranged themselves into three convenient clusters, with the exception of the patrol leader and a couple of enlisted men who seemed to be trying to satisfy their master. It was a perfect setup. From the grenade in his right hand, Werden let the spoon fly free and threw. Next two quick movements of grenades from left hand to right and two rapid throws toward the nearer groups. Before the first grenade found its mark, the second and third were in the air, and Werden had flattened out on the jungle floor. There was the *boom, boom, boom* of three rapid explosions. Then Werden was on his feet firing a long burst from his tommy gun at the patrol leader and the men around him. Once again he dropped flat, rolled away a half dozen yards, rose, and trotted unhurriedly into the jungle. Behind him there was a gradually diminishing cacophony of terror and pain and, after some time, the sound of rifles and machine guns blasting wildly away. Some weeks later, when a Marine patrol passed that way, they found what remained of the bodies of fourteen men. Apparently terrified and presumably carrying their wounded, the rest of the patrol had left their dead and rushed away.

For the next two months Bill Werden and others of Captain Certin's scouts operated in and out of New Georgia, Vangunu, and the big Japanese base at Kolombangara. The 1st Raiders had also put scouts ashore, and these men scouted around Enogai Inlet and Bairoko Harbor, important supply bases the Japanese had established on New Georgia northwest of Munda airfield. By 30 June, when companies A and D of the 4th Raider Battalion sneaked ashore on Vangunu, the scouts had even cut secret trails through the jungle so that once we left our landing area we could move quickly toward our objective—Wickham Anchorage, another harbor where the Japanese had a supply base.

Led by Flake, now captain, our company approached Wickham Anchorage from the jungle side in the early morning of 30 June 1943. Within four hundred yards of the beach the jungle began to thin, and we spread out in a skirmish line. Daylight was breaking as we approached the Japanese base. We had been told to expect perhaps three hundred fifty Japs armed with rifles, mortars, machine guns, and several cannon.

If our scouts were right, we would not have to worry about the heavy stuff. Werden and others had been watching the Japs at Wickham for several days and had reported a regular early morning ritual. Much as we did in rear area camps ourselves, they began each day with a half hour of exercise. During this period, even the few guards posted at the jungle's edge put aside their rifles and joined in the exercise routine, all of it characterized by shouting and loud communal grunting.

For many of us in the stealthy line stealing toward the Japs, this would be our first combat, our first direct contact with the enemy. My tommy gun held at ready, its bolt back, its safety flipped to "fire," I crept forward with the others—to my immediate right Faltynski, to my left Cannon and Cole and Bontadelli. At that stage in our development as combat Marines, we were too ignorant to be afraid.

We were within fifty yards now. A Jap with a booming guttural was chanting the exercise cadence. A few yards ahead Flake raised his arm. When he dropped it we would charge shooting full blast. At that second I saw a BAR man in the 2d Platoon stumble and fall. As he hit the ground, his BAR went *Boom! Boom! Boom! Boom!* The worst thing that could happen to a Marine Raider had happened— an accidental discharge.

Into the few seconds of absolute silence that followed came the startled cry of a bullbat from the depths of the jungle and then a scream of command in Japanese. Flake, recovered now from his five seconds of paralysis, threw his arm forward and down; we charged toward the clearing firing from the hip as we ran.

It was not a very productive charge—perhaps a dozen Jap bodies spread about the clearing. The battle that followed went on all day, the Japs having quickly organized and gotten to their machine guns and mortars, quickly firing. Toward day's end we forced their survivors back toward the beach and finally to the water's edge where a few, defeated and desperate, left their weapons and tried to swim away. These we picked off one by one.

Torrents of rain came down that night and washed the blood away, but it did not thin out our memory of the eight Raiders who were killed that day. We had had fourteen men wounded, but almost all of them would recover and return to the outfit.

While those of us in companies A and D were busy at Vangunu, the other 4th Raider companies that had landed at Segi Point were conducting their own war. Leaving Segi on the evening of 30 June, they paddled rubber boats the eight miles across Panga Bay to the native village of Regi. From there they would hike to Viru Harbor to attack a Jap stronghold.

Scouts who had been in this area some weeks before had predicted that the Raiders could hike to Viru in a day. Their prediction was made on the basis of good weather; but the rainy season had set in, low areas were now mangrove swamps, and trails and channels were filled with mud and slime. The march to Viru required four fifteen-hour days.

In addition to Raider skill and courage, two things made the Viru raid successful. A half hour before the attack, several American dive bombers hit Viru and startled the Japanese out of their prepared defenses. And late in the day, just when they had our men stopped, the Japs cooperated by making a disastrous banzai charge. In a few minutes the Raiders had advanced over stacks of Jap bodies and Viru was ours. Compared with the tremendous losses experienced in the big battles of 1944 and 1945, our losses at Viru were light: ten men killed, twenty-four wounded.

Two days after the 4th seized Viru, our two-stack destroyers came plowing into Wickham Anchorage and anchored as close to the inner harbor as they dared. In a half hour we were on board and steaming off into the open sea.

"What new hell are we in for this time?" said Cole. He and Faltynski and I were stretched out on the steel deck plates of the fantail.

"Probably down to Munda to rescue the damned Army from some trap," said Faltynski.

Sergeant Floyd was standing nearby. "You'll be surprised where we're going. Back to Guadalcanal for a rest."

Cole was skeptical. "We're probably going to attack Truk."

Floyd's information was correct. A day after we left Vangunu, we were back on the Canal, where for a week we actually did enjoy a badly needed rest. Every man in the battalion was suffering from at least one and usually several tropical ills. For cases of malaria and dengue, Dr. Wilson prescribed quinine, Atabrine, aspirin, and maybe twenty hours of sleep a day. For the skin ulcers and other jungle rot that plagued us all, he prescribed at least a half hour of lolling on the beach each day in the fierce tropic sun. For other lesser ailments, he prescribed exercise, prayer, and an attitude of hopefulness and good cheer.

During that week of rest and recuperation, we assembled in formation twice—once to receive an issue of six cans of beer per man, a second time to hear that Colonel Roosevelt had been evacuated to a San Francisco hospital for treatment of a bad case of stomach ulcers. Our new commanding officer would be Colonel Maxim. A tough campaigner who had been in the Marine Corps nearly twenty years, Colonel Maxim was already known to us. Back at Tent Camp 3 he had been around for about six weeks helping out with the Headquarters Platoon, and we had had several encounters with him during the frequent night problems in the hills of Pendleton. Later he had been sent out to Samoa to help in the organization and training of the 3d Raiders.

Although we were sorry about the departure of Colonel Roosevelt, we were pleased to have Colonel Maxim come aboard. He had been a kind of troubleshooter for the 1st Marine Division in the early days of the battle for Guadalcanal and had later seen action against the Japs with both the 1st and 2d Raiders.

With Colonel Maxim's arrival, a happy piece of scuttlebutt circulated: the 4th Raiders would be excused from further battles for a few months while the new commander got acquainted with his men. But when reveille sounded on the morning of our eighth day of rest and we gathered in formation on the company street, we saw our two-stackers waiting a half mile or so from shore and knew at once that we would soon be going north to visit the Japs again.

In the fighting on Vangunu, we had lost Captain Flake, badly wounded by several machine gun bullets in the right thigh and hip. Now our new company commander, Captain McNail, gave us the word. "We're heading back north," he said. "To New Georgia again. The 1st Raiders are having a bad time at a place called Bairoko Harbor. Get your gear together. We'll be loading aboard in two hours."

It was a quick trip: a day and a half up the Slot in our increasingly familiar two-stackers to a landing near Enogai Inlet. Then a forced march to a ridge a few miles south of Bairoko Harbor. There we waited five days, sending out patrols and losing some point men. Except for the twenty-man patrol Werden and the rest of us wiped out on the Munda trail, the battalion killed only a handful of Japs in that five-day stretch.

The killing really began on the sixth day when, along with the 1st Raiders, we pushed north toward Bairoko. As we approached that nest of Japanese Marines waiting there with all their mortars and machine guns, we encountered more and more patrols. There was a typical pattern to each encounter. Either our point man or their lead scouts would burst out of the jungle or round a turn on a narrow trail and be shot at or shot. The survivors on each side would dive for cover and blast away, mostly at unseen or non-existent targets. Then the Japs would scurry off, leaving a torn body or two behind and some of our men wounded or killed. After that, silence. Forward again, more contact, more shooting—a few Japs down, a few Marines hit. Then silence once more.

As we drew ever closer to our objective, we occasionally came across evidence that some efficient ally had been there before us: a lone Jap with his neck broken; two machine gunners huddled at their Nambu, their throats cut deeply from ear to ear; a Jap sniper hanging by one leg from a banyan tree; a six-man demolition squad apparently surprised while eating their fish and rice in a hut. From the look of it, someone had tossed a grenade among them.

"Werden!" we said to one another each time we came across one of these grisly scenes.

Within a half mile of Bairoko, C Company, moving cautiously along a wisp of a trail a few hundred yards to our right, walked into a Jap fire lane. They lost seven men in the first blast and four more while getting the wounded out. It was late afternoon before things settled down, and the word soon came from Colonel Maxim to dig in where we were for the night.

Although we expected the Japs to attack or at least send a few infiltrators into our lines, the night was quiet—except for one long burst of machine gun fire off toward the arc where the 1st Raiders had established their line. In our few hours off watch, we slept fitfully.

We attacked just as the jungle night was beginning to gray into morning, the 1st Raiders on our right charging into the Jap machine guns and fire lanes that had delayed them the afternoon before. We heard a cataclysm of fire and wild, distant yells and screams before the firing died down. Presently word came that the 1st had made about two hundred yards and then had been stopped. Just before the 4th Raiders attacked, we heard the Jap .90-millimeter mortars crashing in the distance, presumably in that area where the 1st Raiders were pinned down.

A few minutes later the 4th Raiders attacked, made several hundred easy yards, and then rammed into the enemy's outer defense line. The Japs had had plenty of time to prepare. They had dug machine gun pits in the natural shelter provided by the roots of banyan trees and cut fire lanes through the underbrush out front. To get caught erect in one of those fire lanes guaranteed almost instant death. Jap snipers were all around, and there were always mortars exploding among Marines caught in these deadly traps.

But somehow the men up front made progress. The three-man fire teams worked together, gave each other covering fire, crawled forward, threw grenades or demolition packs, killed Japs, wiped out machine gun nests, shot snipers out of the trees—always with

71

streams of bullets whistling by and mortars bursting in the trees overhead, showering the men below with falling branches and hot fragments of cast iron.

For the first few hours of that bloody day, Dog Company had been held in reserve; but even in our sheltered area a hundred yards or so behind the main attack, we lost men to Jap mortars, stray machine gun bullets, and the ever-present stalking snipers. An hour or so into the afternoon, still in reserve, we waited along a narrow trail. Up front the firing had lessened so much that instead of flattening out behind whatever cover we could find, we were sitting—Faltynski, Cole, and I—with our backs against the trunk of a large tree.

"They can leave us in reserve for the rest of the week for all I give a damn," said Cole. "I quit being a hero that first day on Vangunu."

Faltynski was slicing a chunk off a ration that looked like a chocolate bar but tasted like cheap soap. "You ain't just—" He did not finish the sentence because there was the sharp crack of a sniper's rifle, and a bullet whacked into the tree inches above his head.

In battle there are many frightening sounds: the scream of an incoming shell, the quick blast of a mortar, the whistling rush of machine gun bullets going by close overhead, the sharp crack of a bullet hitting some small object like a leaf or a twig, the whine of a ricochet—but none are so unnerving as the sound of a bullet striking a solid object like a tree or wall, especially when it is close by. There is such a smashing finality to it—and the instant comprehension of its force can drive the courage out of all but the very bravest of men.

A split second later we were flat on our bellies and filled with fear. There was a second shot that also slammed into the tree immediately above where Faltynski sprawled. A third shot hit the ground close beside him. Then a fourth.

"Son of a bitch seems to like Polacks," said Cole. He spoke out of the side of his mouth because his face was pressed almost into the ground.

"Jesus Christ! Jesus Christ!" said Faltynski, rolling this way and that. "I'm thinking of changing my name to Cole!"

The sniper fired one more time. Right afterward we heard the heavy bang of an M-1 from a few yards up the trail and a shout from our platoon runner: "I got the son of a bitch!"

Cole and I straightened up slowly, but Faltynski was still rolling.

"You can quit racking around and get the hell up out of there, Polack," said Cole.

Faltynski sat half upright, holding his right leg. "The son of a bitch got me with that last one," he said.

It was a clean wound through the right calf. A corpsman who came running up announced that it was only a small bullet hole, no more than a scratch, and helped Faltynski limp off to find Dr. Wilson. We would not see our Polack buddy again for nearly a month.

As Faltynski disappeared toward the rear, there was a spurt of machine gun and rifle fire and the emphatic crash of grenades in the direction of our attacking companies. It sounded very close—only a couple of hundred yards away. About that time too word came along the line that Captain McNail wanted to see all platoon sergeants and squad leaders on the double. They weren't gone long. No more than ten minutes after he rushed forward, our acting squad leader, Bill Bontadelli, was back. Our two companies up front, B and C, along with a reserve company from the 1st Raiders, had pushed to the edge of a clearing perhaps thirty yards wide and been stopped. In the jungle across that clearing, the Japs seemed to have half a dozen Nambus and some knee mortars and a platoon of riflemen. Colonel Maxim had decided that there was only one thing to do—line up and charge. Dog Company could quit loafing, he'd said, and do the job. It was not welcome news.

"Hey," said Cole, "we ain't banzai people."

Bontadelli gave him a hard look. "We will be in about fifteen minutes," he said.

The company, still in single file, was already moving forward at a rapid trot and forming a skirmish line directly behind what was

73

left of companies B and C. Our three platoon leaders had synchronized their watches. At 1425, each platoon leader would toss a white phosphorous grenade into the clearing ahead. That would be the signal for B and C to give us covering fire, and the men of Dog Company would charge across the open space and in among the Japs.

For a few minutes there was an odd silence along the front. Then from the Jap line across the way came the sort of yells and screams that preceded a banzai. As their screaming and shouting reached a climax, three smoke grenades went off out front, and Dog Company charged.

We were more than halfway across the narrow clearing before we realized that not a shot had been fired our way. It was incredible. We had expected to be greeted by machine guns or blasted by mortars, yet no man in our charging line had gone down. Right then a line of Japs rose at the edge of the jungle immediately to our front and banzaied. It all happened so fast that they were right on top of us in just a few seconds.

It was a thing that was not supposed to happen: both sides charging toward each other almost simultaneously. So unexpected was it that both Marines and Japs forgot to yell, forgot to fire. Going at top speed in opposite directions, they ran right past each other. A Jap rifleman with his long bayonet fixed ran by a yard to my right. I could see that he was struggling to angle toward me, but momentum and the fixation of the banzai took him past. Meantime, I was struggling to overcome my own momentum, my own fixations of the charge, but as he rushed by I could not bring my tommy gun to bear.

Our momentum carried us into the underbrush. A few Jap machine gunners were there looking dazed, reacting slowly. We tossed grenades into gun pits and destroyed guns and gunners. Behind us we heard rapid fire as the line of Japs that had banzaied right through us ran into B Company's guns.

We huddled in small, uncertain groups before squad and platoon leaders herded us into an organized force again. Although the jungle immediately ahead was so dense that we could see no more than five yards into it, we were certain that Bairoko Harbor itself was no more than three hundred yards away.

Meantime, our company had not been ordered to delay its attack. We would, our platoon leaders decided, make another try. We would form into columns with from six to eight men single file three yards apart in each column, the columns themselves about ten yards apart. Again the strategy was elemental: move forward through the jungle until someone got shot. Then we would know the Japs were there.

In our 3d Squad column, it was my turn at the point. I was, of course, concerned about running into the Japs. I was concerned also about trying to keep a straight line. To get too far to right or left was to invite disaster. If the columns of Marines to one side or the other fell behind and our squad crossed in front of them, they might mistake us for the enemy and shoot us down.

We had progressed about thirty yards when we heard voices directly to our front. They were Japs, jabbering excitedly. We flattened out and peered into the green wall ahead. We could see nothing but jungle. Presently the voices faded away in the direction of Bairoko. A sudden feeling of hope spread through our small column. Maybe the Japs had had enough. Maybe they were finally in retreat.

"Slow it down, Moe," came a stage whisper from immediately behind me. "Let 'em run all the way to Tokyo." It was Cole, his words summing up the thoughts going through my mind.

Some ten yards to my front was an exceptionally large banyan, its trunk about ten feet in diameter, with a cluster of vines extending from ground level to its lower branches. Stepping cautiously, my tommy gun at the ready, I eased around the protruding roots and into a small clearing.

A Japanese soldier stood in front of me, his long sniper's rifle at his side. He was alone. I still wonder why. He was only a pebble's toss in front of me, his look of instant shock and surprise mirroring my own.

There was a sudden tremor in the arm that balanced the rifle at his side. Nothing more. His fingers were a foot from the trigger. On my left Cole had pushed forward, on my right Bontadelli. They raised their weapons. Just before they shot him, he shrugged and almost smiled.

In the silence of that clearing, the sound of their shots echoed and reechoed through the jungle. Then, from not far ahead, a Jap Nambu clattered and bullets crackled through leaves and vines. We dived for cover, spread out, made contact with our columns to the left and right, and very soon moved into the attack again.

Here the Jap defenders had introduced a cunning technique. Like fingers fanning outward from each machine gun in their line, fire lanes had been cut through the dense underbrush. The lanes were like low tunnels or animal runs, about three feet wide and two feet high. An attacker moving forward through the jungle could see only a few yards ahead; but when his advance took him, as it usually did, into one of the tunnel-like fire lanes, he would never realize it until the bullets from the enemy machine gun cut his legs from under him. Once down in the fire lane, he was a dead man. Dog Company lost a dozen men before we began to understand the lethal aspects of this cunning trap.

Giving up on any direct approach, we backed off a hundred yards and circled to the left toward what we assumed was the end of the Jap line. Flanking movements had worked at Vangunu and Viru, but here at Bairoko when we turned to our right once again, we were confronted with Nambus.

As we stopped and peered into the jungle ahead, we saw one of our scouts, Mother Callahan, moving on alone. Threshing through a dense tangle of bamboo and vines, he had gotten a few steps beyond our advancing skirmish line and had attracted the attention of a Jap machine gunner.

The gunner, probably shooting in the general direction of all the racket Callahan was making, fired a couple of introductory bursts. As the bullets went crackling by, Callahan made a lunge, dived five yards forward, and wound up behind a fallen tree. Un-

76

fortunately, this last lunge put him directly in front of the Jap machine gunner hidden behind some logs a few yards away.

Mother Callahan, at six feet six inches and 230 pounds, was one of the big men in the 4th Raiders, but the fallen tree provided considerable protection. Except for an inch or so of Callahan's prominent rump, which protruded above that rough shelter. In a few seconds the Jap machine gunner took notice of it and began cutting an inch-deep groove right across the outer limits of Callahan's buttocks. For a little while Callahan endured the insult. Better to sacrifice an inch or two of flesh than to stand up and accept four or five .31-caliber slugs in the chest or gut.

Unexpectedly the Nambu gunner ceased his firing, either to recover from a fit of giggling or to insert a new sleeve of ammunition into his machine gun. During that brief pause Callahan pulled a pin on a hand grenade and, still lying flat, gave it a kind of backhand pitch toward the machine gun. He waited for the explosion and then, leveling his BAR, leaped up and charged. The exploding grenade sent the machine gunner and his two loaders sprawling. Before they could recover, Callahan introduced them to twenty rounds of .30-caliber ammunition.

The 3d Platoon rushed through the small opening Callahan's heroic action created in the Jap defense, knocking out several machine gun nests on either side and sending the Japs into a retreat of perhaps a hundred yards. At the tip of this tiny salient, a dozen of us stopped to consider our situation. We were at the point. Dog Company, now minus half the men who had started that day, was strung out in a widening triangle for probably two hundred yards to our rear. Back of that, in a still wider triangle, was what remained of the 4th Raider Battalion. Darkness would soon be falling.

We had been killing Japs in droves all day, but for every one we killed, two more seemed to be shooting at us. Those of us at the point of the advance lay on the edge of a jungle clearing waiting for more men to come up and the order from Colonel Maxim to attack one more time. A weird silence settled over the jungle.

Suddenly, Bill Werden emerged from the tangle of trees and vines in front of us. "Where's Colonel Maxim?" he said.

"About a hundred yards back getting ready to order us to get our asses shot off," Cole said.

"Your chances for that are getting better all the time," said Werden. "An hour ago the Japs landed five barge loads of troops. I threw my last grenade into one of them, but there are plenty of the bastards left."

He disappeared in the direction of Colonel Maxim. Twenty minutes later the order we had been waiting for came up the line. But it wasn't an order to attack; it was an order to pull out. Bill Werden had saved us a lot of pain.

We would have to leave our dead, but we would take the wounded. There were hundreds—so many that nearly every healthy man in both the 1st and 4th Raiders was needed to carry them out. Men whose wounds were considered slight stayed behind with those of us in the rear guard to help in case of a Jap attack. But though we moved slowly, very slowly, back toward Enogai where several PBYs and a couple of two-stackers waited to evacuate the wounded, the Japs did not attack. In fact they did not even follow.

Back at Enogai after two days on the trail, we dug in and waited while the last of our seriously wounded men were loaded aboard PBYs or destroyers and hauled away. A few of our walking wounded were still on hand, being treated by Dr. Wilson and our corpsmen in a temporary sick bay they had established in a native hut.

There, late the second afternoon after our arrival at Enogai, as Cole, Cannon, and I happened past Dr. Wilson's temporary sick bay, we saw Mother Callahan. His dungarees were at half mast, his white buttocks sticking out into the gray world of New Georgia. He was leaning forward from the waist, supporting himself with his grounded BAR while a corpsman painted with iodine the bloody furrow. A few minutes later, Dr. Wilson began doing some preliminary stitching. A small crowd gathered to view this, and Callahan was red-faced with embarrassment and rage.

Cole moved up close behind Dr. Wilson. "By God, Callahan," he said, "when Doc Wilson gets finished you'll be the only Raider in the Marine Corps with two bungholes."

"Come in handy next time he has diarrhea," said someone. There was loud laughter. Callahan, still bent far forward, his feet solidly planted, swung his head half around like a horse bothered by flies.

"You son of a bitch, Cole," he shouted. "When I get loose I'm going to pitch your ass over a damn banyan tree."

Dr. Wilson stopped in mid stitch and held his wicked-looking needle aloft. "Goddammit, Callahan," he said, "stand fast. If I accidentally ram this needle into a testicle, *you'll* be flying over a banyan tree." He turned to the corpsman. "Go tell Sergeant-major Bleak to get over here and drive these goddamned kibitzers away. We'll never get Callahan's ass back together with this gang of slopeheads hanging around."

"It's time to take off," said Cannon, who had no wish to tangle with Sergeant-major Bleak and, accompanied by the rest of the crowd, we hurried toward the cover of the jungle. Some time afterward when Callahan, still in a rage, came looking for Cole, we were so well hidden that, after banging about in the brush a bit, he gave up.

"I think," said Cole, as Callahan went crashing away, "that from now on we'll call him Two-Bung Callahan."

The 4th Raiders had fought well and had sustained a considerable number of casualties in three separate campaigns in the northern Solomons. We were not sent back to our pestholes on the Devil's island of Espiritu Santo. Instead, we were assigned to a camp the 3d Raiders had set up and occupied on New Caledonia before heading north for the invasion of Bougainville.

In New Caledonia, because so many of our men were recovering from minor wounds or suffering from malaria, we were for several weeks excused from our rigorous daily training programs. It wasn't long, however, before Colonel Maxim perceived a disgusting indolence creeping into our conduct and ordered us back to work.

Even though the colonel was a hard taskmaster, he did have common sense. We would, he commanded, observe our usual routine of calisthenics and five-mile hikes—in the mornings only. Afternoons, unless we had caught a working party or had mess duty or the guard, we played baseball and basketball on the diamonds and courts the 3d Battalion had left behind. We wrestled, boxed, ran races. We swam in the small river at the edge of camp. We hiked the mile or two to the main road and caught a jeep or truck into New Caledonia's capital city of Noumea. We visited Army, Navy, and Seabee camps. We were also encouraged to improve our marksmanship at the range a detachment of Army engineers had bulldozed out of the hills three miles away.

A few days after our return from Bairoko, I had traded my tommy gun in for a BAR. It was about nine pounds heavier than a tommy gun and its seventy separate parts made it more difficult to disassemble and assemble, but we were convinced that the tommy gun's .45-caliber slugs were too easily deflected by the jungle's tangle of branches and vines. Several other Raiders traded tommy guns for BARs too.

"Don't shoot any cattle or natives," Captain McNail had warned. "If you do, Colonel Maxim will stop handing out ammunition."

Often when Cannon and Cole and I grabbed our weapons and headed out to fire two or three hundred rounds, Werden would join us to practice with his new pistol. Through some unofficial machinations, Captain Certin had come into the possession of a half dozen special-service pistols, each equipped with a silencer. The pistols had been originally manufactured for a Marine marksmanship team. The silencers, it was said, were the creations of an armorer at the Marine base in San Diego. With its silencer screwed into place, Werden's pistol fired with a sound only a little louder than a sigh. From fifty yards away, he could snap a shot and cut off a stick about the size of a pencil. His marksmanship continually improved.

Our daily exercise in shooting ended, we would return to camp in time for evening chow and then hang around our tents playing cards, writing letters, or talking about the war. By the end of 1943 we knew that America was winning, but we were all convinced that the war against Japan would go on for at least ten years. We had kicked the Japs off Guadalcanal, although the battle had gone on for six months. We had nearly succeeded in pushing them out of the northern Solomons, yet that campaign had lasted three months longer than anyone had expected. The attacks in New Guinea and New Britain were bogging down. The large and formidable Jap bases at New Ireland, Truk, and Yap would have to be taken. Distance itself posed a continuing problem, and the Japanese mainland was still several thousand miles away.

One night, shortly after we lit the lantern in our tent, Werden drifted in and not long afterward our company runner, Duff Chapman. Duff Chapman tried hard to be liked, but he had had two years at Stanford University and occasionally seemed to try to exhibit his intellectual superiority. He brought fascinating news: a half dozen Japanese soldiers had surrendered on New Guinea. It was hard to believe. None of us had ever seen a Jap surrender.

"Are you sure they were Japs?" Faltynski asked. "Maybe they were Korean workers like a few of those that surrendered on the Canal."

"Captain McNail said they were Japs," said Duff. "The word came down from Fleet Marine Force."

"It's got to be some damned Jap trick," said Cannon. "The six of them must have been wounded so bad they were going to die anyway."

"Or they were trying to set somebody up for a banzai," Faltynski suggested.

"I'd like to kick hell out of the people that let them surrender," said Werden. "It was probably some Army shitheads. The Raiders aren't going to let any of the bastards surrender. They come in with their hands up, we'll blast their guts out before they get within grenade-throwing range."

Duff appeared shocked. "You don't mean that, Bill. You're just having a bad day."

"Bad day, my ass, Duff," Werden said. "I had three good hours on the range today. I can shoot straight enough to knock the slant eyes out of any damned Nip that tries to surrender while he's still a hundred yards away."

"He ain't just yodeling 'The Polecat Polka'!" Finished cleaning his tommy gun, Cannon stepped forward and placed it carefully in the rack next to my BAR. "Moe and I were out there with him today. Old Bill is getting so sharp he can shoot the eye out of a mosquito at two hundred yards."

"With a pistol," I added.

Our interruption had given Duff time to recover. "I still think we should try to get some of them to surrender," he persisted. "It would save a whole bunch of men on both sides. Maybe Mrs. Roosevelt is right. Japs are human like the rest of us."

"Human?" said Werden. "Not unless hyenas are human."

Duff turned to me for help. "What do you say, Moe?"

"I'm with Bill," I said.

"You usually are," said Duff dryly.

"You're right," I said. "I don't shoot quite as straight as he does, that's all. But we're wasting time arguing. Like the judges say when they get tired of a case, it's a mute question. The Japs aren't going to give up. They don't believe in giving up. Even when they're half dead, they're always looking for a chance to take you with them. It ain't smart to try to talk them into giving up. All you're going to get is a .31-caliber bullet in the head or a grenade fragment in your guts."

"That's *moot*, not *mute*," said Duff.

"Moot, mute! It don't make a damned nickel's worth of difference!" said Werden, his voice rising. "The Japs shouldn't surrender to us, and we shouldn't surrender to them. As long as things stay that way, both sides are fighting the right kind of war."

Duff was looking as if he wished the discussion had never started. "Hey! Don't get mad at me, Bill!" he said. "I'm not a Jap."

"I'm not getting mad, Duff. You been a friend of mine ever since you jumped out in the open and blasted that Jap sniper on Vangunu. But sometimes when you start sounding like one of those queer Stanford professors, I wish you were a Jap just long enough for me to take my K-bar and cut you a new asshole."

Right then Bernie Cole, who had heard all the racket from half-way up the company street and was afraid he was missing something, rushed into the tent, stumbled on Cannon's boondockers, and knocked over three recently polished M-1s, Cannon's clean tommy gun, and my BAR. By the time we finished cursing Cole and straightening out the mess, Werden and Duff had gone off in the direction of Captain Certin's tent to see if they could drag him into the debate.

With one last blast at Cole, Cannon grabbed his tommy gun and began to clean the latest deposit of sand out of the receiver.

"I'm like you, Moe," he said suddenly. "I'm with Werden. But what's he talking about both sides fighting the right kind of war?"

I had been around Werden long enough to be pretty sure I knew. "I'll tell you exactly what he meant. In the kind of war we're fighting with the Japs, there's no favoritism. Everyone gets what he's got coming to him. In Europe a German machine gunner kills ten of our men and when things get hot for him he hangs up a white flag and comes out with his hands up. Even though the son of a bitch is a member of the Nazi party and has killed your brother and your best friend, you're supposed to pat him on the head, hand him a ration of Texas steak, and give him a free ride to a stockade way out of range of his own artillery. Next thing you know he's in Louisiana cutting cane or in Illinois picking sweet corn. Then when the war is over, he applies for American citizenship, grabs our own girls, has a family, and enjoys the beer. All the time your friends are six feet under and missing all the fun.

"Out here when we hit the beach, that Jap machine gunner knows he's dead. He might last thirty days and kill twenty Marines, but when we land on his island he knows he's a dead man. We're going to get him sooner or later, and it ain't no use for him to come out with his hands up either. If he does he gets five slugs in the guts. If he holds out, he gets fried with a flamethrower. There ain't no Japs cutting cane in Cajun country. That's what Werden means when he says we're fighting the right kind of war."

Cannon, who had continued cleaning his tommy gun, was just putting the finishing touches on the job.

"I'm with you and Werden," he said presently. "To hell with Duff Chapman. To hell with Mrs. Roosevelt too."

Right after taps that night, a high wind full of lightning and rain howled in from the west out of the Coral Sea, and the whole battalion got wet and cold driving in extra tent pegs, tying down flaps, and deepening the drainage ditches around and about the area. For a half hour or so after we finished digging and pounding and settled into our cots, the wind increased in intensity until it threatened to blow our camp clear off to Fiji or Samoa. As I lay there waiting for our tent to go flying away, I thought about Werden's statement. It was an idea so foreign to the thinking of most Americans in the war years that I marveled at it. To practically all Americans, the Pacific War was the dirty war; the Americans fighting it were to be pitied and appreciated, even admired, more than those battling Germans and Italians on the other side of the world. Back home, they saw the Japs as yellow devils—slant-eyed, alien. The Germans and Italians, with the exception of Hitler and Mussolini and a few of their vicious followers, looked and acted and sounded like our neighbors across the street or field.

But in Werden's eyes and mine and Cannon's and most other Marines, the Pacific War was the right kind of war, the simple war in which there were not the distractions of things like pity or Geneva conventions. It was a war that did not require hatred, although hatred was neither forbidden nor condemned. In fact, the whole psychology of the Pacific War allowed a perfect objectivity to those in the act of shooting down Japanese soldiers in a banzai

84

charge or pouring high-octane gasoline into a Jap tunnel and tossing in a lighted match.

It suited perfectly what I knew was Werden's concept of the
cosmos. He neither liked nor hated the Japanese. He killed them
without anger or mercy. To him they were a part of the forces of evil
and had to be destroyed. But they were no worse than evil forces
elsewhere, whether in Germany or Russia or in the America he
called home.

Werden professed to be an agnostic, but I saw him as a member
of a militant one-man religious order in a perpetual war against
wrong. The struggle in the Pacific was only one battle in a continuing war in which he had begun fighting years before World War II
and in which he would go on fighting long afterward. That private
war was his religion, and killing was more than a necessity. It
seemed to be for him a special event, a victory of good over evil, a
kind of sacrament—the sacrament of killing.

Outside, the storm ripped and tore at all things unstable, and
loud cries from down the company street indicated that somebody's tent had gone. Water rushing in over the drainage ditches
and under the flaps was turning the dirt floor of our tent into a
mudhole. In a few minutes the storm had ripped my thoughts away
from Werden and things philosophical, and I reached for my shoes
and shovel. It was going to be a long, busy, miserable night.

By the time Galvo sounded reveille through a wet bugle, the
storm had just about blown itself out. Our tent had held fast, but
about thirty others had sailed off toward Noumea.

The Scouts and Snipers Platoon had lost eight tents, including
Captain Certin's and Bill Werden's. After a crust of bread and a
canteen cup of black coffee for morning chow, some of us helped
Werden and his group erect new tents. During this brief workout
we found time to continue the discussion Duff Chapman had
started the day before. The consensus was that the Japanese would
never surrender.

Cole summed things up in his stentorian way. "We'll never live
to see the day a Jap surrenders," he announced. "Duff and Captain

McNail are getting light in the head. Both of them are probably coming down with malaria again."

"If that's the case," said Werden, "there must be an epidemic of it at Fleet Marine Force Headquarters. They're the ones who started the crazy rumor in the first place."

For the next several months, practically every report we received confirmed our convictions. We did hear that of 4,836 Japanese on Tarawa, 17 had surrendered. The 17, we believed, were either Korean laborers or Japanese troops so badly wounded that they were paralyzed. Elsewhere, in places such as New Britain, the Japs, suffering nearly as badly from starvation and disease as they were from Marine bullets, were not surrendering. In the Marshalls at Kwajalein and Eniwetok, they fought to the last man. In each battle when the end approached, disillusioned and disgraced Japanese generals and admirals committed hari-kari; the last holdouts in the lower ranks shot off their heads with their own rifles or blew themselves apart with grenades, true to their Bushido tradition.

The Japanese were also busy working captured soldiers and civilians to death in the Philippines, the Dutch East Indies, Singapore, and Burma.

Emirau

In late December 1943, the Marine Raiders received welcome news. General Alexander Archer Vandegrift, the brave, determined leader in the American victory at Guadalcanal, was to become on 1 January 1944 the new Commandant of the Marine Corps. General Vandegrift had always relied heavily on the Raiders, and after each of our victories he had been generous with medals and praise. The 1st Raider Battalion had seized Tulagi, saved Henderson Field, and bolstered the regular Marine outfits whenever the Japanese threatened to hammer a hole through the American lines. Also on Guadalcanal the 2d Raiders, after they had stunned the Japanese military with an earlier raid on Makin Island, had constantly kept the Japanese army unnerved and off balance with their month-long foray behind enemy lines. More recently the 4th Raiders at Vangunu and Enogai and the 2d and 3d Raiders on Bougainville had fought extremely well and had helped throw the Japanese back nearly a thousand miles.

Now that Vandegrift had moved up to the powerful office of Commandant, we Raiders could surely expect exciting combat assignments, new and better weapons, well-trained replacements, improved rations, and higher pay.

By late January, however, the men of the four Raider battalions, now all together, for once, in a camp on Guadalcanal, were hearing some alarming rumors from well up the chain of command. It seemed that our ultimate masters at Marine Corps Headquarters

87

had decided that the Raider battalions were no longer needed in the Pacific. Our units were too small, our armaments too light, our organizational philosophy too frivolous, our objectives too limited and unproductive to be of any further use in the rapidly increasing momentum of the island-hopping war.

This new and lofty view, apparently, was the product of Alexander Archer Vandegrift.

The chief source of this scuttlebutt was Private B. Cole, who for once on a Sunday afternoon had been diverted from his usual practice of combing the beach for cat's-eyes. "Move-the-Line Sledd," Cole reported at top volume, "says that the Raider battalions are going to be combined into a regiment—the new 4th Marines."

"Move-the-Line Sledd has been into the Aqua-Velva again," said Faltynski. "We already got the 4th Marines."

Cole gave Faltynski a look of superiority and scorn. "That's the 4th Marine Division, you moron-o-Pole. This is the old 4th Marines I'm talking about. The ones the Japs wiped out on Corregidor."

"You mean the ones the chickenshit Army surrendered on Corregidor," said Bill Werden, who had arrived in time to catch the last sentence of Cole's most recent rumor. "We don't need to be named after that pack of give-up bastards." He looked around for a place to light, spotted Cannon's seabag, and plopped down on it heavily. It was a ritual he almost always performed when he dropped in for a visit. He knew, as we all did, how carefully Cannon folded his khakis and dungarees before stowing them away in his seabag.

"Get yourself another damned place to put your rear, Bill," Cannon said. "Or I'll take a meat axe to you."

Werden winked at the rest of us and moved to a seat on Cannon's cot. "Now I suppose I'm putting wrinkles in the scivvy shorts you got under your mattress," he said.

"Hey, knock it off, you slopeheads!" Faltynski pointed toward Cole with the pistol he had been oiling. "This Hebrew boy ain't finished with his screwy scuttlebutt yet."

"It's not screwy scuttlebutt," said Cole. "Move-the-Line Sledd fried up a couple of steaks for Colonel Maxim yesterday, and the colonel gave him three drinks and the bad news. Colonel Maxim says that right after the 4th Marines got wiped out—"

"You mean chickened out. You mean surrendered," interrupted Werden.

"Right after the 4th quit on Corregidor in 1942," Cole went on, "old General Holcomb, the Commandant, announced that a new 4th Regiment would be formed within two years from Marines who had distinguished themselves in combat. That's us."

"And that's bull!" I said. "The whole damned rumor is bull. The Marine Corps would never be stupid enough to knock off the Raiders. We fight their damned battles for them, and we always win. That's why they call us Nimitz's private army. If it hadn't been for the Raiders on Guadalcanal, the 1st Division would've been wiped out, and old man Vandegrift would be sitting in a Jap prison camp on Truk or Formosa right now."

Faltynski seemed to be losing patience with the way a solemn session of rumor-mongering was going awry. He gave me a rap sharp enough to raise a bump on the muscle of my left arm. "Knock it off, Moe, or I'll put a knot on your head next. This is straight scuttlebutt."

Right after roll call next day, we got the official word from an unhappy-looking Colonel Maxim. The four Raider battalions would be combined into a new regiment, the 4th Marines, with three rifle battalions of about twelve hundred men each. The 1st Raiders would become the 1st Battalion; the 4th Raiders the 2d Battalion; the 3d Raiders the 3d Battalion. For the 2d Raider Battalion, proud of their reputation as Colonel Carlson's own, came the ultimate degradation of becoming the Regimental Weapons Team.

Many months before, the Marine Corps and the government itself had come to each of us and asked us to volunteer for hazardous duty without hazard pay and for extra hardships without recompense. For various reasons, one of which was patriotism, we had volunteered; and we were convinced that we had done well. We had lost comrades and friends. Now as our reward, the Marine Corps and our own government were breaking their contracts with us. We were—all of us, officers and enlisted men alike—filled with fury, resentment, and despair.

But we were still Marines. The bitterness of the facts and the abruptness of the change were hard to accept, but accept them we did.

For the three rifle battalions, the adjustment was mostly psychological. We had lost status; we had lost prestige. We had been demoted from elite to ordinary. We didn't like to consider the effect our change in status might have on the folks back home. But our relatives, sweethearts, and friends, perpetually fearful of our fate, were proud of our high standing; for them, whether as Marine Raiders or 4th Marines, we were the bravest warriors among the world's best men.

For the 2d Raiders, the change to Regimental Weapons meant more than a loss of prestige. They had hardly had a chance to curse Marine Corps Headquarters before they began receiving a whole array of exotic new weapons: heavy machine guns, 81-millimeter mortars, and 37-millimeter cannon. They were summarily informed that they had until 1 March to master these weapons and be ready to use them in battle. It meant that for the next five hectic weeks, the old 2d Raiders were back to working seven eighteen-hour days, a burden so unfair and unreasonable that they were for some months in a state of fury that was almost mutinous.

For the three other Raider battalions, however, life went on pretty much as before. Our squad was still the same legendary 3d Squad, 3d Platoon, although the company was told that two men would soon be added to each squad.

We were now F Company, one change we actually welcomed. Originally we had been D—Dog—Company, but for a short time in recent months, as a battalion in the 1st Raider Regiment, we were Company Q, a label we despised. Brawls frequently broke out when our Raider brothers from companies N and O referred to us as Company Queer. Finally Father Redmond promised from the altar one Sunday that he would slap the next Raider he heard making insulting references to Company Q. The battalion corpsmen, he told us, had enough work to do without having to be constantly involved in repairing battered noses, bloody abrasions, and black eyes.

We also received, from the 22d Marines, a new top-sergeant, named Brushmore. The day Top-sergeant Brushmore reported for duty with F Company was the anniversary of his tenth year in the Marine Corps. He had been a Marine so long, he announced the first time he spoke to the company, that he couldn't remember where he came from, and it was no use to ask him. For him, he said, the Marine Corps was home, and, being a homebody, he intended to stay. For a week or two after Brushmore bounded onto the scene, we watched him warily, a daily surveillance of which he was well aware. But he only waved at us occasionally and smiled and revealed nothing of his character and objectives.

Nevertheless, from friends in the 22d, we knew a few things about him. For instance, it was considered a bad mistake to cross him. Brushmore was said to be a past master at getting even. We also knew that he liked to booze but had never missed a roll call. We had been told that he played practical jokes once in a while, that he was tough and determined, and that, so far as anyone could recall, he had never had a sick day in the Marine Corps. And we had been warned that he was very good with his fists, having once been the welterweight boxing champ of the Fleet Marine Force.

We doubted this last bit of information. Brushmore's face showed none of the scars and bumps of anyone who has spent time in the ring. Although agile and strong, he was not otherwise especially impressive, physically. Nor did he cut any particularly trim military figure. In fact, he looked a little out of GI step. He had a thin red moustache that was carefully waxed to turn up at each end, and bright red hair that he kept plastered against his head as a flat base for an ancient campaign hat that looked as if it had been around since the Marines battled against the wild Moros right after the Spanish-American War. The crown of the hat had been flattened to about two inches all around, and what was left of the brim up front was pinned back against the crown by a large Marine Corps emblem.

The first thing Brushmore did when he rolled out at reveille each day was to slap that hat on his head. He then pulled on green dungarees, socks, and boondockers, and emerged into the alien world of Guadalcanal.

As we moved north in our relentless approach to Japan, Brushmore smiled and chortled often. He saw humor and entertainment where other men saw only ugly land crabs, scraggly palm trees, ominous thunder heads, and surfing sharks. He perceived constant humor too in the men of Company F.

Early each day for at least a half hour, Top-sergeant Brushmore read the dusty collection of regulations that govern the Marine Corps. He knew them intimately, and, being a man of the highest possible principles, saw that they were promptly and properly observed in his F Company feifdom. If he thought an uncooperative or wayward Marine had earned a five-day vacation in the brig, he would recommend gleefully to Captain McNail that the sentence be doubled to ten. "He'll appreciate the extra time," he would argue. "A man likes to get away from the old routine for a few days once in a while. And he'll find a diet of bread and salt and water just as good or even better than he'd find it at that garbage dump run by Move-the-Line Sledd."

But he was not exactly malicious. "I never hold a grudge against some eightball I've had to send off to the brig," he would say, "even though to guarantee that he gets the proper consideration, I have to waste a lot of valuable time organizing a court martial and filling out a stack of damned forms."

And after the court martial, as the offender was being marched smartly away, Brushmore would come out wearing his most benign smile and wish the brig rat well. Ten days later when, weak from overwork and undernourishment, the man returned, Brushmore would hurry out to welcome him home.

Not long after Top-sergeant Brushmore arrived, our squad got its two extra men. The first, Dan Dorning, a solemn veteran from the 1st Raiders, was back from a long stay in the Navy hospital on Tulagi. His skin still a leathery, unhealthy tan and his eyes yellow from jaundice and quinine, he appeared to be about twenty pounds underweight. Nor had he recovered altogether from the concussion he had suffered from a heavy Jap shell during the attack on Rice Anchorage or Bairoko Harbor a few months before. As ordinary medicos worked to cure his malaria and jaundice at the Tulagi hospital, Navy neuroexperts had labored diligently to pull his thought processes back into line. Apparently they had not entirely succeeded.

Assigned for the time being to light duty only, Dorning sat most days on a five-gallon water can in the company street observing the curl of smoke from his cigarette or cleaning his rifle for the fiftieth time. Once in a while he would brighten long enough to ask any of us who happened by a favorite question or two. "Ever nock an arrow? Ever get a cat drunk?"

Then he would angle to his feet, wander into his tent, lie down on a cot, and doze off. At first we thought he was faking his punch-drunk routine, perhaps bucking for the psycho discharge we called a Section 8. But as the corpsmen stopped plying him with quinine and sulfa, "Nock" Dorning began to regain his weight and strength, and the yellow faded from skin and eyes. Three weeks after he joined the squad, he asked to be returned to regular duty. Although our battalion medical officer, Dr. Wilson, sent word that any close, heavy explosions or other distinct shock might tilt Nock a degree or so off an acceptable mental balance again, he certified him as fit for duty. In our daily training grind, he kept up with the rank and file and on the range fired his M-1 quickly and well. He continued to act a bit addled, but we heard no more questions about nocked arrows and intoxicated cats.

The Marine Corps, in spite of all its inconsistencies and whimsies, had great patience with men like Nock Dorning. If during his lapse into the land of the befuddled he had asked for a psycho discharge, he would have been shipped back to San Diego, separated from the service, pensioned out, and sent to a hospital or home. But Nock, like every Raider, was sustained by pride. A veteran who knew his way around invasion beaches, foxholes, and firefights, he was, even in his confused state, too proud and too tough to quit. We were pleased to have him stay.

Our second newcomer, a tall, skinny eighteen-year-old, came to us right out of boot camp bearing the imposing name of Casimus C. Shuttleforth. From the low mountains of northern Alabama, Casimus—Cosmo, we called him—was especially well liked because he was a talented listener. You could bounce stories, theories, future plans, past disasters, and present woes off him all day long, and he would listen attentively and sympathetically.

Cosmo was a listener with so much endurance that in all the weeks he was part of the 3d Squad, we never learned very much about him. We knew he had a father, a stern, powerful, Bible-toting man; a mother, humble and subservient; five older brothers; three sisters; and a sweetheart named Maidie Sue.

Cosmo Shuttleforth had joined the new 4th Marines in time to be a small part of a major undertaking: a massive attack on the Japanese bastion of Kavieng on New Ireland. Although we accepted the news of this campaign with enthusiasm, we knew that the fighting would be fierce and our losses heavy. Intelligence reported that the Japanese had 100,000 men at Kavieng and an impressive collection of big guns, many of them captured from the British at Singapore.

We were not disappointed when, thirty-six hours before we were to board the troop transports that would haul us off toward an incipient slaughter, the New Ireland operation was canceled. Instead, the 4th Marines loaded aboard destroyers; three days later, on 1 March 1944, we sneaked ashore on the small island of Emirau, seventy-five miles northwest of Kavieng. The natives of Emirau, all of them Seventh Day Adventists, greeted us on the shore and announced that the Japanese garrison had left in a hurry a couple of weeks before.

For a few days, F Company camped in a rain forest a half mile from the beach. Except for the ever-present mosquitoes and the silent trees, it was a strangely lifeless place. No birds flew nearby, no land crabs crawled their random ways, no bullbats screamed in the highest branches. But it wasn't long before we realized that we had a legion of equatorial companions: the place was crawling with leeches. How they had sustained themselves before our arrival we couldn't guess; judging from the way they feasted on our blood, they must have been on starvation's edge for generations.

When Captain McNail sent word that we would be pleased to move to a less bloody side of the island, an order came right back to stand fast and thank God that we had only a few leeches to worry about. Colonel Maxim was almost certain that the Japs would try a counter landing from Kavieng. The Navy was also worried about the possibility of a Japanese task force coming our way from Truk. One of our search planes had spotted a half dozen battleships, including the 70,000-ton *Yamato*, at anchor there, along with a cluster of cruisers and destroyers. Colonel Maxin figured he could predict exactly where a Japanese assault force would land, and he wanted us to know that he had put us right in what he guessed their path would be.

After receiving this information we considered the leeches less sinister, especially when the company corpsmen assured us that leeches seldom killed anyone. In fact, they said, medicos sometimes deliberately enlisted leeches to clean infected wounds. Nonetheless, when Captain McNail came by late that day seeking a squad to man an outpost on an island about a mile from the mainland, the 3d Squad leaped up as one man and volunteered for the job.

Hauling our regular gear and as much extra water, ammunition, and rations as we could carry, we waded out at low tide to the tiny island that would be our playground for the next twenty days. The clear water was full of fish, small sting rays, and an occasional eel. A few sharks cruised in the deeper channel a hundred yards to our left hoping, we supposed, that we would blunder and provide them with fresh meat.

Our island was perhaps a third of a mile long and not more than two hundred yards wide. From a broader base on the main island side, it narrowed to a point aimed toward the sea. As we explored our haven, we soon discovered that the Japs had been there before us and had only recently moved out. Several pillboxes constructed of logs and covered with sand had been positioned about twenty-five yards inland. The usual debris of bottles and cans was scattered haphazardly around the pillboxes, the amount of it indicating that the unit stationed there had eaten well and drunk often.

After searching until we were satisfied that the Japs had left us no worthwhile souvenirs, we set about establishing some defenses of our own. At the island's point, a low tree with its roots on the water's edge spread its branches over beach and water. On these low branches we nailed a platform, surrounded it with several feet of sandbags, and emplaced a .50-caliber machine gun pointing out to sea. Along the beach to left and right, we dug our foxholes and placed our lesser weapons in them. Confident now that we could repel a company or even a battalion of Jap Marines, we introduced a few comforts into our daily routine.

Twenty-five yards behind our machine gun, we built several small huts from leaves and branches and spread our ponchos over the tops to provide shelter against the rain. In a hard downpour the ponchos leaked and the water dripped onto us for a half hour or so, but a few minutes after the storm had passed the water percolated away in the sand, leaving us partially dry.

Once a day at low tide three or four of us waded to the main island for water and rations, dodging the sting rays. Back on our island we built small fires and, using our steel helmets for cook-pots, prepared a mushy stew from our rations of meat and beans, beef hash, and hardtack broken into small chunks. The deeper water at the reef's edge teemed with fish. Here we occasionally threw a hand grenade, the muffled explosion sending a few dozen fish floating to the surface. They were small—a pound or so, with

wildly bright and varied colors—but now and then we pulled out a larger brownish species about the size and shape of a grouper.

Natives, who apparently watched us from the main island, paddled quickly to us across the mile-wide channel whenever we fished. These friendly Melanesians showed us which fish they considered poisonous or otherwise inedible. To warn us, they pointed to the suspect types, held their stomachs tightly with both hands, and howled as if in pain. We threw the presumably toxic species back for the sharks and rewarded our teachers with a good share of the fish. Then we cleaned and fried our own share on a skillet we hammered out of a coffee can. No fish I've eaten since has tasted half as good.

Well before dark we put out our cook fires, and the smokers puffed furiously on their last cigarettes before the end of day. As darkness fell we counted our blessings. There were no bullbats, no land crabs, no leeches, no mosquitoes—only the soft sound of a breeze from the sea and the gradually increasing rhythm of the incoming tide. A few of our troop turned in early each night, lulled by the sound of breeze and tide, preparing themselves for the late-night watches.

Because we had the early watch or wanted to talk part of the night away, the rest of us gathered at our favorite spot—the machine gun platform—two men on official watch, the others full of restlessness and words and wonder as we watched the moon rise out of the sea. In the pleasant shadows, there was none of the banter or horseplay of the regular troop areas. We occupied an oasis, a place out of the reach of authority and war. There on our gun platform with its moonlight and shadows and sounds from the sea, we sat like Greek rationalists on the Aegean. We became solemn and philosophical; that, too, was part of our island's elemental charm.

The fifth night, Cole, Faltynski, Cannon, and I were perched on the gun platform discussing what we planned to do if the war ever ended and we made it back home. With us were a pair of semi-official visitors: Bill Vahey, who had the company's machine gun squad, and John Reardon, the patient leader of the 60-millimeter mortars. They

had waded out late that afternoon to inspect our defenses and to deliver a message from Captain McNail. They had really come to escape the main island leeches for a few hours, and the inspection was over in ten seconds. The message was that toward morning we could expect rain and then, for an hour or so, heavy fog.

This was true every day, so the message was not received with much concern. We treated Vahey and Reardon to a fried fish supper, cleaned our mess gear and frying pan by rubbing them with sand and rinsing them in the sea, and then, as the full moon edged into the night sky, directed our visitors to our favorite location for discourse.

Vahey sat down with his back against a couple of sandbags and considered our .50-caliber machine gun. "Looks professional," he said. "What I'd expect from this gang of old warriors."

Reardon had gone to the far edge of the platform and was staring into the clear water. The sea was motionless now that the tide was in and about to turn once more. Reardon swung around, smiling briefly. "They'll never be warriors, Bill. Professionals maybe, but not warriors."

"If we can keep this war going for another five or ten years, they might get to be warriors," said Vahey. "By then I might be a warrior myself."

"You're already an old man," said Cole. "Twenty-five years old. You'll be worn out and gone before you ever qualify."

"Twenty-four," Vahey corrected. "Three years in the Marine Corps already; going on two years out here."

Reardon had turned away to study the water once more. Sometimes on bright nights, we could see luminous fish sporting there. "What we are," he said, not looking up, "is a bunch of amateurs. We weren't born to be warriors. We weren't raised to fight and kill. All we've got is training and discipline."

"And old bastards like Colonel Maxim kicking us in the ass," Cole added.

"We're like people who grow up in a city and who've never seen horses or cattle and think asphalt is the stuff that's turned at plow-

ing time," Reardon continued. "You could put them in the country for fifty years and they'd never be farmers."

"Wait a minute!" said Vahey. "I happen to know you're from Chicago. You're a big city jerk yourself. You wouldn't know a cow from a cucumber."

"That's what I'm talking about," said Reardon. "I'll never be a warrior."

"Hold it!" said Faltynski. "I don't think I can take all these noble sentiments on a night like this. Keep talking all that crap and my head gets so cluttered I can't think about May."

"What you think about when you think about May is probably not very proper anyway," said Cole with one of his insolent laughs. "What you need to do is think about May only once a week. Probably best on Sunday when you're at Mass saying the Apostles' Creed. A Polack like you is in danger of damaging his prostate if he starts thinking abut women on a bright night. So knock it off."

When the laughter had died away, we sat there silent and thoughtful for a while. All of us had grown up in a vast, peaceful land where people seldom spoke of war, and when they did, it was usually about the Civil War. Because of the hard times of the late 1920s and all through the 1930s, we, as our fathers, had developed a consciousness focused on getting a job, supporting a family, putting food on the table and clothes on our backs. We had become a nation of gatherers, planters, harvesters, builders, and suppliers. War and warriors were not to be either glorified or abhorred. They were not to be thought of at all.

If a hundred years earlier we had grown up among the Apaches, Comanches, or Sioux, or the scouts and rangers or frontiersmen who had battled them for generations, then we would have been warriors. We would have been indoctrinated in the conviction that war brings status, wealth, honor. True warriors were spontaneous fighters; we had to think before we pulled a trigger or armed a grenade. Discipline, training, pride, and firepower were what made the Raider system work.

As I sat there half submerged in thought, I became aware of the faintest possible shimmer in the light and shadow at the side of the platform away from the sea and sensed, rather than discerned, a presence. It was Bill Werden, emanating from nowhere.

"What the hell," said Cole and Cannon simultaneously.

"You gooks got anybody on watch?" Werden asked. "I'm going to have to tell McNail that when I got here the whole island was asleep."

"Yeah," said Cannon, "and if you'd quit playing ghost or phantom or whatever the hell you are, we might be able to get some serious thinking done without these interruptions."

"You're here for a reason, I guess," said Reardon. "Does McNail miss Vahey and me?"

"How the hell could he?" asked Cole. "All you guys have got to offer is a little seniority."

"Seniority?" Vahey was puzzled. "In this outfit, we got only about five days' seniority on you."

"That proves my point," said Cole. "When we left the States all those years ago, you and Reardon were already acting corporals because you had five days' seniority on the rest of us."

"And," Cannon put in, "because of your five-day seniority, you yahoos are already real sergeants going on captains. A few more firefights and a few more casualties among the brass and the two of you will be colonels or generals."

It was Werden's turn to laugh. "Daniel Eugene Cannon used to be a simple, friendly tool, a contented meat cutter, before he was corrupted by that damned Cole. Now listen to him yammer."

"Used to be a meat cutter," I said. "But now he's moved up to master of Spam."

Reardon seemed impatient. "What's the message, Bill? You got to be here for a reason."

Werden stopped laughing and found a seat on a sandbag. "I've got word for you guys from Maxim and McNail."

"We're ready. What's the bad news?" Reardon asked.

"OK," said Werden. "First Battalion sent a patrol over to Saint Matthias Island this morning." Saint Matthias was about twelve miles away, and there had been persistent reports that a few Japanese were still there. "We were a day too late. The natives said there'd been a platoon of Japs—about forty-six of them—on the island but during the night they paddled away in a half dozen outriggers. Late this afternoon, one of our destroyers came up on an outrigger maybe ten miles from here." He paused. "Now here's the part that's hard to believe: the Japs in that outrigger started shooting at our destroyer with rifles. They wouldn't surrender. Our people had to blow them out of the water. Before the sharks came, the swab jockeys counted twenty-six bodies."

"And two months ago," said Faltynski, "Fleet Marine Force said we could expect the Japs to start surrendering soon."

"Now here's the dope," said Werden. "The rest of those Japs are out there somewhere. Colonel Maxim thinks they might be heading this way, hoping to kill a few Marines. He says to keep a man on watch in every foxhole tonight."

We passed the word. There was no grumbling; we could sleep tomorrow. Vahey, Reardon, and Cole stayed at the gun platform and shared the watch there. Faltynski and Cannon patrolled the beach on the Emirau side of the island. Bill Werden and I took the unguarded stretch from the point where our line of foxholes ended to the base of the island. It was not a difficult watch. Even after the moon had set and a few clouds drifted across the heavens, we could have spotted a small boat while it was still a couple of hundred yards out.

For an hour or so past midnight there was nothing, not even a suspicious ripple beyond the reef. Halfway toward morning three ships appeared, gliding silently toward the main channel and the big island. Still well out, their blinker lamps signaled to the watchers on shore. We soon determined that the ships were part of a small convoy of destroyers, probably bringing in supplies. We were too close to the Japanese air bases on New Ireland for our admirals to risk anything bigger than a destroyer in the waters around Emirau.

That bit of excitement over, we continued our patrol; about a half hour later we saw what we first took to be a floating log but soon after recognized as a small boat—a native outrigger still several hundred yards away and heading in rapidly. There came a soft call from the nearest foxhole. Our watchers there had seen it also.

"Pass the word not to fire," Werden said. "Let them come in. Moe and I will take 'em on the beach."

Well back in the shadows, Werden and I eased along toward the point where the outrigger was heading. As it came closer, we saw three men paddling furiously. Slowly we eased along until, when their boat grounded, we stood quietly there in the shelter of a tree watching from a few yards away, Werden with his pistol in his right hand, I with my BAR cocked and ready.

They were Japs all right. Apparently sure that they had landed unseen, they pulled their boat toward the tree line, one man—an officer or sergeant—giving low commands in the rough male guttural forbidden to Japanese women.

"Hands up! Surrender!" Werden said suddenly. I must have jumped six inches, and I nearly pulled the trigger of the BAR. For an instant the three men were rigid with surprise. Then they reacted, the leader reaching desperately for his samurai sword, the two others scrambling for the rifles in their boat. Werden's pistol went *Pfft! Pfft! Pfft!* and the three men were down, each one shot neatly through the head.

Very slowly Werden eased his pistol back into its holster. "The damned Japs are never going to surrender," he said.

"Shall I put a couple of more rounds into them?" I asked.

"No need to waste ammunition," he said.

We waited the hour until daylight before we searched them. During that time, Werden didn't have much to say. I knew what was bothering him. He was trying to bring himself to apologize for deviating from what he knew I had assumed was the game plan.

"Moe," he said finally as dawn was breaking over the sea, "you know how I think about things. A man should never do anything he has to apologize for. But I owe you one."

"All right," I said. "I almost put twenty rounds of .30-caliber slugs into the Pacific Ocean."

He laughed. "You're full of surprises, Moe," he said. "Jumping three feet straight up from a standing start. Not many people can do that."

"I'll thank you not to tell the others," I said.

"Trust me," he said, but of course he told everyone several times, until I had the reputation of being the most talented high jumper in the 4th Marines.

When at daybreak we searched the dead Japs, we didn't find much: a rough map of Emirau, a few cards and letters, cigarettes, matches—no more. Werden cleaned his pistol and went off to give Colonel Maxim an account of our experience and the few documents we had retrieved. Cole grabbed the rifles and the samurai sword. He would trade them to the Seabees or the Army officers for bourbon or whatever else he could get. It had been a quiet episode. I had not had time to make any racket with my BAR, and Werden's silencer had worked with its usual precision. Our sleepers not on watch had continued their slumber.

In a few hours Colonel Maxim sent word to go ahead and bury the three men or throw them in the deep water for the sharks. We decided it would be much less trouble to bury them in the soft sand and in a quarter of an hour the job was done. What happened to the other seventeen Japs who had left Saint Matthias we never learned. They certainly did not try to land on our island, and we never heard that they had either encountered or attacked an American destroyer. One thing was certain: they did not surrender.

Two days later Captain McNail sent word for Cole, Cannon, and me to report to Captain Certin of the Scouts and Snipers Platoon. Certin had his headquarters in a small, dry bunker on the main island of Emirau. Bill Werden and a couple of other scouts were there with Certin studying a large map as we hurried in.

103

Certin looked us over. "You slopeheads look fed and healthy," he said, in a tone that implied he was surprised that we didn't look half starved.

"We get plenty of good C-rations, Captain," said Cole. "Fills your gut with fat and your head with hazy ideas."

Certin did not appear convinced. "You're lying, Cole," he said. "Nobody ever got fat on C-rations. If I know you bastards, you got something else hid out there on Paradise Island. Couple of these charming native girls to go fishing for you, I'll bet your marbles."

"We got grenades to go fishing for us, Captain," I said. "We throw in a grenade or two, and Cole's fat girlfriends swim out and take the dead fish away from the sharks. Those girls all got moo-moo, so they float like tubs."

"You mean they all got elephant-something-or-other," said Cannon. "That's why they float like tubs."

"Elephantiasis," said Captain Certin. "Half the gooks on this island have got it. Better not cozy up too close to any of those ladies." He paused. "Now then!" He was finished with the introductory chatter. "What we need is three people to volunteer to take a short excursion with Bill Werden. He says you three eightballs helped him knock off the Japs a few nights ago and are crazy enough to volunteer for an exciting mission like the one we have in mind."

"Bill Werden had the bastards shot dead the other night before I had a chance to lift my BAR, Captain," I said. "What did he volunteer us for this time?"

"About a three-day visit to one of the little islands near Vela. We think the Japs have one or two coast watchers there keeping tabs on our air and naval activity. Admiral Nimitz doesn't like that."

"How do we get there?" said Cannon.

"Submarine," said Certin. "The good old *Porpoise*. Leaves here right after dark. Already got a rubber boat aboard for you. They'll get you to about two miles off shore. You paddle in very quietly so you don't wake up the land crabs. Won't be no trouble at all."

104

"How many Nambus will be on the beach pointing our way?" asked Cole.

"Oh, I don't think there'll be any Japs waiting for you. Maybe a couple of Jap radio people out there and maybe a native or two."

Standing behind Captain Certin, Werden was laughing soundlessly. He flashed four fingers, four times. Captain Certin half turned just in time to see this signal.

"Only one or two Japs, Bill," he said. "Only one or two. Intelligence has assured me of that."

Werden grinned. "Two or twenty, we'll take care of them."

"And smash up their equipment. Smash up their damned radios!" Certin exclaimed.

"Won't be no need to smash them radios if they're anything like ours," said Cole. "A few drops of sea water will put them out of commission forever."

Captain Certin, usually all serious business, almost smiled. "If it makes you feel better," he said, "soak the damned things in sea water and afterward smash them all to hell."

There was a rustle at the bunker entrance, and Mother Callahan stuck his head in.

"Jump in here, Callahan," said Captain Certin. "You just volunteered to take a boat trip with Bill Werden and these screwball buddies of his."

Cole's face cracked in a broad grin. "Here's our old buddy—"

Callahan had raised his hand. "Damn you, Cole, don't say it! I don't need to hear any of your Two-Bung Callahan crap."

"I didn't say Two-Bung," said Cole. "You said Two-Bung." He swung around in my direction. "I didn't say Two-Bung, did I, Moe? Mother is the one that said Two-Bung."

Callahan handed me his BAR, reached out, took hold of Cole's dungaree jacket, lifted him about two feet off the sand, and gave him a shake that would have rattled the teeth of a water buffalo.

"What the hell is going on?" said Captain Certin.

Callahan gave Cole one more furious shake. "I'm just teaching this slopehead some damned manners, Captain."

"Well, drop him somewhere, will you?" Captain Certin said. "So I can give you gooks the scoop." All of us were laughing, even Cole, whose boondockers were now in contact with solid ground; and Callahan had started to smile.

We were pleased to see Mother Callahan. Suddenly, Cannon came out with a question already in my mind. "Captain, how did you happen to pick us to go along with a couple of pros like Werden and Callahan? How the hell did we get included on this ride?"

"I already told you. It's one of your rewards for being friends of Bill Werden," he said. We all laughed, cynically. Certin went on. "Two reasons we volunteered you slopeheads," he said. "First is that we got teams going out to six other islands where we expect to find Jap outposts. So we're shorthanded. The second reason is that Bill Werden says you guys are good paddlers and smart enough to stay the hell out of his way." It made sense. We had all had enough experience with Werden to be ready if he needed us. And we did know our way around rubber boats.

Months before, way back on the California coast south of San Clemente, we had had our first strenuous exercise with those sometimes awkward and obstreperous sea vehicles. Back then the rubber boats we rode toward shore were designed for eight-man crews: one man in the bow, three paddlers kneeling on each side, and, in the stern, a steersman who used his paddle to keep the bow pointed toward shore. We tied our weapons in the bottom because, two times out of three, our boat flipped upside down as we hit the heavy surf close to shore. Once we reached the islands of the Pacific, however, we worked with smaller five-man boats—two paddlers on each side and a steersman at the stern.

During our jungle training on Espiritu Santo, we had practiced frequent night landings with those five-man boats and had become very good at sneaking silently onto small islands. A month or so after we had made camp on Espiritu, there had been some excitement about the possibility of a Japanese coast watcher on Pentecost, a large island across the way. The channel between the islands was filled with cruisers, destroyers, transports, and an occasional battleship or carrier—all refueling or in other ways preparing for some big push to the north. Japanese watchers on Pentecost equipped with powerful field glasses and radios could alert commanders on Rabaul or Truk, and submarine captains in between, about the ship traffic in and out of the New Hebrides.

One dark, quiet night, our company had launched rubber boats from our destroyer well out to sea from Pentecost and paddled in. The trip required nearly two hours of very hard exercise. A couple of hundred yards offshore, we began an especially silent approach, dipping our paddles into the sea at a slight angle to smother any sound. After a few moments we felt our boats scrape the sand, and we leaped out to pull them under the trees. Now, quickly, we organized and slipped into the jungle, moving inland for at least an hour in the pitch dark. In the lead, Bill Werden used his compass to stay on a prescribed azimuth toward at least one point where a Jap coast watcher was likely to be. Behind him we followed, single file, our only guide the bit of luminescent material picked from the jungle floor or trees and plastered on the pack of the man immediately ahead.

In an hour or so, Werden stopped. The word came whispering along the line to settle down where we were until daylight. It was an eerie, three-hour wait in absolute darkness, the silence broken only by the slight sound of a nearby buddy's breathing or restless shifting about and the occasional scream of a bullbat.

Daylight came and we set out, weapons ready, to hunt Japs. There were none on Pentecost. There were, we soon discovered, friendly natives, clean jungle trails lined with small stones, a chapel, and a few French nuns who were busy educating the children and attempting to spread some Christianity around. Pentecost seemed to have something the other islands of Melanesia seldom did: structure, order, and peace.

Reassured after a couple of hours that no coast watchers could operate there without being discovered and reported by nuns or natives, we made our way back to our boats, which by this time the natives had found and pulled to the water's edge for us.

A few miles out, our destroyer waited. The sea was calm, the late afternoon beautiful. We were in no hurry to leave this pretty, peaceful spot for our miserable camp in the swamps of Espiritu. We paddled along at a leisurely pace; I was thinking that if we could stall the remainder of the day away, the torpedo nets would be drawn across each end of the channel and we could spend at least one night at sea.

It was not to be. Late in the day, as we boarded our destroyer, the captain headed full speed for the protected channel between Espiritu and Pentecost. An hour before, he had received a report of several Japanese subs lurking close by, and he was anxious to get home. As darkness fell we were back on Espiritu hiking the last several miles to camp, small clouds of mosquitoes already surrounding us, the day's last legions of flies making their final passes before the black night settled.

Months later, far from Espiritu Santo, we had paddled our rubber boats on a few scouting parties in the northern Solomons and again made practice landings on New Caledonia and Guadalcanal. So, like most Raiders, we could do what had to be done with rubber boats, whether the year before at Pentecost or now on some small, ominous island up near the equator.

The tiny island that was then called Veritatas is southwest of New Ireland in a sea lane much used at that time by warships of both the United States and Japan and directly beneath the sky paths followed by our planes coming from the south to bomb Kavieng and Rabaul. It was a logical place for the Japanese to station men who watched sea and sky. In fact, by the time our sub had approached to within two miles, we had convinced ourselves that there were Japs, maybe as much as a company of them, waiting for us on shore.

There were five of us in the rubber boat we launched into a calm sea from the deck of the *Porpoise*: Werden, Cole, Cannon, Callahan, and me. Overhead a low, dark cloud cover threatened rain. Along with rain, we could expect wind. With the prospect of wind and rough sea spurring us, we paddled furiously toward shore. A quarter of a mile from the island, we slowed our pace and began a silent approach. The island toward which we headed was small, perhaps only four times as big as the one near Emirau where we had been living so pleasantly for the past two weeks. As we neared the shore I remembered how, a few nights before, Bill Werden and I had watched from the dark shadows as the Japs in their outrigger approached. Now the situation was reversed, and I could feel the tension rising in me.

We were moving very deliberately now, the slight sound of our paddles drowned by the murmur of the tide on the beach ahead. Werden left his steersman's place at the stern, pulled his pistol, and took up a position at the bow. In a minute we felt the scrape of bottom on sand and a few seconds later had pulled the boat into the shadows. We were ashore.

"Stay right here," Werden whispered. "I'll be back at first light."

We lay there in the darkness, the tension that preceded our landing already draining away. If those who occupied the island had not seen us land, there was very little possibility that they would discover us in these dark shadows.

An hour after daylight there was a stir in the undergrowth, and Werden appeared. He crouched beside us. "Directly across the island," he said in a low voice. "About three hundred yards. A hut with an antenna on it. Three Japs."

"Let's go get 'em," said Cannon. He was getting that eager look that modified his features before any action.

"We got to wait," said Werden. "If we kill them now, the Japs on some other island might send over a bargeload of troops to see why they aren't reporting in. We'll wait till after moonrise. That'll be the time to get them. There's good cover all the way."

The day was long and quiet. Once in a while we heard squadrons of planes flying over high above, and twice we saw Japanese destroyers going north all out. Late in the afternoon, a small Jap patrol boat chugged by very close to our side of the island, a squad of soldiers lounging around the deck. Werden had been right about the timing for our small operation. The submarine that had brought us was not scheduled to return to the rendezvous point until an hour after midnight.

The day wore on, the sun beginning to dip slowly westward toward the Bismarck Sea. We took turns napping under the mangroves in the soft sand.

Just after dark, with Werden leading the way, we moved out single file. Slowly we stole forward through underbrush and vines until we could hear the tide rippling against the opposite shore. We came at last to a small clearing already bathed in moonlight and shadow and saw, at the edge nearest the sea, a tiny hut situated so cunningly amid the low trees that it could not have been seen in brightest sunlight from either a patrol boat or a low-flying plane. Knowing nothing about the magic our Navy cryptologists had worked, we were filled with amazement that our Intelligence people had so precisely predicted the presence of Japanese coast watchers on this tiny, isolated island.

Edging into a deep shadow, Werden suddenly stopped. We clustered close around. Ahead we could distinctly hear the low sound of a small generator that apparently powered their radio.

"Wait," whispered Werden. Kneeling, we rested. "They're in the hut," he whispered. We settled down, the moments easing slowly away. It was an exercise we had practiced a hundred times—the night stalk—first, night after night, at Pendleton, later in the rear area jungle of Espiritu and on New Caledonia and Guadalcanal. Night after night, with Jap soldiers nearby, we had observed the hours of silence in the mangrove swamps of New Georgia and on the approaches to Bairoko and Enogai. We had become experts in the cat-footed stalk, the silent wait, the sudden kill. And Bill Werden was by far the most talented and fearless among us.

From the hut came an outburst of voices in Japanese and the clear sound of clinking glasses. "Sake-drinking time," Werden whispered. "They'll be out in a minute."

More laughter from the hut, more sounds of glass against glass. A short time later two men emerged, exchanging exclamations as the bright moonlight struck them. Although we knew no Japanese, we could guess that they were admiring the way the tropic moon had transformed their island from the ugly to the sublime. At that moment I was almost sorry for what we would soon be obliged to do.

Side by side, carrying their quart-size bottles, they walked slowly toward the beach and stood there drinking and watching, listening to the approaching tide. Now the third man stepped out and walked to the dark side of the hut. The generator stopped. Clearly, they intended to radio no more reports that night.

"I'll get them now," whispered Werden. "If I have trouble, I'll whistle. That's your signal to shoot. Otherwise, wait. Maybe I can get the other two so we don't have to make any noise." He paused. "Got it?"

"Got it," we whispered.

"Good," whispered Werden and disappeared. I was looking directly at him, his form indistinct in light and shadow. He was suddenly and amazingly part of the darkness.

The Jap at the generator had turned and started back toward the hut—slow step, shadow; slow step, moonlight; slow step, shadow. From that second shadow, he did not reappear. There had been no sound.

The two men on the beach had turned and were walking now, one slightly behind the other, back toward their small hut. The lead man, maybe a yard ahead of the second, stumbled and went down. The second man jumped back a step as if he had suddenly spotted a tiger or a snake. For just a second he was frozen there in the bright light of the moon. Then he was enveloped by a strange, instant shadow before he and shadow disappeared.

"All right," came Werden's voice. "It's finished."

The three dead men were all within ten yards of their hut, the two killed while returning from the beach lying only a few feet apart. I looked closely at the first man. There was no blood. His head was slightly askew, as if his neck had been broken. The others had apparently been killed by a deep thrust of a K-bar blade, but both had died in a silence broken only by the soft lap of the tide, as if they had been throttled before the intrusion of the cold, deadly steel.

"We'll leave them where they are," said Werden, as we examined the bodies with awe. "It'll shake the guts out of the first Jap patrol that comes by to see why their radio isn't sending."

"You sure did a job, Bill," said Cannon suddenly.

"And I don't even have to clean my BAR!" said Cole.

"OK," said Werden. "Let's get going. Callahan, search those bodies. Cole, bust up the generator. Moe, you and Cannon and I will search around the hut for documents and smash their radio."

In fifteen minutes, satisfied that we had done all that could be done, we headed off across the island to our rubber boat. At midnight we were well out over the reef, waiting at the rendezvous point for the sub. It surfaced right on the dot, and a day and a half later we were back on Emirau wading in the shallow channel toward our island outpost. A few days later the airstrip on Emirau was finished and squadrons of fighters and fighter bombers began to land. About the same time, the Army began moving in defense battalions strong enough, they hoped, to protect the new airstrip against unwelcome visitors from New Ireland or the Palaus.

Our job on Emirau was done. Although only Bill Werden had killed any Japs during the six weeks we had been there, we had accomplished one of the most successful operations of the Pacific War: it put our bombers within easy reach of the Japanese bases at Rabaul, Kavieng, and Truk, and forced the Japanese into a full-scale retreat once more.

Halfway through April 1944, we reluctantly left our quiet island and boarded the two-stack destroyers—our seagoing limousines, as we had been calling them—and headed back toward Guadalcanal.

The Emperor's Birthday

On that quick return voyage, the big event of each day came shortly after sundown when the ship's radio tuned in Tokyo Rose. The radio operator turned up the volume so that she could be heard from bow to stern. After the sweet nostalgia of recorded music from some 1930s dance band like Ted Weems or Glenn Miller, the sexy-voiced lady from Japan would devote a few minutes to dire threats and bloody promises. "If you Marines insist on crossing the equator," she would announce, "you will be decimated by the brave and formidable forces of Admiral Nagumo." We were not frightened by her threats: we knew the Japanese were confounded and in retreat.

Then, as if to bring us back from the shock of her dire portents, she would give us a few Bing Crosby melodies, including a couple of sad ballads like "I'll Take You Home Again, Kathleen." Having nearly reduced us to tears, Tokyo Rose would turn for a while to stabbing a lot of guys where it hurt. First she would sympathize with the poor, brave American soldiers and Marines, most of them boys, far from home and fighting a hopeless struggle against the invincible legions of the Japanese Empire. Then she would give the knife a sadistic twist: "And while you brave Americans are dying by the hundreds of thousands in those miserable jungle islands of the South Pacific eight thousand miles from home, your sexy sweethearts and pretty wives are back there in the good old USA jazzing with all those slackers and draft dodgers. And let me tell you, there

113

are millions and millions of them. Right now, your best girlfriend or your sweet little wife is squirming and squeezing in lover's lane in the rumble seat of a Model A."

Even though by the spring of 1944 the rumble seat of any surviving Model A would have been pretty well worn and, in any case, a bit compact for lusty squirming and squeezing, a feeling of alarm and depression would spread across the deck. Most Marines knew from their own experiences that a goodly number of sexy sweethearts and sweet little wives were young, frolicsome, and generous—and surely, after two or three years of waiting, extremely lonesome. There was just enough substance to Tokyo Rose's contention to alarm men like Faltynski who, whenever he had a moment's repose, was beset by the insidious concern that some stateside bebopper might persuade May to run off with him.

About the third night of our journey, Tokyo Rose deviated a bit from her practice of harassing troubled and doubting Marines and considerately reminded her listeners of a majestic event we might otherwise never have known about: the emperor's birthday. On 29 April 1944, the Son of Heaven would be forty-three. "You Marines out there in the horrible jungles of some Pacific island, listen to me! Listen carefully to what I have to say! You should be especially humble and repentant when you consider this darling of the universe, this offspring of the gods. In his bountiful mercy, he has delayed the vengeful warriors of the Rising Sun. He will not be so merciful forever. You must come forward out of your hiding places and surrender, or the mighty samurai will hunt you out and eliminate you like ship rats from the surface of earth and sea!"

There was more, much more, until the ship's captain, deciding that we would hear no more Bing Crosby that night, cut Rose abruptly off.

"Think of it!" said Cole into the ensuing silence. "Give it some hard thought. April 29 is the emperor's birthday!"

"Maybe if we tell Colonel Maxim, he'll give us half the day off," Cannon said.

114

"Be our luck if the old bastard's birthday fell on a Sunday," said Cole.

"Sunday or not, I think we ought to have some sort of special ceremony," I said. "The Son of Heaven might crawl back into a cloud if we don't do something special."

Several minutes passed while we sat there on the deck and pondered the situation.

"Father Redmond might want to conduct a special prayer service in the emperor's honor," said Cole. He glanced at Faltynski, who sat close to the railing looking disconsolately into the running sea. "Wake up, Polack!" he shouted. "Stop thinking about May squeezed into the rumble seat of a Model A with that big truck driver. You can't do anything about it anyway."

"You son of a bitch, Cole!" Faltynski yelled.

Cole ignored the insult. "We just decided to have a birthday party for the emperor of Japan. Give me five bucks and when we get back to the Canal I'll get beer from the Seabees so we can really celebrate."

"You son of a bitch, Cole," Faltynski reiterated, and went back to his musing.

In the next half hour, until a rain squall drove us off the deck, we made plans for the event. Something special had to be contrived to show our disrespect for the emperor of Japan. A suggestion that often surfaced when we were planning any celebration of this kind was to get a couple of chunks of nitrostarch and blow up the officers' latrine. It was always rejected on the grounds that some officer might be visiting there when the nitrostarch blew, and then embarrassing questions were sure to be asked.

Bill Werden suddenly made his presence felt. "I could take one man and kidnap the island commander," he said. "The old bastard never does anything but chase that fat nurse he fancies." I eased back into the shadows, but he spotted me anyway, with his eyes that glowed in the half dark. "What about it, Moe?"

"I can hear the gates of Leavenworth clanging shut behind us, Bill," I said.

"They got to catch us first," said Werden. "We could drag him off back to that cave on Mount Austen. Make the Navy give us a shipload of whiskey for ransom." His eyes were shining with an increasing intensity.

"Let me think about it for about three years, Bill," I said.

"Maybe it ain't a good idea after all," Werden conceded presently. "We might have to tie up a couple of guards. That wouldn't be such a good thing. It would ruin their reputations."

A few days after we got back to our camp on Guadalcanal, Cole went over to the regimental headquarters tent and loitered there gossiping with Sergeant-major Bleak. Before long, as Cole told it later, Colonel Maxim marched in, sat down on a box to sign some official papers, and took note of Cole.

"What the hell trouble are you cooking up now, Cole?" he asked.

"What I was telling Sergeant-major Bleak, Colonel," Cole said, "is that Tokyo Rose says April 29 is Emperor Hirohito's forty-third birthday."

"Screw Tokyo Rose," said Colonel Maxim. "Screw the emperor too. You can tell them I said so."

"I'll send your message through the Red Cross, Colonel," Cole said.

Colonel Maxim snorted. "OK, I know you got some damned screwy thing up your sleeve, Private Cole," he said. "Spit it out! Spit it out, so I can tell you to go to the Devil and kick your ass the hell out of here!"

"What some of us think," said Cole, "is that we ought to get a half day off in recognition of the emperor's birthday."

"Recognition?" Colonel Maxim said. He was beginning to sputter.

Over in his corner of the tent, Sergeant-major Bleak was bent double.

"Goddammit, Bleak!" Colonel Maxim was launching himself into one of his exercises in seething. "Get some goddamned con-

116

trol of yourself!" He turned his attention back to Cole who was standing there in solemn, practiced subservience. "What the hell are you talking about, Cole? A half day off for the emperor's birthday! I'm going to get Dr. Wilson in here and certify you for the damned nut ward!"

Sergeant-major Bleak now had his head in his seabag to cut down on the noises he was making. "Stop that damned heaving over there, Bleak," Colonel Maxim seethed, "or I'll certify you for the nut ward too!"

Cole was standing his ground. "Tokyo Rose says the emperor's birthday is April 29," he said. "He'll be forty-three."

"And if I ever get a shot at him, that's as old as he'll ever get!" Colonel Maxim shouted.

Just then Major Bank sauntered in. "Am I interrupting a riot?" he asked.

"No!" Maxim shouted. "You just stopped a shooting!" At this, Sergeant-major Bleak fell off his seat and rolled off into the shallow drainage ditch outside the tent.

Major Bank turned to Cole. "I don't know what the hell is going on here, Cole," he said, "but whatever it is, I think it would be well for you to go away."

Reluctantly Cole left, Colonel Maxim's angry howls ringing in his ears. Back in our tent, he told us sadly that the meeting with Colonel Maxim had not gone at all well. Almost immediately thereafter, the word came down the company street for Cole, Cannon, Faltynski, and Moe to report to Top-sergeant Brushmore's tent on the double.

We were greeted by Captain McNail, Top-sergeant Brushmore, and Red Salleng, our acting platoon sergeant. "Stand at attention, goddammit!" said Salleng as we pushed our way in. "Captain McNail wants to have words with you."

Captain McNail was different from the ordinary totalitarian Marine officer: occasionally, he would let a man speak in his own defense. Most Marine officers, when giving a man the hard word, would order him to shut his mouth and keep it shut. If he insisted

117

on speaking, he would be immediately cited for insubordination and marched off to the brig. But McNail had had two years of law school before going into the Marine Corps, and he regarded himself an interrogator of some standing.

"Major Bank just got done chewing my ass out, Cole," he began. "What the hell were you doing over there stirring up Colonel Maxim?"

"I thought it would be a good time to ask Colonel Maxim to give the regiment a half day off," said Cole.

"A half day off!" McNail shouted. "A half day off for what?"

"For the emperor's birthday," said Cole. "It falls on a Saturday."

"What the hell do you know about this, Mr. Sergeant Salleng?" McNail said.

"Not a damned thing, Captain," Salleng said in his clear and clipped-for-the-captain tone. "First I've heard of it. I didn't even know the damned emperor had a birthday."

Captain McNail sat down, pulled off his cap, rubbed his head. "Give me a bottle of that sick-bay brandy, Top," he said. "I got to sort this out." He sat there a moment sipping the brandy and looking dazed. "Tell you what, Top. Schedule these bastards for about three days' extra duty in the gravel pit."

That afternoon as we sweated and shoveled in the gravel pit, we paused now and again for a drink of lukewarm water and a chance to continue our plans.

"I think an appropriate way to celebrate the emperor's birthday," said Cole around sundown, "is to burn him in effigy."

"Effigy?" said Faltynski. "I've heard of burning people at the stake or boiling them in oil, but I never heard of burning anybody in effigy. Is it anything like molten steel?"

"And how are we going to catch the skinny bastard long enough to burn him?" Cannon asked. "Hell, not even Bill Werden could sneak him out of Tokyo."

"Well, I don't know exactly what it means," said Cole. "But I've heard of it, and it sounds like a good idea."

118

I was not sure what an effigy involved either, but I seemed to remember accounts in history books of people being burned in effigy. Benedict Arnold had once been reported as having been burned in effigy, but he had apparently survived the experience and dashed off to Quebec or somewhere up north. That night we borrowed Duff Chapman's dictionary long enough to look up the word. While Duff, always nervous about the possibility that someone might run off with his precious volume, hovered nearby, we copied out the definition.

"It won't be hard to make an effigy," said Cole. "We'll borrow the Jap helmet Bontadelli brought back from Vangunu, put a coconut in it, and paint a nose, a mouth, and slant eyes and a pair of spectacles on the coconut. We can stuff an old sugar sack with some of the crap Move-the-Line Sledd has around the cook tent, mount it on a broomstick, and we're all set."

In an hour of ingenious design, we had created the emperor's effigy. "It's as pretty as the real Son of Heaven. He's a scrawny worm," said Cannon, as we inspected our creation.

"It'll do," said Faltynski. "We're going to burn it anyway, or are we going to hang it?"

Rex Guyman, a troublemaker from the 2d Platoon, had wandered up. "Anybody can hang an emperor in effigy," he said. "What we ought to do is machine-gun the son of a bitch." Delighted with himself, he went on. "Jack Freeling still has that Jap Nambu he picked up on Vangunu. Must have two hundred rounds of ammunition for it. He's fired it a couple of times. It works."

Guyman's suggestion was so brilliant and appropriate that it was accepted without debate. To machine gun the emperor in effigy with one of his own Nambus had a pleasing and cynical irony. Freeling was summoned and informed that he and his captured Nambu were to be honored as instruments in the gunning of an effigy. We expanded the invitation to include Reardon's weapons platoon. The Nambu would be supplemented with three of the company's light machine guns. Reardon revealed that he too had a Japanese Nambu and some ammunition hidden away, and also that

119

the mortar platoon possessed a knee mortar with a half dozen mortar shells, all captured in the fighting around Viru Harbor or Bairoko. The effigy party was rapidly becoming a significant event.

It was not hard to decide on the location for the effigy shoot. It would be at the new range the Seabees had built for us a few weeks before. In addition to the usual bull's-eye targets, the Seabees had constructed a mock village with moving silhouettes and pillboxes, designed so that we could practice for the street fighting we could expect as we hit the larger islands like Saipan and Formosa. As on New Caledonia, the range was also available to those of us who wanted to practice marksmanship in our spare time.

Meantime, word of our party spread throughout the battalion; it was not long before we learned that three other men in the outfit had Nambus along with ammunition for them. They were invited to bring their Nambus and participate. It would be a jungle party as noisy as a firefight with the Japs.

By midafternoon on Saturday, a good part of the battalion was trooping off toward the range, our numbers supplemented by self-invited observers from throughout the regiment. Some of these had brought with them their own effigies of the emperor, along with some rifles, tommy guns, and BARs. There was, for a short while, a heated debate about having more than one emperor, but this was settled by the observation that since the emperor was the Son of Heaven, he could split himself into five or even fifty effigies if he so desired.

Cole made a short speech and then shouted, "Ready on the right! Ready on the left!" He paused for dramatic effect. "Fire!" he shouted and everyone fired at once. There were long bursts from the Nambus, shorter bursts from the Brownings and tommy guns, and the crash of a knee mortar shell. Except for the Nambus, whose gunners were having trouble adjusting to the odd sights on those weapons, the shooters were right on the targets. Even the knee mortar shells were landing close among them. The firing went on with short breaks while new sets of gunners fired, until at last the ammunition was gone. So were the emperor's effigies.

For a brief time we hung around the range like players who have finished a hard game. Gradually the spectators drifted away, speaking in low tones.

We were back at the company area helping Reardon clean his weapons when we heard excited shouts up toward the main island road. A column of six tanks from the 29th Marines went roaring by, followed closely by fifteen or twenty trucks loaded with heavily armed Marines. They disappeared in clouds of dust heading toward the area where a main force of Jap counterattackers had landed back in '42.

As our battalion lounged around wondering what the 29th was up to, a flight of torpedo bombers roared over at treetop level, heading in the same direction as the 29th. Out at sea there was activity, too. A mile or so off shore, a squadron of torpedo boats went by at high speed, their waves hitting our beach like an incoming tide, and four of our old two-stack destroyers, their swab jockeys in position on their 3-inch guns, followed closely behind. The two-stackers were so close to shore that we could see that their decks were covered with Marines in camouflage uniforms, heavily armed. Meantime, on the island road, more truckloads of Marines and a half dozen self-propelled guns hustled by.

As things quieted down, we wandered back along the company street toward our tents. Cole and Faltynski were figuring that in the hour or so of daylight they would have time to pick up a few cat's-eyes. Cannon and I had decided to walk the mile to the nearby river to clean up and wash clothes, when the word came down the line, "F Company, fall out for a combat patrol!" Two frantic minutes later, armed and ready, we were lining up in the company street. Judging from the sights and sounds in every direction, the whole battalion was falling out and getting organized. Our platoon officers came bounding toward us, along with Captain McNail.

"Stand easy!" McNail yelled as he came up. "And I'll give you the hot scoop."

We relaxed. "Here's the dope!" yelled McNail. "The island commander got reports of a Jap landing down this way. Up the island they heard what sounded like a firefight. Jap Nambus and knee mortars and a lot of machine guns. The commander of the 29th thought it came from down toward Tasimboko. I heard it myself a while ago. Sounded to me like it came from off toward our rifle range. Anyway Colonel Maxim wants us to be ready in case we're needed."

For an hour, as darkness approached, we milled around in the company street waiting for the order to move out. But gradually, as the truckloads of troops went by going back the way they had come and then the tanks, we knew that the excitement had ended. The torpedo bombers had headed toward Henderson Field long since, and presently we saw the PT boats and then the old destroyers going slowly back. Not long afterward, we got the word to fall out.

No one needed to explain to us what had happened. A Japanese Nambu machine gun has a rapid rate of fire, perhaps three times as fast as one of our own Brownings. In fact, the Nambu's rate of fire is so rapid that we used to say that if you were hit once by a Nambu, you were certain to be hit twice or three times. And those who had been under fire from a Japanese knee mortar were painfully familiar with its flat, distinctive blast. Our birthday party for the emperor had caused an unexpected stir.

"I hope," said Cole, in an uncommonly low tone, "that John Reardon hides that knee mortar and the other gents hide their Nambus way out in the jungle somewhere."

We all laughed. "I'll bet the island commander is already on the line begging Nimitz to send the Fifth Fleet," Cannon said.

"And MacArthur is sending twenty ships up here to haul the Army off to Australia," I said. "There'll be an inquiry for sure."

Guyman hurried over to us. "Have you heard the latest scuttlebutt?" he asked. "Colonel Maxim thinks some troublemakers from the 4th Marines were firing Nambus on our range today."

"We don't know anything about that," said Cole. "Faltynski and I were on the beach all afternoon hunting cat's-eyes."

"Moe and I were down at the river washing clothes," said Cannon. Our weapons were clean and our alibis spotless.

We never did need our alibis. The island commander, perhaps embarrassed by his massive response to an unfounded report of a Japanese landing, apparently did not require Colonel Maxim to make a detailed investigation of the matter. And Maxim, who surely had heard all the firing at our range, did not institute an inquiry that he probably suspected would have eventually led to Private Cole and the 3d Squad, 3d Platoon.

The Lost Tribe of Israel

The following Monday, Galvo routed us out with a 5:30 reveille. By 5:45 we were in the middle of our regular jumping and arm-flailing wakeup exercise, but at twice the usual rate. By 6:00 we were standing at attention in the company street while various lieutenants and sergeants went about inspecting rifles, packs, and associated gear, an insulting rite we had rarely endured since boot camp. By 7:00 sharp we were already two miles from camp and chopping our way through the heaviest jungle on the Tasimboko end of the island.

It was the beginning of five weeks of intense activity: paddling rubber boats to a landing on Savo Island, tossing practice grenades into old pillboxes, swimming toward the Tenare beach from a mile out, creeping up on designated positions as our machine gunners fired live ammunition a few feet overhead, and running up and down the inland hills of Guadalcanal. By sundown each day we were just able to stagger into camp, line up at Move-the-Line Sledd's garbage dump, and later, with our stomachs rebelling, drag off our boondockers, string our mosquito nets, and crawl exhausted onto our cots. Only those who were in the battalion hospital sweating out or shivering through one more attack of malaria or dengue were excused from what we called Maxim's Revenge.

After five weeks, however, the Colonel tired of his game; it was creating more work for him than he had anticipated. We returned to our old, more civilized training ways. We rolled out at 6:00 each morning, had rifle inspection only once a week, worked a mere twelve-hour day, and got Saturday afternoon and Sunday off, unless of course we happened to catch a working party or guard duty.

Halfway through Colonel Maxim's five weeks of calculated revenge, the 3d Platoon was assigned a new leader to replace Don Floyd. Floyd, who had received a battlefield commission during the Emirau campaign, was being transferred to the 5th Marines. Our new leader, Lieutenant Merrill McLane, hailed from Rockport, Massachusetts.

An enlisted Marine in the early 1930s, McLane had, after completing his four-year hitch, left the Corps and earned a degree at Dartmouth. An intellectual, he was more democratic than some of the other officers. He liked to play chess, and because I was supposed to be one of the best chess players in the company, he would show up at our tent and challenge me to a match. He was a good, methodical player, but every now and then I managed to checkmate him. A few times he retaliated by finding my BAR dirty and my appearance slovenly during inspection the following day. Although I considered this reaction whimsical, I liked McLane, and so did the other guys. He got acquainted with the platoon fast.

One Sunday afternoon a month or so after he joined us, McLane came by with his chess set and, after we had played a few games, sat gossiping with Bontadelli and Cannon and me about the platoon. We told McLane that for nearly two years, Cole had been stoutly and stridently maintaining that he was a Jew but had been unable to convince us or anyone else that he really was.

"There are people who don't appear to be what they actually are," McLane said, "and there are some who want to be what they are not."

We sat there considering this observation for a few seconds. "What I mean," said McLane, "is that he's probably a pseudo Jew."

About that time some kind of ruckus occurred in the company street, and McLane went out to investigate. We listened as he tried to calm down the hotheads before going off toward Top-sergeant Brushmore's tent.

We sat there in an amazed silence.

"Well, I'll be damned," said Bontadelli, finally. "Our boy Cole is a Jew after all. What's a Sue-Doe Jew?"

Cannon was scratching his head. "It's probably the name of one of the lost tribes of Israel," he said. "When I was a kid and they made me go to service, I heard the preacher talk about Galileans and Samaritans and the lost tribes."

As if propelled by fate, Private B. Cole banged into our presence at that precise moment. Seeing the extraordinary looks on our faces, he applied the brakes. "What the hell's eating you morons?" he said.

"Lieutenant McLane says that you're a Jew after all," I said. "A Sue-Doe Jew. One of the lost tribes of Israel." McLane had said nothing about either Israel or the lost tribes, but no one corrected me.

Cole gave me a peculiar look, as if organizing his next words very carefully. Bontadelli and Cannon were waiting. "That's what I've been trying to tell you stupid slopeheads for two years now," he said. "It was on my mother's side. My mother is a Sue-Doe Jew." He paused and considered his audience. We were spellbound.

"The Sue-Doe Jews," Cole continued, "were the ones that farmed the land of milk and honey before the other tribes came charging out of the desert to try to take it away from them."

Right then, Faltynski arrived.

"Hey, Polack, Cole really is a Jew," Cannon announced. "McLane says he's a Sue-Doe Jew. One of the lost tribes."

Faltynski gave Cole a disgusted look. "Sue-Doe Jew, my ass. What kind of shit are you trying to pull now, you little bastard?" It was time to produce the surprise he had been saving. "If you really are a Jew, why ain't you circumcised?"

Faltynski had waited too long. "Because," said Cole, "us Sue-Doe Jews don't circumcise. Right before that became the law, the Sue-Doe Jews got lost in the desert."

"Oh, for Christ's sake," said Faltynski, "go ahead and be a Sue-Doe Jew this week for all I give a damn. Next month, you'll be a Sue-Doe Apache!"

He lay down on his cot staring at the canvas above while Cole lectured us on how the Sue-Doe Jews had always provided leadership among the tribes of Israel, how Herod had always envied and hated and persecuted the Sue-Doe Jews, how a multitude of religious leaders had believed that Christ was actually a Sue-Doe and not a Galilean, how the Romans had suffered their greatest military disaster in a masterful Sue-Doe ambush. Cole spoke in an increasingly loud and commanding tone; as the oratory attracted a group of the curious, the tent and surrounding area became more and more crowded until Russ Galvo blew chow call.

Next Sunday morning, Cole and Faltynski were up early, banging around to wake the rest of us so that they could proclaim their intention to search a new stretch of beach for cat's-eyes.

Cannon and I grabbed our mess gear and went off to morning chow. Right ahead of us in line was Mel Blum. "Hey," he said, "where's our part-time missionary and full-time troublemaker this morning?"

"Cole headed down the beach," said Cannon. "His latest thing is hunting for cat's-eyes."

"What're cat's-eyes?" said Blum.

"They're little stones, or maybe they're chunks of coral. They're about as big around as a nickel. Cole polishes them and makes jewelry—beads, crosses, stuff like that."

"And peddles them for large amounts of money, I bet," said Blum. "If he makes it through the war, that boy's going to be the head of General Motors someday."

"Or maybe he'll be the king of the Sue-Doe Jews," I said.

"What in hell is that?"

We told him. Blum laughed so hard he nearly dropped his mess gear. "Sue-Doe Jews!" he said a few moments later, as we sat with our backs against a coconut tree. "What'll that crazy bastard think of next?"

"It wasn't Cole. It was McLane," I said. "McLane said Cole was a Sue-Doe Jew."

Blum was puzzled. "I never heard of any Sue-Doe Jews," he said, "but let's have some fun. Ask Cole what a yarmulke is. See how he gets out from under that question."

The cat's-eye business must have been especially good that Sunday because when darkness fell, Cole still had not returned. A full moon was rising out of the Coral Sea as Cannon, Bontadelli, and I set out to find him. "Why do we want to ask Cole what a yarmaluke is?" said Cannon as we hurried along. "Hell, everyone in Arkansas knows a yarmaluke is an Eskimo dog."

"That's a malemute," said Bontadelli.

"It's not a yarmaluke," I said. "It's a yarmulke."

"What's the damned difference?" said Cannon. "He ain't going to know the answer."

We found Cole in the small tent Move-the-Line Sledd had scrounged from the Seabees down the road and erected near the cook shack. On rainy days it provided a rough shelter for mess cooks peeling potatoes or kneading dough. At night it became a lantern-lit casino. The poker game was run by Cole, Sledd, and Top-sergeant Brushmore, one of whom was always on hand to extract 5 percent from every pot.

"We got the big question for you, you little bastard," said Cannon, as we ducked into the tent.

Cole was intent on the six-dollar pot that a crowing winner was ready to rake in. Quick as a sand shark, he reached into the pot and grabbed thirty cents. "What's the question, butcher boy?" he asked without turning around.

"Blum says if you're a true Jew, you'll know what a yarmaluke is," said Cannon. His voice had a slight rasp: he had frequently emphasized to Cole that he was a meat cutter, not a butcher.

Cole was watching the cards flip out for the new hand. "That's not a question, you dumb-assed mick!"

Bontadelli intervened. "What he means is, what's a yarmulke?"

Cole reached into a newly won pot and pulled out the house share. "I don't know about the other tribes," he said, "but in the lingo of the Sue-Doe Jews it's a password like we use for the Japs—like lollapalooza or lilliput."

We hurried back to Blum, who chuckled contentedly. "We got him. Now ask him about the story behind the shibboleth."

"We got you this time, you crazy bastard," said Cannon next evening, when we finally caught up with Cole again. "What's the story about shaddowbreath?"

Cole laughed. "You mean *shibboleth,* don't you, you dimwit?"

"You said it," Cannon said. "I don't believe it. You said the word."

"Hell," said Cole. "I can tell what you cretins are thinking by looking at your faces. A shibboleth is a password."

"Damn all," said Cannon, "you told us last night a yarmaluke's a password."

"A yarmulke," said Cole, "is a small hat worn by the members of some Jewish sects."

"All right," I said, "what about the shibboleth?"

"When the other tribes came charging in to try to steal the land of milk and honey away from us, we asked them to give the word for *ears and corn.* If they said 'shibboleth,' we gave them two feet of the long spear and enough stones and arrows to stop a Jap tank."

Later, Blum was disappointed. "That's pretty much it," he said. "That Cole has spies listening in on every conversation. He's better organized than the Gestapo."

From then on, Cole entertained us from time to time with stories about the Sue-Doe Jews; but the stories became less frequent as our training program intensified and we began to anticipate our next big battle.

The Flamethrower Volunteers

Shortly after the celebration of the emperor's birthday, the regiment was happy to welcome a platoon of half tracks and a battalion of light artillery, along with additional men to operate them. Each rifle company was also promised three flamethrowers, those evil but practical devices for incinerating pillboxes or encouraging Japanese soldiers to come out of their caves. Everyone in the regiment was pleased to hear about the flamethrowers. Captain McNail positively rejoiced, as did Top-sergeant Brushmore.

But then an ominous rumor began to spread: the flamethrowers would arrive without men to operate them. The ten-man squad would have to come from our very own rank and file.

Some time before the arrival of the flamethrowers, Captain McNail sent word to the men of F Company that he would be pleased to get ten volunteers. To no one's surprise, there was a total lack of response. Although Marines are not ordinarily squeamish, the act of squirting jets of blazing fuel on even the hated Japanese did not seem quite sporting. It had to be done, but the average Marine was happy to let someone else do it. Worse, the flame-thrower was ugly, heavy, and unglamorous. Its very presence on the field of battle excited a great deal of interest among enemy troops, although they never seemed interested enough to crowd forward for a closer look. They were more inclined to fire every rifle, machine gun, and cannon in their repertoire in the direction of the flamethrower. All of this attention made the life of the Marine with the flamethrower extremely stressful and often brief.

Captain McNail was aware of all these negative aspects, but he was still disappointed. At inspection the morning after his first informal request for volunteers, he made a speech during which he reminded us of our reputation for patriotism and bravery and our penchant for volunteering; he tendered a joke about being able to get volunteers to guard the beer dump when a ship from the States brought a few cases of beer; and he cited statistics proving that the trigger man on a flamethrower was the most likely of all Marines to live to a ripe old age.

There were no volunteers.

Captain McNail was one of those good-natured men who become cross when people and circumstances confound them. He was obviously confounded now, because he began to make loud, threatening cries that ended with, "By God, if I don't get ten volunteers in the next ten minutes, I'll tear this company apart!"

No one spoke or stirred. Nearly every man among us had been in a half dozen battles; something more than violent language would be required to frighten us into a response.

For the moment, then, Captain McNail was defeated. But we noticed that right after he shouted "Fall out!" he summoned Top-sergeant Brushmore for a consultation and conspiracy session. If no one would step forward like a man and volunteer for an early and violent demise, by God he and Brushmore would oblige us to.

Two days passed, during which four men answered Captain McNail's call. The first was a hulking character named Swader. Several months earlier while we were on New Caledonia, Swader had become annoyed with a noisy, gasoline-powered generator. Claiming that it had insulted him, he fired twenty rounds from an automatic rifle into the generator and snuffed it out.

Colonel Maxim sentenced Swader to ten days in the brig and reimbursement to the Marine Corps for the generator, which was listed at $18,000. It was understood that a Marine private was not likely to have $18,000, so the colonel decided to extract five dollars a month from Swader's pay until the debt could be retired. Even at no interest, Swader would be in debt to the Marine Corps for three hundred years.

At the suggestion of Top-sergeant Brushmore, the colonel agreed to restructure Swader's payment schedule to three dollars a month if he would volunteer for the flamethrower squad. Even though this meant that he would be in debt to the Corps for five hundred years, Swader decided to become a flamethrower man.

Three more old-timers volunteered the next day. They had been involved in another incident on New Caledonia, when the officers began to live better than the rest of us.

Marine Raider officers shared the same stark living quarters and the same chow as the enlisted men. No one saluted or said "sir" in the Raiders. Officers—commissioned and non-commissioned—were called by their last names. But in the New Caledonia rest camp, the officers established their own officers' country and set up their own mess. They even threw a party one night, at which nurses and young French women could be seen cavorting. It was too much for privates Hodsgill, Barnett, and Braun, all 4th Raider mortarmen. Halfway into the night, they fired three shells from a 60-millimeter mortar in the direction of the officers' mess. Miraculously, there were no casualties, and no attempt was ever made to find the culprits. Shortly thereafter the officers began to settle down and to act like Raiders again.

Top-sergeant Brushmore, through his little band of informants, was pretty sure he knew the identity of the men involved. In their presence, he recalled the incident and badgered them about their poor marksmanship. They admitted nothing but did get nervous, especially when Brushmore told them that an investigator from the office of the Commandant of the Marine Corps was poking around asking questions. If the three inexpert marksmen would volunteer for flamethrowers, Brushmore would ask Colonel Maxim to send the investigator away.

The fifth volunteer was a tough Texan named Rule Donner. An F Company machine gunner, he looked sluggish and deliberate although he was as nimble as a nervous mustang and the best heavyweight fighter in the battalion. Donner volunteered for the flamethrower squad after receiving a letter from a young lady in Texas who, a year before, had promised him her hand in marriage. The letter informed Donner that she had decided the war would never end; she was planning to accept the proposal of a bomber pilot.

Donner leaped up and headed blindly off through the coconut grove toward the evening chow line. Then, as we all watched from the line, he ran into Kleck and Clark.

Kleck and Clark were two among a handful of F Company clowns. Each day as they prepared to make their way back to their tent from evening chow, Kleck would adopt the attitude of a Marine drill sergeant and call Clark to attention. Clark, shirtless, his dirty dungarees sagging, his old campaign hat sideways on his head, would snap to, feet together at the exact angle prescribed by regulations, his arms rigid at his side, and await the command.

"Forrud harch!" Kleck would shout, and off they would go, Kleck counting cadence, in a straight line toward the company area.

Clark always kept in step and obeyed Kleck's commands with a flawless precision, whether the command was forward march, rear march, left flank march, or right or left oblique march. But his military attitude could not have been said to reflect the relaxed-at-attention, arm-swinging marching perfection of a parade-ground Marine. As he marched, Clark kept his arms rigid, palms outward, and he bent forward at about a 30-degree angle from the waist in a clownlike mockery of the whole serious Marine business of routine and discipline.

Everyone in the battalion knew about the Kleck-Clark routine. Clark never deviated from his line of march, whether or not it intersected with animal, man, approaching tide, or tree, unless Kleck ordered him to.

When Kleck saw Donner angling along on a collision course with Private Clark, he assumed that Donner, as every Marine always had, would step aside. Of course, he had no way of knowing that Donner's mind was smoking with explosions. By the time Kleck realized a collision was imminent, it was too late. Donner and Clark had slammed into each other head on.

Kleck gave a strangled cry of "Halt!" as Donner hit Clark with his left fist, right at the beltline, and Clark rolled on the ground, struggling to let out a squawk of pain but powerless to do so because all the wind had been blasted out of him.

"Halt!" Kleck shouted again.

"Halt, hell!" muttered Donner, and gave Kleck a left to the middle. As the force of the blow tilted Kleck forward, Donner caught him again with a left to the jaw.

Right then Colonel Maxim was hurrying by on his way to watch the guard detail pull colors. The colonel had just drawn even with Kleck and Clark and was, as always, seething with resentment at their disgusting charade. He'd seen everything. "Corporal of the guard!" he shouted. "Sergeant of the guard! Officer of the day!" The call was repeated by Marines throughout the battalion area.

By now Clark was on his knees still fighting for breath, and Kleck was stirring. Donner, appearing shocked at what he had done, was mumbling apologies to Clark and slapping Kleck to revive him.

"Arrest these men!" Colonel Maxim ordered. Then he returned to his tent and no doubt did a bit of administrative tinkering, drank a few triumphant drams of sick-bay brandy, and hit the sack for several hours of contented sleep.

Next day, McNail and Brushmore offered the three a choice: volunteer for the flamethrowers or spend six months at hard labor in the rest camp for incorrigibles on nearby Florida Island.

After that, Brushmore and McNail seemed to relax their recruiting campaign. They had enough men to form a talented cadre; the weapons themselves had not yet arrived.

Raisin Jack

Right after chow one Tuesday morning, when all of us in the 3d Platoon were relaxing, Red Salleng hollered down the tent row for Moe to round up eight volunteers from the platoon and report to Brushmore on the double. Out of the corner of my eye, I saw Cole sneaking out the back of the tent.

"Mr. Private B. Cole, sir. You have just volunteered for a working party!" I yelled. I wasn't being vindictive: Cole hadn't caused me any physical or psychological harm for a week.

Cole stopped. "You bastard, Moe," he said. "Why pick on me?"

"Because working parties are more interesting and educational when you go along, Mr. Cole. I have no grudge against you right now—none that I know of, that is."

"Before, by God, the day is over, I'll give you fifty reasons, you idiot mick," he said.

I looked at Cannon and Faltynski. "Do you gents want to party with us?"

Faltynski grabbed his cap. "I guess it's as good as a ten-mile hike."

"I'll go," said Cannon. "I didn't want to help Sledd gut shark this morning anyway."

"On the double down there, goddammit!" It was Red Salleng.

I went into the company street and corralled Nock Dorning and Cosmo Shuttleforth. Nick Zobenica and Bill Drapp had heard

Salleng's call. Apparently not wanting to sweat out a ten-mile hike that day either, they also volunteered for the working party.

I needed one more man. Rex Guyman was wandering by. "Hey, Acting-private Guyman," I said, "tell your slopehead squad leader you're going on a working party with us aristocrats from the 3d Squad. Then hustle right up to Brushmore's tent."

Up at company headquarters, Brushmore was waiting for us with three gadgets that I first took to be flamethrowers. "Hot dammit, Top," I said, "we ain't volunteering to haul no flamethrowers around."

Brushmore had been standing there smug and smiling, but now confronted by incipient insubordination he flushed, and the smile disappeared. "Knock that crap off, Moe," he said angrily, "or I'll have your ass in the brig for thirty days. These ain't flamethrowers. They're for spraying DDT."

We had all heard about DDT. It was a powerful new chemical that was supposed to eliminate all insect life, including the mosquito population. What else it would eliminate nobody in the Pacific knew and nobody cared. What we did know was that all of us human inhabitants wanted to be rid of malaria, dengue, and blackwater fever.

"Will this mean we can stop taking those damned Atabrine pills, Top?" Bill Drapp asked. Atabrine, like quinine, was supposed to be effective in warding off malaria. But rumor had it that Atabrine not only killed off bacteria, it also put a man's sex drive in neutral and eventually smothered it altogether.

"Will this DDT eliminate Japs, Top?" said Rex Guyman. "Let's start dumping the stuff on them."

Brushmore ignored the questions. "All right, Moe," he said. "You and your gang of thugs have volunteered to take this equipment and spray this DDT crap in a big circle around camp."

For the benefit of any noncom or officer who might be listening, we greeted this announcement with bitching and groaning about being shanghaied for such a miserable fate. In fact, though, we were pleased. For a few days, we would escape the boring calisthenics, the close-order drill, the rifle inspections, and the ten-mile romps through the jungle.

Top-sergeant Brushmore listened to all our phony protests with disgust. "All right, Moe," he said finally. "Order your eightballs to knock it off. I ain't got all day to listen to howling hounds." He twirled the ends of his red moustache. "I think I'll tell Captain McNail that this spraying job is the ideal way of getting a gang of volunteers in condition for hauling a few flamethrowers and fuel tanks around."

"Load 'em up!" I hollered. "Let's move out." It was past time to pick up the cans of DDT and the sprayers for spreading the stuff before the idea that had crept into Brushmore's head had hardened into resolution. As we hurried away, we heard Brushmore laughing.

Brushmore had said that we should start the spraying job each morning about three hundred yards south of camp, then head directly inland for about seven hundred yards, then left again until we came to the beach three hundred yards north of camp. It was a simple enough assignment, one we figured we could complete in five hours each day, after which we could swim off the beach, wash clothes in the river, play cards, or nap.

One thing we discovered quickly: after the first hundred yards of easy going through the coconut groves, the land slanted steeply upward and the jungle closed in. Before long we were struggling on the rocky slopes as we hacked our way with machetes. The going was difficult and slow until we finally reached a rocky ridge where, although banyans were numerous, the underbrush thinned out.

We turned left along the ridgeline and knew very soon that we were directly inland several hundred yards from the inner boundaries of our camp, but the jungle was so dense that from the direction of camp we could see and hear nothing.

"Damn all," said Nick Zobenica, "the Japs could move a regiment through here, and back at camp we'd never know it."

"You're right, Nick," Faltynski said. "But you can probably relax. The Japs are a thousand miles away and heading toward home."

"How's the DDT holding out?" I said.

"Still too damned heavy," said Bill Drapp. "Why don't we dump the stuff here and let the mosquitoes come and help themselves?"

We had, at first, been too generous with it, but by now we were learning that for pools and damp places where mosquitoes might breed, a small squirt would do. The DDT spread quickly over whatever surface it touched.

We moved on, gossiping, joking, laughing. It was great to be free of the usual routine. The jungle closed in again for a short while, then surprisingly opened to a pastoral clearing with low grass and trees thinly spaced. There we came suddenly onto the site of an ambush or a surprise attack that must have occurred during the furious fighting back in 1942. Within a fifty-yard radius were shattered rifles, rusting bayonets, and helmets—almost all of them Japanese—the shredded remnants of belts, packs, cartridge cases, canteens, grenades, and the skeletons of many men.

We lingered there considering these records of one small, savage struggle, one of dozens and dozens like it that had occurred on Guadalcanal in the summer and fall of 1942—an incident so trivial that it had probably not even been mentioned in the daily reports.

"This shootout must have happened early," said Faltynski. "Maybe a few hours after our first wave hit the beach." He kicked at a Japanese cartridge case, its cracked and ruined leather covered with green mold. "We were still in boot camp then, most of us. Almost two years ago already."

Nock Dorning moved into the clearing, picked up a rusting Japanese helmet, and stuck a finger through the neat bullet hole drilled into it. He kicked several more helmets toward us. All had similar holes, some neatly cut, others with rough, jagged edges. "No," he said. "It wasn't the first day. It must have been two or three weeks later."

Cosmo Shuttleforth was eyeing the helmets. "I'd sure admire to meet the Marines that knocked over these Japs. I mean to say they were shooting straight."

The rest of us laughed. Cosmo gave us a hurt look, surprised that what he had said had set us off. "What's so funny? What's so darned funny?" he asked.

"You're still a Boy Scout, Cosmo," said Cannon, "but you'll learn fast." He picked up another helmet, this one with two holes through the crown. "What Nock means," he said, "is that these bullet holes weren't made by sharpshooters. These bullet holes were put there by the possum patrol."

He tossed the helmet away. "The damned Japs never surrender, Cosmo. At least I ain't never seen one surrender. And the wounded ones always play possum. When you come up to look them over and maybe even try to give them a shot of morphine, they'll stick a bayonet into your guts or blow your balls off with a grenade. Nowadays, when we stop a banzai charge or overrun their lines, we send a few guys out on possum patrol. They put a bullet or two into each of the sons o' bitches to finish 'em off."

"The possum patrol," said Faltynski. "It's cheap insurance. A bullet only costs about a dime."

"You'll get used to it, Cosmo," said Cole, still kicking here and there in the debris in the hope of finding one more souvenir that could be palmed off on some trusting dogface or swab jockey.

"It takes some getting used to," I said. I was remembering my first possum patrol. It had been on Vangunu, and I was only one of twenty-five Marines. Even with that number, the job took a half hour or more because we had to check out the bodies of maybe three hundred Japanese Marines.

They had come, probably from Kolombangara or Vella Lavella, shortly after midnight in three large barges to reinforce the Japanese garrison we were battling on Vangunu. Although Vangunu's coastline is many miles long and contains countless beaches and inlets where the barges might have landed safely, these three had beached where we had dug in that night. In fact, we had dug in with our lines and weapons facing inland because we had expected an attack from that direction. That attack never came; but when the three Japanese barges were spotted a half mile away, all we had to

139

do was turn around in our foxholes, train our weapons out to sea, and prepare to fire.

It was a slaughter. Only a few Japs got out of the barges, and they were shot down immediately. The remainder were blasted before they even made contact with land. When dawn came, however, out went the possum patrol. The twenty or so Japs on the beach were all dead, except one badly wounded man who, true to form, was waiting with a grenade. Someone shot him before he had a chance to arm it. Amid the carnage on the barges, about fifteen Japs, badly wounded and near death, were still conscious, still waiting patiently with grenades or bayonets, still hoping to get in one last thrust for the emperor. These we eliminated without hesitation, without anger, and without remorse. Hesitation and anger, we believed, were for the unprofessional; remorse a thing to be exercised by those who are paid to mourn. Even so, as I had told Cosmo, it was a job that took some getting used to.

Cole, still kicking here and there in the debris of that long-ago firefight, was not having much luck.

"Knock off that scratching around, Cole," said Bill Drapp. "You'll kick off an old land mine or a pack of explosives."

Cole gave him a disgusted look. "Close your trap, Drapp. They would have disarmed that stuff long ago."

"Maybe," I said. "Maybe not. Get the hell out of there."

Cole gave up the search and joined the rest of us at the edge of the clearing. "Two years," he said, echoing Faltynski's earlier words. "We been fighting the Japs almost two years down here, and we're still way south of the equator. We'll be old men before this war is over."

Nick Zobenica, who had not done much more than grunt all morning, spoke now. "We'll all be dead old men. Dead, or wounded so bad we'd be better off dead."

"Maybe there'll be a miracle," said Rex Guyman.

"There ain't going to be any miracles," said Zobenica, "unless we get some heavier stuff to throw at the bastards. They're digging in deeper all the time."

"Maybe the new flamethrowers will do that job," said Nock Dorning.

"Don't count on it," said Cannon. "The flamethrowers will fry 'em all right, but a lot of guys are going to get hurt bad getting close enough to do it."

"Pray for a miracle," said Rex again.

"And drink more booze," said Cannon. "Sometimes a belt of sick-bay brandy makes you a lot happier, makes you forget the war for a while." He took another look at the Japanese remains. Marines had died there too, no doubt about that. You couldn't kill that many Japs, even in ambush, without losing a few of your own. Of course, the grave's registration unit had removed the American bodies and put them in the Lunga Cemetery long ago.

"About now," said Bill Drapp, "I'd like to have a whole bucketful of sick-bay brandy."

It was time to move on. "At least we got a new weapon that'll kill mosquitoes," I said.

We picked up our gear and moved on, solemn and silent, our earlier cheerful, relaxed mood disrupted by the grim reminder that the war was far from over and that we were fighting a cruel enemy who had nothing but contempt for the inconsistent rules of warfare established by the western world. Like the possum patrol, the attitudes and methods of the Japanese military took some getting used to.

The Japanese way had been at first fantastically different, yet those of us who had fought in the Pacific for any length of time were gradually beginning to respect their concept of war—a war waged without mercy, a war in which those who surrendered were executed by their captors as spineless cowards and traitors to their own cause, a war that increasingly dictated the use of dumdum bullets and flamethrowers, napalm bombs and possum patrols. It was a war without privilege or favoritism, a war in which admirals and generals were killed as quickly and as objectively as Marine privates or sailors of the meanest rank.

141

There were people who were already calling it a good war; but, as Bill Werden and I had agreed, the word *good* was not quite accurate. It was not a good war. It was the right kind of war.

As we tramped silently along spraying our DDT into the bushes and vines and banyan roots, Cannon broke into the general reverie. "At least we got booze," he said. "Even if the war goes on for ten more years, at least we got booze."

"Not enough booze," said Drapp. "Not near enough, unless enough for you is three bottles of green Pabst Blue Ribbon beer every Saturday night."

Still gloomy, we worked our way on and on until, about a half hour later, at a spot three or four hundred yards from the north edge of camp, we discovered a clear, apparently pure spring at the base of a natural rock wall and, only a few yards away, half-hidden behind a screen of vines, the entrance to a shallow cave with a floor of clean sand.

Cosmo stepped forward wearing the same look of happiness and wonder that crossed his face whenever the mail brought another picture of Maidie Sue. He put down the DDT can he had been carrying and flung his arms up and outward like a Bible-thumping preacher. "Ain't never seen a fancier place for a still!"

This pronouncement would propel us toward a life of ever-increasing complexity.

"What," said Faltynski, who had once visited a brewery in Milwaukee and considered himself something of an expert on things alcoholic, "would a young Southern gentleman like you know about a still?"

For once, Casimus C. Shuttleforth was ready with an answer. "More than any other Marine in this man's Marine Corps, that's what," he said. "The Shuttleforth family has been making corn liquor in the hills around Princeton, Alabama, since before we busted the British at New Orleans." He stopped only long enough to draw a breath of new air. "My great-grandfather made more whiskey than Jack Daniel. Right now my pa has three stills going full bore within ten miles of the Scottsboro Courthouse. He can make corn liquor, bourbon, applejack—anything with alky in it."

We were amazed. This was by far the longest oral presentation Cosmo had ever made in our hearing.

"A man could put a cooker right here," he went on, pointing to a spot a few feet left of center in the cave. He gestured toward the ceiling. "You could run a stovepipe out here to take off the smoke. There's water aplenty in the spring for mixing and cooling. You could run a water pipe in along that wall." He paused and the happy look gradually faded. "The only trouble is we ain't got no equipment; we ain't got no corn."

"We got raisins," said Bernie Cole. "We ain't got corn or apples, but we got raisins. There are stacks of twenty-five-pound cans of raisins in the mess shack. The Marine Corps thinks raisins are good for our guts, so they send raisins by the ton to Move-the-Line Sledd. Trouble is, nobody eats 'em. They're piled up all over the place."

"Yeah," said Cannon, "me and Sledd have tried to brew raisin jack a half dozen times, but it always comes out swill."

"Sledd?" said Cosmo contemptuously. "Sledd don't even know how to make pancakes. I know how to distill spirits. I was running one of Pa's cookers before I was ten years old."

"But applejack. Do you know how to make applejack?" Cannon persisted.

"Applejack? Sure. That's just a different kind of hard cider."

It was time to reassert my leadership. "And raisin jack? If you know how to make applejack, you must know how to make raisin jack, right? What would we need to set up a raisin-jack still?"

Cosmo's eyes gleamed with the sudden realization of opportunities. While doing an impromptu dance, he ticked off a list of the things required to establish a respectable distillery. There was not one thing on his list that we couldn't get our hands on in an hour. Our two superscroungers, Cannon and Cole, could borrow the equipment we needed from their Seabee friends a mile down the island road, and any tricky work with copper coils, water pipes, stovepipes, and cookers could be done by our ingenious armorer, Blackie Arnold.

Cosmo reeled off the ingredients for the raisin jack itself. Fifty pounds of this, ten sacks of that. Move-the-Line Sledd, with a prospect of high-grade liquor in the offing, could provide the ingredients instantly and by the ton.

Right there and then we formed a partnership, the nine of us, and swore each other to secrecy. Cosmo was unanimously elected our master distiller; I appointed myself president and maker of grand strategy. Cannon and Cole were in charge of equipment and supplies; Faltynski was declared treasurer. We decided that we would not offer any of our excess liquor for sale but would ask imbibers for donations. If the donations were not forthcoming or were less than we considered generous, the cheapskates would be temporarily severed from the source of supply.

Bill Drapp, Zobenica, Guyman, and Nock would be worker ants ready to fetch and carry, keep a proper fire beneath the cooker, boil water, clean pots, or whatever else Cosmo might require. As we stood there glorying in mutual admiration, we nearly forgot why we had gone out into the jungle that day.

"First things first," I announced. "We still have a few hundred yards to go on our spraying job. Guyman, Nick, Drapp, Nock, and I can take care of that. Cosmo, you stay right here and make your plans for our still. Faltynski can help. Cannon, you and Cole head straight out to arrange for our equipment and supplies. Mark the trail so when we collect all the stuff we need, we can find our way back here tonight. And for Christ's sake, don't let Brushmore or Captain McNail sniff out what we're up to."

Late that afternoon as we straggled wearily back into the company area, we were immediately confronted by Red Salleng and Top-sergeant Brushmore. "What the hell took you bastards so long?" said Salleng. "Top and I were getting ready to send out a search party."

"And not one of you damned, stupid slopeheads took a rifle along," said Brushmore.

"Why the hell would we need a rifle, Top?" I asked. "There hasn't been a live Jap on this island for over a year."

"How in Christ do you know that, Moe?" said Salleng. "You a goddamn prophet or something? Tomorrow you guys take a couple of M-1s along."

"Tomorrow?" said Cole. "Do we got to haul this damned gear all over the jungle again tomorrow?" Now that we had big plans for our secret raisin-jack still, we wanted desperately to continue working the DDT patrol.

"Damned right you're going to haul it again tomorrow," said Salleng.

"And the day and the week after that," said Brushmore. "Might educate you dimwitted jerks to organize the right kind of patrol."

"It wasn't a patrol, Top; it was a working party," I said.

"Never mind your damned technicalities," said Brushmore. "Get the hell out of here before I send you out to spray DDT all night. Or maybe I ought to volunteer you for the flamethrower squad."

As we hurried along to the platoon area, Red Salleng caught up with me. "Come into my tent a minute, Moe," he said. He had a clipped, abrupt, expressionless speech pattern, something I had never noticed while he was a member of the privates' brotherhood, but that seemed officious now that he had moved up to platoon sergeant.

Once inside he pulled a bottle of beer out of his seabag, uncapped it, and handed it to me. "Drink the top half, Moe. I'll drink the bottom half."

I had drained it beyond the halfway mark before he jerked it away.

"One of these days I'm going to kick your ass good, Moe," he said. "You and Cannon and that goddamned Cole."

"Why leave out Faltynski?" I said. "He's one of us."

"He ain't gonna be much longer," said Salleng. "He's moving up to squad leader one of these days soon."

"Oh, shit!" I said. "There goes another one of the good guys."

145

"Now that's the kind of wise-guy talk that keeps you on the hot list every damned day, Moe. You bitch that the people who run this outfit are on your ass all the time, and then you shoot off with some smart comeback like that. Maybe if you'd watch your damned mouth and say 'sir' to Lieutenant McLane and Captain McNail once in a while, you'd get on a whole hell of a lot better in this outfit." Red was about out of breath.

"I didn't join the Raiders to say 'sir' or dance around saluting some half-assed officer," I said. "My grandfather was Swiss, and Swiss people don't like anybody trying to lord it over them."

"Yeah, and if your grandfather was half as stupid as you are, he must have been a Swiss bull," said Salleng. "Going around half-cocked all the damned time butting your head against the world and bucking for the flamethrower squad as hard as you can go."

"What the hell are you talking about now?" I asked.

Red went to the tent entrance, looked up the company street, and came back. "What I'm talking about," he said in a half whisper, "is Brushmore. I don't know what he's got against you and Cole and Cannon and that Polack, but there's something stuck in his craw. He hasn't done anything yet because he ain't sure you guys did what he thinks you did. Stay on his good side. Don't get him riled. He might decide you guys ain't the ones he's after. Otherwise he'll have your ass in that damned flamethrower squad before you know what hit you." He paused and looked me directly in the eye. "You're a dumb son of a bitch, Moe, but you're a good BAR man. So is Cole. I'd hate to see you guys waste away in the flamethrower squad." He drank his half of the beer in one gulp. "Get on out of here, now," he said. "And tell your stupid-ass buddies to go easy with Brushmore."

When I got to our tent the others had already left for the chow line. I sat there alone considering Red Salleng's warning. I knew, and, although Salleng had said otherwise, I knew that he knew what Brushmore suspected, because Salleng had been there when the incident occurred. It had been during the landing at Emirau, and it had happened mainly because Top-sergeant Brushmore was an inveterate practical joker.

Emirau has several much smaller islands close by, as do most Pacific islands. During the landing the 3d Platoon was given the job of attacking one of those small islands, perhaps two hundred yards wide and a half mile long. In the early morning darkness we unloaded from the destroyer that had brought us from Guadalcanal into a landing craft large enough to contain the whole platoon. We hung the cargo net over the side and down we went hand over hand on that tricky ladder. Because the sea was smooth, we filled the landing craft quickly. Top-sergeant Brushmore, who had elected to land with our platoon so that he could be sure we conducted ourselves properly, was the last man over the side. As he stepped onto the first crossline of the cargo net, he dropped a grenade in among us. It happened so fast that no one reacted in time to catch it. We heard it hit the bottom of the boat and roll; for the briefest instant we were frozen with fear.

In those days we carried eight grenades in our packs and two more with the arming ring fastened to a metal loop in our pack straps. If we needed to throw a grenade in a hurry, we reached up and jerked it free. When we did, the arming ring remained on the shoulder strap, and the grenade was primed and ready to fire.

When Brushmore's grenade fell, we knew that somehow the pin that fixed the grenade to his pack strap had come loose; the grenade was live and ready to explode. A dozen of us nearest the point where the grenade had fallen scrambled on the bottom of the boat hoping to find it in time to throw it over the side. We had five seconds. Darkness defeated us. I don't know what the other men in the boat were thinking; they may have been saying their morning prayers. I was counting: one-a-second, two-a-second, three-a-second, four-a-second, five-a-second, six-a—.

There was no explosion. Badly shaken, I rose very slowly on legs from which all the strength had drained. My buddies were rising too. We discovered the grenade, pin still in place, for the moment a harmless chunk of metal and gunpowder.

From the deck above us came laughter—wild, raucous, undisciplined. It was Top-sergeant Brushmore. "First time I ever saw a

147

bunch of silly bastards that call themselves Marines trying to dig a foxhole in the bottom of a boat!" He started over the side, still howling gleefully. It was too much for some of us. As he let go the cargo net to take his last step into the landing craft, the four who were nearest the destroyer—Cannon, Faltynski, Cole, and I— pushed powerfully against its side. The landing craft gave a sudden lurch, and Top-sergeant Brushmore stepped forward into thin air and down to the sea.

He wasn't going to drown: we knew we could snag him with a boat hook or toss him a line. He was too valuable a combat Marine to throw away. We only intended to let him get good and wet. But in seizing the opportunity for revenge, we had overlooked one important thing: he was loaded down very heavily with clips of ammunition and grenades, and he had brought along extra ammunition in bandoliers strapped around chest and shoulder. He went down fast.

Somehow, in spite of all that weight and all those encumbrances, he floundered to the surface and fought to stay. His battle with the sea was complicated still more by the fact that he was too stubborn to let go of the tommy gun he carried. We gathered along the side of our craft clapping, cheering, and shouting words of encouragement. Still struggling, he went under once again, and once again fought his way to the surface. He was struggling more desperately now, and we suddenly realized that if he went down this time, we would not see him again.

There were some quick thinkers in our platoon who could convert thought to immediate action. Led by Red Salleng, three of them had already thrown off packs, weapons, and ammunition, and together they went over the side. Two minutes later Brushmore was back among us. He was shivering, red-faced, breathless—and mad with rage. When he was able to breathe with only the roughest regularity, he began making promises. He would find out who had pushed the boat, who had planned to let him drown, who had stood on the edge of the boat and led the cheers. He would personally castrate these enemies and then gut them with his K-bar knife.

We heard him out respectfully, but we were coming apart with laughter inside.

With a sudden jerk our landing craft headed toward the beach, its .50-caliber machine guns firing long bursts into the jungle ahead. The war had to go on. All the way to the beach above the heavy voices of the machine guns, Brushmore raved and cursed and raved and threatened and raved some more. It was the shortest, happiest combat landing we ever made, and in this rare instance the Japs weren't shooting back.

Darkness fell as I sat there thinking about Brushmore's early morning swim on Emirau, and just as I started laughing aloud, Cannon came in with a steak sandwich Move-the-Line Sledd had sent over. "Sitting here in the dark laughing like a mad hatter," Cannon said. "Did you get too much DDT today? Some of these new sprays burn out the brain."

In a low voice I reminded him of Brushmore's desperate swim off Emirau and then mentioned what Red Salleng had told me. Cannon was skeptical. "Hell, it was still dark," he said. "He didn't see us push that boat away. He was trying too hard to flap his wings and fly."

"I hope he never figures it out," I said. "Hauling a BAR around is bad enough. I don't need a flamethrower."

"Nor I," said Cannon. "I've never liked my meat burned."

For the next five days we rolled out mornings an hour before reveille and, sustained by the chunks of bread Move-the-Line Sledd sent us, headed into the jungle on our DDT patrol. By noon each day we were at our cave working feverishly to erect the most productive distillery ever seen in the Solomon Islands. Stacked high and dry in the confines of our pretty still were twenty-five-pound tins of raisins, one-hundred-pound sacks of sugar, and small boxes of yeast. A master distiller like Cosmo Shuttleforth almost never used yeast, but it was there in case of an emergency requirement.

On Sunday morning, while most men in the 4th Marines—Catholics, Protestants, Jews, agnostics, and atheists—had gone to

Mass to hear Father Redmond promise to knock hell out of the next Marine he heard uttering a forbidden epithet, we gathered at our still to watch Cosmo Shuttleforth run off the first batch of the stuff we called raisin jack. Each of us had brought a canteen cup; into each cup Cosmo poured a taster's share.

"Sniff it good," said Cosmo. "Bet your bottom you never smelled anything better in your life." He stood there immensely pleased, a master artist in rumpled cap and dirty dungarees.

Even without Cosmo's promise, I knew when I first gazed into my cup that I was in the presence of something remarkable. The stuff appeared to be vibrating and thrashing about like a living thing, and the fumes rising from it were clearly visible. I sniffed the fumes and coughed—a hacking, lingering cough. I had heard of strong drink, 80 or 90 proof, but Cosmo's inspired product must have hit at least 170. I raised the cup to my lips with both hands and took a tiny, tentative sip. The stuff went down as smooth as lemon and sugar water, but when it hit bottom it exploded like a bazooka shell. I know I took two steps and staggered, and so did the others who had swallowed their first sips.

We sniffed again, sipped once more, and gazed at each other in awe. It was clear that this brew, this unrivaled liquor, was the key to fortune. As we stood there shaking hands with Cosmo Shuttleforth and congratulating each other on one more of our great and continuing achievements, a harsh, familiar voice issued from the mouth of the cave.

"Just the gang of volunteers for the flamethrower squad I wanted to see." It was our tireless nemesis, Top-sergeant Brushmore. He stepped into the cave and looked quickly around—at our cooker, our fire, our sacks of sugar, our tins of raisins, our ingenious arrangement of pipes and smokestacks. "I could smell this garbage scow when I was still one hundred yards away," he said. We stood there speechless.

"I followed you gentlemen out here," Brushmore went on, "because I have welcome news. The latest model flamethrowers will be here in two weeks, and we already have seven brave volunteers. As you know we need three more, and Captain McNail has asked me to go round the company and offer the opportunity to every one of you." He gave us all a sweeping, kindly look.

Peering steadfastly down at our boondockers, we said not a word.

Top-sergeant Brushmore sighed. "Well, I tried. I told Captain McNail it wouldn't work, but I tried," he said. "I guess we'll have to do something special to inspire more of the old Raider spirit into our company."

Probably because of his special standing as part-time meat cutter, Cannon seemed less alarmed by Brushmore's presence than the rest of us. Now he held out his cup. "Try some of this imported stuff, Top."

"What is it?" said Brushmore suspiciously.

"It's the first batch of raisin jack ever produced at this still," said Cannon, the few sips he had taken already beginning to spin in his cranium.

"It smells like something you ought to light a match to," said Brushmore. "Let me see you drink it first."

"This is hot liquor. This is burning, howling, fence-hopping, women-chasing, fist-fighting liquor." Cannon tipped the cup, took a healthy drink, and spun half around. "Dogfaces, swab jockeys, and other perverts cut it with water or grapefruit juice. We drink it straight." He drank once more and rocked a bit but with a clever stutter step regained his balance.

Brushmore regarded him expectantly. When Cannon neither turned purple nor collapsed, Brushmore reached for the cup, took a heroic swallow, smacked his lips, turned gray, and sat down heavily on one of the hundred-pound sacks of sugar.

"It smells like gunpowder and tastes like gargle water, but it's good. It's better than good. It's grand." He took another swig. "What in the hell is it?"

We had attacked his senses. Now it was time to assail his sensibilities. "We got seventy more gallons where that came from, Top," I

151

said. "And in a few weeks' time we can make enough to float a battlewagon."

Brushmore took another long drink, and a slight shudder shook his frame. "I only want a fifty-gallon barrel," he said.

I stepped forward and refilled his cup with what was left in my own. He studied it carefully—the heavy fumes, the agitated ripples, the crackling noises.

"I don't suppose you're selling any of this illegal stuff to your unfortunate comrades in arms, are you?"

"We voted on that," I said. "We decided it would be better to pass out samples and then ask for donations."

"An obvious attempt to circumvent Marine Corps regulations," said Brushmore.

"What do you mean circumvent, Top?" I said. "Here we are planning to run a charity for boozers and you start talking about circumvent."

Brushmore didn't answer my question immediately. Instead he crouched on his sugar sack a minute, shaking the liquor in his cup and appearing to be wandering through deep and tortuous thought. "Moe," he said finally, "you and your crackpot buddies, Cannon and Cole, and that Polack whose name I can never remember, are going to wind up behind the walls of Leavenworth Prison one of these days. I'd say about fifteen years hard labor and no booze, no smokes, no steaks, no women." He hesitated and looked toward our master distiller, who, always shy around Brushmore, had backed into a shadowy corner behind some raisin tins. "I ought to turn all of you in for corrupting the morals of this simple-minded woodhick you call Cosmo. By God I think I'll call the corporal of the guard and have the four of you put away right now."

It was a masterful performance by a great showman, but I knew he had no intention of calling the corporal of the guard. It was the preamble to something else, which was certain to be bad.

"Do you animals know anything about the structure of a corporation?" Brushmore asked.

"Huh?" said Zobenica. "Corp of what?" Nick's surprise had betrayed him.

Brushmore stopped. Born with a quick temper, in his years as sergeant and top-sergeant he had honed it to a hair trigger. "Knock it off, idiot boy!" He gave Nick a disgusted look. "Tell you what you do, Zebon-enema. Tell you what you do. Take a run down to the beach and back here on the double!" Zobenica was amazed. The beach was half a mile away. "Go! Get the hell out of my sight! You need exercise so your brain wheels will spin!"

Nick turned to me. I shrugged and nodded. Defeated, he ambled off. "Now we can get organized," said Brushmore. "I learned about corporations in the arithmetic book I had in fourth grade. What you do to start a corporation is issue shares of stock. I'd say, in this case, about fifty shares. I'll issue myself twenty-six. That makes me the prominent or dominant shareholder, I forget which. But it doesn't make any difference because that way we'll have somebody in charge who really knows how to run a corporation. We'll give a share to Captain McNail, one to Major Bank, and one to Colonel Maxim. That will guarantee cooperation at the top of the pile. You guys can split the rest of the stock any way you please." He paused. "One thing to damned well remember. We ain't passing out any of this stuff free and asking for donations. You idiot boys would have so many freeloaders scrambling around here they'd knock over every palm tree on this end of the island. No, sir! We'll sell this stuff at three dollars the canteen cup. By the time we leave here to invade New Ireland or Truk or some other hellhole, we'll be rich as sultans or politicians. Agreed?"

We had listened with open mouths. "Hold it a damned minute, Top," I said. "We ain't agreed to nothing. How'd you end up with all those shares?"

Brushmore gave me an autocratic wave. "Eminent domain, my man! Eminent domain!"

I had never heard of eminent domain, but I could recognize a shakedown. "My ass," I said. "It's robbery."

Brushmore had apparently decided, for the moment, to maintain a diplomatic calm. "It ain't a robbery if I don't have a pistol. What it is is the doctrine of lazy-fare, as the French say. All that means is 'Let's play fair.' You see it in all the books about corporations. Someone who understands the system has to run the show. It's the aberration of nobility."

"Hey, Top," I said. "Somewhere about four sentences back, I fell off the train. How the hell did the nobility get into this?"

"Yeah," Cannon put in. "Who wrote this damned book you're talking about anyway? Imminent domain. What the hell is it?"

Right then Brushmore's hair trigger went off. In an instant his complexion went from a healthy pink to a deep, furious red. "Insubordination is what it is!" he shouted. "And you bastards are the ones that's insubordinate! I organize a corporation and give you morons half the stock and you still ain't satisfied!"

As the fury reached a grand crescendo, I remembered Red Salleng's warning of a few days before. Although I suspected that there was something faulty about his logic and all his talk about eminent domain and aberrations for nobility, I also knew there was nothing limited about a Marine top-sergeant's powers. Brushmore was struggling for control of his temper. "Well?" he said suddenly. "Well? Am I right?"

As any other Raider, I did not believe in retreat; but an attack in another direction is sometimes the prudent alternative. Still, I hesitated.

"Well?" said Brushmore, his face taking on the color of beet juice.

"All right," I said, "but when do we get our stock?"

"Tomorrow," said Brushmore. "You get it tomorrow. That is, if I get around to issuing it."

The stock Brushmore produced next day was pretty crude by the standards of large corporations and other cutthroat entities: a statement typed on plain paper that Moe, Cosmo Shuttleforth, D. Cannon, B. Cole, R. "Fal-whatever the hell his name is," and "certain others to be named by the aforementioned" are issued twenty-one shares of a total of fifty shares of a corporation to be entitled the R. J. Distillery. We had been outflanked, outmaneuvered, and robbed by a smiling fox with a red moustache.

Also on Monday, with the exception of Cosmo Shuttleforth, we found ourselves still on DDT patrol. Cosmo's name that morning appeared at the head of the sick list. But when Cosmo protested to Top-sergeant Brushmore that he had never been in better health, Brushmore seemed unconcerned. It would only confuse matters, he told Cosmo, if his name had to be removed. Better to get on out to the R. J. Distillery where he could stay out of sight and make raisin jack for a few days.

The exceptional aspects of Cosmo's case were not lost on the other members of our group. One by one we tried to persuade Brushmore that if the demand for our liquor spread beyond battalion and regiment, Cosmo would be unable to handle the distillery duties alone. Top-sergeant Brushmore, sensing profit and success, agreed that our reasoning was sound. One by one we were pulled off the DDT patrol and placed on the no-duty roster.

In the first few days of its operation, the R. J. Distillery produced a good many more gallons of raisin jack than we were able to sell. We had merely let it be known around the battalion that excellent liquor was available at a modest cost and then waited for the world to come to our door. A few early customers did find their way to us, paid the price, were mightily pleased, and spread the word through the 2d Battalion and beyond. Along with these early consumers from our immediate area, a steady stream of curiosity seekers and other interested visitors, perhaps attracted from a half mile away by the intriguing smell, dropped by. Some of these, especially Army and Navy wanderers, no doubt distressed because the Marines had gone one-up on them again, became insistent about receiving free samples of our brew.

Apprised of this development and much concerned about the health and welfare of his master distiller, Top-sergeant Brushmore went to Sergeant-major Bleak with a gallon of our finest stock and suggested that a guard post be established at the distillery to run

155

off such riffraff. After a few hearty sips of Cosmo's raisin jack, Sergeant-major Bleak not only acknowledged that such a post was necessary but also, as his enthusiasm for our product intensified, directed that the guard be armed with a Browning automatic rifle. Inspired by his presence, Cannon put up a crude but instructive sign.

> R. J. Distillery
> A Non-Profit Project of the 4th Marines.
> No Trespassing! No Skulking Around!
> (The guard is a Marine Raider. B.A.R.
> loaded with dumdum bullets.
> Small hole in front, big hole in back
> where guts come out.)

There was some debate about the word *guts*. It might, we thought, be too emphatic, too much like the real thing. So Cannon, in his good-humored, practical way, painted a thin blue line through *guts* and substituted *chunks* in the space above the line.

A few days after we went into production at the R and J, as we called it, Faltynski, feeling the importance of his position as company treasurer, argued that we should hang a price list on Cannon's sign: two dollars for a canteen cup full, three dollars for a full canteen. Cannon objected. His sign, he said, had poetic dignity that would be lost if it were cluttered with price lists and advertising gimmicks.

The other members of the corporation hooted at the idea that Cannon's sign was poetic and dignified, but we eventually did vote Faltynski's idea down. For one thing, we had a few privileged customers who paid less for a cup than ordinary folk. For another, we might want to increase our prices dramatically if demand began to surpass supply.

During the first week or two of its existence business at the R. J. Distillery increased gradually, but production stayed well ahead of demand. We minor stockholders were content with the profits of our humble capitalism. Life in those days was an extended tropical vacation: an hour's work around the still in the morning; a flurry of customers, easily handled, in the late afternoon or early evening. Except for those brief periods of business activity, we went our happy way. We lolled on the beach; we swam in the river nearby; we fished off the reef with grenades; we explored the island from end to end; we visited the main hospital, where we could lean against the barbed wire perimeter and observe the shapely nurses in the distance; and we drank only enough of Cosmo Shuttleforth's magical beverage to maintain a pleasant glow.

For two idyllic weeks, while the demand for our product was still modest, Cosmo juggled his recipes to create three distinctive brands. The first—the one we had sampled that first afternoon— featured a goodly percentage of alcohol. This was not a drink for novices. Even old salts with a high tolerance for powerful liquor found it prudent to absorb their drinks while firmly seated. We christened it Quickjack. It guaranteed deep and peaceful slumber.

A second brand, Slapjack, was much weaker than Quickjack, containing about the same percentage of spirits as ordinary bourbon. For some reason, Slapjack promoted sleeplessness. It was thus popular with those who liked to play poker and curse their luck or shoot craps and fight.

Cosmo's third creation was Hijack. Tasty and mild, it was about as strong as 3.2 beer. Hijack could be sipped all day without producing any symptoms other than contentment. It was a drink much admired by people such as sharpshooters—who like to look out over their sights and see something more definite than a blur—and navigators, who like to head off in the right direction and stay on course.

Meantime, as the days passed and the reputation of the R. J. Distillery spread up and down the coast of Guadalcanal, across to Savo and Tulagi, and even to the ships at sea, the demand for our products increased, and our work days gradually lengthened. A time came when, what with the demands of our thirsty and numerous customers, we were reduced to the embarrassing state of having to go around sober ourselves.

In addition, Cosmo Shuttleforth, our gentle and usually pliable master distiller, developed a rebellious streak. It was not that he minded the hard work and long days at the still; he was used to that. What concerned him was that he was losing touch with the war. "I joined this outfit to shoot Japs," he told us. "I like making spirits, but I can do that anytime and anywhere. I want my rifle back. We need to get ready for the next big fight up north."

Cosmo's concern was understandable. Before our first experience in battle, all of us had shared a similar concern. Even though the war in the Pacific promised to go on long enough to accommodate prospective warriors who were still in kindergarten, there was always the lingering fear that peace might come before a man had a chance to fire at least a few rounds at a fanatic Jap machine gunner or rifleman. How could a Marine who had never been in battle explain such a thing to the folks back home?

We all knew the horror stories about Marines who had never had a chance to fight because they had been stuck in some miserable rear-echelon job like repairing fighter planes at Henderson Field or guarding some damned admiral in New Zealand or Honolulu. All of us were familiar with the predicament Stud Van Fleet had gotten himself into some months earlier when he volunteered to spend a few weeks running a sawmill near Tasimboko. When the time came to invade Bougainville, he had been told that his job was to go right on running the sawmill and that his old mortar squad would have to get along without him. Stud had been obliged to desert his sawmill post in order to get back into combat again. When the Bougainville campaign ended and he returned to Guadalcanal, he had been sentenced to five days in the brig and continued duty at the same old mill.

Although those of us who had been in battle were less concerned than Cosmo about missing out on combat, we too were disenchanted. Aside from the fact that we had an ever-decreasing opportunity to enjoy the products of our labors, we were bending under the heavy burden of work. We never seemed to have time to get the day's labor done. For a while we tried rolling out with the company at reveille and working at the R and J until the end of the day's regular routine. But our customers approached in ever-lengthening lines; ships' captains sent orders that had to be filled in ten-gallon lots.

Shortly after sundown each day, along came a happy Top-sergeant Brushmore to check on the day's profit, to extract his share, and to threaten us with immediate induction into the flamethrower squad or a one-way trip to Florida Island unless we speeded up production.

We tried rising an hour before Galvo blew reveille and working a seven-day week. But just as we began catching up on our work-load, the crews of two minesweepers and a subchaser came ashore and wiped out our stock. We ran out of raisins and collapsed on the sand for a day of rest. A half hour later, we were abruptly awakened when a working party brought in raisins by the ton. Our supply of sugar vanished. A convoy of trucks arrived with more, much more. And always we were hounded by Top-sergeant Brush-more or one of his henchmen demanding a stricter devotion to duty and higher and higher levels of production.

Finally one morning, almost overcome by exhaustion and de-spair, we sat down for a nine-man council of war. But just as we collapsed onto convenient sugar sacks, an indignant snort came from the mouth of the cave. Top-sergeant Brushmore stood there, his fierce pirate eyes gleaming beneath his red eyebrows.

"On your feet!" he shouted. The nine of us made a concerted leap. "I came by to let you fine young Navy mules be among the first to inspect our new flamethrowers." He gestured outside. In the open area out there stood seven Marines in camouflage dungarees and helmets, each man breathing hard under a heavy load. We recognized them all: the flamethrower volunteers, each one bent forward at the waist beneath the burden of three-foot fuel tanks, pressure tanks, nozzles, and all the other ugly equipment necessary for creating and projecting accurate streams of fire.

"Our flamethrowers!" Brushmore cried joyfully. "Our flame-throwers are here!" He stepped up and patted one of the fuel tanks. "Napalm!" Brushmore said. "Napalm! Jellied gasoline is what it is. Whatever it hits, it sticks to and burns. Captain McNail says the stuff was invented by some geniuses at Harvard University." He looked into the cave and spotted Cosmo, half hidden behind a pile of sugar sacks. "Cosmo!" he cried. "Our raisin-jack genius! Get out here and have a look at these beauties!"

Cosmo emerged from his hiding place and came hesitantly forward. "Put your hand on these two tanks," Brushmore said. "That one on the right is full of napalm; the other is full of pres-surized gas. All you have to do is pull the trigger on this nozzle and the fire, liquid fire, shoots out 150 yards. Sticks to anything it hits. Great for burning Japs out of pillboxes. By God these things will get their attention, and they only weigh about twenty-five pounds." He turned to Cole and me. "Not much heavier than a BAR. Fact is, BAR men make good flamethrower volunteers because they're used to drawing enemy fire and hauling a lot of weight around."

While Brushmore was finishing his pep talk, I was looking more closely at the seven volunteers. They were surely hoping desper-ately that Brushmore would soon round up three more so these heavy loads could be spread around. "All right, you volunteers!" Brushmore suddenly shouted. "The show is over! Get back to the company area and check in with Blackie Arnold so he can show you how to load and fire these things!" Their loads appeared to be about four times the twenty-five pounds Brushmore had men-tioned so easily.

"My brave and faithful seven volunteers," he said. "The Marine Corps needs more men like those boys." He paused and patted Cosmo on the back. "We won't let you volunteer unless we get desperate, Cosmo," he went on. "We couldn't run this raisin-jack business without you." He looked hard at the rest of us. "But we'd never miss any one or any three of these slopeheads. We need three more for the flamethrower squad. Ain't any of you slopeheads

160

getting tired of this raisin-jackin' twelve hours a day, seven days a week?"

We assured him that, far from feeling overworked, we were happy as Santa's elves. After Brushmore headed back toward camp, we collapsed on sugar sacks and tins of raisins and resumed our council of war. Cosmo, who had actually touched the flamethrower tanks, was trembling as a result of his experience. Apparently expecting the tanks to be hot, he had been startled to find that they were cool to the touch. The others appeared stunned, especially Cole, who was shaking like palm fronds in a brisk breeze. "Easy, Cole," I said. "Old Brushmore ain't got us yet. He can't make you volunteer."

"He made seven guys volunteer," said Cole. He stopped shaking. "I'm practicing my sick bay routine. I'm thinking about seeing the doctor and telling him I got malaria."

"Stop taking your Atabrine tablets for a few days," Faltynski said. "You won't have to shiver on purpose." Faltynski had suffered attacks of malaria twice, both times when, after fretting about his manhood for a week or two, he had started throwing his Atabrine pills over his shoulder.

"I think I'll go to the doc and turn myself in for a Section 8," Zobenica muttered.

"I'd check into the nut ward too," Drapp put in, "but I don't think I could get used to the company you have to keep."

"Maybe we should go to Colonel Maxim," I said, "and tell him we want out of this job."

"Maxim?" Drapp was incredulous. "Maxim? He's a stockholder in this company. You go and bitch to Maxim and you'll end up in the flamethrower squad for sure."

Cosmo stirred. He seemed to be returning from another world. "I wonder," he said in a low, conspiratorial tone, "if we couldn't accidentally blow this place to hell. Blow it to hell. That's what the revenue folks did once to one of Pa's stills. Pa's best still. His biggest producer."

161

"Blow the R. J. Distillery to hell?" I could scarcely believe what Cosmo had just said. Yet if we were to be emancipated from serfdom, some drastic approaches had to be taken.

"It might be a good deal," said Cannon. "Let me think on it awhile." Cannon knew more about explosives than the rest of us, having once done time in the demolitions platoon. "A two-pound block of nitrostarch would scatter things around this cave; might even scatter the cave." He grinned. It was the first indication of happiness I had seen on his face for a week.

I stuck my head out of the cave and looked around for the guard. He was thirty yards away trying to conceal himself behind a banyan tree while he smoked a forbidden cigarette. I ducked back inside. "We'd better put it to a vote," I said. "If we don't count Brushmore and his three other stockholders, the R. J. Distillery is a democracy."

"Hold it! Hold it a damned minute! Before we vote, we need to think this out!" said Nock Dorning. "You don't want to blow up the guard, do you? He might be sleeping in the cave tonight and catch the blast."

"And that BAR of his is loaded," said Guyman, who until now had said nothing. "Be all right if one of the old guys had the guard. If one of the old guys spotted anyone sneaking around the cave at two in the morning, he'd shoot up a case of ammunition, but he'd shoot twenty feet over your head. But these kids they got on guard now are replacements right out of boot camp. If they happened to see you, they might blow your guts out first and cry about it later."

"Those boot-camp refugees can't shoot straight," Cannon said. The thought of blowing something into the far beyond had apparently filled him with a false and dangerous courage.

"Who says so?" said Zobenica. "You know as well as I do that the guy on the R. J. post carries an automatic rifle. Don't you ever read our own sign?"

"We could crawl up through the drainage ditch. The guy would never see us. When the blast goes off, he'll dive for cover and stay there."

"But what if he's standing close to the still? The blast might tear him up. We ain't paid to kill Marines."

"Cannon and I will figure it out," I said. "You guys stay the hell away from here tonight. Go to the movie or something."

"What about the guard?" said Cosmo. He seemed to be regretting his impulsive suggestion.

"Don't worry," I said, "we won't hurt the guard. Let's vote." Unanimously we voted to rid ourselves of the R and J. We knew it was the only way.

The fateful decision made, Cannon and I filled a gallon tin with Quickjack and went off to the F Company area to visit Blackie Arnold, who enjoyed the honor of having a tent all to himself. That is, he had about one-tenth of a tent for himself and his cot and seabag. Otherwise, about a quarter of the space in the tent was taken by a large work table hammered together from rough lumber, and the rest was filled with ammunition boxes, crates of hand grenades, mortar shells, gasoline cans, and weapons in various stages of repair: machine guns needing new barrels; mortars with shaky bipods; M-1s with worn firing pins; and BARs with jammed operating rods or uncooperative male and female brackets.

The first thing we saw when we walked in was the company's three new flamethrowers piled near the tent pole. Blackie was standing at his work bench attempting one more time to adjust the spring he had designed for the two BAR magazines he had welded together into a single unit that he hoped would hold thirty-six rounds. It was a spare-time project, one he had been working on for the past three or four months.

"Any luck today, Blackie?" Cannon asked.

"None! None! Not no damned none! I can't get a steady tension when I fuse the springs." He put the double magazine down and focused his attention on our can of Quickjack. "What heaven-sent firewater have we here?"

"It's really sent by us special messengers from the R and J," I said. Blackie, having apparently decided that his day's work was

163

done, reached for the Quickjack and took a hearty swig right out of the can.

Cannon had drifted toward the tent pole to get a closer look at the flamethrowers. "Are these the new ones?" he said.

"Yeah." Blackie took another quick gulp. Once any drinker started on Quickjack, it was hard for him to stop or even slow down. He smacked his lips and drew a deep breath. "Yeah, them's the new ones, and we got trouble with 'em already."

"Brushmore says they'll throw a stream of fire 150 yards," I said.

Blackie chortled. "Yeah, and if crawfish ate tabasco, they'd taste like garlic. If we can get the damned things to work right, they might throw it out there forty yards."

"Jeez," said Cannon, "that ain't even half a football field. If you got to get that close to a Jap pillbox, you might as well throw dynamite."

"I'm damned glad it ain't going to be my game," said Blackie. He went over to the nearest flamethrower and seized the nozzle. "Right here is the big clinker in the system. Half the time the cotton pickin' igniter don't work. We get napalm squirting out like water from a hose, but no fire. You give a Jap in a pillbox a squirt of napalm without any fire to it, and the next thing you know he'll be chasing your ass off the premises with a Nambu machine gun." He threw the nozzle down in disgust. "Maybe we can figure out how to get the damned fire going before we hit Guam." Shaking his head in frustration he returned to his workbench and sampled his Quickjack again.

"What we came for, Blackie," I said, "is a grenade and a good-size piece of nitrostarch."

Blackie raised one eyebrow. "You going fishing for shark?"

"We got plans to screw a shark," said Cannon. "We aim to do it right after dark."

"I got what you need," said Blackie. "I'm going to point to where it's at, and then I'm walkin' out of here. If you find what you're looking for while I'm gone, slip out the side of the tent and take off. I'll never know whether you found anything or not. I don't keep count of that small stuff anyway." Cuddling his can of Quick-jack, he sauntered out into the company street.

By 8:30 that night, Cannon and I set out in the darkness for the R. J. Distillery. Cannon carried a large block of nitrostarch. I carried a hand grenade from which the powder had been extracted to render it harmless. Only the fuse remained. By 9:00 the two of us were easing along the shallow drainage ditch that a working party had dug six weeks before and approaching the cave. The moon was rising but in the shadows of palms and banyans, we had all the cover we needed. We had only the guard to watch for—and his automatic rifle with its twenty-round magazine.

When we were still twenty yards from the still, I saw the guard. Or rather, I saw him by the glow a cigarette makes when it is not prudently shaded beneath a poncho. He was crouching near his favorite tree, thirty yards to our right and well out of range of the explosion we were planning. Nevertheless, we wanted to be certain that when trouble started he would not make a sudden rush toward the still. The grenade we had carefully prepared would, we were convinced, take care of that.

We crawled a few yards closer to the target. The guard smoked on. It was time to start.

"OK," I whispered to Cannon. "We're close enough. Light her up." Lying on his belly to shield the first tiny flare of his cigarette lighter, he ignited the fuse.

Pulling the pin from the grenade, I rose to one knee and released the spoon. With a sharp metallic click and the pop of striking fuse, the spoon sprang free, and I arched the grenade, trailing a satisfactory wake of red sparks, a few yards to the left of the guard. At the same time Cannon tossed the block of nitrostarch into our raisin-jack still and turned to move away. By snatching desperately at his legs and dragging him into the drainage ditch, I saved his life. A stream of tracer bullets splitting the night slammed over our heads and into the underbrush behind us. We could hear those bullets popping, crackling, whistling all around.

In an instant I realized what had gone wrong. The guard, an innocent novice fresh out of boot camp, had not even recognized the sight and sound of a hand grenade coming his way. Instead of diving for cover as we had expected, he had let the harmless thing of cast iron fall at his feet, stood his ground, and fired in the direction from which it had come. Insanely I was thinking: Browning automatic rifle, model 1918-A-1, .30 caliber, gas operated, magazine fed, air cooled, hip or shoulder weapon.

"We gotta get outta here!" Cannon was shouting. "We gotta get outta here! That nitro's gonna blow!"

"We can't! Don't move, you stupid son of a bitch. He's got us pinned down!"

In the direction of the camp, a sentry was yelling, "Corporal of the guard! Corporal of the guard!" Back there, I knew that, alerted by the unscheduled firing, the whole guard platoon was turning out. Soon, very soon, they would be heading our way. Then, suddenly, an inspiration born of desperation and fear struck me. Frantically I scratched around in the drainage ditch for something to throw. My hand found a small coconut. "Grenade!" I yelled and flung the coconut toward the guard. In a single desperate leap he cleared three logs and disappeared into the jungle on the run.

"Take off!" yelled Cannon. "She's gonna blow!"

Only one escape route was open. It led right across the patch of jungle where the guard had disappeared. Like madmen we ran for the beautiful protection of that dark, deep jungle. As we ran, I yelled "Grenade!" and every Marine within range of my voice dug four holes where his elbows and kneecaps hit the ground. And while they lay there and we ran, there was a magnificent crash, an ear-splitting roar. The R. J. Distillery was gone.

All the long, circuitous route back to camp we laughed—at Cannon's luck, at the alarm we had felt during that desperate moment when we lay pinned down, at the stupidity of a boot sentry who ignored a grenade and dove for cover at the threat of a harmless coconut. We came out of the jungle near the movie area and slipped unnoticed onto a coconut log seat at the edge. The movie

166

featured a sexy blonde named Lana Turner. The crowd sat spell-bound by the sight of creamy skin and platinum hair. Not many Marines would desert her for a two-pound explosion and a few scattered rifle shots five hundred yards off in the jungle.

"By God," Cannon said exultantly, "it ain't everybody can blow up a brewery and see Lana Turner on the same night."

And Three Makes Ten

Next morning, along with a score of other curious Marines, I inspected the results of our night's work. Our fifty-gallon vats were shattered; our supplies of sugar and raisins were scattered; and all kinds of rock and coral blasted from the ceiling of the cave were piled onto the debris.

The affair was disposed of in the guard book as an explosion of undetermined origin. The only other official notice taken of it appeared on the bulletin board that afternoon. Our names were back on the duty roster.

Five days passed, five blessed ten-hour days of ordinary duty in the torrid Guadalcanal sun. In contrast to the weeks of slave labor around the R and J, the mild exercise we experienced in hacking a trail through the jungle, unloading cargo barges, or stacking one hundred-pound cases of ammunition was merely a pleasant pastime. We learned that Brushmore had been handed one more volunteer for the flamethrower squad—a veteran of the 2d Raiders who had grown weary of pulling a cart in the 81-millimeter mortar platoon.

As Brushmore welcomed his eighth volunteer, the level of morale in the 4th Marines and among many other outfits on Guadalcanal and Tulagi was experiencing a dramatic decline. Men who had long been models of proper conduct became snappish, even mutinous. There were frequent outbursts of temper. Father Redmond was constantly dashing around to try to settle ridiculous disputes and maintain peace.

No such breakdown in morale affected us former R and J stockholders or our favored associates until we had consumed our last bottle of Hijack. Then we began to feel a slight and gradual change. We first noticed it in the chow, which for weeks had improved under an increasingly happy Move-the-Line Sledd but, within a few days' time, had reverted to the old slop. It was clear, as Cannon reported, that, deprived of his nightly ration of Quickjack, Sledd had been dipping into the Aqua-Velva.

One evening as Cole, Cannon, Faltynski, and I sat in our tent grumbling, Father Redmond entered. A visit from Father Redmond was rare. A busy man when he had been chaplain of the 4th Raider Battalion, his workload, mostly self-imposed, had quadrupled now that he was the shepherd for a whole regiment. He shook hands all around and, looking for a place to sit, selected Cannon's seabag. Cannon winced but said nothing.

"I wish we had a drink to offer you, Father," said Cole, knowing that Father Redmond let no spirits touch his lips other than communion wine.

"As a matter of fact," said Father Redmond, "I came by to talk about strong drink. I have been sitting in on a session with Colonel Maxim. He's extremely worried about the recent sharp drop in morale."

"Something's wrong, all right, Father," I said. "They didn't even act this crazy when the Marine Corps killed the Raiders."

Father Redmond chuckled. "I don't think General Vandegrift would like to hear you put it that way. The change is only superficial, in any case." None of us believed that, including Father Redmond, but we let his statement stand. "I believe I know, and Colonel Maxim is sure he knows why the regiment's morale is down. It's been skidding since a very few days after that unfortunate explosion at the R and J." As Cannon and I glanced quickly at each other and then down at our toes, Father Redmond paused for a moment.

"You know," he went on, "Marines aren't much for thinking about consequences. They attack without any thorough plan. They blow up raisin-jack stills without much thought of what's to follow. It makes one wonder. Even though I am opposed to alcohol in principle, I know that, with the way this war is going on forever out here, the men don't have much else to look forward to but a strong drink now and then."

We looked at each other again, wondering what all of this was leading up to. "It would probably be a fine thing if somehow the R and J could be restored," Father Redmond said and smiled. "Even though, as I have said, I am, in principle, opposed to alcohol."

He rose to go; Cole delayed him. "Maybe you'd better say a blessing over these two Catholic eightballs before you go, Father," Cole said, pointing to Faltynski and me, "so they don't end up in the flamethrower squad."

Father Redmond gave Cole a quizzical look. "What about you and Private Cannon, Mr. Cole? I can't ask the Lord to shower his favors on Catholics alone."

Cole turned to Cannon. "Well, I guess a little blessing wouldn't hurt us would it, butcher boy? Might even help us stay out of the flamethrower squad."

Father Redmond went through his ritual and departed. It seemed to do Cole and Cannon no harm.

One afternoon a few days later, Jack Freeling, a rifleman in the 2d Platoon, bumped his way in front of me in the evening chow line. He and several of his people had inherited the 3d Squad's job on the DDT patrol. "Hey," he said, "I saw something interesting today. They're putting up a Quonset hut where the R and J used to be."

"Who's they?" I asked.

"Danged if I know," said Freeling. "The Seabees maybe. I saw a bulldozer, trucks, and a dozen guys working to beat hell."

Such an out-of-the-way location for a storage building seemed odd, but of course there was no predicting the Marine Corps planners. For a few days I thought no more about the mysterious Quon-

170

set hut and continued to participate contentedly in our daily exercises: one day a practice landing onto the beach at Tassafaronga; the next morning a two hundred-yard crawl through the jungle with Bill Vahey's machine gunners firing streams of tracer bullets two feet over our heads; the day after that a simulated attack with live ammunition against a mock village the Seabees had built for us; on the fourth day a demonstration of the new flamethrowers against several old coconut-log pillboxes the Japanese had left behind.

It was pleasant playing the role of spectators for once; we applauded when Hodsgill and his flamethrower gang emerged suddenly from a patch of bamboo stalks, clumped heavily to within thirty yards of the ancient pillboxes, and blasted away. From Hodsgill's flamethrower came an impressive stream of liquid fire flush on the target, but from the squad's other two came only a few impotent squirts of fireless napalm.

Top-sergeant Brushmore and Captain McNail seemed taken aback by these failures, especially since they had invited Major Bank to view the show; but they recovered quickly. "Even if it doesn't fry the Japs inside," Captain McNail explained to Major Bank, "the fire and heat will suck out all the oxygen so the bastards will suffocate anyway."

"I see," said Major Bank, who sounded as if he didn't see anything except a few coconut trees nearby.

As Blackie Arnold, Hodsgill, Kleck, Clark, and Swader huddled over the two flameless weapons, Top-sergeant Brushmore headed our way. "Did you see that beauty shoot fire?" he asked.

"Hell, Top," yelled Cole, "I'll bet those guys can pee farther than that, and with a lot hotter stream."

"And it would use up all the oxygen and carbon dioxide and hydrogen too," said Cannon. "How the hell did you get those nuts to volunteer to commit suicide, Top?"

"Same way I'm going to get you and Cole or you and Moe or that screwball Polack to volunteer!" Brushmore's voice was rising. "Those bastards that pushed me over the side up at Emirau!"

Captain McNail had come over. "Knock it off, Top," he said mildly, "old Cole and his buddies will be so happy to volunteer in a few days that they'll be fighting each other to get hold of one of those nice, lightweight napalm tanks." He turned to Cole. "Right now we're considering a policy of issuing a quart of sick-bay brandy to the flamethrower squad every night after chow."

"I don't know, Captain," said Cole. "Maybe the best policy for those guys would be a life insurance policy for about fifty thousand dollars each."

Captain McNail smiled, but Brushmore standing behind him looked angry, determined, and grim. As they walked away discussing some urgent plan in low, intense tones, we saw Red Salleng, his face as red as his hair, stomping toward us on the double.

"I heard that! I heard that, you dumb bastards!" he said. "What the hell are you shitheads trying to do? Cole, you dumb bastard. Can't you ever keep your fool mouth shut?" He fixed me with his number-one glare. "What the hell is the matter with you, Moe? Why the hell are you stirring up Brushmore all the time? Did you hear what he said about you guys pushing him over the side?"

"I didn't say a word, Red," I said.

"Yeah, but by God you had the wrong kind of look on your face. The next working party we get, you and Cole and Faltynski are on it."

"That's nothing new," said Cole. Red Salleng raised his fist. This time I was certain that Cole was going to catch a ham-size blow right in the mouth. But at the last instant Cole gave Salleng that boyish, innocent, insinuating smile and turned away; Salleng, frustrated, dropped his hand in disgust.

That Saturday night, Colonel Maxim, still concerned about declining morale, managed to round up enough beer so that each man received five bottles. It was a nice gesture, but to those of us who had become accustomed to the varying joys of drinking Quickjack, Slapjack, and Hijack, five bottles of 3.2 beer were not much better than water.

172

Late Sunday afternoon, Cole brought more news about the new Quonset hut. He and Faltynski, on the way back from peddling cat's-eye necklaces throughout a newly arrived Army regiment, had detoured to within fifty yards of the old R and J. The Quonset hut was finished, and a ten-foot fence of barbed wire had been erected around it. A large "off limits" sign was prominently posted. They had just started to crawl under the wire when a jeepload of officers had driven up and gone inside.

"It must be another damned officers' club," Faltynski suggested, as we sat around the tent that night.

On Monday, Red Salleng kept his promise about working parties. All that blistering hot day, Cole, Faltynski, Bill Drapp, Guyman, and I slaved away on the beach loading 81-millimeter mortar shells, crates of hand grenades, and cases of .30-caliber ammunition onto barges that would take them out to a fleet of LSTs anchored a few hundred yards off shore. Nock Dorning and Cosmo Shuttleforth had been sentenced that day to a working party shoveling coral in the island pit. Nick Zobenica had been given a special assignment as regimental runner. Of the R and J nine, only Cannon had escaped by volunteering to cut meat in Move-the-Line Sledd's domain.

The tropic sun was heading well down toward the horizon by the time we returned to the F Company area. Standing in front of company headquarters, smiling blissfully, was Top-sergeant Brushmore. Right beside him was Private D. Cannon, wearing a hangdog look.

"Halt!" said Brushmore as we tried to slide by. We halted abruptly. He gave me a hard look. "Here's that great demolition expert, our good BAR man named Moe, with his gang of thugs. Mr. Moe, would you kindly step right over here beside your high-explosive butcher friend, Mr. Buck Private Cannon? You other jokers, get in there beside them." Brushmore, still smiling, crashed his hand down on my back and shouted, "Be happy! Relax! Cheer up! We're not looking for brig rats. The brig's too crowded already. We're looking for two volunteers for the flamethrower squad."

173

As the bent and dejected figure of Cosmo Shuttleforth, followed by an exhausted Nock Dorning, shuffled wearily up to our group, Brushmore added, "Get over there by Moe and Cannon and those other slopeheads, Mr. Cosmo." He turned a pitiless glare toward me. "See what you and Cannon and Cole have done to this poor hill boy. The best distiller in the southwest Pacific, and you've brought him to this sorry state, a slave in the pit, a candidate for the flamethrower squad. Yell for Nick Zebenema or whatever you call him. Nick's been running all day long. Yell real loud."

"Nick," I called.

"Louder!" said Brushmore. "You can yell louder than that. Yell as loud as you did the night the R. J. Distillery blew."

"Nick Zobenica!" I yelled.

"I could recognize that voice in a crowd." Brushmore gave me a sly wink. "Even at nine o'clock at night when it's all dark outside."

There came the sound of shambling footsteps and then Nick Zobenica arrived. He had that day carried so many messages that by mid-afternoon the mist in front of his eyes had tricked him into scraping his shins on coconut logs, catching his dungarees on thorny vines, and colliding at regular intervals with unyielding trees.

"Now," said Brushmore, "I believe our whole party is here." He stopped and cleared his throat. "Captain McNail, as you well know, needs two more volunteers for the flamethrower squad. Does anyone in this group want to volunteer?"

There was a bit of foot-shuffling. No more.

Brushmore pointed a threatening finger at me. "By rights you should volunteer for demolitions, Moe. You and Private Cannon, that screwball sidekick of yours."

"Not me, Top," I said. "I'm satisfied with a BAR."

"All right then," said Brushmore. "All right. I would be pleased to have you fine young gentlemen form a column of two's and follow me. We have a special surprise for you."

Marching at attention, we followed him down the company street and into the jungle in the direction of the old R and J,

Brushmore counting cadence as if he were in charge of a boot-camp platoon.

"What the hell goes on?" muttered Cole.

"Knock it off, you eightball! You're at attention!" shouted Brushmore.

Presently we arrived at the clearing with our sign, now freshly painted, still posted on its banyan tree. Before us was a brand new Quonset hut. Just inside the building's barbed wire perimeter stood a small group of khaki-clad officers; bland and smiling in their midst was Colonel Maxim.

"Halt!" bellowed Top-sergeant Brushmore. "Stand at ease!"

Colonel Maxim clicked his heels and assumed an air of happy omnipotence. "So," he said, "my raisin-jack people." He looked us over one by one. "Why, here are some of our old merrymakers from way back at Tent Camp 3. The two Irish hooligans Cannon and Moe, and Ski, and that creator of Japanese banners, Sir Bernard Cole." He turned to his officer audience, among whom were Major Bank and Captain McNail. "This fine group," he announced, "is the foursome that knocked me on my ass one night back at Camp Pendleton. Ran right over me like a herd of wild jackasses."

We looked at each other and, in spite of ourselves, grinned. The 3d Platoon that night in the hills above Tent Camp 3 had spent a half hour creeping up on the Headquarters Platoon, lying carelessly in an open, moonlit area without any sentries posted. It was a surprising omission on their part: they understood the game. Night after night we played it—squads, platoons, companies sneaking up on one another and making rough and tumble attacks. It was great sport unless you caught a fist in the face or a boot in the groin.

That night as we crawled to within twenty yards of the Headquarters Platoon, Colonel Maxim had strolled out a few yards from the rest and stood there peering through his field glasses at some movement on a hillside a quarter of a mile away. He had just returned the glasses to their case and had half turned toward his platoon when we charged right through them. The Colonel had

had only enough time to utter the "son" in *son of a bitch* when Faltynski and I bowled him over and Cole and Cannon trampled him as they went by. Then we had plunged into the underbrush beyond him and were gone. Somehow he had recognized us and kept the knowledge tucked away until now.

"Strictly unintentional, Colonel," said Cole.

"We thought you were a Headquarters Platoon scout," I explained.

Now Cannon joined in. "A sad case of mistaken identity, Colonel Maxim," he said.

"A sad case of one hooligan lying and the other swearing to it." Colonel Maxim was grinning too.

"They're like that, Colonel," said Brushmore. "They're the same damned bunch of cutthroats that pushed a boat out from under me on Emirau."

"I was on the other side of the boat, Top," I said. "There wasn't any way I could have done any pushing. The other guys were over there with me. Ask Red Salleng. He'll tell you."

Colonel Maxim was laughing. "Ask and you shall receive, Top-sergeant," he said. "A lot of lies and jack manure. What I'd like to know is why you haven't volunteered these four bungholes for the flamethrower squad."

"I'm working on it, sir," said Brushmore. "They'll volunteer right after they see what we got waiting for them inside."

The colonel moved on to inspect our newcomers—Cosmo, Dorning, Zobenica. "And these three, I presume," he said to Brushmore, "are innocent youngsters who have been dragged into the raisin-jack business against their will."

"Yes, sir," said Brushmore. "I mean not exactly, sir. This one—" he said, pointing to Cosmo, "is the expert. He knows how to make the jack."

"Remarkable," said Colonel Maxim. We shifted warily.

"Stand easy," he said. "Stand easy while I make a short speech." He paused. "What I'm going to say to you is unofficial." He spoke

176

in a low, conspiratorial tone. "But you people have no idea what you've done to raise morale in this outfit and up and down the island."

"Thank you, sir, we do our damnedest," said Cole in his loudest, most impertinent voice.

"Knock it off, Cole!" Brushmore yelled.

"I know that when you founded the R and J," the colonel continued, "you had no intention of doing anything else but beat the system and make money, a great deal of which, I understand, has gone into the pockets of our good friend Top-sergeant Brushmore."

Brushmore acknowledged this recognition with an uncertain nod.

"In any case," Colonel Maxim went on, "I must say that publicly I condemn you. Privately, I want to say well done!"

He paused dramatically while we squirmed in the last hot rays of the sun, wondering what unpleasant pronouncement would come next. It came quickly. "We heard about the unfortunate incident when your old place exploded. Whatever the cause, we know that you gentlemen regret that it happened. It was unfortunate for regimental morale too, you can bet on that. In fact, in the past week or so, we have been so concerned about the effect on morale that, while you people have been getting a good Marine workout each day, we arranged to put everything back in order for you again." With a signal for us to follow, he headed toward the Quonset hut's double front door.

As we followed, our hearts sinking with a slow realization of what we would find inside, Top-sergeant Brushmore hurried forward, swung the doors open for us, and bowed as we passed.

Inside everything was squared neatly away. Along one wall of the long single room that stretched for thirty yards in front of us, one-hundred-pound sacks of sugar were piled to the curved ceiling. Stacks of tinned raisins stretched for several yards beyond. A row of fifty-gallon drums occupied the opposite wall. Extending outward from them, a jumble of copper pipes joined in a single spigot over, of all incredible things, a squat and shiny metal bathtub.

"We confiscated the tub from the Japs," Colonel Maxim said grandly. "If there are any venereal disease germs left in it, your excellent Quickjack will eliminate them." He approached the tub, which was big enough to hold several Jap officers and a half dozen geishas, and gave it a slight kick. "It's stainless steel," he said, "an ideal settling tank for your product. Yes, sir. Confiscated it from a Jap general on New Georgia. Sent a destroyer up there to pick it up and bring it down here. In fact, I might say that everything in the building has been confiscated from the Japs." He waved grandly at the sacks of sugar and tins of raisins, ignoring the "U.S. Property" stamped on every sack and tin.

I glanced at my partners. Poor Cosmo's eyes were glazed, and he seemed to be rapidly settling into a state of collapse. Cole appeared to have suddenly contracted an advanced case of the bulkhead stares. Cannon was muttering an obscene litany that must have included every limb and twig on Top-sergeant Brushmore's ancestral tree. Faltynski, Drapp, Guyman, and Zobenica had fallen into a trance. Nock Dorning looked as if that 150-millimeter blast he had experienced at Bairoko had just exploded again, this time inside his head.

Top-sergeant Brushmore, standing behind Colonel Maxim, waited silently, smugly. He made a series of motions with arms and hands—a man going into action with a flamethrower. I was spellbound. Brushmore mouthed a curse and turned toward the others. Stunned and desperate, they made not a move.

Now Colonel Maxim, whose back had been turned during this exercise, swung around to speak. "I'm afraid," he said, "that your new distillery will have to wait a few weeks before you experts will be able to resume your alcohol-making pursuits. A few minutes before we came over here to inspect this magnificent new facility, I got word from General Sheepherd that the 4th Marines are to invade an island in the Marianas. A wonderful opportunity. Cannon and mortars everywhere, pillboxes all over the place, Intelligence says."

"Our new flamethrowers will come in handy for that one, Colonel," Brushmore said.

"Yes, indeed," said Colonel Maxim. "Those new flamethrowers will burn the bastards out in a hurry. And when we finish that job and get back to Guadalcanal, our new distillery will be waiting right here for you and your boys."

Brushmore cleared his throat. "Colonel, do you think it might be a good idea to transfer Private Shuttleforth to the rear echelon so he can stay behind and make raisin jack while we're gone?"

Cosmo, wearing a look of dismay, leaped forward. "I'm volunteering for the flamethrower squad!" he shouted.

This seemed to startle Nock Dorning out of his shock; stepping forward, he saluted Colonel Maxim smartly. His words were like an echo. "I'm volunteering for the flamethrower squad!"

In the excitement and confusion that followed, Brushmore's suggestion was forgotten. Colonel Maxim seemed delighted. He shook hands with Cosmo and Nock and then, calling his officers' group together, hopped into his jeep and drove away.

Top-sergeant Brushmore, bewildered and surprised by this unexpected success, stood there eyeing our group. "By God," he said at last, "we finally got our flamethrower squad."

"Ever nock an arrow, Sarge?" said Nock Dorning. "Ever get a cat drunk?"

"Dismissed!" shouted Brushmore, and, except for the newest flamethrower volunteers, we sprinted quickly away.

And so, in the late spring of 1944, the ten brave volunteers, disillusioned and uncertain about their futures, began their exhausting training program. Others, though, seemed to be filled with glee. To celebrate the birth of the flamethrower squad, Captain McNail and Top-sergeant Brushmore threw a party in Brushmore's tent where hidden stocks of Quickjack, Hijack, and Slapjack were unearthed, toasts were offered, happy speeches were made, and cheerful songs were sung.

The men of the flamethrower squad convened a bitter caucus at which it was decided that during the next campaign, certain portions of McNail and Brushmore would be fried in napalm. They created a committee of five to be sure that the job would be properly done. They would soon have an opportunity: we were about to journey far to the north for the invasion of the island of Guam.

Guam

Three weeks before we loaded our weapons, our ammunition, ourselves, and all of our hopes onto a convoy of LSTs and pushed off from Guadalcanal for Guam, our acting squad leader was selected to attend Officer Candidate School. The very next day, as Red Salleng had promised, Faltynski moved up to squad leader. Those of us who had been in the 3d Squad, 3d Platoon, since Tent Camp 3 did not welcome the change. There was no way, we were convinced, that the old easy sense of equality could be maintained, especially now that our longtime friend would be required to spend part of each day in the company of sergeants, officers, and other despots who were constantly plotting new strategies against us. It was almost as bad as having a buddy fall to a sniper's bullet.

Cole, Bontadelli, and I watched Faltynski sew his only set of sergeant's stripes onto a khaki shirt he would never wear unless we got liberty in San Francisco or Tokyo. "Our friend from the old 4th Raiders couldn't wait to get hold of needle and thread to put the damned stripes of authority on his arm," said Bontadelli mournfully. "You wait long enough and you find out what a guy is really like underneath his sixteen coats of base paint."

"What he ought to do," I said, "is tattoo the damned stripes on."

Cole stuck his head out of the tent and spotted Guyman and Drapp. "Get in here!" he yelled. "We need witnesses. A good guy, one of the originals, is selling his soul to the high brass."

Guyman and Drapp, happy to participate in any event that promised to spiral out of control, rushed in along with a half dozen others who had been loafing nearby. By this time Faltynski, surprised and redfaced at all this unwelcome attention, was trying to shove shirt, stripes, needle, and thread into his seabag.

"Hey Polack, we don't mean to embarrass you!" Cole turned to me. "What do you think about it, Moe? You've known this Polack a day or two longer than I have."

"Going on three years now," I said.

"What do you say about his sellout to the brass?" Cole's voice had risen another notch to accommodate the listeners who had not been able to crowd into the tent.

"The same thing I told Red Salleng a few days ago," I said. "There goes another one of the good guys."

"Goddammit!" Faltynski shouted. "I ain't goin' nowhere. I'm still right here where I've always been."

"But not for long," said Cole. "Not for very damned long." He turned to address his audience, now swelling to about thirty. "You've all seen it happen a hundred times. A good buddy, a good Raider, gets three stripes on his sleeve, and in no time at all he starts acting like a lieutenant or captain or major."

"Yeah," said Guyman, "and we all know what bastards they are."

From the appreciative audience came rowdy agreement and applause. Faltynski leaped up and rushed at Cole. He swung a hard right, missed, fell over a seabag, and went to his knees. Cole ducked out one side of the tent and ran off to report to Red Salleng that his newest squad leader had attempted to strike an innocent subordinate for no good cause.

The whole episode, we all knew, was the sort of hazing every newly appointed squad leader could expect from old friends; but beneath the clowning there was an undercurrent of resentment and maybe some envy. Our old friend would be giving us orders now.

Faltynski turned out to be a good squad leader. He was the same friendly and efficient guy we had always known, but he could also be as firm and tough as a situation required. Nevertheless, in the months that he ruled our small domain, Cole and I believed and complained that he assigned us to more working parties and other unsavory tasks than the newer guys in the squad because he didn't want to be accused of playing favorites. He had his own direct way of dealing with our complaints about working parties. "While you're doing that," he would say, "you won't be doing anything else."

A few days after Faltynski's promotion, two replacements arrived to fill the slots vacated by Cosmo Shuttleforth and Nock Dorning. The first was a slight, sardonic character named Mauvin, a kind of easygoing copy of our Private Cole. Only a month or so out of San Diego boot camp, he had been assigned to the 4th Marines and eventually to F Company. The second man, a cheerless, humorless private and one-time sergeant, Steve Bledco, was a veteran whose combat experience went back to the 1st Raiders and the early battles at Bloody Ridge, Matanikau, and Tenaru.

Bledco arrived one day just as Cole and I were returning from noon chow, slammed his seabag down in the gravel in front of our tent, unslung his rifle, and stuck it out in front of us like a policeman's baton. Surprised, we stopped and looked him over.

"What the hell are you stupid gizmos lookin' at?" he said.

"Nothing!" said Cole, staring him straight in the eye. "Not one damn thing I really want to see. What the hell are you looking at or for?"

"I'm looking for the 3d Squad, 3d Platoon, of this half-assed outfit," Bledco said. "I'm supposed to report to some son of a bitch named Katinski or Zabrynski or some such crap."

"He's right behind us," I said. Faltynski had been only a few yards back, hurrying to assign us to a work party before we tried to hide out. He was just in time to catch Bledco's last three or four words.

"I'm Faltynski," he said, pulling to a stop beside us.

"I'm Bledco. They told me to report to you."

"Who told you?" asked Faltynski.

"Hell, I don't know." Bledco's tone had changed from challenging to surly. "That redheaded son of a bitch with the moustache and the flat hat."

"You mean Top-sergeant Brushmore," said Faltynski.

"You got it," said Bledco, "that's the GI bastard."

Cole had stiffened at my side, and I could feel my hackles rise also. Although we ourselves were often impatient with Brushmore and sometimes disrespectful in our descriptions of him, he was our top-sergeant, our own man. We didn't take kindly to mean-looking strangers referring to Brushmore or anyone else in our company in this way.

Faltynski looked Bledco over curiously. During his growing up days, he had known some hard characters. He talked to Bledco calmly, guided him into the tent next door, and pointed him toward an unoccupied bunk in the back.

Bledco, we learned later from Red Salleng, had been one of Edson's original Raiders, and he had been wounded severely in the Bloody Ridge battle. With his wound far from healed, he had volunteered for duty within a couple of weeks, only to be wounded again. Back from the hospital after a lengthy stay, he had been thrown into the 3d Raiders in time for the Bougainville campaign, during which he had been wounded a third time, getting some grenade shrapnel in the back. Returning to the 3d Raiders, he had been brigged for being drunk and disrespectful to his commanding officer. All those qualifications had apparently persuaded Colonel Maxim or Major Bank that he might fit right into the 3d Squad, 3d Platoon, of F Company.

In fact, he was ill-tempered, uncooperative, and withdrawn. He had been ordered to join us, but he never really came aboard. There was no doubt about his qualifications for the line of work we were in—he had been around so long that he knew practically every weapon in the Marine arsenal. He had a rare skill in jujitsu, was good with knife or bayonet, was a crack shot with an M-1 or a .45. And he could hurl a grenade twice as far as any other Marine I'd ever seen.

184

In the single week he was with us, Bledco pushed Mauvin over a bunk, tripped up Guyman intentionally, and got into a fight with Bill Drapp. The fight lasted about five minutes. Bledco was far too big and too strong for Drapp, who did cut him up here and there, but Bledco eventually landed a punch that cracked Drapp's nose and put him on his back in the company street.

Bledco was stepping forward with the idea of kicking Drapp around a bit when four or five of us, including Salleng and Faltynski, jumped in, but not before he had landed two kicks squarely on Drapp's ribs.

After that incident, Red Salleng visited Captain McNail and told him that the 3d Platoon had had enough of Bledco, and McNail transferred him to E Company where Captain Walker needed a runner.

While Bledco in one week had attracted the resentment of the entire 3d Platoon and half of F Company, Mauvin had made a dozen friends. We especially appreciated him during the workday: he was quick, cheerful, efficient, and willing. But then, from sundown to lights out, he played his mouth organ. He had found it in a San Diego pawnshop and bought it for fifty cents some weeks before shipping out, and he insisted that it be called a harmonica.

Every evening, especially in the hour or so before Galvo blew taps, Mauvin would produce it and treat us to a few tunes. Unlike most Marine mouth organ blowers, who preferred mournful melodies, Mauvin generally puffed out snappy pieces like "Old Ben Turpin" and "MacNamara's Band." Mauvin's music was complicated by a missing reed here and there, so that in his performances there were critical gaps. This did not diminish the zest with which he expended breath and energy. However, we all agreed, we could steel ourselves against Mauvin's nightly concerts with the realization that we would soon be shoving off for Guam.

The week before we left Guadalcanal, Colonel Maxim called a halt to our regular training routine, and the working parties began. We loaded the heavy stuff onto the LST assigned to F Company. Into the huge bay below deck went amphibious tractors called alligators; jeeps loaded with ammunition, rations, and five-gallon cans of water; heavy mortars and pack howitzers, shoved in and tied down in any open space we could find; and, in cribs along the bulkheads, thousands of 5-inch shells.

Only a day or two before the journey, we spent a twelve-hour shift covering the deck from bridge to bow with fifty-gallon barrels of high-octane aviation gasoline. These we locked into place with heavy chains so that the barrels would stay put even in a heavy sea. Between the barrels and the ship's rail we left enough space for two men to walk abreast. We spent our last day before boarding ship loading stack after stack of freshly sawed boards about ten feet long, an inch thick, and ten inches wide. These we spread across the tops of the gasoline barrels to form a broad deck, which we lashed to the chains that held the barrels in place.

"OK," said Captain McNail when the job was done. "Here's where you people are going to live for the next few weeks. We only got room below deck for the crew and a few of the company officers. You guys can make tents out of your shelter halves. You won't get very wet even when it rains. The water will run down between the barrels and drain away. It'll be a lot healthier for you up here than living down there in one of those alligators."

Each squad had been assigned to an amphibious tractor that would haul us to the beach on D-day; in a heavy storm or some other emergency, we could seek shelter there. But after we loaded aboard on the day we left Guadalcanal and stowed our packs, weapons, and all our other gear into our alligator, we realized that it would be a pretty crowded and even less comfortable place than that provided by our shelter halves pitched on the boards and barrels.

We left Guadalcanal on a peaceful, moonlit night and headed northeast toward the Marshall Islands. Six days later we went ashore to stretch our legs on Kwajalein, which had been seized by the Marines some months before. The Navy had pounded the main island with so many tons of bombs and shells that only one torn tree and a shattered Japanese blockhouse remained.

When we dropped anchor at Kwajalein and observed the many ships and the forest of masts around us, we knew that no matter how long the individual battles went on, the United States had won the war. Within our view there were fourteen carriers, eleven battlewagons, thirty cruisers, maybe seventy destroyers, minesweepers, PT boats, and cargo ships too numerous to count. That night probably half of them pulled out for the invasion of Saipan.

Those of us who were destined to invade Guam lingered in the lagoon at Kwajalein for four quiet days. One of the islands of the atoll had been declared a recreational area, and each day a few Higgins boats came by our LST and hauled those of us who wanted to go ashore the few hundred yards to the beach. The island did not have much to offer except sand, four palm trees, and a sort of canteen where a few bored swab jockeys handed out occasional cans of warm beer. It was a place so devoid of things to do that Bontadelli and I even helped Cole patrol the beach for cat's-eyes.

On the fourth afternoon, our dull routine was broken by the appearance of an outrigger propelled by three paddlers heading our way from the main island. As it skidded onto the beach, out jumped Chris Mazini, a friend we had not seen since the attack on Vangunu months earlier. Mazini, one of the first to volunteer for the old 4th Raiders, was something of a rarity: he was a regular Marine and a corporal at that. With such a rank, he had been immediately given the 1st Squad, 3d Platoon. On Vangunu he had been severely wounded by a machine gun bullet and evacuated. We had neither seen nor heard anything of him since.

Now, when all the handshaking was finished and he had introduced us to the two Marines who had come with him, he told us that after being evacuated, he had been taken with a boat load of other wounded men all the way back to a Navy hospital in Honolulu. When finally judged fit to return to duty, he had been sent to Kwajalein to a Marine Support Group. There for some months he had been working as a supply clerk, a humiliating comedown for a combat Marine. "We hear your convoy is pulling out of here tonight," he said. "When you do, the three of us are going to be aboard. We're fed up to the ass with this rear echelon crap."

Red Salleng had come up. "You'll get your balls in a sling with your commanding officer for sure," he said.

"Screw him!" Mazini said.

Red considered the two younger Marines. Neither looked as if a razor had ever touched his face. "Do you two boot-camp refugees know what kind of trap you're getting into?" he said. "If you make it through Guam, the only decoration you're going to get is a big P on your back and about three months in the brig." Red was shirtless so no sergeant stripes showed on his arm, but they recognized the voice of authority.

"We're with him," said one, and the other kid nodded.

"OK," said Salleng. "When you get aboard, hide out somewhere for a couple of days. I hope you brought your canteens and rifles."

Thus when the Higgins boats returned late that afternoon to take us back to the LST, the three stowaways went along. Two days later and a long way west of the Marshall Islands, Red Salleng took them to see Captain McNail. "Well," said McNail, looking them over, "you guys and five others who sneaked aboard on Kwaj are technically over the hill. Hell, I'll bet that supply outfit doesn't have any men left. But we can't send you back now, and we sure can use you." He put them in the 1st Platoon.

The two kids, seventeen years old, had never fired a rifle in anger, but we figured they would do all right. After all, both of them had survived San Diego boot camp.

There was frequent opportunity for argument, discussion, and tale-telling as our LST lazed along during late June and early July 1944. Not since we had joined the Marine Corps had we had so much time on our hands. Far to the west of us the 2d and 4th Marine divisions had run into more trouble from the Japanese on Saipan than leaders like Admiral Kelly Turner and Howling Mad Smith had anticipated. Since for a time it appeared that help might be needed there, we were for several weeks kept in the limbo of floating reserve.

We were accustomed to intense physical activity each day, and boredom quickly set in. We did our best to combat it. Our officers bustled us through an hour's exercise each morning and another hour in the afternoon. The twice-a-day chow lines helped us kill a couple of hours. We read a great deal from tattered pocket books and magazines six months old. These we traded back and forth until we had read each one twice. Games of cards, checkers, chess, and salvo went on all day long.

At night with lights out, these pastimes stopped. Then in the hours before we turned in for the night, those of us in the 3d Platoon would gather near a gun platform on the bow for what we called tall-tale time. The only rules were that the subject should not involve religion, politics, or conquests of females, and that it should be one we had not heard several times before.

Sometimes we talked about work we had done before the war. No one among us had ever worked in a white collar job. Red Salleng had cut timber in Oregon; Faltynski had worked as a section hand; Mauvin had operated a punch press; a few of us had cut trees and helped build small earth dams in the CCCs; Bontadelli had planted and hoed and shoveled until, as he said, his back was bent; Cannon had been a butcher; Anderson had driven a truck; Kessinger had worked in a foundry; Cole had loaded and unloaded freight cars at a hardware factory. No one had ever made much money. Most of us had no more than a year or two of high school; not one had the money or the inclination to go to college. How, we asked, does college prepare a man to drive a truck, dig a ditch, hammer spikes in railroad ties, or fire machine guns? At the time, these seemed to be appropriate questions.

There was a submarine scare on our ship early one morning. One of our destroyers reported pings on its sonar and the word spread quickly throughout the convoy. After flipping out a few hasty depth charges, however, the destroyer signaled all clear and the convoy cruised on.

189

A submarine contact or any other contact was unlikely at that time because the Japanese on and around Saipan were pretty well occupied with their Marine invaders, and the Japanese fleet was moving toward Saipan for the Marianas Turkey Shoot. Nevertheless, the day after the submarine scare, a few enemy torpedo planes did arrive.

A half dozen of them came in late out of the setting sun. We were lounging on our fifty-gallon barrels of gasoline when we heard a lookout shout a warning and sprang up to see one of our destroyers blasting away at something far out on the periphery of the convoy. The next thing we knew, a Jap torpedo plane was heading directly toward our LST. Why he selected our clumsy tub for a target is not easy to explain. There were scores of larger ships in the convoy, including several cruisers and perhaps twenty destroyers. He may have mistaken us for a small carrier. In any case, by the time he was only a half mile away and boring purposely toward us, it became clear what he meant to do. He was, fortunately, no kamikaze: the day of the kamikaze came six months later. He was not the most determined pilot in the Japanese Navy either, because he launched his torpedo from a considerable distance out and made a quick, low bank to get away. Our ship easily dodged the torpedo, which continued through the convoy without hitting anything.

No one is ever pleased to see enemy torpedo planes, but on our LST we were less concerned about the torpedo than we were about the possibility of a tracer bullet setting off the fifty-gallon foundations of our homes on the deck. It would have made one grand funeral pyre.

Impressed by that brush with six planes and six torpedoes, all of which hit nothing but the ocean, our convoy commander took us east for another few hundred miles. We saw no Jap planes for the next several days. Then, finally, official word came that the Japanese defenses on Saipan had started to crack. The invasion of Guam was back on the calendar. The date: 21 July 1944.

Very early that morning we were up and about, running quickly through the chow line, gathering at our alligator, checking our equipment, and finally, with a roar from a dozen alligators, splashing into the sea. We hit the water not far from one of the old line battleships, which was shelling the island with 16-inch guns. In the predawn darkness, we could see those great shells in their red-hot clusters of three seeming to move very slowly across the sky. When they finally landed far inland we could hear, after a minute or so, a tremendous explosion. I imagined that I felt the concussion even a mile at sea, where we waited. It was pleasant to know that these monster shells were going the other way.

Our company was in the first wave. We were to land on the west side of the island several miles south of the old Marine barracks and the airstrip on the Orote Peninsula. The small Chamorro town of Agat was located a half mile to the north of our landing beach. Just as dawn was breaking, our alligators formed a line and started in. The trip from starting line to beach required about fifteen minutes.

It was a typical Marine landing: no fancy stuff, no decoy craft, no smoke screens, no early morning delays for Hollywood con men to snap dramatic photographs of brave warriors clambering down cargo nets, no glamorous generals armed with sunglasses and corncob pipes. The Marine Corps is a blunt instrument. In the early days of the fighting on Tulagi and Guadalcanal, it was a sledge. Now at Guam, driven by the momentum of victory after costly victory, it was a pile driver, a battering ram. Its object was to smash with a first wave of amphibious tanks, tractors, rifles, machine guns, grenades, nitrostarch, mortars, rockets, flamethrowers, cannon, and determined men.

While that battering first wave slammed into the beach defenses, a second wave was already well on its way, and behind that a third and a fourth and a fifth and, if necessary, a sixth—until the enemy was obliterated. For the Marine Corps, the blunt instrument had worked in battle after battle. It would work again.

For this invasion, at least in that landing area south of Agat, the planners had contrived a maneuver that was novel and daring. Instead of halting and dumping us at the water's edge as in all past invasions, the alligators and buffaloes hauling the first wave would keep on going slam-bang through the Japanese defenses and inland eight hundred yards. The second wave would do the same except that they would unload four hundred yards inland. The third and subsequent waves would dismount at the beach and mop up there. Meantime, those of us in the first two waves would have caught the Japanese troops in a large and deadly net.

It was an ingenious concept, and we were enthusiastic about it. We could expect to lose some tractors and men hammering our way through the Jap pillboxes and trenches on the beach. And very demanding fire discipline would be required if we were to avoid shooting our own men. It would mean that those of us in the first wave would be for a time isolated a half mile inland. If succeeding waves could not break through to us rather promptly, things might get very hot indeed.

We were not concerned. We were, in fact, buoyed by a powerful confidence. We were Marines, many of us veterans of battles going back to the Solomons, more than half of us Raiders. It would be sweet, for a change, to be shooting at the Japs as *they* advanced from the beach.

Somewhere on the Orote Peninsula side of the bay, the Japs had a nest of 77-millimeter cannon. As our long line of alligators, still half a mile from the beach, drew abreast of them, they opened fire. We saw boats hit and Marines flung up and outward by the explosions. All we could do was huddle and hope and keep plowing along until we were close enough to see objects clearly on the beach. Now the two machine guns mounted up front on our boat began to pour a stream of bullets into the tangle of brush and trees at the water's edge. Our coxswain gave a yell: "Fifty yards! Fifty yards to paydirt!"

"Keep rolling when you hit that beach!" Red Salleng yelled. "Don't stop! Keep it rolling!"

But when our first wave of alligators hit the beach on Guam, we ran into an unexpected obstacle: the big guns of our bombardment fleet and the five-hundred-pound bombs the Navy and Marine aircraft had dropped all along the water's edge had ripped up chunks of coral as big as small buildings. Our alligators could not go around those monsters, nor could they surmount them. Our coxswain tried until our alligator was tilted at such an extreme angle that it nearly went over backward. We yelled for him to give it up, stop the vehicle, and let us leap out before we were crushed beneath it. When he did finally stop butting and banging about, we jumped over the side and landed in deep, loose sand churned up by the bombardment. On either side of us other alligators had ground to a halt, and the rest of the men of our platoon were leaping clear. Up and down the beach we heard the rattle of Nambus and the crack of enemy rifles, but right where the 3d Platoon gathered a few yards off the beach, all was quiet. We had landed at a spot where either the Jap defenses were very thin or the shells and rockets of the bombardment had knocked them out.

McLane and Salleng were conferring, but only for a few seconds; then the word came down the line. We would leave the beach and run to our objective. Red Salleng was already leading the way, fifty yards inland, moving at a rapid trot directly toward a ridge six hundred yards ahead. Single file at five-yard intervals, we followed. Halfway down the line came McLane.

We stopped once for a brief rest on our dash toward that ridge. A few bullets from somewhere far ahead clipped leaves and branches above us, but there was no serious resistance. From three hundred yards behind came the sound of heavy firing that increased in intensity as our second and third waves hit the shore.

"Let's go!" came the shout from up front, and we were running forward again, our breathing more and more labored, our leg muscles increasingly strained, until finally we reached the ridge and spread out a few yards below its crest. Exhausted, we threw ourselves down in a line about two hundred yards long and, too

193

breathless to speak, looked around. Very soon we made a remarkable and disconcerting discovery: we were alone.

The platoons on our right and left had fallen far behind and, judging by the volume of fire well to our rear, they had been stopped a few yards off the beach. Except for a single Jap sniper firing a shot now and then from some distance to our right, our run had gone unnoticed.

The grass where we lay gasping for breath in the ninety-degree heat was dry, yellow, and a couple of feet high. Several hundred yards to our left the Navy bombardment had started a fire, but it had not spread in our direction. A few yards directly behind where Mauvin and I lay, McLane and Salleng and the squad leaders had gathered, trying to decide what to do next. "Our biggest danger right now," said McLane, "is from our own people. If some artillery observer back there mistakes us for Japs, we're going to have every gun in the fleet coming in on us."

"We'd better get over the ridge then," said Salleng. "We'd have a lot better chance."

"Better wait!" said Faltynski. "As we came up I thought I heard Japs yelling over there."

As they hesitated there for a moment silent and undecided, I saw, just below the ridge line and directly ahead, a small movement—the briefest possible rustle in the knee-high grass. There was no breeze. I clicked off the safety on my BAR, swung the barrel toward that spot, and waited. Right where I had fixed my sights and only a few yards ahead, five men rose very slowly into a half crouch and stood for a second, peering left and right. They were squat, alien, four of them with rifles ready, their helmets covered with grass, their hooked bayonets gleaming in the sun. The fifth, their leader, his eyes flickering, held a samurai sword, its blade long, curved, shining. As the realization hit him that he was looking directly into the barrel of a deadly weapon, he raised the samurai sword and gathered himself to leap. I was neither startled nor afraid. My BAR was aimed right at his middle and set on full automatic. I pulled the trigger.

Of the various sporting rifles and military weapons invented by John Browning, the Browning automatic rifle is the most remarkable. Although labeled as "automatic," it can be set on single and fired as a semi-automatic weapon or put on automatic, whereupon, as long as a shooter keeps the trigger pulled, the rifle goes right on pumping bullets until, in a few seconds, it exhausts the twenty-round magazine.

The BAR is a very accurate weapon if it is handled correctly. Two characteristics, however, make correct handling a bit difficult. Some shooters, even among weapon-loving Marines, can never accustom themselves to the fact that when the BAR is fired, there is no kick, no recoil in the usual sense. There actually is recoil, but because of the gas action involved, the recoil, although very slight, is forward instead of back. Novice riflemen are always surprised by this characteristic when they fire the weapon on single fire. When they have the rifle on full automatic, they must be very carefully coached and very strictly forewarned, or the weapon will pull them forward, then upward, and then over onto their backs. This can also be an unhappy event for anyone standing near and, especially, directly behind the shooter.

The BAR has another characteristic that surprises the novice: it fires on the forward motion of the bolt. With an ordinary rifle like the older Springfield '03 or the M-1 of World War II, the bolt is used to slam and lock a cartridge into the firing chamber. When the trigger is pulled, a firing pin strikes the cartridge and the shot fires immediately. On the BAR the bolt is pulled back several inches and locked in place. Immediately a powerful spring at the base of the magazine pushes a cartridge upward. When the trigger is pulled, the bolt is released and pushed forward by another powerful spring. As the bolt moves forward, it slams the waiting cartridge into the firing chamber. The instant the cartridge is in place, the firing pin springs forward and fires the round. Thus, with the ordinary rifle, there is a delay between trigger pull and firing that is so brief as to be undetectable. With the BAR, there is always a very brief but detectable wait.

195

In that fraction of a second while the bolt of my BAR was moving forward, the Jap officer had raised his samurai sword, already in frantic motion, a few inches higher. Then the bullets, probably three or four of them, hit him and flung him away. Without conscious thought I swung the BAR toward the others, the remaining bullets from the twenty-round magazine pounding squarely into them. They were flung here and there by the powerful impacts, two of them lifeless as they fell, the other two squirming and bouncing about in the grass and making those strange gurgling noises so often produced by dying men.

As I rammed another twenty-round magazine into my BAR, Mauvin, an amazed look on his face, rose to one knee for a better view of the bodies sprawled to our front.

"They're on the reverse slope, all right," Salleng said calmly from a few yards behind us. "No telling how many. Spread the word. Spread the word to get ready for a banzai."

In an instant the three squad leaders had rushed off to spread that word all along our thin line.

Mauvin was still on one knee looking at the downed Japs. "I couldn't even move!" he said, his voice full of self-reproach.

"You will next time," I said. "You'll get plenty of chances." One of the wounded Japs had ceased his spastic movements. The other one had actually reached out with both hands and was pulling himself toward the crest of the ridge.

"Better finish him off," someone behind us ordered. "Mauvin, put a couple of rounds into that bastard."

Startled, Mauvin hesitated and looked toward me. The Jap had stopped his tormented crawl and was, incredibly, reaching very slowly toward a grenade on his belt. It was a thing to be marveled at. This small man, a private in the emperor's army, surely of peasant stock, considered by those who governed and owned him as only a little more valuable than some draft animal—this small alien, his guts ripped apart by three or four .30-caliber bullets, nearly paralyzed by shock and pain, nevertheless commanded that hand to move in a last dim impulse to struggle against a despised enemy. To this day I distinctly remember that brave soldier of Japan with admiration and awe.

"Shoot the bastard." It was the same even voice that had given the first command. Mauvin raised his M-1 and fired two shots. The hand stopped its movement.

"Put a round into each of the others," the voice said. This time Mauvin didn't hesitate.

The banzai we had expected had not yet come. Salleng, McLane, and the platoon runner went off toward the middle of our line. Fifteen quiet minutes went by. I crawled forward a couple of yards for a closer look at the dead Japs. There was a great deal of blood. Flies were already buzzing round, and a crimson trickle was worming toward us through minute openings at the roots of the sword grass.

"That was close," said Mauvin softly. He had crawled up alongside me. "I wonder why they stood up so slow."

I wondered too. Why had they risen from the grass so deliberately? Why had they given me a target that Marine riflemen dream about? If they had leaped quickly to their feet and moved fast, they might have cut us to pieces while we were still getting into position to fire. Perhaps their actions were dictated by some strange military theory that an enemy is less likely to see a man who moves very slowly. If so, it was a theory that made about as much sense as the belt of a thousand stitches so many Japs wore, believing that it would divert enemy bullets away from their vital parts.

As we waited there spread out in a thin line along our two hundred yards of that shallow ridge, I heard heavy footsteps and spun around to see Steve Bledco. Breathing heavily, he threw himself down beside me. Between gasps, he said that a machine gun had opened up on him as he left the beach and fifty yards farther along, a Jap mortar shell had blown him off his feet. He was no longer the mean and angry man who had been briefly part of our squad. Instead, he was nearly rigid with fear.

"What's over the ridge?" he asked through chattering teeth.

"Don't know," I said and pointed toward the five bodies sprawled in front of us. "These came over a few minutes ago. McLane's making up his mind whether or not to send us over."

For a moment there was a silence around us. Bledco got to one knee, his head cocked to the right. "They're over there. Over the ridge. I can hear the bastards."

I could hear nothing except, way back on the beach, the crackle of machine guns. I looked at Mauvin. He shook his head. He had heard nothing.

"They're over there all right," Bledco said. "I've heard 'em fifty times before." He made a supreme effort to still his chattering teeth. "Gimme a grenade," he said, apparently forgetting that he had four of his own hooked here and there on his web gear.

I reached into my dungaree jacket for a grenade and handed it to him, although he was shaking so hard I was not so sure he wouldn't arm it and drop it at our feet. But when he wrapped his hand around that grenade his shaking stopped. He paused just a second to square his feet, then pulled the pin, let the spoon fly, held the grenade a count, and threw. It was a long throw, maybe fifty yards to the reverse slope of the ridge, but the grenade soared as if it had been fired from a launcher. From over there came the heavy sound of an explosion and then screams, wild cries, and shouted commands. Bledco had heard correctly. The Japs were there.

Now Bledco remembered his own grenades and one after the other he threw them. More screams from the reverse slope and suddenly a line of armed men led by an officer with a samurai sword came rushing toward us over the ridge. In the middle of the line, they hurled themselves in among our men, slashing and stabbing with their bayonets, screaming and hacking before they went down. On our end of the line, the rush lacked momentum. The fifteen or so men who came over seemed to be half blinded by indecision or fear. We blew them down. As the few survivors ducked back to the reverse slope, we rammed in new clips and magazines and pumped extra bullets into the scattered Jap bodies.

198

Bledco had crawled several yards closer to the top of the ridge. Now he turned and called back. "There's more of them over there. I can hear them jabbering. Toss me some more grenades." I took off my pack with its load of eight grenades. One by one I tossed them to him. One by one he threw them over the ridge. There was a steady stream of explosions followed by cries of pain and anger. With my grenades gone, Mauvin pulled off his pack, and he and Bledco began the same routine.

By this time the Japs were apparently getting reorganized. A Jap grenade sailed our way, rolled down the hill, and exploded behind us. Then a second grenade came and another and three together and a dozen. We rolled this way and that to escape the explosions.

Somehow, those of us closest to the ridge line escaped unhurt. Behind us, though, came cries for a corpsman. Perhaps encouraged by the cries, the Japs attacked again, a larger group coming over on the dead run. We reacted more quickly this time; our automatic weapons blasted them away before they had taken ten good steps.

A hundred yards behind us we heard shouted commands. Captain Walker was coming with E Company at a steady trot. Bledco looked around and crawled back toward me. "That's what I came up here to tell you guys," he said. "Captain Walker sent word that he was on the way as soon as he could get off the beach."

"Line 'em up," Walker shouted at Lieutenant McLane as E Company drew even with us. "We're going over."

On the reverse slope of the ridge, dead and wounded Japs were everywhere. Others of them were already running back toward another ridge line two hundred yards away, but a few were holding on and firing as fast as they could work their weapons. These holdouts didn't last long, and many of those running away were cut down by rifle and machine gun fire.

As E Company moved steadily on toward that next ridge, our platoon stayed behind. With Bledco and Mauvin beside me and a dozen others of our platoon spreading to left and right, we conducted the possum patrol, shooting extra bullets into each of more than a hundred bodies.

The possum patrol over, we rested in the shade of a small stand of large-leafed trees waiting for the rest of our company to come up. Bledco sat down on a Jap ammunition box, looked at me, and smiled. It was the first time I had ever seen on those heavy features anything but a snarl or a sneer. "I feel great," he said in a low voice. "I been so goddamned scared the last three months I could hardly crap." He held out a steady hand. "You saw me shaking back there," he went on, "but I'm not scared now. I've come back." He reached out and tapped me on the helmet. "We had it going back there with those grenades, didn't we. I ain't scared no more. I'm back. I'm staying with you guys for a while. That Polack squad leader of yours is not such a bad guy. I might even get so I like that damned bastard I kicked hell out of back on the Canal."

There was a warning flutter and a mortar shell exploded ten yards away. The air around us was filled with purple smoke.

"A goddamned marker!" shouted Faltynski from somewhere behind us. "Bail the hell out of there!"

We rolled frantically toward any cover we could find and lay clutching the ground as a barrage of shells came in. Then silence. Minutes passed. No more shells came. I sat up, still shaking as I always shook when the Jap mortars found us. Bledco laughed. "Now you're the one that's turning chicken," he said.

That night just before midnight, as we fought a desperate battle to beat off one more banzai, Bledco stood to throw a grenade, and one of our men, mistaking him for a Jap, shot him three times through the back with an M-1.

We took other casualties in that banzai, and we used up much of our ammunition, but at daybreak we attacked toward Mount Alifan, as if our leaders believed we had chased all the Japs off our end of the island. In this rare instance, they had guessed right. Most of the Japs had gone north toward Orote Peninsula. A few machine gunners fired at us, and a sniper here and there. We disposed of them quickly, and by noon had not only reached our objective but had gone a half mile beyond. Finally, we stopped and rested until a convoy of amphibious tractors brought rations, water, and ammunition.

Halfway through the afternoon, Captain McNail, somewhat thick of tongue from a few swallows of sake the Japs had left behind, assembled F Company for a special assignment. It was, he said, one that we would be certain to enjoy. A three-man reconnaissance patrol had sneaked that morning to the outskirts of a Chamorro village on the east side of the island and about eight miles south of us. There were Japs in the village—maybe a platoon of them—and they seemed to be holding the villagers as virtual prisoners. Our job would be to get down there as soon as possible and save as many people as we could before the Japs decided to cut them to pieces with samurai swords.

It turned out to be an unusual mission. We hadn't gone a mile when both McNail, who had decided on a few more swallows of sake, and Top-sergeant Brushmore, who had sampled twice as much, passed out and had to be folded over the backs of a couple of horses we had liberated somewhere. Lieutenant McLane appointed himself temporary company commander, and we moved right on.

There were, in fact, only nine Japs in the village, and they had arranged themselves for our convenience around a meal of rice, seaweed, and fish heads in a small hut on the north side of the village. We didn't bother to invite them to surrender. Instead, at a signal from Red Salleng, twenty-five of us fired simultaneously with M-1s and BARs, the bullets penetrating the hut's flimsy walls and the hides of the Japs inside. There was no answering fire; each of the nine had been hit at least a half dozen times.

The villagers needed only a few minutes to realize that they had been delivered from the slave camp in which they had existed for the past two years. They were wild with delight, hugging us and each other, laughing, crying, patting us on the back so enthusiastically that we began to believe we would be casualties of the Chamorros before we saw the Japanese again. In no time at all the

Chamorros had organized a fiesta: baked fish, fried chicken, pies, and taro bread—all washed down with a home-brewed liquor almost as powerful as Quickjack.

An unusual thing about the whole affair was the large number of possessions the villagers had managed to hide from the Japanese during the occupation. Two natives, both retired from the U.S. Navy five years before World War II, appeared in their old uniforms not more than ten minutes after we had finished off their overlords. They criticized us for taking so long to fight our way back to Guam.

Two days later we were back in serious action. The 22d Marines had cut across the base of the Orote Peninsula where the old Marine barracks were located before World War II. They had trapped several thousand Japs; now we had to line up and go in after them.

The night before we were to launch our attack, the Japanese treated us to a major banzai. We welcomed it: it was much easier to shoot them down when they were out in the open coming toward us than when they were dug in and firing from a trench, tree, spider trap, or bunker. But in all the running, shooting, and screaming, the Japs managed to get in among the foxholes of our 1st Platoon and bayonet Mazini, who took a half dozen of them with him. A few minutes after that, a suicidal Jap bearing a pack full of explosives leaped into a foxhole occupied by our two other young stowaways and blasted them into unrecognizable parts.

During our counterattack the next day, the flamethrower squad lost Cosmo Shuttleforth and Nock Dorning. A Jap rifleman shot Cosmo at short range, not an unusual way to depart. Dorning's way was more spectacular. On the Orote Peninsula the Japs had prepared a deadly surprise, especially around the airstrip. Because for some time they had not been able to send any planes out on bombing missions, they were left with an excess of five-hundred-pound bombs. In their ingenious way, they had converted these to land mines that were easily tripped by the pressure of a footstep. To kill only one man with a five-hundred-pound bomb may be considered wasteful, but the Japs surely reasoned that the bombs would otherwise go entirely to waste.

The flamethrower squad had had a demanding day, having been called on a half dozen times to rush forward and discourage stubborn Japs holding out in revetments or pillboxes. Nock had gone back to get an extra canister of napalm, and he was running forward with it, no doubt far more concerned with a Jap machine gunner who was landing bullets close around him than he was with where he was putting his feet. He was still seventy-five yards from his squad when he stepped on the trigger mechanism that set off the bomb. The tremendous explosion that followed was extraordinarily bright, probably because the napalm had become a fiery part of it. We saw no more of our friend Nock Dorning.

Coming off the line late that afternoon, we saw Cosmo Shuttleforth one more time as the graves registration people loaded his body, along with the bodies of twenty other Marines, onto the back of a six-by-six truck.

Home to Guadalcanal

After the battle on Orote, the heavy fighting on Guam was over for F Company. What Japs were left had gone off to the north end of the island, where the 3d Division and the 77th Army Division gradually destroyed them. We had daily patrols and a few skirmishes, but the fight had pretty much gone out of the Japs. We even heard that a few had surrendered to the Scouts and Snipers Platoon.

The scuttlebutt being spread at that time by Private Cole and others was that the 4th Marines would return from Guam to a camp on the Marshall Islands or perhaps the Gilberts. Instead, we took the long journey back to our camp on Guadalcanal.

In our tent, everything was exactly as we had left it three months before—our cots with their small mattresses rolled up according to regulations, our seabags arranged neatly around the tent pole, our incidental belongings right where we had left them. It was a tribute to our rear echelon, the small group we had left behind to stand guard and keep things in order.

The morning after our return, Colonel Maxim sent word that for a few days we would have a period of rest and recreation. *Rest* to Colonel Maxim meant two days of unloading ship followed by a Saturday night issue of three bottles of New Zealand beer. The recreation consisted of six weeks of hard training, or light physical conditioning as the colonel called it—up every morning at 5:00 for the jumping and arm-flailing sessions, a quick breakfast of powdered eggs and New Zealand bacon, and a two-hour hike through the jungle. It was thought that during our long journey to Guam and our several weeks of shooting Japs there, we had spent far too much time loafing atop barrels of gasoline, crouching in foxholes, or otherwise lounging about. This meant that our muscles had suffered grievous deprivations and our reflexes had become dulled. Once back home, we obviously required some fine tuning.

Because of Colonel Maxim's sense of propriety, wounded men, returning from the clean sheets and crisp nurses of a Navy hospital, were generally given a few days to regain their enthusiasm for the old routine; but the colonel was concerned about the health and welfare of these shirkers too. Thus the walking wounded could often be seen limping through close order drill or trotting laboriously up and down the company streets getting their damaged joints and muscles stretched properly again—under the command of a kindly gunnery sergeant. They almost seemed happy when they were finally released to regular duty.

It was not that Colonel Maxim was displeased with our performance on Guam. In fact, a week after we had moved back in on Guadalcanal, he spent a day going from battalion to battalion informing us that he was proud of the way we had shot the Japs to pieces wherever we had met them up there. But he was concerned, he emphasized, that on several occasions we had reacted somewhat sluggishly against Jap night banzais, and he believed we had been too reluctant about firing on distant targets. This was especially true of our mortarmen and machine gunners.

"I'm not excusing the rifle platoons either," he shouted. "Sitting around with their heads in their helmets while fifty Japs are grabassing around five hundred yards out front. Shoot the bastards! At least shoot at them and make them quit whatever the hell they're doing. They aren't doing anything that will help you live to see the Golden Gate in '48. You can count on that!"

The upshot of all this ranting was that for five weeks we spent a couple of hours every afternoon crawling around in the Guadalcanal hills aiming our weapons at designated targets off in the distance. Although most of us had fired anywhere from eighty to eight hundred rounds of ammunition at various Japanese individuals and formations on Guam, we did have to admit that there was much truth in Colonel Maxim's complaint. We resolved to do a better job of interrupting distant Japs at their play next time we met up with them.

During that first week after our return to Guadalcanal with all the frantic activity of unloading ship, moving back to our old camp, and cranking up for the old training routine, no one seemed to recall the raisin-jack still for which Colonel Maxim and Top-sergeant Brushmore had had such high hopes. All those months it had waited at the jungle's edge, carefully guarded by the faithful watchdogs of the rear echelon.

But Top-sergeant Brushmore had not forgotten, nor had Colonel Maxim. Midway through our third vigorous week, word filtered to us that the battalion might be able to excuse several key members of the 3d Squad from duty each afternoon if we would be willing to resume production. Now that for the moment the Japs were far away and not so often in our thoughts, we had been hearing some talk about the happy times when Quickjack and Slapjack improved the minds and spirits of many a 4th Marine.

Our master distiller was gone, though: one more reason for being relentless and uncompromising in any future dealings with the Japs. But in a nostalgic and positive mood, our raisin-jack group sent word to Colonel Maxim that we would try to go into limited production again. Cannon, because he had often watched Cosmo during his artistic performance at the site of our original still, thought he might know the correct formula for Quickjack. But sadly, in the first batch he brewed, either he omitted some of those ingredients that would have rendered a proper critical mass, or he did not know the magic words that Cosmo recited. In any case, the Quickjack produced by Cannon came out more like quicksilver or quicklime or quick diarrhea. With Cannon's reputation in question, Move-the-Line Sledd and Private Cole teamed up to exhibit their skills. What they produced, after two or three disastrous attempts, would have dissolved an anvil or the stomach of a shark.

Top-sergeant Brushmore was beside himself. He ranted, he threatened, he accused us of sabotage, and he reminded us that the flamethrower squad had lost four men on Guam. There were immediate openings for uncooperative wretches like Cannon, Cole, Guyman, and Moe. Alarmed at our dismay, Mauvin revealed that before being fired for tippling, he had once worked briefly for the Jack Daniel's distillery in Lynchburg, Tennessee. He would try his hand as master of raisin jack. He was, as anyone except a sergeant, officer, or other dreamer, might have predicted, an immediate and dismal failure. Stud Van Fleet announced that he knew how to distill raisin jack. No luck. He went back to his sawmill. John Reardon, Bill Vahey, and George Wilbert volunteered. They merely wasted two hundred pounds of sugar and six tins of raisins. It became gradually and painfully obvious that without the spirited genius of Cosmo Shuttleforth, we would never tip up a canteen cup of Quickjack again.

There was so much disappointment in the battalion that several guys from Captain Walker's company went out and hijacked a Navy beer truck, and we had something liquid with which to smother our sorrows for a couple of days. This approach promised such easy returns that Walker's boys hijacked three more Navy beer trucks in a two-week period and, to vary the pattern, broke into an Army Air Force club down at Henderson Field and made off with thirty cases of quality bourbon. The Army flyboys retaliated by buzzing our camp a few days later with a squadron of B-25s. The Navy's response was more positive. They began mounting .30-caliber machine guns on their beer trucks—an ominous development, although not because we were concerned about a few machine guns. What worried us was that the Navy gunners, being the world's poorest marksmen with small arms, might shoot at us and hit some innocent soldiers or Seabees a half mile away. To top it all off, Colonel Maxim received word from Admiral Halsey or some high monkey-monk on Halsey's staff that if we did not cease our reprehensible practice of interfering with the prompt delivery of Navy beer, the battleship *Washington* or the *North Carolina* would pull up a mile off shore and bombard us with its 16-inch guns. That was a threat that had some gusto to it, and those who had been interfering in the spiritual affairs of the U. S. Navy decided to give it up.

Defeated and sorrowful, Top-sergeant Brushmore, although not convinced that only Cosmo Shuttleforth knew the formula for Quickjack, finally recommended that the unproductive raisin-jack distillery be converted to a regimental brig where members of the 3d Squad, 3d Platoon, might receive the incarceration they deserved. Knowing of Brushmore's discontent, Cole, Cannon, and I began to be concerned about the flamethrower squad again. Before Brushmore had a chance to enlist us, however, four young, ignorant replacements volunteered.

Meantime, Faltynski was leaving. The campaign on Guam had been an especially tough one for him. There had been a great deal of walking and running and leaping into holes and hauling heavy loads. The leg wound he had received way back on Bairoko had been bothering him for several months before we'd landed on Guam, and by the end of that campaign, the leg had become infected. Now the bone was involved. His chronic malaria had struck again on the voyage from Guam to Guadalcanal, a severe case this time. Both these medical problems were probably aggravated by the fact that he was suffering an acute case of lovesickness. The girl called May was more and more frequently on his mind in spite of Cole's warnings. "You need to get hold of yourself, exert your will, purify your thoughts!" he shouted at Faltynski one Sunday afternoon as we wandered along the beach a mile or so from camp. "You're not the cat's-eye hunter you used to be. You're limping around like you got your feet on backwards."

"Goddammit, Cole," Faltynski said. "I got a sore leg. I'm just getting over malaria. I ain't feeling too great."

"There ain't a damned thing wrong with you," retorted Cole, "except some gonad trouble."

Faltynski was startled. "Did the corpsman tell you that?" he asked. "What the hell are gonads anyway?" The look on his face indicated that he didn't want them.

"They pop up from nowhere," said Cole. "They're caused by an advanced case of lovesickness. You have to quit thinking about May or whatever that gal's name is. She'll be there when you get back in 1948 or 1950. If she's not, you can find a hundred others walking the streets in South Bend as pretty as she is, and younger and hotter too."

Cole had a point. The pictures May frequently sent Faltynski showed a plump, pretty, and sexy young lady. But by 1950 she would be nearly thirty years old, definitely moving on in years.

"What about it, Moe?" said Cole.

"I think he ought to tell her to marry that truck driver she's always talking about."

"I'm going to punch your damned mick teeth out, Moe!" Faltynski shouted.

"What's wrong? What did I say?" I asked. "I can't do anything about some damned squareheaded truck driver moving in on a guy's girlfriend. Hell, they're both eight thousand miles away. My reach isn't that long."

"You got a mean streak, Moe," said Faltynski. "One of these days I'm gonna kick it out of you."

"He's just trying to be his usual helpful self, Ski," said Cole. "It's only that he doesn't have any big-city finesse. Maybe I can translate what he said into more sophisticated Indiana English."

The debate went on for the next three days. In the end, Faltynski went off one day to sick bay where Dr. Wilson declared him unfit for duty and sent him down the island to the hospital. The next thing we knew, he was scheduled to return to the States for further hospitalization in San Diego, where, against all of our thoughtful advice, he had already arranged to have May meet and marry him. We had lost our old friend and sometime squad leader to an infected wound, a case of malaria, and a fatal sickness called love.

Two weeks after Faltynski left, Colonel Maxim relaxed the training program. We would, especially because the Christmas season was approaching, follow our old rear-area schedule of half-day work and half-day rest or play. For a few weeks life was almost pleasant on Guadalcanal. That December of 1944, the rain clouds had gone north toward New Ireland and Truk to harass the Japanese garrisons there.

Even the occasional night guard duty was pleasant, especially for those on beach patrol. The shoreline at our Tassafaronga camp curved inward for a couple of miles and then swung outward in a long, graceful arc of sand and palms. Under the moonlight, the water shone and the sand softly glowed. Here, just over two years before, armed men were landing, big guns were firing, bombs were exploding, men were dying; and off across that rippling channel of blue, moonlit water the guns and the torpedoes of two great naval forces had torn men to pieces at their posts or flung them into the flaming sea.

Each time I reached the far end of my beat, I stood awhile looking off toward Tulagi. I watched the moon reflect in the water and in the froth far out where the onshore breeze pushed the waves across the high reef. It was a time for thinking back.

On several nights I thought of our brief liberty in New Zealand, already more than a year ago. Auckland, our liberty port, was a fair-size, beautiful, and civilized city. There we were quartered in long, narrow, one-story barracks, perhaps one hundred men to a building. A half mile from camp, a commuter train made regular stops at a small depot. For a few cents we could ride quickly into the city, visit the pubs, and hurry to one of the wonderful restaurants for steak and eggs, fresh coarse bread, and sweet, ice-cold milk. Afterward there was a rush for the servicemen's clubs where friendly and mostly generous young women waited.

On the third day of our New Zealand adventure, I happened upon the public library and, on an impulse, decided to do some research on chess. We played it often on boards about six inches by five with small pegged pieces that could be stuck into the tiny holes drilled into the squares. I entered, banging the door and stumbling into a large, bright room. There were a dozen oak tables in neat rows with a half dozen readers at each one. Here and there were leather easy chairs, each occupied by an elderly gentleman with the morning newspaper. In unison, they snapped their papers, frowned, and harrumphed before returning to their reading.

Behind me I heard a tiny, tinkling, spontaneous laugh and turned to see, behind a large administrative-looking desk, a pretty young lady about my own age. She smiled understandingly and beckoned. "This," she whispered as I came forward, "is the Auckland Public Library."

I nodded. "Yes, I saw the sign. I knew it wasn't the Ashes and Coals." I realized as soon as I uttered the words that my whisper, probably intensified by two years of exposure to exploding artillery shells, shouted commands, howling sergeants, and raucous buddies, had carried clearly across the reading room. There were snickers from the tables and more harrumphs from the leather chairs.

"Shhh!" whispered my pretty librarian, raising a finger to her lips.

It was embarrassing, and I turned to leave. "Please don't go!" she whispered quickly, a little louder this time. "It's just that we've never had a visit from a Marine." She rose gracefully and pointed toward a small office at her end of the reading room.

"Now," she said, as she closed the door. "What is it you wish?"

She was so pretty that I nearly forgot my original intent, but I finally managed to explain what I had hoped to find there. After a few minutes of bustling about through card files and stacks, she produced a small book by Paul Morphy, one of the first great American chess masters. In that first hour of study, I learned enough to guarantee mastery over all who had in the past easily disposed of me. Duff Chapman, John Reardon, Cole—they would soon suffer the same frustration and humiliation they had gleefully unloaded onto me. At the end of an hour, I reluctantly returned the book to the pretty librarian.

"I would never have believed that Marines play chess," she whispered. She had a delightful accent.

"Some of them do," I whispered.

"Did you finish your book?" she whispered.

"No. I'd like to have more time to look into it."

For a moment she hesitated as if she intended to hand it back, but at last she pulled open a drawer and very carefully placed the book into it. "Perhaps you could come back tomorrow." She gave the book a little pat. "I'll keep it right here for you."

Next day and the day after that, I caught the early morning train and was waiting at the door when the library opened. On that third day as I waved good-bye to all the readers and tiptoed out, I was seen by three half-soused rowdies from the mortar platoon. It was too late to hide. They came charging up the street toward me— Hodsgill, Donner, and Braun.

"Moe," yelled Donner, "you found a hothouse right downtown!" He eyed the sign, and the expectant look on his face disappeared. "Hey, Moe," he said, "doesn't that say public library? What the hell were you doing in there?"

"Reading a book," I said.

"Reading a book!" Hodsgill was aghast. "What the hell kind of liberty is that?"

Rex Guyman trotted up, took in the situation, and cleared his throat officiously. "No offense, Moe," he said, "but we've got to warn the guys. Our buddy seen coming out of a library?"

"Yes," I said, "a library, and I'm going back tomorrow."

"Jesus Christ!" said Donner. "I don't believe it!"

Word of my incredible behavior spread through the company. Next morning when I caught the early morning train, I was followed closely by a squad of guys from the 3d Platoon. While I sat in the library memorizing more and more of Morphy's strategies, they wandered outside, looking in through the glass now and again to be certain I was still there. As I left, the librarian followed me to the door and out onto the steps. "Perhaps tomorrow you should ask your friends to come in," she said.

"If they're hanging around out there tomorrow," I said, "I think we'll call the MPs and report a disturbance."

As we stood there, Salleng and Faltynski sauntered by, made an ostentatious pivot, and wandered very slowly back.

"They're funny," my librarian said, with one of her quick and attractive smiles.

"They're crazy," I said loud enough for them to hear me. "They've been in combat for two months."

"We'll see you at the Ashes and Coals, Moe!" Faltynski hollered as he and Red went by.

She hesitated. "How long will your division be in New Zealand?" she asked.

"Maybe a week; maybe a month," I said.

She smiled. "Good-bye," she said, and I went off to the pub. Faltynski was there, and Red and Cannon and Cole.

"Hey, Moe," Cole called. "You sure know the right stuff to check out of a library." They were mightily relieved. Their old friend had returned from the very edge of a strange obsession. He had not, as they had feared, actually been going into a library to acquire some mysterious information from a book but to check out a female. This was the sort of conduct that any healthy Marine could appreciate.

As usual, we caught the last train out of Auckland that night, and after a quick steak that Cannon fried up in the cook shack, went happily off to our narrow cots.

At daybreak Galvo sounded a surprise reveille, and Colonel Maxim told us that the Army was having trouble up in the northern Solomons. We would have to cut our liberty short and go to their rescue; we had one hour to get ready to board ship. I thought of the librarian. There would be no time to say good-bye.

I was so preoccupied with these thoughts of the year before that I had forgotten I was on guard patrol. I nearly blundered into Frank Anderson, corporal of the guard that night, who was out making his rounds of the guard posts. "Hell, Moe, if I'd been a battalion of

Japs you'd have wandered right by and never seen me. Were you walking in your sleep?"

"No, Andy," I said. "I was wide awake but a long ways away."

Christmas was made more pleasant by the news that a minor stroke my father had suffered was not serious and he was much improved and in no danger. The extra beer ration we received on Christmas Eve helped too, and mail call Christmas Day brought a surprise—a few packages from home. There was, unfortunately, a widely circulated rumor back in the States that we needed socks and sweaters; we really could have used whiskey, knives, pistols, and watches with luminous dials.

Christmas had barely passed when we learned that the 29th Marines, a new outfit, would be combining with the 4th and the 22d into what would be called the 6th Division and that we would soon be heading north once more, this time to hit the fortress island of Formosa.

All through the late fall of 1944 and into January 1945, replacements had been drifting in at an ever-increasing rate until by early February we were almost up to strength. The last group of replacements, eighteen men fresh from the States, checked into F Company on Valentine's Day. They were kids a few months out of boot camp, although there were a handful of regulars, rear echelon types pushed out of cushy Stateside jobs by a new breed called women Marines.

Of the eighteen replacements the 3d Platoon got three—one man for each squad. Loafing in our tent, Cole, Cannon, Mauvin, and I watched the newcomers as they labored along under seabags, rifles, and other gear. They halted in front of Red Salleng's tent. He hustled out, looked them over, and yelled for his squad leaders. Frank Anderson, who had been made temporary leader of the 3d squad, was first to arrive.

"You got any preferences, Andy?" Salleng asked.

Andy shook his head. "No. They all look like pogey-bait Marines to me."

"Well, hell, then," said Salleng, "flip a coin to see who gets which."

The 3d Squad drew James Albert LeGrand, soon to be known as Jamal. Jamal LeGrand moved into our presence very slowly. In fact, he backed in because his attention was attracted to an unusual activity in the company street. Private Kleck, who had been among the first to volunteer for the flamethrower squad, was busy counting cadence for an imaginary squad of women Marines. Suddenly Kleck shouted "Halt!" and LeGrand stopped so suddenly that he sat down hard on the dirt floor of our tent. "What the hellation is going on out there?" he demanded of Cannon, who was standing just inside the entrance way. LeGrand was still watching as Kleck began scolding a nonexistent young lady who did not seem to be able to execute a proper about-face.

"That's our famous drillmaster Private Hee-hoo Kleck," Cannon said. "He's put himself in charge of pounding some soh— sophis— oh, shit, what's the word, Moe?"

"Sophistication," I said. "He's getting those young ladies ready for the big female inspection tomorrow."

"What young ladies?" said James Albert LeGrand. "Looks like he's yowling at a bunch of coconut trees."

"They're out there all right," I said, "in Kleck's head. When he heard about how the Marines are now recruiting women, he decided he was going to apply for a job drilling them as soon as they get out here to Guadalcanal. He's practicing. Don't pay him any attention. If he wasn't doing that he'd be doing something nuttier."

LeGrand pushed to his feet and dusted off the seat of his dungarees. "Kleck must be an old Raider," he stated.

"One of the originals," I said.

LeGrand took another look at Kleck, now backing expertly up the company street so that he could be in the proper position to watch every step of his phantom platoon. "There are a lot of old Raiders in this outfit, aren't there?" LeGrand asked suddenly.

"About half or two thirds." I turned to Cole. "How many are left in the 3d Platoon, Sir Bernard?"

"Hell if I know," said Cole. "Half the ones we still got are off in sick bay with malaria, and the other half are trying to talk Doc Wilson into sending them to the booby hatch."

"Exactly nineteen left," Mauvin piped up from his corner of the tent. "I toted it up for McLane one day last week."

"Why's he want to know that?" asked Cole, who, like the rest of us, always suspected some sinister motive behind any superior's request for information.

"Probably so they'll know how big to build the stockade to hold all you old Raider bastards when the war is over," said Mauvin.

"They must be building one big as Missouri then," announced LeGrand, watching as Kleck reversed direction and marched his phantom females smartly by. "Everybody says you old Raiders are crazy, but you don't know it because you all went crazy at the same time."

Guyman had crawled into the back of the tent in time to hear this. "I'm Rex Guyman," he said to LeGrand. "You a head shrinker or what?"

"I ain't no head shrinker. I'm a watchmaker," said LeGrand, "but I can recognize a bunch of crazies when I see them."

"Maybe the guy is right," said Cole. "What I'd like to know, though, is if we all went crazy at the same time, when did it happen?"

"The day we volunteered for this damned outfit," said Cannon.

"That's too easy," I said. "I think it happened the first month we were on Espiritu Santo, especially that time we all had diarrhea for a week."

"Move-the-Line Sledd caused that commotion," said Guyman. "He was so drunk he put salts instead of salt in that shark and mutton stew. Worst crap I ever tasted."

"I think we all lost our minds when the Japs trapped us on that trail near Bairoko," said Cannon. "All bunched up and zeroed in. Go left, drown in the swamp. Go right, get sucked into the quicksand. Go ahead, get shot three times with a Nambu. Go back, get shot three times with a Nambu. Mortars blasting overhead, 150-

millimeter shells falling in, snipers picking our guys off one by one!" The more he talked, the louder his volume, so that in the end he was nearly shouting.

LeGrand stood there among us, his look of amazement steadily deepening. What he was hearing only seemed to confirm his original assessment, and several weeks went by before he believed that a few of us might be only temporarily mad.

"James Albert LeGrand," said Cole to Kleck, when he came into the tent. "We're going to call him Jamal for short. He says he's a watchmaker."

Kleck looked LeGrand over closely. "Where do you make these watches? A guy could get rich making watches for this outfit."

"A watchmaker," LeGrand said, "does not manufacture watches. A watchmaker repairs watches. You got a faulty timepiece, I can fix it for you in a jiffy—for a price."

"This is a screwy world," said Cole, looking first at Cannon and then LeGrand. "We got a butcher who tells us he's a meatcutter but doesn't do anything but open cans of Spam and vienna sausage, and a watchmaker who doesn't make watches."

"Well," said Kleck, "a fox is not supposed to smell like a drillbit anyway."

There was a shout from up toward Blackie Arnold's tent. "Flamethrower squad! Front and center!" Forgetting about Jamal LeGrand, Kleck turned and trotted away. "Coming! Coming! To one and all, I'm on my way!" he shouted.

Guyman was standing in the middle of our tent looking at Jamal LeGrand with respect. "I ain't never considered it before," he said, "but if the rest of us are as far off as Kleck, our new boy might be right: all of us crazy, but we don't know it."

"Kleck's gotten worse since he enrolled in the flamethrowers," said Cannon.

Jamal LeGrand had been with us only a few days when his reputation as a repairer of watches whipped through the battalion grapevine. It was amazing how many men owned watches that no longer worked. Late afternoons, evenings, and Sundays, there was always a mob of guys hanging around our tent pleading or demanding to be put first on the list to have a watch rejuvenated.

Jamal did his best, and, considering the tools he had to work with, his best was very good. He had a razor blade, a nail file, a safety pin with the point ground fine, and a pair of tweezers. Unless the parts of a watch were rusted together or so badly damaged that repair was impossible, he tinkered around until the timepiece started ticking again.

After Jamal had been in the squad a few days, we found out that back on the rifle range at Camp Matthews, he had qualified as expert, so we took his M-1 away and armed him with a BAR. That change worked an immediate alteration. Although Jamal was tall, he had narrow shoulders and a narrow head. Until he got the BAR we would have referred to him as skinny and slight of build. All of a sudden he seemed bigger, much bigger. As always, it was taken for granted in the outfit that BAR men were big, whether they were big physically or not. I had observed the same transformation before, when short guys had suddenly become extra large animals after donning the special web suspenders of a BAR man and shouldering that awesome weapon. I always felt that I grew three inches taller and twice as broad whenever I picked up my own BAR.

Okinawa

Jamal LeGrand did not have much time to repair watches or to get intimately acquainted with his BAR. Not long after a couple of Marine divisions landed on Iwo Jima, we began boarding ship. Once more our invasion convoy headed off toward Japan, and after a few days at sea we were told that the convoy's objective was not Formosa after all, but Okinawa, an island much closer to the Japanese homeland.

On 1 April 1945, F Company landed on Okinawa in the fourth wave. As we neared the beach we saw to our amazement the Marines of the waves that had preceded ours spread out in three long skirmish lines, moving easily inland. There were none of the usual sights and sounds—no machine gun fire, no shellbursts, no men running or falling or crawling inland, no casualties being carried toward the beach, no doctors working desperately at the aid stations. Only mounds of supplies already piling up on the beach, lines of tanks, half tracks, cannon, jeeps, and trucks going steadily ashore. And way in the distance off to the south a single long burst of machine gun fire from a Japanese Nambu.

"The only Jap on the island," somebody said. Those of us who survived would learn that there were also 109,999 other Japs on the island and probably 9,999 other Nambu light machine guns.

The only excitement that first day occurred shortly after dark. We had crossed the Japanese airstrip at Yontan as the sun was easing into the East China Sea, and we had dug in waiting for the

219

Japanese banzai that was sure to come. There was no banzai that night. There were no infiltrators, no incoming artillery, no grenades, no mortar shells. Shortly after darkness fell over the quiet land, a Japanese Zero landed on the airstrip and the pilot, obviously not having heard that a new landlord had moved in, stepped out of the plane onto the runway. No one fired. He stood there alone, probably wondering why the usual welcoming committee was not there to greet him. Presently, a Marine in a nearby foxhole called softly to him to surrender, whereupon the lost pilot reached for his pistol. The end came swiftly with the arrival of perhaps a hundred bullets.

There was nothing much to shoot at the next day either, although our platoon did file past one dead Jap who had been surprised as he was planting a few land mines along a trail we were following. Shot in the groin, he sprawled there, a dozen saucer-size mines that had spilled out of his box scattered nearby. Tiptoeing warily, we skirted around man and mines and passed the word back for Blackie Arnold to come up and at least dispose of the mines.

The third day as we headed east, we encountered six live Japs. Apparently a recon patrol, they blundered into our line as we paused in a heavy stand of trees for a short break. Rifles slung haphazardly, they came toward us chattering and giggling, as if no one had bothered to warn them that the Marines had landed. When they finally saw us, we were looking at them over the sights of our rifles from a few yards away. They did not offer to surrender, nor did we issue them an invitation.

Halfway through the fourth day, we burst suddenly out of a heavy stand of pines into the winding street of a small village, and saw immediately beyond a sandy beach and the blue Pacific. Trotting along silently in single file, we were into the village so quickly and unexpectedly that a half dozen Okinawans, grouped and gossiping in front of the village's largest hut, were unaware of our presence until we were right on top of them.

"Search the houses!" Captain McNail shouted.

There were only about thirty-five people in the village, mostly women and children and a few old men. As on Saipan and elsewhere, their Japanese overlords must have spread horror stories among them about how the Americans tortured and killed all civilians. Heads bowed, eyes downcast, they clustered in the street practically overcome with fear.

"We ain't going to hurt you damned gooks none!" McNail shouted, a roaring reassurance that probably converted their fear to terror.

Over at the north edge of the village, there were shouts as Cole and Guyman flushed two more civilians from under a dilapidated hut. They were young men, clad as the other civilians in the long, black gowns worn by every Okinawan we had seen on our way across the island. Top-sergeant Brushmore headed toward them.

"These bastards look too well fed to be civilians, Top!" Cole hollered. He had turned half away from the two of them.

"Hey!" Guyman yelled suddenly. "These guys are Japs!" He was pointing his rifle toward their feet. "They got split-toed shoes!"

As Cole turned back to see for himself and Brushmore began running toward them, Guyman, never a man to require much prompting, reached out and ripped the black gown off the nearest man. Underneath was the familiar Japanese uniform. In a desperate reaction, the Jap grabbed for the pistol at his side. The second man let out a squawk and ran for the cover of the trees. Before the Jap with the pistol could raise it, Guyman fired a single shot from his M-1 and the man was down and dead. Meantime, the Jap who had let out the squawk of surprise and fear had taken perhaps three steps when Cole raised his BAR and fired a burst. The impact of the bullets took the Jap onward a step or two—no more.

The violent drama had unfolded so quickly that the rest of us were mere spectators. I looked toward the Okinawan civilians. Probably thinking that their turn would soon come, they had gone down on their haunches and there they squatted, quaking in fear and despair.

221

"Check every one of them!" McNail ordered. Somewhat apologetically, a half dozen guys from the 1st Platoon went through the terrified villagers, pulling black gowns back far enough to look beneath them. There were no more Jap uniforms, no leggings wound in place, no split-toed shoes.

By this time, McNail and Brushmore were inspecting the two bodies. "Japs all right, Captain," said Brushmore.

McNail was puzzled. "I wonder what the hell they were thinking of," he said. "Why the hell were they hanging around here?"

"Maybe deserters, Captain," Brushmore said. "Maybe spies. Either way they got the best we had to give them."

McNail was examining the two dead men with an extraordinary interest. A frown crossed his face, and he looked over at Guyman and Cole, who were standing there well pleased with themselves. "Guyman! Cole!" McNail said sharply. "Get over here!" He peered more closely at the dead Japs. The whole face of the one who had reached for his pistol had been shot away, and the wounds in the body of the second man were very large.

"Yes, sir!" They were obviously expecting a word or two of praise.

"You aren't filing off the tips of your cartridges are you, Guyman?" The question caught Guyman by surprise. He opened his mouth to respond, but no words came forth.

"Answer up, goddammit," said Brushmore. Guyman was struggling to react. Back during the fighting on Guam, some of our men had suffered such gaping wounds that we began to believe the Japs were using dumdum bullets. On the way to Okinawa, there had been a suggestion that we could get even by filing the tip off each .30-caliber bullet to create a snub-nosed missile that would smash whatever body parts it might hit.

Guyman had found his tongue. "No, sir!" He released the clip from his M-1 and handed the seven remaining rounds to McNail. McNail studied them carefully.

"All right," he said. He handed the cartridges to Guyman and turned to Cole. Cole had already released the magazine from his

BAR. Now he passed it across to McNail who flipped out three or four cartridges, inspected them closely, and without a word handed cartridges and magazine back to Cole.

"I think it's time you two slopeheads got some new weapons," McNail said. "The rifling must be about gone in yours. Maybe those slugs are tumbling."

Guyman and Cole were recovering their poise, and Cole had opened his mouth to utter some impulsive, bitter protest when McNail held up his hand. "Good work!" he said. "Good shooting, both you bastards!"

We dug in late that afternoon between the village and the sea. Shortly before dark, Top-sergeant Brushmore came along inspecting the line and took note of the two Japs still lying exactly where they had fallen earlier that day. "Guyman!" he shouted.

Guyman came running up from his foxhole thirty yards away. "Yeah, Top?" he said.

Brushmore pointed to the two Japs. "Get Cole and bury those bastards!" he ordered.

"What?" Guyman was stunned.

"Have you lost your damned ears? Bury the bastards," Brushmore said. "We might be here two or three days."

"Bury them?" Guyman said. "You mean me and Cole? Hey, Top, we're the ones that shot 'em!"

"Right!" said Brushmore. "You shot 'em; you bury 'em."

"Goddammit, Top, that ain't fair!" Guyman exclaimed.

"Fair?" It was Brushmore's turn to bristle with indignation. "Who said anything about fair! This is the Marine Corps. Now get your damned entrenching tool and dig a nice hole to drop those bastards into."

As Cole came running up to add his words of protest, Mauvin and I sat there doubled over with glee. Brushmore turned toward us and seemed to reach an instant decision. "You too, Mauvin," he said. "Take Moe with you and that damned Frank Amo. Give your buddies a hand."

"Damn, Top," I said. "How the hell did we get into this? We didn't shoot anybody."

Brushmore was turning red, always a bad sign. "Goddammit," he said, "if you hadn't been standing around half asleep, you would have!"

The five of us dug the hole quickly in the soft clay, rolled the two dead Japs in, and threw a few shovels of dirt over them; but it was well after dark before we stopped our loud bitching about the constant injustices dumped on all the enlisted men who struggled and sweat in the subterranean levels of the Marine Corps social order. As we crawled into our foxholes, still mumbling our bitter complaints, a cold breeze blew in from the sea. In our two and a half years of tropic living we had forgotten that the world can get cold; a blanket and poncho may not offer enough cover to keep the chill away. But this was quickly forgotten when we began to encounter the Japs in larger and larger numbers.

The first of these encounters was on the fifth night. From dawn to dusk, F Company, reinforced by the Scouts and Snipers Platoon, had ridden Sherman tanks on a combat patrol up the gravel road along the east coast of the island. Although we made several stops for brief skirmishes with small Jap patrols, our progress was steady. By day's end, we were fifteen to twenty miles north of the nearest American units.

Captain McNail and Major Bailey, who had charge of the tank platoon, were becoming increasingly lonesome and nervous as the day wore on. They knew—all of us knew—that the Japs had to be close at hand and waiting to attack or ambush. At sundown the column halted while Major Bailey reported our position to the regimental commander. Instead of being recalled, we were ordered to dig in where we were for the night and to keep going north next day.

We dug our foxholes about ten yards apart in a huge circle the military calls a perimeter defense. Well within it, the tanks with their guns pointing outward formed their own smaller circle. As we began to dig in, Captain McNail sent out the Scouts and Snipers to patrol about a mile or so to the north.

Since the 3d Squad, 3d Platoon, had been riding the lead tank in the patrol, we drew the unpleasant assignment of digging in close to the road on the northernmost arc of the perimeter. If the Japs decided on a night banzai, our position was the one they would be most likely to hit first. We felt better about the situation when Captain McNail posted several machine guns close to us on either side of the road. As Bernie Cole and I dug our foxhole quickly in the soft dirt, Top-sergeant Brushmore strolled by. "Dig it wide enough for three men," he said. "We're going to put a man from the Scouts and Snipers in each of the holes on this side."

"Let the bastards dig their own holes," said Cole. "They got shovels just like we do."

"You damned slopehead!" said Brushmore. "Didn't you see them go out on patrol? Maybe if you get tired digging, I'll send you out there with them. Now get your ass in gear and dig."

The digging was easy. In fifteen minutes we had a hole three feet deep and wide enough for three men. Darkness came. We checked our automatic rifles, placed a dozen hand grenades on the parapet, and stuck our K-bar knives in the side of the foxhole within easy reach. As we squatted there eating our C-rations, a low call came out of the darkness. It was Captain Certin. "Scouts and Snipers coming in!" From foxhole to foxhole, the word spread left and right around the perimeter. "Scouts and Snipers coming in!"

One of the most dangerous ventures during the Pacific War was to blunder into a Marine defense line unannounced in the dark. In a few minutes the Scouts and Snipers crawled into our line and scattered to the waiting foxholes on either side of the road.

"Where's Bill Werden?" I called softly into the darkness.

From ten yards away came Werden's voice. "Here, Moe."

"Crawl in here, Bill," Cole and I called in unison. With Bill Werden in our foxhole we would have a better chance of surviving the night. In a few minutes Werden was sitting on the edge of our hole eating cold beef hash from a can of C-rations.

"Anything out there, Bill?" I said.

"About a company of Japs," he said. "They're screwing around a mile or so up the road and two or three hundred yards inland. They'll be by to see us before morning."

The word was already passing. "Expect a banzai tonight right down the road."

"Goddamn!" said Cole with so much feeling that Werden and I both laughed.

"How did God get into this?" Werden said. "Let's keep God in reserve for the invasion of Japan. We can handle this bunch of Nips with BARs and machine guns."

"Knock it off!" came a call from twenty yards behind us. It was Top-sergeant Brushmore trying to get his unruly brood to settle down for the night.

We settled down for a typical front-line night. In every foxhole one man stayed awake and on watch, alternating with others in the hole hour by hour until the break of day. Some time well after midnight, Werden shook us awake.

"They're out front," he said. "I can hear the bastards."

They were out front all right and unusually noisy. We heard shouts, screams, and even a few shots. One of our mortars put up a flare. The Japs were within three hundred yards and marching, not charging, but marching toward us right down the road, and they were driving a mass of Okinawan civilians ahead of them.

They were within two hundred yards now coming steadily on, the Okinawan civilians sort of moaning in one weird, despairing chorus, the Japanese soldiers behind them yelling what we took to be threats and commands. Now they were only one hundred yards away. Still we hesitated, fingers on triggers, but frozen with indecision. Even Captain McNail, usually quick in desperate situations, was baffled and silent.

Then a Jap soldier burst out of the mass of civilians and opened fire with his Nambu.

"Fire!" McNail shouted. In an instant there was one simultaneous blast from our machine guns on the road, from all our rifles, tommy guns, and automatic rifles on our arc of the perimeter, and from six or eight of the tanks behind us.

The Jap with the machine gun was hurled five yards, a target for perhaps twenty bullets. The mass of Jap soldiers and Okinawan civilians melted away. In perhaps forty seconds we stopped firing. No one had given us a command to stop. There was simply nothing to shoot at. As the smoke from our weapons drifted off, we looked at each other in disbelief. We had stopped banzai attacks before but never so quickly and never without taking casualties. This time, we soon learned, not a man among us had been hit.

Our mortars put up a couple of star shells. In that shifting light we saw bodies littering road and roadside. There was an eerie silence. From out there came none of the usual sounds—the gasps, groans, screams, and wondering laments of the wounded and dying.

"Are they all dead?" whispered Cole incredulously.

Bill Werden was putting another drum magazine in his tommy gun. "Either that or they sure know how to play dead."

We waited. Surely this wasn't the end of it. Surely there were other Japs out there somewhere. Surely another attack would come. But as the time ticked by—a half hour, an hour—we began to believe that there would be no more banzais that night.

Then, out of the darkness came a small muffled cry, a little more than a whimper—lonely, unearthly, sustained.

Cole started so quickly he almost dropped his rifle. An involuntary shiver rippled the muscles of my back. Werden crouched at the front of the foxhole peering into the darkness. Our mortars put up another flare. It hung and drifted and spread its greenish light, flickering across the field of the dead before us. Then darkness again.

And again the cry, the muted whimper, the same loneliness, the same note of despair.

"For God's sake," said Cole.

"Quiet," Werden whispered. "I want to hear it one more time."

We waited. And then again the sad, lonely whimper on the chill night breeze.

"It's a baby, a little one," said Werden. He laid his tommy gun on the edge of the foxhole and pulled out his pistol.

"I'm going to bring him in!"

I grabbed his arm. "You'll get it for sure if you do," I said. "If some Jap doesn't stick a bayonet into you, our own men will blast your head off."

"Pass the word down the line that I'm going out," said Werden. "I'll take care of the Japs." He pushed my arm away. "Nobody can keep me from going out, Moe," he said. "Nobody."

"All right. I go too then," I said.

"Not this time, Moe," said Werden. "You'll slow me down." He slid out of the foxhole and disappeared.

After spreading the word, Cole and I sat there in our foxhole in dead silence staring into the darkness. A faint, pink line on the eastern horizon meant that daybreak was not far away. Fifteen minutes went by. Not a sound. Five or ten more minutes passed. The first light of dawn showed in the sky. Still no sound. Then a faint scratching on the road directly in front of us, and Werden was there. Cradled in his right arm was the little one, an Okinawan boy two or three years old.

"He's in good shape I think," Werden said. "His mother is dead. She shielded him with her body. That's why he was whimpering. He was pinned under her in the cold water along the road. It's lucky he didn't drown."

In the faint light of the new day, that little one examined us. He examined us curious creatures with our strange, white, rectangular faces and round eyes—and was not afraid. Captain McNail trotted up, and then Brushmore and then twenty other men, leaving their foxholes to cluster around and see what daylight and Bill Werden had brought.

"I think he'd like something to chew on," said Brushmore.

He produced a piece of hard candy we sometimes found in our

C-ration cans and popped it into the little fellow's mouth. He rolled it around in his mouth a bit and smiled. That small smile brought an absolutely incredible surge of joy through our company of Marines. We shouted and laughed and jumped up and down and clapped each other on the back and spread the word that our boy was hardy and healthy and would survive.

"I'm putting you in for the Silver Star, Werden," said Captain McNail.

"Silver Star, hell," said Captain Certin. "I'm putting him in for the Navy Cross!"

From the direction of the tank perimeter there came a shout. "What the hell's going on over there?" It was Major Bailey. "We got to saddle up and move out in fifteen minutes." A corpsman came up and relieved Werden of his small burden, and we went back to war. By the early light of day we dragged the dead off the road and tumbled them into the ditches alongside. Major Bailey and his tankers, all of them fastidious gentlemen, did not relish grinding a hundred yards of bodies under the treads of their tanks.

Bill Werden never received either Silver Star or Navy Cross. In all the fighting of the next seventy days on Okinawa and all the furor and excitement of the war's sudden end, Captain McNail forgot his promise. And Captain Certin? By the time he got around to submitting his recommendation, the officers who award medals were busy with the surrender of the Japanese.

I saw Werden again on our fifteenth day on Okinawa. A regiment of Japs had been bottled up on the Motobu Peninsula, which juts out into the East China Sea on the west side of the island. There they had fortified a low mountain called Yaetake, and the 4th Marines made a direct attack against it.

Right at the base of the mountain our company ran into trouble. We were moving at a rapid trot single file through brush and low trees, each man about five yards behind the man ahead. One by one we had to cross a narrow road not much wider than a cart path. From three hundred yards ahead, a Jap heavy machine gun, a half dozen light machine guns, and what seemed to be a company of riflemen were firing steadily in our direction. Our plan was to cross the road and spread out left and right into a skirmish line, then attack straight up the mountain and shoot it out.

So far, though Jap bullets from the ridge line were raining around us, we had not had a casualty. But as we came to that narrow road, we got hurt. Of the first twelve Marines to cross, a Japanese sniper somewhere close by shot every fourth man through the head. Those men were dead before they fell. As I rushed down toward that road I could see what was happening ahead and, at that moment, I was more nearly paralyzed with fear than at any other time during the war.

As I skidded across and joined the others who had made it ahead of me, I heard from behind the voice of Captain McNail ordering the rest of the company to halt and take cover.

A few minutes passed. Then from some vantage point across the road came a command from McNail. "You guys up there!" he shouted. "Get that son of a bitch sniper!"

We looked at each other. We had no notion of whether the sniper was firing from right to left, left to right, from spider trap, tree top, or bunker. The sniper could not see us, we knew, or he would have already been picking us off. In our short skirmish line, we lay there anchored by the terrible inertia of fear and confusion.

Two or three minutes went by. The Jap machine gunners on the ridge, with nothing to shoot at, ceased their fire. Then from a bush close to the narrow road we had crossed came once again the enraged voice of McNail. "You bastards up there! Get the lead out of your ass! Get after that son of a bitch!"

A single shot rang out—the sniper getting off a quick round toward McNail's voice.

"He's somewhere to our right," I called to Sergeant White, the only NCO on our side of the road.

"I thought it came from the left," said White.

At that moment Bill Werden rose to one knee from a patch of shrubs about twenty yards to my right. Where he had come from or how he had gotten there, I do not know. He had not crossed the road with the rest of us. Perhaps he had gone out before daylight to scout ahead of our attack forces, had learned that we were held up, and had come back to help. He waved me toward him. I made a low rush—four or five lunging steps—and was at his side.

Werden pointed toward a patch of undergrowth about thirty yards away and perhaps twenty yards nearer the road. "He's in there," he whispered. "I heard him work his bolt after that last shot. We'll work up a few yards closer and each throw a grenade. Then in we go—you go right, I go left."

Weapons ready, we eased forward. Suddenly from a few yards ahead, the crack of a rifle, the sniper firing down the road again. Now clearly came the sound of the rifle bolt being pulled back. We were very close. I looked at Bill Werden, now about five yards away. There was the distinct sound of a rifle bolt being slammed forward. Werden nodded. We threw our grenades toward the sound and flattened out. There were two quick explosions.

"Now!" Werden shouted. The sniper, right hand on his rifle, was pushing himself to his feet. The .45-caliber slugs from Werden's tommy gun and the .30-caliber bullets from my BAR caught him right across the middle. As the bullets hit him a small cloud of dust rose from his uniform, and then he was a crumpled bundle on the ground.

We moved forward. This was no Japanese veteran. He was just a boy, a young Okinawan who appeared to be maybe twelve years old. I picked up his rifle. It was an old .25-caliber Arisaka. The long-barreled model, it was longer than he was tall. Somewhere along the line it had been so badly damaged that the spring clip no longer fed the cartridges to it. Each time he had fired, he had had to pull the bolt back and insert another cartridge; then he levered the bolt forward and fired again. That explained why he shot only every fourth man. He needed time to reload. But he was a natural-born crack shot, and three of our friends would never go home.

"He's a kid," I said. "The damned Japs gave him that rusty old rifle and left him here to get killed. He's just a kid."

"He's a kid all right," said Werden. "But when the Japs gave him that rifle, he grew up to be a man."

There was shouting from our left. It was Sergeant White. "Let's go, Moe! We're moving out!"

Up on the ridge, the Japanese machine gunners were rattling their sabers again, and our 81-millimeter mortars were beginning to blast them.

"You going our way, Bill?" I said.

Werden took the Jap rifle out of my hand, extracted the bolt, and threw it off into some bushes twenty yards away. "No. I'm trying to locate Captain Walker. He's supposed to be attacking a hill a half mile off there to the left."

"OK, Bill, hang loose," I said.

"You too, Moe." He turned and was gone.

The battle to eliminate the Japs on Motobu lasted four days. The second, the day after Werden and I eliminated the sniper, was a fairly easy one: a brief firefight in the morning with considerable shooting and shouting on both sides and then a sneak attack up a shallow gully to the flank of a ridge defended by about fifty Japs. We had them outguessed, outgunned, and outnumbered; in this rare instance, they abandoned their defenses and ran. As we lay there on our newly won position, we saw, three hundred yards to our right, G Company assaulting a wooded hilltop. There the Japs did not retreat. As G Company spread out and charged the hilltop, we saw a company of Japs charging from the opposite side. There was a savage medley of shots, howls of "Banzai!" and rebel yells. In five minutes the Japs were eliminated, but in all the infighting G Company had taken some heavy losses.

Inspired by our costly success, we attacked again. By late afternoon we had fought our way toward the crest of yet another ridge. Fifty yards ahead of us four Jap 77-millimeter shells exploded. Although the shells caused no casualties, they did set the dry grass and low trees afire; as we continued our advance, we were presently in the black belt of ashes and smoldering embers the blaze had left behind. Single file at five-yard intervals, the 3d Platoon trotted through this blackened area, our boondockers getting hotter at every step. Up ahead the 1st Platoon had been temporarily stopped, and the word came back for us to hold where we were.

It was not a pleasant resting place, but there we knelt for a few minutes beating out the small fires around us and searching for a bare spot that was beginning to cool.

"Moe," came a call from behind me, "pass the word that we're getting our balls burned off back here."

It was Cole, always impatient to get on with any attack. Now he was doubly so. I turned and opened my mouth to yell something like "Relax your ass!" But the words stuck in my throat—to his immediate left, a wicked-looking snake had risen about two feet off the ground and was poised to strike.

Okinawa, the experts say, is not as hostile to man as the jungle islands to the south. On board the transport bringing us to the island, the battalion doctor had reassured us that, except for the usual mosquitoes, flies, dengue fever, typhus, and filariasis, along with an occasional typhoon, there was not much to worry about. Of course, he did want to remind us that in the island's fresh water streams there were snails that spread liver flukes. These could infect a man with a disease called schistosomiasis, so it was unwise to swim or even bathe in Okinawa's creeks, canals, and rivers. The doctor also mentioned that if we met a snake on Okinawa it might be a Habu, one of the world's deadliest. But the Habu population was very small, he said, so we were not likely to get within a mile of one.

The snake that now poised beside my unsuspecting Sue-Doe friend was somewhat blackened by the fire that had swept through its domain, but it appeared to be still full of fight and fury. It may have been one of a harmless species, unrelated to the deadly Habu, but I raised my BAR and shot its head off, the bullet passing within inches of Cole and whining off into the distance. Cole stared at me open-mouthed and stunned, until he glanced down and saw the headless creature writhing across his shoes. With a howl he sprang away from it.

233

While he was leaping, I was already congratulating myself on my skill. "Settle down!" I yelled. "Nobody has ever been bitten by a headless snake!"

It took Cole a few moments to calm down. "When you aimed that BAR in my direction, Moe," he finally said, "I thought you had gone Asiatic and took me for a Jap."

And then, for the rest of that afternoon, whenever we stopped Cole hurried around telling everyone that his old friend Moe had tried to shoot him and had hit a snake instead.

The incident left us all badly frightened: there wasn't a man in the company who was not more afraid of a snake than a Jap. But this was the only snake that Cole and I encountered during our travels in the jungles and mountains of the Pacific.

By mid afternoon that day, we reached our objective. While our company waited for the companies on our left and right to move up, those of us who weren't on watch lay around in the warm afternoon sunshine. Cole and I had just dozed off when McLane called for the 3d Squad to go with him on a hunting expedition. About an hour earlier and three hundred yards back, we had passed a tunnel the Japs had dug into the face of a shallow cliff. Just in case several of them were hiding there, we had fired a few bursts into it from our BARs, and someone had tossed in a white phosphorous grenade. Then we moved on.

Now, after McNail had had a half hour to reflect, he had ordered McLane to take a few men back to the tunnel for a closer look. In five minutes we were there, careful not to approach from directly in front. At first we took quick looks into the darkness of it. No fire came our way. We became bolder until presently Cole and I were at the tunnel's mouth. We could see several yards into it. Still no sound, no bullets coming our way. Increasingly bolder, we crawled in toward the darkness. Still no sound.

The smoke from our phosphorous grenade had pretty much cleared away. Only a slight acrid smell hung in the air. "We need a little light," said Cole. "This place might be full of souvenirs." Here and there on the tunnel's dirt floor were scraps of Japanese newspapers. "We'll make a torch," he said.

I backed out of the tunnel, left my BAR with Bontadelli, and borrowed McLane's pistol. "Don't go in more than ten yards," he said. "In fact, you and Cole had better get your asses out of there."

It was not an order. He was just thinking out loud. Before he could make an order out of it, I ducked back in to join Cole, who by now had wadded several sheets of paper together and touched a match to it. We had crawled forward not more than ten yards when we heard a slight sound, a kind of low whine, and saw suddenly a pair of gleaming eyes. Cole backed up so fast that his shoes caught me in the helmet. The blow was not a jarring one because I was scrambling backward too.

There came another whine, low and eerie as it echoed off the tunnel's walls, and then a low bark. We stopped, waited a few minutes, and resumed our forward crawl, Cole extending his torch, the fire now burning toward his fingers. There, perched back against the tunnel's end, was a small dog. Stretched out in front of him was the body of a Jap soldier.

Our torch was nearly burned out. We backed out of the tunnel into the sunshine and told McLane what we had found. "A dog," he said, "a Japanese war dog I'll bet. They mostly train theirs to carry messages. We can't leave him there to starve. I'll crawl in and get him."

"You might need your pistol," I said. He took it and crawled into the cave. In a few minutes he and the dog emerged. The dog sat there shivering while McLane opened a can of beef hash and fed him. He took off the steel half of his helmet, poured water into it from his canteen, and put the helmet in front of the dog. The dog whined and lapped up the water quickly.

We stood in a small circle watching. It was a handsome dog, resembling a small collie but with short white fur. For four days it followed at McLane's heels, first into the attack of the next two days and then to a three-day bivouac where we waited for further orders. On the morning of the fifth day, while McLane sat there patting him, the dog howled, rolled over, and died. All of us except McLane had been expecting it. The white phosphorus had surely burned the war dog's lungs.

On the third day of our attack toward Mount Yaetake, we started early, moved down into a shallow valley, and then attacked all day up the steep southern slope of the mountain itself. At sundown we drove the last Jap defenders off the mountain's south side and dug in a few yards short of the crest.

Our company was very low on ammunition, and we had neither rations nor water. But no supply trucks or jeeps could make the rough climb to our mountain stronghold. Top-sergeant Brushmore hollered for volunteers to go back a mile or so to a point supply jeeps could reach. With Brushmore leading, Frank Anderson, Cole, and I and twenty other Marines went back down the way we had come that long day. Even on the down slope, that mountain was rough going. But when we started back up, each man hauling a case of .30-caliber ammunition or two five-gallon cans of water or a couple boxes of C-rations, we found the going a good deal more demanding. By the time we were halfway to the ridge line, darkness had fallen and we were exhausted. But we persisted and at last staggered to our destination.

In a few minutes we had parceled out ammunition, rations, and water to the company, and Anderson and I returned to the shallow foxhole we were to share that night. I took the first watch—an hour staring into the dark. Andy slept. Then I woke him and he took his hour on watch. It was a familiar pattern. Some time well into the night, Andy shook me awake. I reached for my BAR and took the watch. In fifteen seconds he was asleep. For perhaps a half hour, all was quiet. Then he began to snore.

I was concerned. The Japs were close. They had been close all day and stubborn in their resolve to kill us. The sounds of firing here and there along the line meant that scattered groups of them were trying to infiltrate. Inspired by Andy's symphony, some of them might decide to drift in our direction to discover the source. I poked Andy in the ribs. He sat up and fumbled for his carbine. "Is it time already?" he mumbled.

"No!" I whispered. "You still have about a half hour. You've been snoring."

"I'll stop," he muttered, and went immediately to sleep.

A minute went by, perhaps two. Suddenly Andy let out a snore that rivaled the bellow of a fog horn. I began to imagine things moving about in the darkness in front of the line. I shook Andy awake. He stirred and fumbled once again in the bottom of the foxhole for his carbine.

"What the hell now?" he whispered harshly.

"You got to stop snoring," I said. "You'll wake the dead."

"You, Moe, by Christ, have got to let me sleep!" He stretched out once more and in thirty seconds was breathing in the deep rhythm of sleep.

I sat for a few minutes peering out front. A star shell split the night, its flickering light revealing nothing but small trees and knee-high brush in the direction of the Japanese.

The star shell fizzled out and the black of a moonless night settled in again. I had begun to relax when Andy stirred slightly and blasted off another snore. Far superior to any he had produced before, it was loud enough to have startled every Marine and every Jap for one hundred yards up and down the line. I woke him with a sharp kick in the rump. He came awake slowly, shaking his head like an aggressive tackler who has just speared a goal post. This time he didn't pick up his carbine: he reached for his .45 pistol and rammed it into the soft spot under my chin.

"Damn you, Moe," he whispered. "You wake me up one more time and I'll blow your ass off."

It is difficult to talk with the barrel of a pistol stuck under your chin, but I managed. "OK, Andy," I gurgled. He eased the pistol away. "But if you start snoring again, I'm getting out of this hole and under that bush." There was a small shrub a yard or two to the left.

"Go! Get the hell out! For Christ's sake, let me sleep!" he said. I crawled out of the foxhole and slid under the bush. I was even more vulnerable there than I had been in the foxhole, but I felt a little more comfortable.

In thirty seconds Andy was snoring once more. A small pebble hit close to the foxhole. "For Christ's sake, Moe," came a hoarse stage whisper from the foxhole a few yards to the left of me. "Shut him to hell up!"

Right then there was a pop out front, and a grenade exploded only yards away. Dim figures rushed toward us. I cut loose with my BAR, twenty rounds fast. There were screams, men falling, more figures rushing. Then they were gone past, through the line, crashing down the steep slope behind us. From a hundred yards back there came the explosions of grenades, rifle shots, and bursts from submachine guns. One of our heavy machine guns opened up to our right. The firing spread all up and down the line. Star shells bloomed. Our mortars came to life, and a salvo of 105-millimeter shells exploded several hundred yards ahead. It was one magnificent demonstration of firepower, and the best thing about it was that, as far as I knew, no Marines got hurt. The Jap infiltrators lost half a dozen men as they came through our line. Another bunch who had been trying to get at our 60-millimeter mortars were blasted as they hit the defensive perimeter the mortar platoon had set up a hundred yards behind us.

As the firing died down I crawled over to Andy, thinking that he might have caught a grenade fragment or been scared out of his wits. He was sound asleep and snoring contentedly. It was almost daybreak. I looked again at the pistol still clutched in his right hand and decided not to disturb him. Next night I shared a foxhole with Cole, and the night after that with Mauvin. By that time we had disposed of the Japs on Motobu.

All during the fighting on Motobu, we had been receiving ominous news that the Army was running into increasing resistance to the south. By the time the Motobu fight ended, the 1st Marine Division had already moved south to relieve the Army's 27th.

We were not surprised to hear that the 27th Division had not been able to keep abreast of the other Army divisions in the line. On Makin Island and later at Saipan, the division had become whipping boys for Howling Mad Smith, a Marine general so impulsive and so unconcerned about casualties that we were inclined to sympathize with the men of the 27th. But when we heard that here on Okinawa they had made a hasty, disorderly retreat, leaving tanks and artillery for the Japs to capture and wounded men with whom the Japs could amuse themselves, we began to wonder.

A few days later as we headed south to go into reserve behind the 1st Marine Division, we met a column of the 27th on trucks going in the opposite direction. As they rolled by on their trucks heading north for rest and recreation and we walked south to thirty days of combat, they entertained us with calls of "The undertaker is waiting for you bastards!" or "Keep going south to an early grave!" We were ordered not to shoot them off their trucks, but we were tempted. After that experience, any sympathies we had held for them vanished once and for all.

The day after relieving the 27th Army Division, the 1st Marine Division attacked and took back the mile the 27th had lost. That night they stopped a Jap banzai led by several Sherman tanks the Japs had captured from the 27th. The next morning the 1st attacked again and pushed the Japanese back an additional half mile.

As we hiked steadily south we began to hear, about midday, all the booming fury of Marine attack and Japanese defense. Late that afternoon, moving slowly and very carefully through the area the 1st had seized the day before, we came up on the chaotic leavings of battle: at first the scattered Japanese dead and soon thereafter piles of them in and around the scores of Okinawan tombs the Japs had converted to deadly strongpoints. Our own wounded had been borne off to aid stations hours before, and most dead Marines had already been collected and hauled north toward Yontan, piled like logs on the trucks we had met from time to time during the past four hours.

239

The Japanese dead, lying where they had fallen, were beginning to decompose, especially those unfortunates destroyed by flamethrowers. Even in this place of death and destruction, even here, there were a few, grievously wounded and overlooked by 1st Division possum patrols, waiting in their patient, single-minded way with grenade or knife or bayonet or rifle, hoping for a last chance to kill one more Marine.

Jamal LeGrand earned his keep that afternoon. He had a quick eye that immediately perceived the smallest blink or tremor among the seeming dead; and on at least three occasions he saved a buddy from grief. Thankful, we were slow to reprove him for his habit of rushing into any shattered pillbox or tomb to hunt for souvenirs and to extract the gold. An hour or so after we entered this wasteland, he was beginning to smell like a Jap incinerated by napalm and five days dead. It was not long before we referred to him as Jamal the Ghoul, and Red Salleng, getting a bit disgusted, ordered Jamal to stay away from the tombs and to have some respect for the dead, even if they were dead Japs.

"None of us are angels of mercy," he said to me, "but it's time for Jamal to mine for gold some other way. Keep him close to you, Moe!"

"Hell, I'd rather keep an outhouse close to me," I protested. "We can smell him from thirty yards off."

"Keep the bastard away from those dead Japs then," Salleng shouted, "or I'll kick both your asses up to your ears."

I assigned the job to Cole, who never had been one to worry much about unsavory odors, and, for the rest of the afternoon, he kept such a close watch that Jamal, defeated, finally left off his ghoulish rummaging about and returned his pliers to his pack.

The following day we waited while the 1st Division went over to the attack once again. As their objectives took them farther and farther inland toward Shuri Castle, however, the 22d Marines, one of the regiments from our division, moved up and began attacking on the right. About a mile back of the front from a vantage point on a ridge overlooking the area under attack, we could see the tiny figures advancing in a thin line behind a platoon of flamethrowing tanks overrunning hill after hill, blasting and burning out pillbox after pillbox, tomb after tomb. They were beginning to move up the steep slopes of a hill fortress soon to be known as Sugar Loaf when the Jap artillery, which had earlier been concentrating their fire on the 1st Division, began to shift their attention to the 22d Marines. At the same time, the Jap forces counterattacked. We saw suddenly the small figures scrambling about in hand-to-hand fighting, with airbursts from the Japanese artillery exploding above them, the shrapnel killing Japs and Marines alike. Meantime, heavy shells from the Japanese 150-millimeter cannon began falling around the flamethrowing tanks. The tanks gave ground. The attack stopped.

"They don't have enough men up there to drive the Japs very far," said Red Salleng. He had come quickly up to join us at our lookout point.

"Where's the 29th?" I asked.

"Off to our left in reserve," Red said.

"Why the hell they got two regiments in reserve?" Cole was amazed.

Brushmore had wandered up, bending low to stay below the skyline. Now he chimed in. "General Sheepherd thinks one regiment is all we need on a one-mile front."

"General Sheepherd doesn't know his ass from a butcher block," said Cannon, who had come back to the squad the day before.

"The trouble is," said Salleng, "a regiment is not a regiment and a battalion is not a battalion up where the bullets are whistling by. If the 22d had all 7,500 of its men up there, they'd be going through those Japs like a tank through a tent camp."

There was a sudden commotion behind us and from close at hand a half dozen shots.

"What the hell?" said Red, and started back toward the 2d Squad. Several men were clustered now near one of the many tombs scattered around the area.

241

"Banzai!" came a scream from the tomb and a Jap, samurai sword in hand, rushed into the open. He was met by a hail of bullets and went down.

As Salleng hurried to join the 2d Squad there was another "Banzai!" from within the tomb, a single shot rang out, and Salleng swung half around, a look of surprise on his face and a splash of red on his right arm.

"Goddammit!" he said.

The Jap who had shot Red erupted into the open now, waving his rifle and screaming. He was immediately shot down. Now two guys from the 2d Squad ran to the tomb and tossed in a couple of grenades. There were no more shots, no more cries.

Salleng was not grievously wounded, but his arm was thoroughly torn and bleeding badly. He and our corpsman went off to find Dr. Wilson. We would not see Salleng again in this campaign. In an hour he had been replaced by Coon-ass Brown who, for some time, had been the assistant platoon leader.

The excitement of the moment over, we went back to our watch point. The 22d Marines had not yet resumed their attack. "They ain't goin' nowhere unless they get some more men up there," Brushmore said. "We're always shorthanded up front."

It was an old, frustrating story that all front-line fighters everywhere know by heart: generals and colonels have an exaggerated idea of the number of riflemen they have up front.

Here on the lower one-third of Okinawa, we had a division of Marines, roughly 18,500 men, attacking on a narrow, one-mile front. Even though some 7,000 Japs were defending that front, if we had attacked with all of our tanks and artillery and 18,500 men, we would have ripped through the Jap line like, as Red Salleng had said, a tank through a tent camp. Inexplicably, the division commander had decided to attack with one regiment—a third of his force—slightly more than 6,000 men. It was a significant number, but already 1,000 fewer than the defenders who, of course, were dug in and possessed great firepower.

242

Of the 6,000 men, 2,000 would not be a part of the attacking force. They were the regimental headquarters people, jeep and truck drivers, medical and first aid specialists, artillerymen, heavy weapons people, and so forth. Of course, 4,000 attackers in line and charging forward are capable of accomplishing much, except that the regimental commanders of the 22d or any other regiment always keep a battalion in reserve.

So now the attacking force has only 2,700 men. Unfortunately for the men up front, each battalion commander holds a company in reserve, leaving the attackers with perhaps 2,000 men. Good military dogma dictates that each company commander keep a platoon in reserve, which means that the actual attacking force is now less than 2,000. A third are mortarmen, machine gunners, flamethrower operators, demolition men, and other specialists who wait back of the attacking force until their specialties are required. Thus the attack forces are further depleted.

In any attack the bulk of the casualties are among the members of that thin first line—those men who go forward knowing that there is nothing out there in front but someone waiting to kill them. Ten miles back, in the comfort of some bombproof cave, the division commander is waiting to hear the good news. He has, he believes, sent a regiment of men to the attack.

But in fact, he has sent perhaps 1,600, and the news he ultimately hears is likely to be bad. After all, some heroic work is going to be required of the men in his thin front line in order to overrun a force of 7,000 veteran defenders firing from protected positions and with plenty of ammunition to spare.

Sugar Loaf Hill provided a classic example, and every Marine who fought up front in southern Okinawa knew why the hill proved so difficult to secure. Day after day, the news reports proclaimed, the 6th Marine Division attacked that grim fortress defended by 7,000 Japanese troops. Even so, 18,500 Marines should have taken it quickly. Eleven times the division attacked the hill; eleven times the division was thrown back. In fact, the attacking force never numbered more than 75 men, those at the very point of a great triangle. Behind them thousands and thousands of men and a bevy of generals and colonels watched and waited in reserve. Each day the report came back that the attacking force had fought their way up the hill, dug in on the crest, and were then driven off. The first two-thirds of each report was correct. The Marines did attack and did reach the crest of the hill, but they were not driven off. They were decimated: assisted out of this world by Japanese bayonets, rifles, machine guns, mortars, and cannon. They were in fact betrayed by the blissful self-deception of their commanders.

But our job was to attack as ordered. Those of us who survived would wonder about it for the next fifty years—and be thankful that we did not in the end have to invade Japan.

A few days after the initial unsuccessful attacks on Sugar Loaf and another hill called Half Moon a half mile inland from Sugar Loaf, the 29th Marines moved up and the remnants of the 22d went back into division reserve. Next day the 29th Marines attacked where the 22d had failed; again the assaults and counterassaults, the temporary successes and bitter failures, all the while black air bursts from the Japanese artillery exploding like thunder overhead. Four days the 29th tried; four days they failed. Then it was our turn to go in—into a shambles, a charnel house.

For some incredible reason, our leaders sent us up to relieve what was left of the 29th Marines in broad daylight. It was a costly maneuver. The Jap machine guns and cannon were blasting us while we were still a mile from the front line. Marine historians have said that the 4th Marines lost 39 men during that relief. It was probably 139. The 2d Platoon of one company lost 16 men to a single 14-inch shell. As we came up to the foxholes occupied by the 29th Marines, the Japanese were counterattacking. Their riflemen were everywhere, firing recklessly from spider traps, small pillboxes, and the few ruined trees that remained. We were in the midst of a fierce battle while we were still two hundred yards behind the 29th Marines' line.

Dusk was settling over the ruined land as we finally approached the main line and jumped into the foxholes and trenches the 29th had dug or captured from the Japs. The men of the 29th were desperate to get out and away—they hardly took time to brief us before they crawled back and then dashed off to the north. Before they were out of sight, the 3d Platoon, which had wound up on the far left of the line, had three dead and two wounded in a firefight with the Japs on Half Moon Hill, a hundred yards away.

For twenty minutes there was bedlam, the Japs on Half Moon firing our way with everything they had; the Marines firing .30-caliber machine guns, rifles, and BARs back at the Japs full blast. John Reardon brought the 60-millimeter mortars right up behind us, set them up in a few seconds, and began shelling all along the top of Half Moon Hill. In no time at all Jap knee mortars were answering. It was a battle with neither Japs nor Marines sending men forward, yet there were heavy casualties on both sides. We could hear the firefight going on all along the line to Sugar Loaf and on to the shores of the sea.

Perhaps thirty minutes before dark the firing suddenly stopped, and we at last had time to look over the edge of the hole and down the slope in front of us. There were bodies everywhere out front, both Japs and Marines, all in various stages of decomposition, perhaps two hundred within our immediate belt of sight.

On our left where the ridge facing Half Moon Hill petered out onto a flat no-man's-land, the fighting had been vicious for our 1st and 2d squads. The 3d Squad was luckier: we were not in the direct line of Japanese fire. The foxhole that Cannon, Mauvin, and I had jumped into was extra deep and large, probably a mortar pit the 29th had driven the Japs out of and then used themselves.

From our foxhole, a tunnel with enough crawl space for a man and his rifle led down toward the forward slope. I crawled a few yards through the tunnel until I could see daylight twenty yards ahead. If I could crawl down, a Jap infiltrator could crawl up during the night, a possibility the Marines who had lived there for two days had apparently not considered. I backed out, borrowed Mauvin's entrenching spade, crawled forward about ten yards, and blocked the tunnel with fresh dirt.

For the time being, our only serious threat was coming from a sniper firing occasionally from somewhere close by, his bullets kicking up the loose dirt piled up front. It was not exactly a steady fire—just every four or five minutes the sharp crack of his rifle and the dirt from our parapet splashing over us.

We could judge from the sound that he was not more than fifty yards away, and we wondered how he could have worked his way so close to the defensive line of the 29th Marines. Because he was so near and so intent on our foxhole, we were finding it difficult to survey the torn slope that fell away to the narrow strip of valley one hundred yards below us. We wanted to know especially the route an infiltrating Jap might take if he crawled toward us during the night. We solved that problem by filling a couple of sandbags the 29th Marines had left in the hole and throwing them up on the parapet. We left a small space between the bags, angled so that the sniper, who seemed to be off to the right, could not hit us as we peered through to study the land out front. The sniper reacted immediately. His next shot skimmed just across the top of the right side bag. We looked at it closely. The shot had angled in from our right front. We repositioned the bags so that we could look warily over that way. There were dead men scattered all along the forward slope, but we saw no movement, no telltale wisps of smoke or dust.

Twenty-five yards to our right and perhaps thirty yards down the slope was a Japanese 20-millimeter cannon that appeared to have caught a blast from one of our flamethrowers. There it squatted, its long barrel pointed toward our line, its gun crew still in the positions they had assumed when the fierce flames had reached them—the gunner still kneeling behind his gun, his blackened fingers on the trigger; the loader on his knees leaning against the cannon's right side; an ammunition bearer tilted into the gun from the side opposite; and at the end of the barrel a fourth man, his seared hand grasping as if he had reached down to pull the weapon forward when the full force of the burning napalm had fixed him in the act.

246

"We need to get that damned gun out of there," said Cannon. I knew what he was thinking. If during the night the Japs sent another gun crew crawling forward, they could make things very hot for us.

A few minutes later when Coon-ass Brown crawled into our hole, I pointed to the cannon. He studied it through the crack between our sandbags.

"It's probably burned out," he said.

"Maybe," said Cannon, "maybe not."

"What do you think, Moe?" Brown said.

I shrugged. "Maybe, maybe not."

Brown hesitated a couple of counts. "OK," he said, "I'll be back right after dark. We'll go out and get it. I'll pass the word so our own people don't open up on us."

"We'll have to watch for that sniper. He's somewhere out there," Cannon said. The sniper had stopped firing and a peculiar quiet was settling across the torn land.

"Probably cooking up a five-course dinner," Mauvin said. He had been very quiet ever since we'd moved into our hole. "You think maybe that sniper is one of the guys on the gun?"

Cannon laughed, and I joined in.

"They're a little too dead to do much sniping," I said. But the shots were coming from somewhere near the gun. It was a thing to remember. When Coon-ass Brown, bent low and trotting quickly, came back to us, however, I had shoved Mauvin's comment to the back of my mind.

Now that darkness had fallen, we didn't have to be so careful about sticking our heads up. We crouched there peering off toward the gun, a blur below us.

"OK," said Brown, "when I head out, follow as hard as you can. I'll grab hold back by the trigger. Moe, you get hold of the barrel up by the front sight. Mauvin, take hold in the middle. Then we'll run it back to our side of the ridge. Cannon, you're our bodyguard."

Carrying our weapons, we were on top of the gun and its gunner in a few seconds. Up close, we could see that the dead Japs were practically welded in place, skin to steel. We kicked them away, our

247

nostrils assailed by the vile stench of decomposing flesh. As I reached for the barrel I saw, out of the corner of my eye and a few yards off, a Jap rifleman rising from a shallow hole and swinging his weapon toward me. It was our sniper, hidden near the gun just as Mauvin had suggested, but so cleverly concealed by brush and dirt that we had not been able to see him. There was a burst from Cannon's tommy gun, and the sniper fell back into his shallow hole.

"Go!" hollered Brown. I tightened my grip on the gun barrel, and we rushed back toward our line and to our side of the ridge.

Into the darkness, a star shell intruded, and in its drifting light we looked over the gun. It was a 20 millimeter all right, only slightly damaged by the napalm that had killed its crew.

Cannon was grinning. "Say thanks, Moe," he said, "as soon as you can find your tongue."

I was trembling from my toes to my ears. "You'd swallow your damned tongue too," I said. "The barrel of that rifle looked like a 16-inch gun."

Mauvin seemed put out with Cannon. "You were the trigger man," he said. "You should have shot the son of a bitch sooner."

Cannon didn't answer. He went on grinning. All he had done was save my life.

We attacked Half Moon Hill next morning with 21 men. We needed about 521. Until some time the night before, the Japs had probably had 200 men armed with rifles, mortars, and machine guns defending the hill. During the night, as we learned later, they had very quietly begun a general retreat all along the line from Shuri Castle west to the sea. Next morning Sugar Loaf Hill finally fell to K Company, although a couple of other companies helped out. The murderous firefight of the afternoon before was probably the rear guard shooting off their ammunition to cover the retreat. With Coon-ass Brown leading, our 21-man army hustled toward Half Moon. A lone machine gunner was shooting at us, and some Jap riflemen were firing our way too; somebody got in a lucky burst from a BAR to eliminate the machine gun. The riflemen we dealt with more deliberately. Maybe 50 of them were still on the hill, enough to stop us for an hour about two-thirds of the way to the crest. While we lay there, E Company attacked from the east side of the hill and pushed the defenders toward us.

Fifty yards ahead of us a squad of Jap soldiers appeared. Because they were looking back toward the E Company attackers, they did not see us crouching there. We hesitated briefly while we made sure they were Japs and then, in a few well-aimed bursts of fire, ended their service to the emperor. Five minutes later as we toiled up the hill to meet E Company, we lost Coon-ass Brown to a Jap in a spider trap. It was a hard loss.

Nine bloody days passed before we secured Okinawa's capital city of Naha. Even though the Japanese were pulling back what was left of their main army, there were a couple of thousand determined defenders between us and our objective. To complicate matters, rain fell in torrents night and day. Even the tanks couldn't get up to help us, but the attack moved on. We got into the northern outskirts of Naha on the sixth day of fighting and attacked again the next day.

Much of that seventh day the 3d Platoon had been in company reserve, the 3d Squad in platoon reserve. We were not pleased to be in reserve. In any battle when things get complicated up front, there is always an agonized plea to send up the reserves. So when we heard from several hundred yards ahead the sudden clatter of a Jap machine gun, the 3d Squad sprang to their feet without even being told. Cole, his BAR at the ready, was already inching ahead like a horse at the starting gate when the call came pounding back, "Third Squad! Up front!"

Single file we hustled forward past the other squads in the platoon, past Lieutenant Harris who, a few days before, had replaced McLane, and a hundred yards beyond to Captain McNail. He pointed to a hillock about fifty yards ahead. At its base a half dozen Marines were taking occasional quick potshots at some target out front.

"Machine gun platoon ran into a pillbox up there. Sounds like a water-cooled machine gun. They need a rifle squad to get the damned Japs out."

There was no point in asking McNail why the machine gun platoon couldn't handle its own problem. Whenever the mortar or machine gun platoons blundered into a trap or an ambush, they yelled for help from the rifle platoons. When they had finished yelling and we had gone to help them, they stood respectfully aside and let us do their dirty work. The rifle platoons were expendable. This was the way the Marine Corps worked.

Taking care to keep the hillock between the Jap machine gun and our six-man squad, we trotted forward. It was Bill Vahey's platoon. They had, he told me, been sent forward to plant a couple of guns on a hill some 150 yards ahead and had drawn fire twenty steps after they left cover. "We already lost Hall and Belinski," he said, gesturing toward two still figures lying in the open.

"Dead?"

"You know it," said Vahey. "That Jap put about ten extra slugs into each of them right after he knocked them down." I had known the two old professionals since Tent Camp 3.

The only positive aspect of this situation was that we could tell at a glance something we rarely knew at the beginning of any attack—the exact location of the enemy machine gun. Out front, a shallow triangular valley narrowed to a point in a bank about forty feet high. Right into the base of that rocky bank, years before, respectful Okinawans had built a tomb to accommodate the bones of their honored dead. The tomb was a large one, perhaps twenty feet high and fifteen feet across. The Japanese Army, in their practical way of dealing with the sensitivities of others than their own, had merely shoveled out the ancestral bones, reinforced the tomb with concrete, and created a small fort. Through a narrow aperture in the concrete wall they were firing a .30-caliber machine gun that, if we could judge by the extended duration of its bursts, had to be water cooled.

Cole and I studied the problem for a few minutes. There was no way we could work our way along the ridge on either side of the triangular field. If we tried edging along the outer slopes, we would be exposed to fire from Jap defenders there. A frontal assault could not succeed. My six-man squad would be shot down.

We looked at each other in dismay, looked once again at the deadly field in front of us—and perceived a possibility. Some twenty yards ahead, all across the base of the triangle, was a depression. Beyond the depression in the direction of the Japanese, the triangular field had once been a rice paddy, the highest in a series of several that dropped off toward us. The spot we occupied was about a foot and a half lower than the field directly in front of the tomb.

"Get a bazooka man up here!" I shouted to Vahey. The bazooka was a fairly new weapon that we had first used on Guam to knock out enemy tanks. On Okinawa, it had proved useful against the countless small forts and pillboxes the Japs had created from Okinawan tombs. While the word for a bazooka man went back down the line, Cole and I huddled and planned.

If the two of us with our BARs could crawl out to that parapet across our end of the rice paddy, one at the far left end, the other the far right, we might be able to keep the Jap gunners so preoccupied with sporadic fire from our BARs that a bazooka man stationed at the middle of the triangle's base could rise above the parapet long enough to get off a rocket.

Five minutes after the call went back, the platoon's bazooka expert came puffing up. Our explanations required only a few seconds: Cotton Kessinger was one of the old Raiders and didn't need a blueprint or even lines drawn in the mud. He understood what had to be done and was immediately ready.

"Burn 'em good with those BARs," he said as the three of us began our crawl forward. "I only got two rockets. I'll need a little extra time to be sure of a hit." With Cole and me each taking a half dozen extra twenty-round magazines for our BARs, we crawled forward. The Jap machine gunner, although he had a very small chance of hitting us, got off an occasional nervous burst in our direction. My one real worry was about the shortage of rockets, the bazookas we used in those days being notoriously inaccurate. As I crawled, I brooded about timing and fate. If the bazooka failed, Captain McNail would order a frontal attack during which our squad would be wiped out. After that, with the evidence of 100 percent casualties, McNail could probably persuade the strategists that any further attack should be postponed until morning, when a tank could be sent up to help out. Meantime we would be lying cold meat in the mud.

As Cole and Kessinger and I reached our positions, I waved at Cole. He raised up just enough to level his BAR toward the Jap pillbox and fire a quick burst aimed at its narrow aperture. As the Jap gunner, firing one long, steady blast, swung his machine gun toward him, Cole dropped behind the parapet. When he did, I straightened up and fired a long burst. Since I had had more time to aim than Cole, my bullets hammered against the pillbox, chipping the concrete and coming very close to the Jap's fire slot. Frantically, he swung the gun toward my end of the line, his bullets kicking up mud and debris all along the way.

Now Cole jumped up, fired, and dropped under cover again. As the Jap, pivoting his gun back toward Cole, worked quickly past the middle of the parapet, Kessinger, rising to his feet and standing for a moment motionless in full view of the world, fired the bazooka and dropped back down. Halfway to the target the rocket veered suddenly, hit the ground, glanced, and exploded ten yards short.

Now the Jap gunner clearly understood the fate we had planned for him. He fired a long burst directly over Kessinger, who was on his back reloading his clumsy weapon. It was going to take time. There was the rocket to be inserted, wires to be attached, and gadgets to be checked and double-checked, all while he lay on his back in the mud, a stream of bullets whipping by inches above him.

While Kessinger struggled, Cole and I resumed our game. We had to persuade that gunner to swing his weapon our way, but now that the gunner and his loaders knew where their worst danger lay, we were obliged to fire ten- or twenty-round blasts before they would even fire a quick burst toward either of our vantage points.

Suddenly our attention was attracted elsewhere. On the ridge line to our left appeared two Japanese riflemen, probably sent forward by a desperate officer in the hope that they could get off a few shots at our bazooka man. Rifles at the ready, long, curved bayonets fixed, they moved slowly in a half crouch like weary hikers battling a gale. Their attitude and actions were so different from those encountered before among the fierce defenders of Okinawa that we could scarcely believe what we saw.

In the early battles in the Solomons and the Marianas, Japanese soldiers from time to time did strangely unmilitary things. On watch they were careless; in attacks they charged blindly and without purpose. Not so on Okinawa. These Japs were determined, disciplined, and very brave. And they did nothing haphazard in plan or purpose. But these two soldiers, although they were going forward to do their duty, looked as if they had lost all hope and knew it was their day to die; and they seemed to have no intention of creating difficulties for their executioners. Cole and I hesitated and marveled for a second. Our angle of aim was good. We shot them down.

Now Kessinger was ready once more. He wriggled around from back to belly, having considerable trouble keeping his bazooka below the parapet yet out of the mud. Somehow he managed. Flat on his belly and ready to leap, he looked at me and nodded.

At once, Cole leveled his BAR and fired off a long burst, the Jap machine gunner once more swinging the gun toward him and arriving a half second late. I leaped to my feet and fired, and the gunner, frustrated and desperate, swung frantically back across the arc. For a few seconds he neglected Kessinger, who, during that brief lapse, rose and took deliberate aim. The gunner, recovering, was halfway back across the arc to center when I saw the rocket shoot out from the bazooka's muzzle, this time traveling straight and true. There was a loud and satisfactory explosion right on the face of the tomb.

As the noise of the blast echoed off across the shattered heart of Naha, we heard cheering from Vahey's machine gun platoon, from the other men in our squad, and throughout the platoons behind us.

Cole and I were already rushing forward. If there were survivors, we needed to finish them off while they were still dazed. A step behind us came Cotton Kessinger, shouting crazily. He had left his bazooka behind, but he was waving a pistol and firing wildly in the direction of the tomb. We were within ten yards of our objective when, on the slope above the tomb, the lid of a spider trap was shoved upward and a bewildered Jap rifleman emerged. He had apparently been stunned by the explosion. As he staggered about trying to discover where he belonged, Cole and I fired from the hip and cut him in two. We would argue at some length that night about whose bullets had actually hit him. Whatever the case, it was good shooting and not the type you learn on the rifle range.

There was not much more to be done. Kessinger's rocket had smashed tomb, machine gun, and the four soldiers crammed into the small space the tomb had afforded them.

"Remember Carrigan?" Cole said as he looked them over. They sprawled there, clearly dead. He put a bullet into each one of them anyway.

We heard shouted commands behind us: Vahey's machine gunners hurrying forward to set up their weapons on the ridge point above the tomb; behind them two of our rifle platoons running to seize the ridge line on each side of the triangle.

We crawled around in the tomb grabbing souvenirs before any other Marines arrived. It was a good haul: two Nambu pistols, both slightly damaged; a half dozen flags; and a Japanese naval officer's saber, its metal sheath pitted with shrapnel. I glanced at Cole and knew what was going on in his head. He was already calculating how much whiskey he could get for the flags and pistols and how much money that beat-up old saber would bring.

Our small squad dug in for the night a few yards from Bill Vahey's machine gunners. They had dug in, piled sandbags up front, and posted their three air-cooled Browning .30s on the point above the ruined Japanese pillbox. Three or four guys from the machine gun platoon were poking around in the pillbox, hoping to locate a few souvenirs we might have overlooked.

With his K-bar, Cole opened our last small can of beef hash. As we sat there sharing it slowly, Top-sergeant Brushmore, loaded down with bandoliers of ammunition, came by. "How much do you need?" he said.

"Between us about 320 rounds," said Cole, who had run an inventory, "and about 200 rounds for the rest of the squad."

Brushmore unslung several bandoliers and tossed them into the fresh dirt we had piled in front of our hole. "I hear you gents had a busy day."

"We did, especially the last couple of hours," I said. Cole and I were stuffing .30-caliber bullets into our twenty-round magazines.

"Well, I hope you don't have a busy night," said Brushmore. He rearranged his load of ammunition and started to move away.

"Hey, Top!" Cole called. "When you come back this way, bring us about fifty cans of beef hash. We shared our last can six ways. Bring up about twenty gallons of water too. We don't have more than a half a canteen a man."

Brushmore stopped. "What you got is what you get," he said. "There's a flood behind us. Washed away the pontoon bridge over the Asato River this morning." He paused and grinned. "Tell you what. Tighten your belts for a few days. Two or three days without chow will make you guys appreciate Spam and shark and Move-the-Line Sledd's fine leather pancakes. If you want a drink, look up at the sky and open your mouth next time we get a few inches of rain."

As Brushmore haw-hawed off down the company line, Vahey and our old friend Donner and a couple of ammo bearers from the machine gun squad, being careful to stay well below the skyline, headed our way. "Just came by to tell you guys you saved a lot of asses out there today," said Vahey.

"Not to mention a lot of horse's asses," said Cole. It was such an obvious joke that only Donner laughed and then kicked a little more mud onto Cole's shoes.

"It's hard to be decent to a bastard like you, Cole," Donner said. "I'll tell Moe that you guys ought to get a medal."

"Kessinger ought to get the medal," I said. "It takes guts to stand out there and deadeye that bazooka the way he did."

"Here comes McNail," said one of Vahey's gunners. "He's probably bringing your tin stars right now."

Captain McNail, still fifty yards away, was toiling toward us through the mud.

"Here comes the guy who's gonna get the medal," Cole announced at the top of his lungs.

"I'm going to recommend," said McNail, looking directly at Cole, "that regiment send us a portable brig, so we can lock your smart ass up every night."

While McNail was talking, Bill Werden had come quietly up. "While you're at it," he said, "order one that's soundproof so we don't have to hear him bitching and moaning all night long."

Cole and I leaped around McNail and whacked Werden a couple of times on the back. We hadn't seen him for three weeks, and we were happy that he was still alive. "What's the word on the little guy you dragged in up north, Bill?" I said.

"I never heard another word," Werden said. "Now that he's learned about the taste of hard candy, he's probably breaking his teeth on a ton of it every day." He turned to McNail. "Captain, Colonel Maxim says to dig in deep. A Hellcat pilot spotted the Japs moving some heavy stuff around a mile or so out front."

"Why don't the Navy shell the bastards?" Vahey asked. "They could have them wiped out by now."

"Navy has a bad case of kamikaze shock," said McNail. "Right up to Nimitz, everyone in the Navy is scared shitless of those crazy suicide bastards. The whole fleet is sitting out there hoarding their ammunition." He swung around intending to say something more to Bill Werden, but Werden was already one hundred yards away heading down the line on the run.

"That guy never rests," said McNail. "What the hell do you suppose they feed him?" He turned back. "OK, you heard him. Grab those shovels and pitch that clay. We'll be lucky if they don't throw the outhouse at us tonight. I'll spread the word."

The ground on the ridge was soft. We dug a hole four feet deep. An hour later, an unusual order came along the line. In ten minutes we were to pull back a hundred and fifty yards and dig in again. It was a tricky maneuver in the dark, and one that did nothing to increase the company's happiness count. Why were they pulling us back? It made no sense at all. If during the night the Japs crawled in from the opposite side of the ridge and occupied those deep foxholes we had so laboriously dug, we would have to fight half of tomorrow and lose some good men kicking them off the ridge again.

But we were Marines. We obeyed—a hundred and fifty yards back and dig in again. As we settled down into our new, much shallower holes, Cole was unusually subdued. In all his days of battle, from Vangunu far to the south to this foxhole only seven hundred miles from the Japanese homeland, he had never been hit by as much as a pebble; but that morning a grenade fragment had lodged in a book on Hebrew history he carried in his pack, and near midday a Jap machine gunner had put two bullets through the tail of his dungaree jacket. "I'll take first watch," he said in an uncharacteristic whisper. "I ain't been sleeping so good lately anyway."

"Maybe you should try counting sheep," I said. "Borrow a couple of thousand from that flock your Sue-Doe Jew relatives used to herd across the land of milk and honey."

Cole accepted my weak joke without so much as a snicker. "If we ever expect to get out of this hellhole, I think I better send up some hallelujahs to the Sue-Doe heaven," he said softly.

Five minutes later, if we had been able to hold still long enough, we would both have been sending hallelujahs, hosannas, and prayers of thanksgiving heavenward on behalf of our brilliant leader, Captain Robert McNail. The Japs began to pound that ridge line we had so very recently vacated with 320-millimeter mortar shells.

Even 150 yards away from those tremendous blasts, we were bounced a foot off the ground by the concussion each time one exploded. Up there where our foxholes had been, the earth leaped in volcanoes of fire and debris. The barrage went on and on right along the ridge line; and we shook, bounced, and sweat with fear that the Japanese soldiers manning those mortars might lift their fire and begin dropping their monster shells right in among us.

In ten—perhaps as many as fifteen—long, long minutes, the barrage abruptly ended. For another ten minutes we went on shaking, stretched out at the bottom of our hole. Our eardrums had been so battered that for a short while we could hear nothing. Then, as the ability to sort out sound gradually returned, we heard a few calls for corpsmen from men who had been damaged by falling debris. But word soon came that, although twenty men had received some cuts and bruises, only one man had been seriously hurt by a chunk of rock or coral.

"I've had about as much of this crap as I need," said Cole, as the smoke drifted off and the acrid odor of high explosives gradually diminished. "I think I'm going to develop a bad case of big-mortar shell shock and go screaming back to the holy place where the colonels and generals hide out." The idea made him more cheerful, and when I volunteered to take the watch for the first hour, he went instantly to sleep.

Midafternoon of the next day as we charged even farther into the city of Naha, a 90-millimeter mortar shell exploded near him, and he took a charge of shrapnel in the calf of his right leg. It was a beautiful wound for a man of Cole's expectations. He came limping back past me, a rough bandage on his leg, a pleased smile on his face.

"Hey, you little bastard!" I shouted. "Get the hell back here! You aren't hurt! I can patch you up in five minutes!" He stopped briefly and pulled back the bandage. It was more than a flesh wound. It was a deep tear and bleeding badly. I would have to let him go.

"I got the one I wanted, Moe," he said. "I'm turning the war over to you and getting the hell out of here." He looked down at his leg, the wound now rapidly turning the bandage crimson. "This one ought to take me out of circulation for a few months. Maybe clear back to Frisco." He stuck out his hand. I grasped it, and we stood there eyeing each other a long moment. I envied him. It was like Cole to arrange for such a pleasant wound. No damage to the parts that really mattered and probably no lasting damage to his leg.

"Leave me the BAR," I said. "You won't need it back there where you're going. I'll pass it on to Mauvin or Pappy Schultz." Pappy Schultz, one of the new men in the squad, had been assigned to us a few days before we left for Okinawa.

Cole unslung the heavy BAR and handed it across. "I'll see you in Dago, Moe," he said.

"Maybe; maybe you will," I said. "We aren't through here yet, and we still got 60 million of the bastards waiting for us in Japan." I watched him as he limped away, dragging his wounded leg pitifully as he passed Captain McNail a hundred yards to the rear.

The next day the battalion, now way under strength, made a frontal attack on a ridge line that cut through the very heart of Naha. In a half hour we had beaten the Japs off the ridge line and dug in along the rim. But we quickly realized that although the Earth's surface was ours, the underground still belonged to the Japanese. They had dug tunnels from the reverse slope to just about every Okinawan tomb on the north side. Almost before we knew it they were firing at us from all around the hill. One by one we blasted the tombs and caves with grenades and blocks of nitro-starch or burned them with flamethrowers. Mel Blum had been summoned, and he was in his glory, laughing happily as he blew tomb after tomb and cave after cave.

Blum had turned away from the tenth hole he had blasted when from a Jap trench two hundred yards ahead came a single knee mortar shell. The shell arrived without even a warning flutter and exploded practically at Blum's feet. From thirty yards away, I saw him go down.

"There goes Blum," I said to Pappy Schultz, who was moving along behind me. Covered with mud and blood, Blum tried to pull himself to his feet. We hurried to him. "Where are you hit?" I said.

"All over hell," said Blum, "but mostly in my back, I think." He fell and was out of it for a few minutes. During that time Pappy and I cut open his dungaree jacket. The wound in his back looked bad, but not fatal. As I slapped a bandage on it, a corpsman came up with a stretcher and four stretcher bearers. They had just lifted it when Blum opened his eyes and winked at me.

"Hey, stop the car," he said. "I got one more thing to tell Moe." The stretcher bearers hesitated. "I been saving a good question for Cole." Another shell from the Jap knee mortar landed about thirty yards to our left. The stretcher bearers were getting nervous, wanting above all else to get the hell out of there. "Next time you see him, ask him if he ever heard of a furtive patah." He was chuckling as they hauled him away.

That day we drove the Japs two-thirds of the way out of Naha, but the 3d Platoon lost five men, including Pappy Schultz, who had been with us only a couple of weeks and had left a wife and little girl behind when he volunteered for the Marine Corps. A Jap rifleman got him through the heart. Minutes later, Mauvin and I located the Jap and evened the score, but the satisfaction we felt didn't bring Pappy back.

F Company dug in that night along one more of the low ridges that cut across the shattered city inland from the sea. Because of our heavy casualties over the past eight days, our defense line was thin, the foxholes fifteen to twenty yards apart.

Mauvin and I shared a foxhole. It was a shallow one the Jap defenders had left behind. Although we were nearing exhaustion, we spent a half hour digging to a depth of perhaps four feet, piling the loose dirt into a parapet up front. Contented finally that we had done what prudence dictated, we shared a can of meat and beans, laid our several grenades at the front of the hole, stuck our knives in the bank where we could grasp them quickly, and prepared to settle down. I would take the first watch. Mauvin stretched out in the bottom of the hole and was instantly asleep.

As twilight gradually changed to darkness, I studied the terrain out front. Our location was not ideal. Because of the winding way the ridge ran, our foxhole was at the point of a shallow triangle that jutted a few yards farther than the others in the direction of the Japanese. To make our situation even less attractive, we were quite close to a cluster of Okinawan tombs. Perhaps thirty paces to our direct front was the angled roof of an extra-large tomb. A sniper anywhere out there could create for us a very unpleasant night.

An hour went by. I woke Mauvin and slept. In what seemed like only a few seconds, he startled me out of my sleep. "Time," he whispered. "It's been quiet. No mortars, no nothing." He stretched out and slept.

I crouched at the front of the hole, peering into the darkness, listening for the faintest noise. Nothing. A star shell popped above, hung, drifted, went out. Nothing. Minutes passed. Another star shell. I studied the slant-roofed tomb out front. No movement there. As I sighed softly in relief, there was the sudden sharp crack of a rifle, and a bullet hit the parapet in front of me. Instinctively I ducked and stayed low. The star shell went out.

At the crack of the rifle, Mauvin had awakened and leaped to my side. We waited. During the next two hours the sniper fired seven times, each bullet striking the parapet in front of us or whistling by close overhead. There was nothing we could do except stay low and hope he could not get the proper angle. Finally, for a long, tense half hour, he did not fire, and we began to hope he had given up the game.

"You might as well stretch out," I whispered to Mauvin. He did not object, and was soon asleep. Perhaps a half hour went by, a half hour of watching and listening and hoping. I was beginning to believe that our friend had actually given up when unexpectedly a star shell popped directly overhead. In its sudden bright glare, I sensed the smallest possible movement right at the top of that

261

closest tomb. I blinked and looked more closely and in the eerie, twisting light saw a small object, oddly shaped but oddly familiar. It was the four grasping fingers of a human hand. I realized in an instant that the possessor of that hand was our sniper pulling himself to a vantage point at the top of that tomb.

The star shell was slowly falling toward earth, gradually casting longer shadows, gradually lessening in its intensity. In thirty seconds it would be gone, and in the immediate darkness afterward, our sniper would pull himself upward into an ideal position to finish us off. I hesitated, hoping that he would make the mistake of pulling himself upward while the light still shone so that I could pour into him a few bullets from my BAR. He was far too wise. The hand remained where it was. The star shell was low and sputtering. Maybe fifteen seconds of light remained. I was hypnotized by the fading light, the still hand, the drifting shadows.

Then suddenly I knew what had to be done, what I should have done thirty seconds before. I raised my BAR, took careful aim, and fired. I saw concrete and fingers flying, heard a distinct scream of surprise and pain, heard a solid object, probably the sniper's rifle, clattering as it slid down the opposite side of the tomb. Then came another scream of pain, desperation, rage. I was pretty certain that our sniper friend would bother us no more.

Awakened by the racket of my BAR, Mauvin grabbed his M-1 and leaped up. "What in Christ!" he said.

"Our sniper," I said. "I sent him away." Mauvin crouched beside me a moment, sleepy and uncertain. Then he stretched out again and was soon fast asleep.

The pounding of my BAR had not only roused Mauvin but had startled watchers and sleepers all along our line. A half dozen star shells turned night into day. In the bright glare, I saw on the gray slant of the tomb a crimson stain, and I experienced a strange feeling of regret. In all the months and months of invasions and firefights, in all the shooting and the killing, I had had few moments of regret or remorse. I had never lost a minute's sleep over the slaughter at Vangunu, the Japs we had shot down in one banzai after another, the men killed at close range on Guam and Motobu and Half Moon Hill and Naha, the executioner's role I'd played in the possum patrols, and all the rest. It was war—kill or be killed. It was the way things were.

Here too, in dealing with our sniper, it was shoot or be killed. He had stalked us with a deadly purpose—to shoot two Marines, in the head if possible. If I had caught him in the open and eliminated him with a shot to his guts or chest or head, it would have been business as usual, an almost routine part of a job I did not enjoy but was certainly willing to devote myself to. But this strange incident culminating in the need to shoot off the back of a brave man's hand—it was somehow grotesque, somehow not quite right, not quite fair.

Perhaps, I thought, I was getting tired. I poked Mauvin awake. "Take the watch," I said. "I'm having trouble staying with it." He let me sleep until break of day.

Late that afternoon, the 29th Marines came up to relieve us. Things had quieted down so much around Naha that they were brought up in a long column of perhaps 200 trucks, each truck bearing eighteen men. After they moved into our shallow foxholes, we hurried to the rear and piled into the waiting trucks. What was left of F Company clambered onto the first three trucks. The whole 4th Regiment required about 50. If from some high, distant point to the south, the Japs were watching that column going north, the first 50 trucks with about fifteen men aboard each one, the next 150 trundling along empty except for the driver, they must have exulted—until they remembered that they had lost five to our one, and all of their fallen were dead.

What we needed first was sleep. For nine days of attack, no one in the outfit had had more than two or three hours' sleep on any night. Now, with only one man in each platoon on guard, we could begin catching up.

On that first night in reserve, however, I had a hard time dropping off. I thought of the guys from the old squad—most of them long gone. And now Cole. Right now Cole was probably on a hospital ship headed for Guam or Honolulu, relaxing on a soft bunk below deck telling his tales of heroic conduct to a galaxy of pretty, sympathetic nurses. More likely, though, he had already limped onto the bridge and at that very moment was busily peddling two pistols and a worthless saber to the captain of the ship. I laughed out loud at the thought, and my laugh woke Art Corella, who was sleeping close by. "I was thinking about that damned Cole," I explained.

"There must be about a thousand better things to think about than that damned troublemaker," said Corella, and almost instantly started snoring again.

Art Corella had been grumpy ever since he had returned to duty from the hospital early that day. I couldn't blame him. He had been wounded only five days earlier, and here he was right back at the same old stand. The letdown was even more acute because back at division hospital he had been considered, for four days, a walking medical marvel. Indeed, his wound had been classified as exceptional because it had not killed him.

Every doctor in the division and numerous associated medical types had agreed that Corella had had a perfect right to die seconds or, at most, moments after the bullet from a .31-caliber Jap rifle had hit him on the right side of his neck. The bullet had entered three inches below his right ear, missed the jawbone, and gone straight through to exit a couple of inches below the left ear. The bullet had not come into contact with anything vital, although that part of the anatomy is so crammed with vital parts that a human being's chances of surviving such an invasion are probably much less than one in a thousand.

Small wonder that after fixing a tiny bandage onto each side of Corella's neck, the doctor in the aid station where he first reported had put him off to one side to die. But Corella, especially since he felt as chipper as ever, was understandably reluctant. He wandered about the aid station being enjoined, from time to time, to find a convenient spot where he could stretch out: comfortable for Corella and convenient for those who figured that in a short while they were going to have to throw his body into the back of a truck.

A couple of hours later with Corella still wandering about asking where he might get a few swigs of water and perhaps a bite of chow, the doctors on duty realized that they might have a medical wonder on hand, and very soon Corella was a celebrity of lofty standing. Shortly afterward, he was taken back to the division hospital. Medical people from all over Okinawa made the pilgrimage to the hospital to view this remarkable case. At first considerably embarrassed and annoyed, Corella eventually came to appreciate his unique position. On the morning of the fourth day, however, Ed Flecher was brought in, and at once became the newest focus of attention. He had been hit in the corner of the right eye by a sniper's bullet fired from above. The bullet had angled along a complex route and had come out under his left ear. There was a widespread feeling the Flecher should have died quickly. For several days he experienced a slight headache, and for a time the vision in his right eye was slightly blurred—otherwise, nothing noteworthy.

Corella's case was forgotten; very shortly, he was handed a rifle and sent back to the front. It was not surprising that his sense of humor had suffered.

The day after we were relieved by the 29th Marines was a Sunday. At midmorning Galvo blew church call, and almost every survivor of our nine-day attack on Half Moon, Sugar Loaf, and Naha went off to Mass. Protestants, Catholics, and otherwise, now convinced that all men are mortal, were eager to fall in, at least for the present, with the legions of the Lord.

In an open area surrounded by Okinawan tombs, an impromptu altar had been created out of a stack of ammunition cases; we gathered there in the sunshine waiting respectfully as Father Redmond, tommy gun slung over his shoulder, strode up and looked us over.

"My flock increaseth on this quiet morning," he said with a touch of irony. "It's a miracle—one that compares favorably with the multiplying of the loaves and fishes." In fact, although the 4th Marines had lost more than half their men in the past week, Father Redmond had rarely witnessed such a large congregation. I looked around and was amazed. Even Captain McNail and Top-sergeant Brushmore stood there a few paces behind me, and, way in the back, Colonel Maxim. There were sheepish smiles all around, but no one walked away.

Father Redmond unslung his tommy gun, placed it carefully on a grenade box off to one side, and announced that he was offering this Mass for all those comrades we had lost on Okinawa. Since more than half the men standing before him were not Catholics, he went on, he would say the Mass in English, not in Latin. He faced the altar. "I shall go to the altar of God," he began in a firm voice, as two Navy Hellcats thundered over heading south.

"To God who is the joy . . ." The Hellcats were swinging around, thundering back, and we suddenly heard the distinctive crackle of their .50-caliber machine guns.

"Hunt cover!" Father Redmond shouted, and we made an unrestrained dash for the Okinawan tombs and the small caves close by. As we huddled there, a few bullets hit above us chipping rocks, concrete, and coral and showering us with small chunks of debris. Then, apparently concluding that they had wiped out another nest of Japanese infidels, the Hellcats winged off.

Father Redmond had not left the altar. Now, as we headed hesitantly back to our places, he was watching the errant flyboys out of sight to the south. "We are five miles back of the front," he said indignantly. "To mistake us for Japanese troops, those Navy pilots must have been drunk or blind or blind drunk. I swear here in the presence of the Almighty that if they return and strafe us again, I am going to blast them from the heavens with my tommy gun!"

No one even so much as snickered or smiled, although we all knew that only the Almighty could shoot down a Hellcat with a tommy gun. Even so, we admired Father Redmond's spirit.

"We'll begin again." We bowed our heads respectfully once more.

Once Father Redmond started something, he was not inclined to tarry. In just a few minutes we had reached the Apostles' Creed, a high point in the Mass. For the moment forgetting his earlier promise, he began in Latin: "Credo in unum Deum."

"What?" whispered Mauvin who was standing beside me. "Whad he say?"

"I believe in one God," I whispered.

"Ah!" Mauvin said. "I get it. I guess I do too."

Right then there was a shrill, ominous whistle and one hundred yards beyond us the black explosion of a Japanese 77.

"Into the tombs!" Father Redmond yelled. We scrambled for cover. A half dozen shells whistled in, none of them exploding within fifty yards. A nearby battery of our 105-millimeter cannon, evidently getting a fix on the Jap emplacement, began firing off toward Naha. No more shells came our way. We emerged slowly from caves and tombs. No one had been hit, but we had all been somewhat alarmed.

"Jesus Christ!" said Brushmore, who had been standing a few rows behind me. "The damned Jap bastards can't even let us say our prayers."

"Probably the first Brushmore's said in twenty years anyway," Mauvin whispered.

Father Redmond had returned to his makeshift altar. "We'll go back to the Apostles' Creed," he said. "Credo in unum Deum," he began, and beside me Mauvin jumped as if he expected the words to be followed by another hail of Jap shells; but this time all went well through the Creed, the Lord's Prayer, and Communion. Father Redmond turned to intone the last blessing. At that instant we heard the whistle of an approaching shell, the sound of it clearly indicating the arrival of something much bigger than a 77.

"Go! The Mass is ended!" Father Redmond shouted.

As one man, the Catholics shouted back, "Thanks be to God!" and rushed toward the tombs. The tremendous explosion that followed shortly afterward shook the earth for two hundred yards around; those of us quivering in cave and tomb were content that Sunday morning that we had done our pious best.

"That," commented John Reardon later, "was the fastest blessing I've ever received."

"Yeah," said Mauvin. "Thank God Father Redmond has a rapid tongue."

A half hour later, Colonel Maxim sent word for us to saddle up. We moved north another several miles, out of the range of the Jap 77s and, we hoped, so far from the front that our Navy's Hellcat pilots, even the ones that had been sopping up martinis at the Yontan Officers' Club, would not mistake us for the Japanese.

For a couple of quiet days we loitered in that so-called rest camp, living in open foxholes except when the showers of late May drove us into the shelter of the tunnels the Japs had left behind. On 29 May we found out what our next objective would be. The generals had decided that an attack on the Oroku Peninsula might allow us to slip in behind the defenders of Naha and Shuri Castle and cut them off from the rest of the Japs digging in on the south end of Okinawa.

The 4th Marines were to provide the invasion force, and we had five days to get ready for the 4 June D-day. The trouble was that, although on paper the 4th Marines had several thousand men, our losses during the nine-day attack on Half Moon, Sugar Loaf, and Naha had been so heavy that less than a thousand combat Marines remained. There was plenty of equipment: tanks, amphibious tractors, trucks, jeeps, cannon, heavy mortars. A few replacements had arrived—guys back from the hospital, some men with minor wounds, a few kids right out of boot camp, and some truck drivers and cooks. But we didn't have the men we needed to do the killing work up front.

The same day that we got the news of the upcoming invasion of Oroku, Captain McNail called out F Company and made an announcement that he believed the old-timers in the outfit would be glad to hear. Marine Corps Headquarters had issued a new directive specifying that all Marines who had been two times wounded would be patched up, spruced up, fed a few square meals, re-civilized, returned to the States, and given a thirty-day leave. The irony for those who had been twice wounded was that the directive was not to take effect until after the Okinawa campaign had ended.

I had been wounded three times—once on Guam and already twice on Okinawa. But the Okinawa wounds were not considered official because they'd been treated on the spot, and I'd gone right back into action.

As D-day approached we were not especially happy, nor did our happiness increase when, late on the afternoon of 3 June, the regiment's combat rolls were increased by two hundred pink-cheeked kids, most of them no more than three weeks out of boot camp. Since my squad was down to five men, Sergeant White, who had replaced Coon-ass Brown, gave me two of the new boys. To-ward the end of the day who should walk up but Bill Drapp, our associate from the raisin-jack still, and Frank Amo, who had trans-ferred into the 3d Platoon from machine guns a few weeks before we invaded Okinawa. Both had been wounded on Motobu but were back from the hospital just in time for the Oroku party. I was pleased to see them, except that to balance things out, Captain McNail took Cannon away from me and made him an assistant squad leader in the 2d Platoon.

Cannon and I protested. "We got to spread the old guys around," McNail explained. "Otherwise these new kids will be shooting each other instead of the Japs. As soon as this operation is over you can have your butcher friend back." We had to accept the verdict. In the first place, there was no place to appeal it; in the second place, it made good sense. Cannon picked up his pack and tommy gun and walked slowly off to join the 2d Platoon.

Even with the addition of the brave and ignorant two hundred, when D-day came we had less than half as many men as we needed, but in we went, just as always. Lots of preliminary bang-bang from the naval guns; lots of rockets, bombs, and napalm from Navy and Marine flyboys; lots of explosions, smoke, and debris on shore; very few hits. The Japs were right there waiting for us, even though we were, as usual, a couple of hours late. As usual, those of us who walked to war had to knock them back. We did it. I don't know how, but we did knock them back a few hundred yards from the beach to a shallow ridge line maybe a hundred feet high. There, right up against the base of that ridge, we stopped. That is, we got stopped, and there we stayed. The morning wore on. Several of our tanks got ashore, fired off a few 75s, and either found cover or got holed by some Jap antitank guns.

Sergeant White and I had made it to a small hill perhaps thirty yards short of the ridge. Some of our men in a skirmish line a few yards ahead of us were trading shots with Jap riflemen, and Jap soldiers were busy throwing hand grenades down on them. Japanese mortars were coming in with an increasing frequency. A couple of Japanese machine gunners had found a spot where the ridge curved toward the sea. They were beginning to be a real nuisance. In short, things were developing beyond our most pessimistic expectations.

At that moment our new platoon leader, Lieutenant Harris, decided it was time for him to leave the good cover he had enjoyed about a hundred yards behind us. Harris had been around for a while, but always in heavy weapons; he had not yet learned that survivors in rifle platoons are men who have learned to move in short rushes, fast. He came strolling out across what had once been a rice paddy as if he were going for a walk in the park. When he saw White and me in our perch behind our little knoll, he began trotting toward us. The machine gunners were going to get him as sure as God made chain lightning. We waved and yelled. "Get down! Get down! Run! Run! Run like hell!" He trotted toward us. He was still ten yards away when a bullet took him right in the chest.

Harris was a big man—six three, 240 pounds, no fat. That bullet stopped him. He rocked there a second or two, put his left hand to his chest, and said, "That's all!" Then he fell on his back in the mud.

"I didn't know he was left-handed," I said. It was an inane observation. White looked at me, a strange, desperate look. "We've got to get him in," he said. "They'll shoot him full of holes out there."

"Wait," I said. "I saw the bastard that shot him." A second or two before Harris was hit, I had caught a small movement on the hill line above us. What I had seen was no sniper, only a Japanese rifleman doing his duty. He would stick his head up again to see what had happened to his target. I switched my BAR to single fire and aimed it at the spot where I knew he would show. In about five seconds, right on schedule, the Jap rifleman stuck his head above the ridge line. I shot him squarely between the eyes. I don't know enough about the laws of mass and momentum to calculate the force of a .30-caliber bullet traveling at maybe 2,750 feet a second, but I do know that it is considerable. The impact threw him up and back, and almost in slow motion his helmet flew straight upward and made a complete turn as it fell. He would kill no more Marines.

"Let's go!" White yelled.

Together we rushed toward Lieutenant Harris. There was not time for fancy work. Each carrying our rifle in one hand, we reached Harris on the run; each grabbed a foot and dragged him to cover. The machine gunners were landing bullets a few yards behind us all the way.

Harris was still alive—not conscious, but alive. We tore open his dungaree jacket. There was not much blood, front or back. He groaned a little. We gave him a shot of morphine and tagged him to let others know what we had done. The Jap machine gunners were firing as hot as ever, the mortars creeping closer and closer. No corpsmen could come up to give Harris even the most basic aid. No stretcher bearers could haul him away.

And then, as so frequently happens in battle, came an inexplicable sudden change. The Jap machine gunners stopped firing. The mortars ceased their seeking. Our skirmish line made a few tentative moves, then rushed the ridge line. We could stand and walk about in a civilized manner once more. No killing fire came our way. A corpsman rushed up and slapped bandages on Harris, front and back. By the time he finished, four men with a stretcher were there and Captain McNail, somber-faced and sad. In a few minutes Harris was on his way to an aid station on the beach. "He'll make it," the corpsman said to McNail. "It's close to the heart, but he'll make it."

"OK," McNail said. He picked up his rifle. "Let's go!"

We went over the ridge into a little valley beyond and up a steep hill to the base of a Japanese radio tower that was still standing after days of naval gunfire. There were a few reinforced concrete buildings half shattered by shellfire. Here the Japs stopped us again. Our men out front dug in while we waited for the tanks to come up.

Captain McNail, Sergeant White, and two or three company runners set up temporary headquarters in one of the slightly damaged rooms of the largest building. Next door, our small squad lazed around waiting for any special assignment Captain McNail or battalion headquarters back on the beach might dream up for us. While we waited, Jamal the Ghoul pulled a pair of pliers out of his pack and went off looking for gold teeth; Mauvin, always restless and curious, explored several rooms off the building's main corridor. In a few minutes Jamal was back, a disappointed look on his face.

"No gold, Ghoul?" Frank Amo said.

"None, goldangit!" said Jamal. "Only a half dozen dead Japs around here, and their crockery ain't full of nothing but enamel."

"Cheap bastards!" Amo said.

There was the sound of rushing footsteps in the corridor. We leaped up, weapons pointed toward the door. It was Mauvin, skidding in at a dead run.

"What the hell!" I said, half expecting to see Japs coming in right behind him.

"Moe!" Mauvin shouted. "Right next door! The room right next door! There's a safe! A big one!"

As one man, we rushed into the room. There was a good deal of shattered concrete lying about, and half of one wall had been blasted away by a heavy shell, but there, perched in a sheltered corner, was an old-fashioned black safe of heavy steel or cast iron. Clustering close around, we gave it a quick once-over. There was no combination lock, just a heavy handle. Frank Amo reached for it.

"Whoa!" I shouted. "It's probably booby-trapped!"

Frank stopped in mid-reach and jumped back.

"But what if it ain't booby-trapped?" said Mauvin. "What if it's full of money? The rear echelon bastards will come in here in a couple of days and steal it from us!" Already sensing riches, Mauvin was ready to defend his wealth—even if it was a wealth he only imagined.

"It's probably full of Jap money," said Jamal. "Not good for a damned thing but starting a fire."

"It might be full of gold teeth," said Amo, smiling sardonically as he perceived Jamal's sudden look of greed.

Mauvin, now staying well away from the safe's handle, was peering intently at the heavy door. "We could take a grenade and blow the handle off, Moe," he said. "Then the door will pop open. If it's booby-trapped we'll find out, and nobody will get hurt."

It seemed like a good idea. In a few seconds we had lashed a grenade to the door right below the handle, loosened the pin on the grenade so that it would pull out easily, fastened a wire to the loop, taken cover out in the hall, and pulled the pin. In five counts the grenade went off with a healthy blast. We ran back in to our safe. Through the smoke and dust of the explosion, we saw it. The handle was now gone, but the formidable door was still closed to us.

"Nitrostarch," said Mauvin.

"Nitrostarch what?" I said.

"We'll tape a block of nitrostarch against the door. That will blow it off." He was already fumbling in his pack, from which he produced a block nearly as hefty as the one Cannon and I had used to blow up the raisin-jack still.

In a few seconds the nitrostarch was in place. Setting the fuse, we ducked into the corridor. Again there was the roar of an explosion, a lot more emphatic this time. Filled with happy expectations, we charged pell-mell into the room and saw first the door blown cleanly away and lying off on one side of the room. The safe itself had fallen forward on its face so that whatever treasures it held were still denied to us.

"The dirty sons o' bitches!" Mauvin exclaimed, although it was not clear whether the people to whom he was referring were the Japs, the manufacturers of the safe, or those workers in some far-off powder plant who had put too much wallop into the nitrostarch.

"The goddamned rear echelon is going to get the gold after all," said Jamal the Ghoul.

Sergeant White stuck his head in. "Amo," he said, "you and Mauvin get out to the 2d Squad. They need a couple of BARs on the line. Moe, you and these other guys follow me." He was so caught up in his duties that he paid no attention at all to our fallen safe, now clearly visible in the middle of the floor. Amo picked up his BAR and, with Mauvin a step behind, trotted off toward the 2d Squad. The rest of us, quietly cursing our bad luck, reluctantly followed White to a room up front and into the presence of Captain McNail.

Through a convenient hole in the wall, McNail was looking back toward the beach. "The tanks," he said, pointing. "Now we'll be able to move."

Still a hundred yards back, five Sherman tanks lumbered toward us, drawing heavy mortar fire all the way. Buttoned behind their carbon-steel cover, they were not concerned about mortars. We were. The mortar shells intended for the tanks were soon falling uncomfortably close to our hideaway.

The tanks fired their 75s and machine guns at what they supposed to be Japanese defenses a few hundred yards to the front. Then, right when they appeared to make several hits, they backed up, turned, and lumbered off toward the beach.

An hour went by, and two. It was late afternoon. Captain McNail was indecisive. He knew from the volume of fire coming our way that a frontal attack on the Japs would get nowhere. But he was being pressured by higher authorities giving their orders from havens far to the rear. He had to make some kind of demonstration. He beckoned to White. I followed, although I had not been invited to the party.

"White," McNail said, "send Moe and six men up that hill." He pointed to a hill a little to the left of where the Jap fire was coming from.

"Captain," White said, "I don't think they can get ten yards."

"Send them!" McNail said. He turned his back and went to his walkie-talkie.

"You heard him," White said. "And thanks for helping with Harris."

"Anytime," I said. I gathered Jamal the Ghoul, Bill Drapp, and four other guys who had just been volunteered to commit suicide. The Jap mortars and machine guns were going full blast right across the path we would have to take. But we had been ordered to go, and off we went.

We had taken about six steps when once again came sudden change. The machine gunners knocked off for rice balls, I suppose, and the mortarmen for a sample of sake. Single file we dragged through the deep mud up the hill in the direction McNail had pointed. Halfway there we saw, about a hundred yards to our left, a line of men down on their bellies, digging. They were Marines from another company. When they saw us plodding along in the open, they began to yell and wave at us to get down.

"You'll get your balls shot off!" one of them yelled. On we went and a few yards below the crest of the hill turned toward the Jap line. Still no fire from the Japs, not a sound except from the Marines we had seen, still yelling at us to get the hell out of there. I stopped. My patrol stopped, spread out to some extent. The whole situation was just too spooky. I called McNail on the walkie-talkie. "Do you want us to dig in here?"

"Keep going," said McNail. "The colonel wants you to keep going until you draw fire."

"Let's go," I said, and as we rose the mortars hit us. We had no warning. The mortar shells had come in without even a swish. We were caught motionless and erect. The first explosion was no more than a yard to my right; I didn't even hear it. There was a mushroom of smoke, a devastating pressure all along my right side, and I was slammed into a mud bank three yards away.

Oddly enough I was still conscious, though paralyzed from the concussion. There came a hail of mortar shells, perhaps twenty-five right in among us. Then sudden change. Silence. The smoke drifted away. There were no cries, no groans of wounded men. I began to move—fingers, hands, my left arm. The right arm wasn't working very well, and I saw blood streaming from a great gaping wound. I crawled to Bill Drapp. Dead! To Jamal the Ghoul. Dead! To my four other volunteers. All dead! I looked back toward the line of Marines we had seen earlier and saw through a haze that they were still there. None moved toward me. I decided that if I could crawl, I might also be able to stand. I made it to my feet and heard a yell. "Stay down, for Christ's sake!"

I started staggering toward that voice, on and on, and at last made it into the line. There was a flurry of activity around me. A corpsman rushed up and looked me over and cautioned me not to move. "Your arm will be OK," he said, "but I think you might be hit in a lung." The next thing I knew I was laid out on a stretcher in an ambulance jeep and on my way back to an aid station on the beach.

The aid station was jammed with wounded men: the day had been a costly one. Four stretcher bearers lifted my stretcher off the jeep and carried me toward a huddle of corpsmen and doctors working like demons on a pile of wounded men. Out of the chaos a couple of corpsmen emerged and cleared a space where my bearers could put me down.

As the stretcher bearers hesitated, I was aware of two young Marines standing there looking down at me—a couple of the replacements who had joined our platoon only a few days before. Their eyes were wide, their faces pale and tense.

I was not a happy sight, my dungarees tattered and burned, bloody flesh hanging from my torn arm, a puddle of blood collecting beside me on the stretcher. The two young Marines looked down at me, repelled but fascinated. One was tall and skinny, the other short and broad. Both were about sixteen years old—a couple of kids who had skipped school one day only a few months back and made the mistake of joining the Marine Corps. They looked at each other. A look of dismay crossed the face of tall and skinny. He stared down at me wide-eyed and gasped with a stunning realization, "There goes the last of the old ones!"

My stretcher bearers moved on. As I faded off into unconsciousness, the words of tall and skinny rang in my ears.

Toward the New World

I awoke to the sound of subdued, urgent voices and realized slowly that I was lying on my back in an immense, dimly lighted cavern. The lights directly overhead were perhaps forty feet above. Soft red gleamed high in the cavern's distant corners.

Leaning forward, I rolled my head from side to side. As far as I could see in every direction were row on row of stretchers like my own, each occupied by a wounded man. The cavern, I gradually realized, was the lower deck of an LST. The huge open area that on its way to Okinawa had been filled with tanks, amphibious tractors, cannon, and ammunition had now become a hospital, a collecting point for wounded men, hundreds of them stretched out side by side, row on row.

On my right the voices murmured again, more urgently than before. Rolling slightly that way I saw three men, a doctor and two corpsmen, working intently on a wounded man. Obviously the situation was critical. A corpsman held an oxygen mask to the face of the wounded man. He lifted it a second, just long enough for me to recognize Lieutenant Harris. By a miracle of coincidence I had been put on the same ship in the same row, exactly beside him.

"Pulse very erratic, getting weaker," the doctor murmured. He was young, probably a recent product of medical school, and he did not at all appear to like what was happening. He and the corpsman worked on and on and on, and in the end despaired. The corpsman lifted the oxygen mask, and the doctor gently returned the limp hand to the side of the stretcher. The three of them stood for a few seconds looking down. Then the doctor leaned— and pulled the poncho slowly up over Harris's face.

"That's all," he said softly, the same prophetic words Harris had uttered when the bullet had hit him early that day. The Japs had cheated us. White and I had risked our lives to save Harris, and he had died on us anyway. The thought faded away, and for a while so did I.

I regained consciousness to much stirring about in that great belly of the LST. Corpsmen and ordinary seamen were scurrying in every direction, lifting stretchers and carrying wounded men toward various elevators and exits. They worked their way toward me with exceptional speed and efficiency, and soon I was out on the deck of the LST in bright sunshine, the first I had experienced in quite a few days.

The LST had nestled alongside a much larger ship, a transport, and load after load of wounded men, still on their stretchers, were being lifted to the deck above. Once on deck, we were sorted out and carted off in a dozen different directions. Although only sporadically conscious of what was going on, I do recall being carried into a compartment one deck down and lifted to a hospital bed just inside the compartment entrance. There were probably twenty beds in that compartment. Within minutes, twenty wounded men had been brought in and the twenty beds were filled. Next there was a flurry of activity as a half dozen corpsmen cut off our blood-soaked dungarees, cleaned layers of dirt off us, and somehow shoved or rolled or coaxed us into hospital gowns. Before we knew it we were tucked in between crisp, white sheets, a pillow was stuck under each head, and a pure white blanket was pulled up over us.

"We ought to have a full house in an hour," one of the corpsmen said cheerfully, "and we can get the hell out of here before we get another visit from the kamikazes." Not long afterward we heard the rumble of the anchor chain, and we were under way.

"Now," said the cheerful corpsman to no one in particular, "we can get down to business."

That business, we soon learned, was the business of healing, and the men in that ship were experts at it. First they examined us in our bunks. Then, one by one, according to the critical nature of each case, they hauled us off to an operating room for a general cleaning, bandaging, stitching, x-raying, cutting, or whatever else might be required.

The ship was a floating hospital, but it was not a hospital ship. It didn't go around nights with its lights turned on like a hospital ship, and it didn't display any large red crosses on its side. Undistinguished in its blue-gray coat of paint, it hid in the smoke screen like other Navy vessels off Okinawa, and it dodged the kamikazes and hoped for the best like the men on the destroyers and frigates out on the picket line. There were no nurses on board.

The evidence of medical logic and prudence was everywhere around us, from the arrangements within the individual compartments to the relationships among the compartments themselves. If I sat on my bed and faced the central corridor, I saw to my immediate right the head—or latrine—with its sink, urinals, and individual stalls. To my immediate left against the compartment's outer bulkhead was a small desk and chair, the corpsman's station. Twenty-four hours a day our corpsman, a man with a friendly, positive attitude, or one of his two assistants, who were just as friendly and cooperative, was at that desk busy with records or rushing around answering to the needs of his twenty patients. If the man on duty needed help, he punched a buzzer over the desk and help arrived on the double.

After a few hours on board that ship-hospital, I began to feel a dramatic improvement. The numbness in my neck and side gradually lessened, and the pain in my right kidney began to be much less severe. My head cleared, and on several brief occasions when the corpsman was out of the compartment, I left my bed, shuffled into the head, and stood for a few minutes in front of the urinal. In three hours I tried four times. Still no luck. After the fourth try, when I turned to take the half dozen steps back to my bunk, the corpsman was standing there, hands on hips, a look of distinct

disapproval on his face. "Damn, buddy," he said. "You ain't supposed to be up wandering around." He grabbed my left arm and
guided me back to my bunk. I told him I was feeling better every
minute, except for this small difficulty.

"Well," he said almost indignantly, "you got so much concussion along your right side, you're lucky you still got a kidney down
there. For a while the doc thought your liver was ruptured. That
wouldn't have been so good."

There was some commotion in the corridor, and he left me for
a few minutes, but was soon back with a mug of black coffee.
"Drink this fast," he said, "and I'll bet your problem will solve
itself." He was right, and in a couple of hours when once again he
had left the compartment for a few minutes, I took the opportunity
to wander slowly down the corridor on a scouting trip.

All along the corridor and, I assume, along the corridors on the
several decks below were compartments much like the one to
which I had been assigned, all filled with wounded men. The assignments appeared to be made according to the type of wound or
condition. Our compartment and several nearby were filled with
arm, leg, and shoulder wounds. There were compartments for
chest wounds, others for stomach wounds, others for burn victims,
and still others for men suffering what was then called battle fa-
tigue. Four doors down from our compartment and in several
other compartments close by were men with head wounds. My
scouting trip was interrupted by a doctor who asked me what the
hell I was doing out of my compartment and ordered me to get
back to it pronto. I didn't argue. I'd had enough wandering about
for one afternoon. It was time to rest.

I awoke a few hours later with a powerful thirst. Apparently,
once my kidneys had decided to begin functioning again, I had
become dehydrated. I drank jugs of water and coffee by the pot. As
I drank my third mug of coffee in less than an hour, I noticed that
across the corridor there was a small compartment the doctors
seemed to be using as a sort of refueling stop. In it was a refrigera-
tor from which they pulled pitchers of orange juice. Several times

that evening when the traffic let up, I slipped across the corridor and helped myself. It was, I thought, a prime example of Raider self-reliance.

Halfway through the next morning while our friendly corpsman was busy with his records, I ducked out to continue my raiding game but was stalled by a couple of doctors who got to the orange juice a step ahead of me. While they stood there sipping, I loitered in the corridor just out of their range of vision. In muted voices they were discussing one of the wounded men.

"They brought him in just before we left Okinawa yesterday. He'd been hit maybe two hours before. It's a remarkable case," the one doctor said. "Here's a man shot with a .30-caliber rifle. The bullet enters between and maybe half inch above the eyes, goes straight through the brain, front to back, and exits without even taking much bone. He's conscious, lucid, cheerful, and not in any pain. In fact, when I came out a few minutes ago he was sitting up in his DMB laughing at the Snafu cartoons in *Yank* magazine."

There was a brief period of silence. "Not a chance, I presume?" said the other doctor. He had a soft, cultured voice and an Eastern accent sort of smoothed over.

"Not a chance. There'll be too much cranial bleeding. And we can't stop the pressure from the scar tissue forming. He'll be OK tonight and tomorrow. Probably lose him late tomorrow night."

"God!" the other said softly. "I wish the Japanese would come to their senses and quit. All this dying is getting far too repetitive."

"Yes," said the first doctor, "there are always some you just can't put back together."

They came out and headed down the corridor, pausing several compartments away to look in and wave at someone just inside. I watched them until they were well out of range, slipped in, poured a mug full of orange juice, and ducked back across the corridor. The friendly corpsman looked up from his desk. "Stealing the Navy's orange juice again, I see."

"It's the only thing that's keeping me alive," I said, and handed him the mug. "Hold this while I get into my bunk. I only got one good arm."

He took the cup and watched critically as I slid into the bunk. "There's not a damned thing wrong with your arm, Mac, except some flesh and fat loss and a hole about the size of your fist. Otherwise all you got is some torn muscle in your neck, a cartilage ripped here and there along your ribs, and a chunk of metal over your liver. You're already about 90 percent cured, and we've wasted a good DMB on you. Every damned ragged-assed Marine I've ever seen is half man and half con man."

"What's the DMB?" I said.

He looked quickly around the compartment. Most of the other men were catching up on their sleep. "It's the bunk you're sitting on," he said in a half whisper. "It's the dead man's bunk, the one just inside the door in each compartment. We put the worst cases there. That way if they die, we can slip them out without disturbing the others."

"What am I doing here?"

"You're a fraud," he said. "A damned fraud. Back on the beach they tagged you wrong. They couldn't even get a needle into you to give you plasma because your veins had collapsed. Also when we looked at your X ray, we saw all that metal in your upper back and thought at first you must have picked it up over on the island when you were hit. Where'd you get all that iron anyway?"

"Last year on Guam," I said. "Grenade shrapnel."

"The Japs have been using you for target practice for some time, haven't they?"

"Going on three years," I said.

"Incidentally," he said, still keeping his voice low and confidential, "don't mention this DMB thing to any of the others. If you do, the DMBs in the other compartments will get nervous. They're not all going to die. More than half of them are probably as healthy as you are."

283

He picked up a pen and went back to his records. I felt pretty good, sitting there sipping my orange juice. I was not going to die. I had, of course, known it all along, from the moment I had pulled myself up from the mud back there on Oroku and staggered into the E Company lines, but it was pleasant to have someone else confirm my conviction.

I had finished the orange juice when a lone officer entered the compartment. He stood there quietly surveying the scene. Suddenly aware of his presence, the corpsman looked up and snapped to attention. "Relax," the officer said. "Keep right on doing what you were doing." He looked me over. "You seem to be beating the odds," he said.

"I'm coming along," I said, "but I'm not ready for the invasion of Japan."

He smiled and wandered off through the compartment, stopping here and there to talk to any man who was not napping. Before he left he stopped briefly at the corpsman's station. "Doing your usual excellent job, I see," he said, and was gone out into the corridor.

"Who is that, the top doctor?" I asked the corpsman as the officer's precise footsteps faded away.

"He's more than that," the corpsman said. "He's the head honcho. He's the captain of the ship."

It was hard to believe. I had never before heard of a ship captain who ever left the bridge except to go ashore. "He'll be back," the corpsman said. "He usually comes by two or three times whenever we have wounded men aboard."

An hour later, after a doctor had come by to put a fresh bandage on my arm, I went off to explore the ship more thoroughly. In an hour I had pretty well reconnoitered everything except the engine room and the bridge. There was not much variation below deck—mostly compartment after compartment full of wounded men. Up on the deck things were arranged as on any transport: blue-gray bridge, bulkheads, and masts. Nothing to indicate that

284

this ship, plowing eastward through a placid sea, was any different from other Navy transports.

I turned, went down the ladder, and headed along the corridor toward my compartment. I had passed the entrance to one of the head-wound compartments, only four doors from mine, when I heard a familiar voice cry, "Moe!" I stopped, turned back, looked in. There in that compartment's DMB sat Cannon, smiling his gold-toothed smile.

"What the hell are you doing here?" I said, and saw the bandage wrapped round his head. In that instant I knew: the remarkable case the doctors had discussed, the bullet hole front and back, the damaged brain, the leaking blood vessels, the scar tissue's slow, implacable pressure, the dead man's bunk. I looked at my friend and managed to smile.

We sat there on his bunk trading stories of that last day on Okinawa. I told him about Harris and the others. He described seeing Williamson killed and a half dozen other men in the 2d Platoon. The six young boots the 2d Platoon had received had all been killed or wounded during the first few hours, victims of their own ignorance.

"I'll tell you how I got hit," he said. "I came around the corner of one of those tombs, and there was a Jap with a rifle about fifty yards away. I got the jump on him but my tommy gun jammed. When I pulled the trigger he didn't fall. He raised his rifle and aimed. His bullet hit me and I was down on my back, and I still couldn't believe that my tommy gun jammed. I've had that same old tommy gun since Tent Camp 3. I've never had it jam before. Here I sit with a bullet hole in my head, and I still can't believe my Thompson jammed."

The duty corpsman got up from his small desk. "Better take off now," he said to me. "That's enough excitement for one day."

"OK," I said. "I'll be back first thing tomorrow."

"After noon chow," the corpsman said. He walked with me down the narrow corridor to my compartment and stood inside the door for a minute. "I brought this wandering bellhop back to you," he said to our corpsman. "He's been jawing with a friend in my compartment. The one in the DMB."

"What are his chances?" I asked.

"You don't know?" Cannon's corpsman said.

"Well, I heard two doctors talking," I said.

"And they said he wouldn't make it to Saipan?"

"They said maybe two days. He must be the one they were talking about." I was finding it more and more difficult to speak. The corpsman put his hand on my arm. "Sometimes they last a little longer," he said. "Sometimes they get an extra day."

I spent an hour with Cannon the next afternoon and went back again that night, but in a half hour or so he began to be weary and went into a deep sleep. Next morning, though, he was wide awake, happy, and smiling when I came in. The doctor's prediction had been wrong. He was still alive. I began to feel a faint hope. Medical miracles do sometimes happen. I remembered the miracles of Art Corella and Ed Flecher. They had both survived wounds that would kill a man ninety-nine times out of a hundred. Cannon, as most Marines, was in great physical condition. If anyone could survive a head wound, he could. Maybe the bullet had cut its way a little lower than the doctors thought.

That afternoon and again that evening before he dozed off, we talked for an hour, mostly about Raider days at Tent Camp 3. That had been a long time ago. That night I went to sleep with a rising hope.

I awoke to someone shaking me. It was the corpsman from Cannon's compartment. "Your friend wants to talk to you," he said. I pulled on my hospital slippers and followed him down the corridor.

Cannon was sitting on his bunk, a strange look on his face. "Moe," he said when he saw me, "what I'd like to do is go up on deck a while."

"I tried to talk him out of it," Cannon's corpsman said. "I don't think it's such a hot idea."

I went down the corridor to find our corpsman. He was in the doctors' compartment filling a thick Navy mug with strong coffee. "He wants to go up on deck," I said.

"Who? Who wants to go up on deck? Oh, you mean your buddy with the head wound." He sipped the coffee. "I'll ask the doc." Putting his cup down, he hurried off toward the duty doctor's small office. In a few minutes he was back. "He says OK. It can't do any harm." He picked up his coffee, took a long drink, and emptied what was left into the small sink. "Somebody will have to stay up there with him."

"I'll be there," I said.

"OK," he said. "Bring your blanket and don't forget your life jacket. I'll get your buddy and help him up the ladder."

By the time I had picked up the blanket, pillow, and life jacket and hurried into the corridor, the corpsman and a couple of sailors were already moving Cannon step by deliberate step up the gangway to the main deck. We settled down on a hatch cover forward of the bridge. At first Cannon was determined that he was going to sit on the edge of the hatch with his feet dangling toward the deck. While somewhat shakily he settled himself onto his seat, the corpsman and sailors stood there patiently looking off toward the bow into the pale light. The night was far along; there would be only a little more than an hour before the break of day. Presently the corpsman looked back at Cannon, who was slumping forward a bit. "Maybe you'd better stretch out on your back awhile and get a look at the stars," he said.

"A good idea," said Cannon. "I'm getting kind of empty headed up here in this high place." He lay back slowly and, as he did, the corpsman deftly slipped the pillow under his head and spread the white blanket over him.

"We're settled in now," the corpsman said to me. "I need to go back to the compartment. I'll check up here every now and then." He and his helpful sailors headed below.

A few minutes passed. A morning breeze from the north was bringing a chill to the main deck. I stretched out on the hatch cover beside Cannon and pulled up my blanket.

"We had it good, didn't we, Moe?" Cannon said in a low voice. "We had it good. Cole and Faltynski and Red Salleng and Brushmore and Bill Werden and Move-the-Line Sledd and all the other bastards. Friends!" He paused. "Whatever happened to Cole, anyway?"

Earlier that day and again a little later, he had asked me that same question. "Hit in the leg in Naha," I said. "He'll be OK."

"Oh yeah," he said. "Whatever happened to Nock Dorning? I ain't seen him since he joined the flamethrower squad."

"He's dead," I said. "Stepped on a land mine on Guam."

"And Faltynski? Did he get it on Guam too?"

"No, Faltynski's OK. He left us last year after we got back to the Canal from Guam. He's back in the States."

"Oh, yeah, I remember now." He was silent for a little while, and I had begun to think that the easy rock of the ship had lulled him. Then he stirred. "Moe," he said quietly, "I ain't going to make it, am I?"

The question surprised me. I felt the tears come to my eyes and my throat tighten. "You'll make it," I choked out. "You got to make it."

"I can tell when you're lying, Moe," he said. "You're the world's worst liar. You always hesitate before you lie. Your tone changes." He laughed, not a very strong laugh. "The world's lousiest poker player."

I could not answer.

"I'm a little dizzy," he said. "The ship is sort of moving round."

I reached out and put a hand on his arm. "Hang on," I said desperately. "I'll get the corpsman."

"No," he said. "Just stay here."

I lay there rigid. The wind had picked up and was beginning to sing in the lines.

"We were the tommy gunners!" Cannon said suddenly in a strong voice.

He didn't say anything else, and for a while he was breathing steadily. The ship rocked on, and I dozed. When I woke, the corpsman was standing there in the first light of the new day and right alongside him four seamen with a stretcher. I sat up and looked toward Cannon. His eyes were already open, and he was staring straight upward into the morning sky.

"I'm sorry," the corpsman said. "We're sorry." I looked at the four sailors. They were solemn, sad. Cannon had not moved. I looked at him once more, his wide-open eyes, his lips pulled back in the familiar gold-toothed grin. Realization came slowly.

Around midmorning the ship's crew gathered on the deck, along with the officers not on duty and some of the doctors and corpsmen. Six men, including Cannon, had died during the night and their bodies had been prepared for burial at sea. Exactly on the hour, the captain appeared and read the ancient words of the ritual. Then the boards were tilted and the bodies slid out from under their covering flags and into the deep gray sea.

I went back to my bunk and sat there thinking about the past three years—not bitter, just sad. Everything had gone to hell, and the biggest battle was still to come.

The corpsman brought me coffee, and I drank, and a short while later he came by with orange juice, and I drank that. Otherwise they let me alone. Midafternoon, the captain of the ship stuck his head into the compartment, saw me sitting on my dead man's bunk, hesitated, then stepped in. He came up close to my bunk and leaned toward me.

"I'm sorry about your friend," he said, and before I could answer he had turned abruptly away and was gone. In the corridor he stood a few seconds talking to one of the doctors in a low tone. A few minutes later our corpsman came in and handed me a mug of sick-bay brandy. "The captain thinks this might help," he said.

It did—for a while. The afternoon passed and the long night and the next day. The ship pushed steadily eastward and on the eighth day anchored off Saipan. While the last of the wounded were being unloaded on the port side, fresh supplies were already coming aboard on the starboard from a flotilla of Higgins boats and barges. The fighting on Okinawa was still going strong, our corsman told us as we said good-bye, and the wounded were piling up back there. The ship was going right back for another load.

I was in a Quonset hut hospital ward on Saipan with doctors and attendants scurrying about getting the latest batch of wounded men settled before I realized that for the time being I was in the care of the United States Army. Marine wounded were usually treated in Navy hospitals, but because of the heavy casualties on Iwo Jima and the even heavier casualties coming in from Okinawa, all Navy hospitals were jammed with wounded men.

In addition to the usual doctors and orderlies (not corpsmen, as the Navy and Marines called them), the Quonset hut I found myself in had something different, something very special: a nurse. Blonde, pretty, in her late twenties, she perched for a while each day in a small office right inside the front door. The office was set off from the rest of the long room by walls of plywood and glass. Those walls were designed so that, sitting up in our beds, we could see only her head and shoulders above the plywood section of the partition, and she could peer out and inspect us whenever she might be motivated by concern about our welfare.

Unfortunately, she left that exclusively to the doctors and orderlies who prowled about the premises. It was her duty, apparently, to arrive each morning at 9:00, preside at her desk for an hour or so, flirt with the youngest and handsomest doctors, knock off for lunch at 11:25, return at 1:00, and, promptly at 2:00, leave for the day. Otherwise, when she was not examining her records, bullying the orderlies, or sallying forth to scold one or another of the wounded men, she sat at her station smoking cigarettes, reading magazines, or leaning back listening like the rest of us to Radio Saipan, which came on about 10:00 each morning and filled the next three hours with musical things like "Falling in Love with Love."

Early the third day I was rolled off to an operating room where two young and optimistic surgeons did a stitching job on my arm. Their optimism was premature. When late that afternoon they came in to look me over, they announced that I could, for a few days, put myself in neutral at government expense while they scheduled me for a skin graft.

"The hole in your arm is too big," they told me. "The stitches aren't going to hold."

"Lucky man," said one of the orderlies as soon as the two enthusiasts were out of hearing, "I guess you know that all skin grafts are done back in Honolulu." A vision of alohas and hulas flashed through my mind.

The cheerful doctors were back next morning. "We got good news," one of them said. "You're scheduled for that vulcanizing job three days down the road."

"Are they going to fly me back to Honolulu?" I asked. The hulas would be swirling sooner than I expected.

Something about my question rocked them into howls of glee. "Word sure gets around fast on the Saipan grapevine," one of them said. "You're the third guy to ask that question today. The answer is no. No plane ride to Honolulu. No trip to Honolulu either. Until last week, all skin grafts were done in Honolulu or San Francisco or San Diego, but we got so many men waiting for the service that the Army felt it would be more practical to send some skin-graft teams out here. In other words, you won't have to travel all the way back to them. They're being considerate enough to come all the way out to the Mariana Islands just for you."

"Somehow," I said, "I can't find the right words to express my heartfelt thanks."

"That way," the second doctor said, "you'll be all healed and ready to take an active part in the invasion of Japan." Doctors, orderlies, and several wounded men propped up in their beds nearby were delighted with this bit of humor. Even the guy in the bed next to mine giggled, although, considering the fact that he was encased in a plaster cast from neck to ankles, some special sense of the ridiculous was required.

"I ain't going for the invasion of Japan," I said. "This is my second officially recognized wound. I'm due thirty days' leave in the States as soon as you experts put me back together."

291

Doctors and orderlies looked at each other, grinning now like happy cats. "You haven't heard the latest?" the younger doctor said. "Since a week ago it's three times wounded. Four-fifths of the Marine Corps has now been twice wounded. They can't dump that many Marines onto the mainland all at once. The country couldn't stand it." They went off laughing.

"Are they kidding?" I said to the nearest orderly.

"It's what we hear," he said. "It's on the grapevine."

"It figures," I said. He didn't hear me. He was already moving toward the nurse, who was beckoning to him through her protective glass partition.

I didn't even bother to feel sorry for myself. I had become perfectly adjusted to Marine Corps logic and Marine Corps ways. It was like growing up in a family dominated by a powerful father who operates by impulse and rules by force. The one constant in such a world is change—often sudden, mostly inexplicable, seldom for the betterment of the individual but almost always for the ultimate benefit of the family unit. When, on Okinawa, Captain McNail had told us of the Marine Corps' promise that twice-wounded men would be returned to the States, I had accepted the news as fact—established, unmodified, unassailable. But subconsciously I knew the promise had to be suspect. Too many of our veterans who were still able to fight had been twice wounded. The Marine Corps, already desperately weakened by our tragic losses on Iwo and Okinawa, could not long endure if it allowed more than half of its remaining men, its veterans, to take the long road home. I relaxed and waited for the arrival of the medical vulcans.

The leader of the skin-graft team, right on schedule, did the grafting without any complications. I had to spend the week afterward on my back while waiting for places to heal: my left thigh, from which a big patch of skin had been removed, and my right arm, where the vulcanizing job had been done. The operation caused me almost no discomfort. A few days later, however, I began to suffer from an agonizing pain in my ears. I suspected sulfa, which was then a new and unrefined drug. The doctor had prescribed it to ward off infection. I described my symptoms to the ward doctor. He looked into my ears and informed me that my pain was in my head, not my ears. I told him I was experiencing side effects from the sulfa. He said he thought I was bucking for a Section 8 and suggested aspirin.

That night was a difficult one. The pain in my ears had become intense; I resolved to take no more sulfa. Sleep came slowly. A few hours later, the pain in my ears subsided. Perhaps the effects of that day's sulfa were wearing off. Trouble was, the orderly would be around with two more pills in the morning, and he would stand there watching to be sure I swallowed them.

Some months earlier, Nick Zobenica, who never took his Atabrine pills, had taught me a little sleight of hand. I resolved to use his trick thereafter and conceal the sulfa pills each day long enough to discard them during a trip to the head.

Nick Zobenica: our associations went back to the raisin-jack still. I had last seen him on Okinawa the day we had attacked Half Moon Hill.

We had not gone fifty yards in our attack on Half Moon when Nick took a bullet through the right heel. Since the machine gunner whose bullet had hit Nick was still shooting in his direction, Nick ignored the inconvenience and raced ahead like an Olympic sprinter. When he found cover about halfway up the hill, though, he felt an increasing level of pain and was compelled to stop. I went back a few yards and looked him over. Although the bullet had gone cleanly through flesh and bone, the wound was not bleeding badly. Our corpsman ran up, also pursued by the Jap machine gunner, and put a quick bandage on it. "You got a pretty wound there, Nick," he said. "It will probably take you all the way back to Guam, maybe even San Diego."

"I'm ready to get started right now," said Nick. "It's a long way."

But the first hundred yards on that long road back was covered by the same machine gunner, and the way he was pumping lead indicated that he had an unlimited supply of ammunition. Nick cursed his fate and grumbled. "Give him a job," said the corpsman. "Give him something to do. Otherwise he might get restless and try something rash."

"I got a job for you, Nick," I said.

"Gee-eezy, Moe," Nick said. "My foot's half shot off. You ain't gonna send me after that son of a bitch on the machine gun, are you?"

"We'll get him later," I said. "You can stay right here and do what I need done."

As we had rushed across the first hundred yards of our attack on Half Moon, Mauvin had seen, some distance out in the open field behind us, a Jap sniper stick his head up far enough out of a spider trap to fire one shot before dropping under cover again. Sooner or later, he would be raising up, hoping to shoot some Marine in the back. Mauvin was a few yards ahead of us. I waved him back and in a half minute he told Nick exactly where to aim. Nick readied his rifle. "I'll get him," he said.

An hour later, when we had moved about one hundred yards closer to the crest of Half Moon, Nick came limping up. "I shot myself out of a job," he said. He pointed to his heel. "It's beginning to smart like hell, Moe," he said. "I think I can make it back." The Jap machine gunner had not fired for some time.

"You better hang on here," I said. "That Nambu man might only be playing dead."

"I can make it," Nick said and limped off across the open space toward our main line three hundred yards away. He had hobbled several steps when the Nambu gunner opened up. In an immediate marvelous recovery, Nick started to run as if he were equipped with two perfectly good heels and an outboard motor, the machine gunner spraying bullets a few yards behind him. Halfway back to our main line, he ran out of breath or dash and took one long dive into a shell hole full of water and mud. There he lay with the machine gun bullets going close overhead until the gunner wearied of his game and turned his attention to E Company, attacking from the left. Some time later, we saw Nick crawling toward our line where, still fifty yards short, he was spotted, and two headquarters Marines rushed out and dragged him in. We figured he was already halfway home.

With the picture of Nick Zobenica's dash still in my mind, I dozed off and awakened to a bright morning made brighter by the realization that the pain in my ears was only half as bad. When the orderly came by presently with my two sulfa pills, I seized them eagerly and transferred them to a secret place before pretending to toss them in and wash them down. A few days later, the pain in my ears was gone.

Although I took no more sulfa pills, by mid July I was on my feet again and had been moved out of the regular hospital Quonset hut to a pyramidal tent with other men whose wounds were healing satisfactorily. Each morning thereafter I reported to the doctor; each morning he seemed satisfied that the graft was doing nicely. After that I spent the day as I pleased.

From the Army hospital it was not far to the airstrip. Often in the afternoon I went down to watch the B-29s take off for Japan. I hung around the strip so much that I began to know a few of the pilots, copilots, crew members, and mechanics. Among these were a couple of Marine flyboys who had a pretty soft assignment. Each afternoon, they flew a C-46 cargo plane the hundred or so miles to Guam and returned late in the day. Their main cargo seemed to be special messages, mail, and booze. They were both very interested in hearing about the fighting on Okinawa. One day, one of them mentioned that the 4th Marines had returned from Okinawa to a camp on Guam for reinforcements and rest.

"Anytime you want to take a ride down there to visit your buddies," he said, "just hop aboard. We'll get you back before dark. If you like, we'll even fly over Rota so the Japs can take a few more potshots at you." Rota, a small island roughly between Saipan and Guam, had been bypassed the year before, but the Japanese still had men and some potent antiaircraft guns there.

"The Japs will get a chance to shoot at me soon enough," I said. "As soon as I get back to the outfit and we lead the invasion of Japan."

In fact, the 4th Marines were destined to invade Japan a few weeks sooner than anyone expected, and, incredibly, the invasion would be a peaceful one. That night, the news came of a magical new weapon—the atomic bomb—that had exploded over Hiroshima and had practically wiped the city off the map. Two days later came word of another huge bomb on Nagasaki and then the even more remarkable report that Japan had surrendered.

Back in the hospital tent, we walking wounded wandered around in a sort of unbelievers' daze. We were, through the intercession of a scientific marvel, not to be killed on schedule after all. Instead we could look forward to going home, the home most of us had expected never to see again.

But there was to be a delay in my homecoming: the next day we heard that the 4th Marines had been selected to be the first American troops to go ashore in Japan. They would be landing all around Tokyo Bay. It was a great honor, and I felt cheated that I would miss out on the historic event. But as I sat on my bunk there in that Army hospital on Saipan, I started to consider some possibilities. I had been in the Pacific thirty-two months, nearly three years of my life. I had fought the Japanese from the Solomons to Okinawa and had been four times wounded. I was a member of the 4th Raider Battalion, the heart of the 4th Marines and the best outfit in the U. S. Marine Corps. Why should I, who had fought in jungle, mountain, and field, miss out on all the glory? I got up from my cot and went off to find my doctor. He had just finished breakfast at the officers' mess. "What can I do for you?" he said as he came out.

I told him that the 4th Marines would need all the men they could get, and I wanted to be discharged from the hospital so that I could get down to Guam in time to invade Japan with them.

He hesitated. "Let's go over to my tent and have a look at that arm," he said. Once there, he removed the bandage, looked things over, and then shook his head. "I'm afraid not," he said. "It wouldn't be medically correct for me to let you go. The wound is 90 percent healed, and there's no point in risking an infection." He saw the look of desperation on my face, and his voice lost some of its professionalism. "If I were in your shoes, I'd want to go too. If they'd waited three more days before dropping those big bombs, you'd be far enough along. It's only that the timing is bad. I'm sorry. I can't see my way clear to let you go."

I thought it over a minute. "All right Major," I said. "Can you give me a one-day pass so I can catch a ride to Guam and visit my friends before they leave?"

"How the hell are you going to get to Guam, let alone back here in one day?"

I told him about the Marine fliers and the C-46. For a couple of minutes he digested that information. Then, reaching for pen and paper, he wrote out the pass, signed it, and handed it over. "Thank you," I said and tucked it into my shirt. When I turned to leave, he held up his hand to stop me.

"In case you get some wild-eyed idea about not coming back," he said, "when that pass runs out you'll be officially away without leave. I think you Marines call that going over the hill. In case you get some idea about going AWOL or over the hill, whichever you prefer, I'm going to wait twenty-four hours, and then after that pass runs out, I'm going to report you. I won't have any choice."

"Can you make that forty-eight hours?" I said.

He sat there shaking his head. "When you Marines go through boot camp," he said, "they must give you a shot of insolence along with the damned smallpox shots. Now get the hell out of here before I call the MPs."

I had taken a few steps toward my tent when he suddenly yelled, "Stop! Halt!" I stopped and looked back. He was sporting a half smile. "All right, forty-eight," he called. "And good luck!"

Once More to Guam

There was no time to waste. The 4th Marines would be loading ship already and in the next two or three days shoving off for Japan. Back at the tent, as I threw my few possessions into a small sack, it occurred to me that I was a pretty ragged looking Marine. On my feet I had a pair of slippers two sizes too big that the medicos had found for me. My loose-fitting pair of trousers of the type worn around the hospital were held up by a frayed cord. My shirt was of ancient Army khaki, the right sleeve cut off about six inches above my elbow to accommodate the bandaged arm. The Army had not issued me a cap; there had been a shortage of them in hospital supply. But I had been going freely about Saipan for several weeks, and no one had challenged me about my unmilitary appearance. I would take my chances down on Guam.

I headed the few hundred yards to the main road and caught a ride on the first truck to come by; very shortly I was at the airstrip. Near the dispatcher's shack, my two Marine flyboy friends were getting out of a jeep.

"I'm ready to take that ride to Guam today," I said.

"OK," said one, "we're taking off in a half hour. We'll fly right over Rota and see if the Japs have really given up." On our trip south, the two idiots not only flew over Rota, they circled it twice. No antiaircraft fire came up.

"I guess the Japs have really called it quits!" one of them hollered back at me.

An hour later we were on Guam. "We'll be heading back in two hours," they said. "Don't drift too far off if you plan to get back to the hospital today."

At the control room I inquired about the whereabouts of the 4th Marines. No one knew anything about them. "This is Army Air Force up here," a sergeant volunteered. He pointed in the direction I took to be the south. "Go out and catch a truck heading that way. Sooner or later you'll find somebody who can tell you where to go."

Three rides later I found a driver who had heard of the 4th Marines. "They're camped over near Pago Bay," he said. "I'm going within a couple of miles of them. I'll let you out where a road goes east. Your next ride should get you pretty close."

I hauled myself, clumsily because of my damaged arm, into the back of the truck. It was a typical six-by-six with a canvas top and narrow, slotted benches on each side. The benches were filled. On one side sat a row of Army privates, on the other a smattering of Navy types, with the places nearest the cab occupied by four Navy nurses—three ensigns and a lieutenant. I looked more closely at the soldiers on the opposite bench. Sitting right in front of me was Leo Rock, a friend from high school days. As I extended my left hand toward him, the truck started up with a jerk, and I almost fell.

"Sit down, soldier!" the nurse lieutenant ordered in about as nasty a tone as I had ever heard an officer use, and I felt a flare of anger. Here I had pulled myself, bad arm and all, aboard a truck where no seats remained, had just met a friend from home, had been fighting for months in the most savage battles of a war I had not started, had not yet recovered from a wound that could have killed me, and I was being called to account by a person, a noncombatant, who had obviously just arrived on the western Pacific scene. Most disgusting of all, she had called me soldier. I remained on my feet.

"Sit down this instant!" Her voice had a note of hysteria. "That's an order!" She peered maliciously at my ragged shirt, my thin, sloppy trousers, my oversize shoes. "What are you anyway, some kind of brig rat!"

"I am a Marine," I said. "Not a damned dogfaced soldier. What are you?" It was not a wise thing to say. After all, she was a lieutenant in the Navy. Leo Rock's face assumed a look of shock, and there was amazement on the faces of the other men sitting along the benches.

"You are insubordinate!" She was furious. "You are out of uniform! You are insolent! Where is your cap? I'm putting you on report!" She pulled out a pencil and pad. "Give me your name, rank, and serial number."

"They call me Moe," I said. "My serial number is 466037, Corporal, just like Adolf Hitler."

The three nurses giggled. She suppressed them with a glare. "What outfit are you in?"

"The 4th Marines, a few days back from a lot of hell on Okinawa!"

"I asked you where your cap is!"

"I have no cap," I said. "I lost my cap on Okinawa."

The truck suddenly stopped and the driver hollered back. "Hey, Marine, the 4th is a half mile down the road and a mile right."

"Good-bye, lieutenant," I said. I looked at Leo Rock. He was sitting there thunderstruck. "Good luck, Leo," I said and jumped off the truck. For a second I thought the nurse lieutenant was going to jump off after me. She had actually risen and taken a step when the truck started up, and she nearly fell over the end gate. As the truck pulled away she was leaning out, still screaming threats about putting me on report.

Twenty minutes later I was walking down the F Company street. Even though this was Guam instead of Guadalcanal, everything looked familiar: same graveled streets, same dirty-green pyramidal tents, same palm trees waving overhead. And down at the opposite end of the street, a corporal counting cadence for a squad of baby-faced Marines.

There was a shout from one of the tents. "It's Moe!" I recognized Bill Bontadelli's voice and thought, That's one guy we didn't lose! "It's Moe!" came another shout, which was echoed and re-

300

peated down the tent row; and in a few seconds I was surrounded by my surviving buddies, shaking my left hand and pounding my shoulders and back. It was a great event: I was the first of the wounded to return to my platoon. Captain McNail hurried out of the headquarters tent and, right behind him, Top-sergeant Brushmore, grinning through his red moustache.

"Where the hell did you come from?" McNail shouted. "We haven't had any word you were on the way back."

"Somebody must have launched him in the right direction," Bontadelli whooped happily. "He never did learn which way a compass needle pointed."

"He looks like he escaped from the hospital," Brushmore said.

"Well," I said, "I didn't wait to say good-bye." I explained to McNail and Brushmore that at the end of forty-eight hours, the Army would officially consider me over the hill.

"Never mind," said McNail, "they won't catch you here. We're boarding ship for Japan day after tomorrow." He turned to Brushmore. "Issue Moe a new BAR. We can't give you your old one, Moe. When you got hit there on Oroku, your BAR got blasted worse than you did. We found it next day right after we chased those damned Nips off that hill." He slapped me on the shoulder. "Hell, you need everything new—dungarees, boondockers, the whole shebang."

"Hey, Captain," Brushmore interrupted. "I think we oughta issue him a flamethrower instead of a BAR. Moe always wanted a flamethrower. Remember how hard he worked to get one back on the Canal?"

I ignored Brushmore's joke. "There's something else I need to tell you, Captain," I said, and described my confrontation with the Navy nurse.

"Hot damn, Moe," McNail said. "You've had a busy day. She's probably calling Colonel Maxim right now. Top, go in and call your friend in Colonel Maxim's office. When her call comes in, have him transfer it to me. I'll tell the bitch we never heard of the guy she's after." He turned back to me. "It will take the Navy a month to sort things out and catch up with you. We can take care of a court

301

martial later." He winked at me. "We're sure proud to have you back, Moe." I was so happy I could have jumped over a coconut tree.

Top-sergeant Brushmore turned toward the company head-quarters tent, stopped, came back. "You know, Captain," he said, "we're so short of dungarees we can only issue one pair to Moe, and I'm not so sure I can find a cap to fit his bull head. What he needs to do tomorrow is look for his seabag in that pile they brought up from Guadalcanal. How about five volunteers to help Moe find his seabag first thing in the morning?"

I wondered why five volunteers would be needed to help find a seabag. Brushmore gestured toward the Quonset huts at the edge of camp. "While we were on Okinawa, the rear echelon moved everything from Guadalcanal and set up camp here on Guam. All the 6th Division seabags were piled in those Quonset huts. The rear echelon guys who did the job must have been drunk, because they didn't store them in any orderly way—just piled them in. The 22d Marines' seabags got mixed in with ours. Some of the 29th regiment's got piled on top. When we got back here from Okinawa, it took most of us a week to dig through the piles to find ours. Wait till you see that damned mess."

There was a generous beer issue that night: it was based on the number of men we were supposed to have in a full-strength company, usually around 186. Since the company had suffered 82 percent casualties on Okinawa, however, and had received only about forty replacements after its return to Guam, each man got eight cans of Pabst Blue Ribbon. Colonel Maxim deliberately delayed the event until about eight o'clock, hoping, he said, that by that time we'd have eaten at least some of Move-the-Line Sledd's liver and beans. As we gathered in the company street waiting for the arrival of the beer truck and trying our best to forget what Sledd's minions had dumped into our mess gear an hour before, Duff Chapman wandered up, spotted me, and hurried over.

"I hear you got a bad one, Moe," he said.

"It was close," I said. "I'm lucky I'm still in one piece. I'm lucky I still got my right arm."

"I'm doing a lot better since I saw you last," he said. "Take a look." He thrust his hands in front of me. They were trembling only slightly.

"You're doing a lot better," I said. I looked at his lips: only a slight tremor there. "A whole hell of a lot better."

At dusk the day we'd driven the Japs off Half Moon, E Company had dug in along the crest of the hill, and what was left of F Company had moved back to fortify a hillock between Sugar Loaf and Half Moon. The night was mostly quiet, the Japs firing a few mortar shells now and then to let us know they were still out there. Early next morning we headed back to Half Moon to relieve Company E so that they could hurry off to Sugar Loaf and attack toward the sea.

We walked up Half Moon single file, no Jap machine gunners shooting at us as they had the day before, only Bill Flann, an E Company sergeant coming halfway down the hill to meet us and guide us to the positions we would occupy on the line. As point man in our column, I was still fifty yards from where Flann waited near a ruined Jap pillbox when Duff Chapman trotted past me with a message for Flann from Captain McNail. Duff was within five yards of Bill and had raised his hand in greeting when a Jap mortar shell came fluttering in, detonated on Bill's helmet, and blew half his head away. His body tumbled forward, practically at Duff's feet.

Duff was not hit by anything that would penetrate. What hit him were bits of flesh and blood and some concussion and a monstrous psychic shock. I rushed up, saw there was nothing left to be done for Bill Flann, and turned toward Duff. He was standing exactly where he had stood when the shell exploded, right arm still half extended, eyes glazed. He was shaking uncontrollably from head to foot.

Our corpsman had arrived, and the other guys from the platoon were coming up. "Keep right on moving! Don't bunch up here!" I hollered. I pulled out my poncho and spread it over Bill's upper body. It would not be an encouraging sight for some of our young replacements.

"Where are you hit, Duff?" the corpsman asked. Duff struggled to speak but no sound came except that of chattering teeth. Finally he did manage to shake his head, and a few minutes later to mutter haltingly that he was all right. The corpsman led him off to a tree stump and sat him down. Duff crouched there stunned and shaking.

The men from E Company began filing by toward the rear, and the F Company riflemen and machine gunners scattered to the foxholes and gun emplacements E Company had left behind. Duff merely sat on his tree stump shaking. He was beginning to regain his ability to speak, and to anyone who approached he mumbled his apologies. "I'm trying, I'm trying. I'm trying to stop. I can't stop this damned shaking."

Captain McNail came up. "Do you want to go back, Duff?" he said.

"No, not back. No, sir."

"Can you take a message to Colonel Maxim?" McNail said. "I'll write it out."

Duff nodded, rose, accepted the note, and headed back across the mile or so to the cave where Colonel Maxim had set up regimental headquarters. For three days Duff did his duty, carrying messages here and there, shaking, always shaking, the involuntary tremors never ceasing. On the fourth day Colonel Maxim ordered him back to the aid station. Unable to eat, scarcely able to hold a canteen to his lips long enough to drink, he required stronger medicine than could be provided in the combat zone.

I had not expected to see him again, but here he was, our company scholar back with the outfit, his hands now nearly steady. Duff Chapman—skinny, intellectual, defenseless—did not look much like a Marine. But he was, and a good one. Even Bill Werden would attest to that.

"Have you seen Bill Werden?" I asked.

Duff smiled. "Thought by association, Moe," he said. "Bill was here until yesterday. He and Mother and a half dozen guys from Scouts and Snipers have gone on ahead. You'll see him in Japan."

A six-by-six pulled up with a load of beer, and Galvo blew beer call, a jazzy, unofficial rip-roaring couple of bars from "Roll Out the Barrel." The first time he had heard Galvo blast out this unauthorized rendition back on Guadalcanal, Colonel Maxim had summoned Major Bank with the intention of placing Galvo inside a small, barbed-wire enclosure. In his quiet way, Bank had persuaded the colonel to postpone that impromptu sentence until after the invasion of Guam. Galvo, Bank argued, might be needed to blow colors when we recaptured the old Marine barracks. Now as the last hot notes of Galvo's beer call floated off toward Agana, Colonel Maxim only shook his head in a kind of groggy disbelief.

"I'd as soon listen to the howl of a banshee or an incoming shell," he muttered and, helping himself to a half case of beer, marched disgustedly off toward regimental headquarters.

The party that followed the beer issue began sluggishly. We were all somewhat subdued. For long months, even before the last great battle on Okinawa, we had been preparing ourselves, consciously and perhaps subconsciously, for the biggest and surely the deadliest battle of them all—the invasion of Japan. It had required all the resources and will of the Navy and Marine Corps and a significant force from the U. S. Army to wipe out the Japanese defenders of Okinawa and Iwo Jima. In those campaigns we had killed nearly 150,000 men. We would have to end the lives of fifty times that many human beings to conquer Japan, and there was no doubt in our minds that in the doing we would lose at least two million men.

Now, in late August 1945, even though the 4th Marines were scheduled to land in Japan right at the hornet's nest in Tokyo Bay, there would be no gunfire, no resistance at all. There would be no boatloads of Marines blasted out of the water by Jap high-speed guns, no men fragmented on the beaches by machine gun fire and shrapnel. No land mines, no grenades, no knee mortars, no samurai swords, no long, wicked bayonets. There would be no pillboxes to be blasted by nitrostarch or burned out by flamethrowers, no fortified hills to be overrun. There would be no foxholes to dig, no fire lanes to select, no barbed wire to string, no grenades to stockpile, no rifles to load nor knives to ready for the long, long nights and the deadly banzais that we always expected. There would be no more days in the mud or nights in the rain. There would be no enemy shells whistling, no stretcher bearers struggling with their torn loads, no doctors and corpsmen laboring frantically over dying men. And, perhaps most incredible of all, there would be no more of the insinuating, oppressive anxieties and fears that precede battle; no more of the euphoria of victory and the bleak despair of defeat.

The whole implication of it was difficult to adjust to and absorb. No longer would we have to postpone or oblige ourselves to forget those simple aspirations involving home, sweethearts, family, friends. No longer would we be required by hard and continuing circumstance to think thoughts of war, our expectations limited to the next firefight, the next bloody invasion, our memories, after nearly three years of gathering, crowded with vivid recollections of fearsome and tragic things. We had had to at least partially obliterate or modify those memories with the protective blanket of a callous cynicism.

Without the slightest warning, we now had to realign our thinking and abandon the whole psychology of war. This would not be easy; it would take time. That night, as we lined up at the truck, each man collecting his eight bottles of beer seemed a bit befuddled, a bit subdued.

Later, beer in hand, about thirty of us gathered in the company street in front of Top-sergeant Brushmore's tent, opened our introductory can, and drank it slowly, speaking at first in low, solemn tones. For a while it was a no-nonsense crowd. We had brought ration boxes, five-gallon cans, and grenade crates to sit on, and we lounged there trading accounts of what unfortunate, permanent thing had happened to whom. Considering the magnitude of our losses, it was not a happy information exchange.

An hour went by. The tropic moon was rising quickly over Pago Bay. Someone produced a mouth organ and blew softly into it. I asked about Mauvin and was told that he had been wounded the day before Okinawa had been secured. We had never managed to steal his mouth organ and throw it over the side of the LST, as we had gleefully planned.

Our present musician, who was not handicapped by several missing reeds, began with a few merry tunes and presently was joined by Galvo and his bugle. As they played a flourish or two in the background, we began a series of toasts.

"May old Arch-your-balls Vandegrift fry in hell for breaking up the Raiders!" Brushmore shouted. We drank heartily.

"May Howling Mad Smith fry in hell for killing off half the Marine Corps!" yelled Reardon. We drank heartily.

"And here's to our old and dear friend Tokyo Rose, for all her dirty stories and clean music!" yelled Reardon. We drank. I couldn't recall that Tokyo Rose had told dirty stories, but her Bing Crosby records were generally superior, although they were beginning to be pretty scratchy and worn by the time we'd taken the ride to Okinawa.

"To the emperor's birthday!" yelled Corella. We realized that we had forgotten to celebrate this event in 1945; we apologized to one another for the oversight.

"It probably wasn't a very happy birthday for him this year anyway," said Reardon. "And we were doing about as much shooting on his birthday this year as we did on Guadalcanal in '44."

"Right," said Brushmore, suddenly serious. "Maybe we should drink to the emperor's birthday in 1946. Here's hoping by that time, the scrawny son of a bitch is dangling by his neck from a rope."

We drank long and unanimously to that. The evening began to move more rapidly. We became cheerful, even boisterous. The mouth organ player was inspired by Galvo, and the melodies became more bawdy and repetitive.

Galvo had blown taps some time ago, but we had ignored the summons. Even as midnight approached, no one tried to remind us that tomorrow would be an active day. We decided to have a shoot-down-the-coconuts contest before turning in. The company had an ample supply of live ammunition left over from the last few days on Okinawa, and we reckoned it was time to rid ourselves of some of it. With the war over, however, we were already beginning to be civilized: we left our mortars and machine guns in our tents and restricted our shooting to M-1s and BARs. I knew my doctor on Saipan would disapprove, but I slapped a magazine into the BAR Brushmore had issued me that afternoon and fired twenty rounds full automatic, feeling once more the deadly surge of power up and forward as the bullets blasted away. It was the last time I would ever fire a BAR.

About one in the morning, the island commander or some other killjoy sent a company of MPs our way; but by that time we had cleaned our weapons and dropped off to sleep. Our slumber was interrupted by the abrupt, demanding rhythm of reveille at exactly 0530. Now that World War II was said to be over, the Marine Corps was apparently rising early to begin preparing for the next one. As a brief concession, however, Colonel Maxim had decided that for at least a week we would spend only twenty minutes on calisthenics each morning, instead of the usual half hour. Captain McNail and Top-sergeant Brushmore, brimming with disgusting enthusiasm, were dancing around right up front.

McNail had been inclined to excuse me from calisthenics, but Brushmore had objected. "Hell, Captain," he growled, "he wasn't hit in the legs—only in the arm and side, and he didn't absorb enough concussion to crack a beer mug. He's been sitting around on his ass getting fat and sloppy like some rear echelon swab jockey."

McNail had thought it over for a minute and then yelled, "You're right, Top! We got to force him to get in shape or he won't

308

be worth a crap when we get to Japan. Get your ass in there with the other slopeheads, Moe. Exercise those legs! Swing that left arm!"

"And don't pull any stitches in your right arm either," ordered Brushmore loudly, "or we'll throw your ass in the brig!" There were yelps of glee from the ranks. Brushmore's red moustache bristled. "Knock it off, you bastards!"

I felt a burst of contentment. It was great to be home.

Once we had for the thousandth time forced down a few mouthfuls of Move-the-Line Sledd's morning bilge, my five volunteers and I headed off to find my seabag. Joining us was Brushmore, issuing orders and organizing the hunt. When we arrived at the Quonset huts and large tents where the division seabags were piled, I realized once again how grievous our losses on Okinawa had been. Dead men do not return to claim seabags, nor do those who have been seriously wounded. Those unclaimed bags were stacked floor to ceiling—6, 8, 10 bags to a stack—row upon endless row. When the 6th Division had sailed from Guadalcanal, some 20,000 bags had been left behind, each packed with the clothing and special keepsakes of the individual Marine, each stenciled on the bottom with the man's first initial and last name. Now there were probably 15,000 to 18,000 still unclaimed. Building after building, tent after tent was piled high with seabags waiting to be claimed. Most of them never would be.

"It ain't going to be easy," said Brushmore.

We lingered for a few solemn moments a step inside the door of the first Quonset hut. It was one of the rare instances when no one of our usually talkative group had a word to say. I glanced quickly at my friends. All of them had the same look, the look of men listening to the last sad notes of taps as they stand at attention near the open grave of an old friend and are determined not to cry.

The seabag: long ago adopted by Marines because of their ancient association with sailors and ships and the sea. A Marine's one private place in a society almost devoid of privacy, it is a cylindrical bag of heavy khaki-colored canvas into which each man stores all those possessions not belted around his middle or carried in pack and knapsack or worn on his person. About three feet long and a foot in diameter, the seabag is usually stuffed with a remarkable assortment of things practical, frivolous, sentimental: dress greens, caps, and low-cut shoes for formal affairs (and thus seldom worn); two or three khaki uniforms for less formal occasions; three or four pairs of green dungarees with caps to match, the everyday dress for routine training and working parties; a couple of blankets and a shelter half or two; an extra pair of work shoes, or boondockers; a half dozen pairs of shorts and a dozen pairs of socks; a three-gallon bucket of light metal and a heavy scrub brush; a small bag or box containing shaving gear and other toilet articles.

What space remains is crammed with more personal belongings: perhaps an extra knife or dagger, a pistol, a book or two, a few extra cans of rations, a half dozen clips or magazines of ammunition, knickknacks, and souvenirs. Hidden away in small containers are the precious, secret things: a special picture of a wife or sweetheart; a sheaf of letters from the girl in the picture or, in some cases, from different girls in several pictures; a collection of letters and photographs from the home folks with their frequent, poignant reminders to their man at war to stay alive, to please come home.

As we stood there quietly that long moment contemplating those seabags piled row on row, perhaps 2,000 in this Quonset hut alone, I thought of Pappy Schultz who had made not a sound when the fatal bullet struck him while we crouched side by side in that shallow Jap trench in Naha. Somewhere among all these bags was one that belonged to him. Pappy would not be coming to reclaim his bag. Neither would Cannon, nor Jamal the Ghoul. What would finally happen to those bags and their contents? What would eventually be done with Cannon's meat axe, Jamal's makeshift tools, Pappy Schultz's letters from home and the pictures of his wife and little girl?

"All right, goddammit," said Brushmore suddenly, his bark a bit husky, "let's get at it!"

310

It was a grim business, made much more difficult because the men who stacked those bags had obviously been in a hurry. Not only had the bags of the 29th and 22d regiments been piled helter skelter with the bags of the 4th, but for a week or so after the remnants of the regiments had returned to Guam, several thousand men had ripped through whatever logical arrangement there might have been and converted it to chaos. Nevertheless we began, gradually checking through the stacks. Where some order remained, our search was easy. But we often came to places where the stacks had tumbled. There we had to go through the bags one by one, searching for that single elusive name.

Every half hour or so we chanced on the name of someone we knew: W. W. Williamson. The night before the attack on Oroku, he and I had promised each other that we would no longer stick our heads up over a ridge line when we wanted to view what was on the other side. We had agreed that the proper thing to do was to stick up head *and* shoulders. Then if a Jap rifleman was out there, he might shoot at your chest and not your head. Chest wounds are not pleasant, but at least the chance of surviving one ranges from fair to good. Those hit in the head seldom survive. Unfortunately, Williamson forgot the agreement.

J. Brown. Shot by a Jap in a spider trap. Brown never saw the Jap that killed him.

B. Barnwell. Bayoneted by a Jap during a banzai. In all the excitement of a Jap charging in his direction, Barnwell pulled the safety instead of the trigger. By the time he realized his mistake, it was too late.

A. Sanchez. Killed by a chunk of shrapnel from one of our destroyer's 5-inch guns. The shell exploded hundreds of yards ahead of us during a softening-up bombardment before our attack on Mt. Yaetake, but one large fragment came whirring back where we waited.

B. Reeves. Shot through the spine during the 4th Marine attack on Half Moon Hill. Paralyzed from the waist down.

311

D. Usalis. Badly burned in a freak accident. The afternoon before we moved up to relieve the 29th Marines, Usalis and a buddy were lounging near an Okinawan tomb when one of our torpedo bombers came roaring in low after a bombing mission against Sugar Loaf Hill. Several miles behind us, a battery of our 105-millimeter cannon were firing, their shells going over only a couple of hundred feet above us. An outbound shell hit the inbound torpedo plane head on. The plane went down, crashed very close to Usalis, and exploded. Although Usalis was burned over most of his body, he was still alive when he was carried away.

J. Leon, 1st Lieutenant, Platoon Leader. Cracked up when a 14-inch shell practically wiped out his platoon.

None of them would ever return to reclaim their seabags.

The morning ended; Galvo blew chow call. "They only got shark for chow today," said Bontadelli. We agreed that we had eaten enough shark to last a lifetime and worked on, searching, searching, through stack after stack, pile after pile, bag after bag. Once in a while we stopped to drink lukewarm water from our canteens and to plot new strategies. Afternoon came and late afternoon. Galvo blew colors. It was sundown. In five minutes it would be too dark to see.

"It's time to call it a day," said Art Corella. "I've looked at so damned many brown bags, I'll be seeing brown all night."

"We must have gone through three or four thousand," Brushmore added. "We'll try again tomorrow. I'll ask Captain McNail to let us off from calisthenics. Sledd can give us a few pancakes, and we'll get over here early." He looked at me. "If we don't find your bag tomorrow, Moe, we'll have to forget it. Maybe we better get five more volunteers to help out."

Next morning we continued the search, this time with ten men and Brushmore. That second morning went on toward noon. Our band of volunteers was tired and pessimistic. An average day on Guam is very hot and very humid. Sweating heavily through our dungarees, we stopped for a short break.

312

"Are you sure you had a seabag, Moe?" said John Reardon. The most patient man in the company, even he was losing his momentum. We were in the fourth Quonset hut we had checked that morning and had not run across a single bag belonging to anyone we knew.

"I think we ain't even in the right regiment," Art Corrella said, giving a disgusted kick to a stack of eight or nine seabags. The pile tottered and fell; we were just able to scramble out of the way.

"For Christ's sake, Art, watch what you're doing. We've had enough casualties," Brushmore said. He looked at the bags scattered by Art's kick. "Well, I'll be damned." He pointed to one of the bags. "Moe, it's right at your feet!" I looked down. There was my seabag.

We ripped it open. The first thing I looked for was the extra pair of boondockers I had left behind. Before leaving for Okinawa, we had each been issued a new pair. Most of the guys had thrown their old ones away, but I had kept mine. They were pretty badly worn, but good for a couple more months. I threw aside the oversize slippers the Army hospital had given me and pulled on the old shoes. My dungarees I pulled out and donned right on the spot. I found a proper cap that fit, and I was ready to go to Japan.

Next day we boarded ship and, sometime during the night, shoved off for Tokyo Bay.

First Wave

Technically the war was over, but we were still wary. The convoy of LSTs, transports, destroyers, and cruisers kept a sharp lookout for subs, and the ships were blacked out at night. There was always the possibility that some Japanese submarine commander might not have gotten the word to surrender, or perhaps might have decided to go on fighting a private war.

During the voyage to Japan, a linguist, one of a dozen hurriedly sent out to Guam from Honolulu, gave us a crash course on a few Japanese phrases. It was not the first time we had been so counseled. Back at Camp Pendleton in 1942, a Marine sergeant freshly returned from Guadalcanal had labored to teach our company the Japanese words for "Hands up!" and "Surrender!" He had been intent on doing what he had been ordered to do. But since he had survived several of the bloodiest battles on Guadalcanal and had discovered a few things about the Japanese attitude toward surrender, he emphasized that the most practical approach was to shoot first and cry "Hands up!" maybe ten minutes later.

Our pragmatic sergeant had ultimately told us that if we really desired to give a Japanese soldier a chance to throw up his hands, the proper expression was something that to my ears sounded like "Data koy!" It had the ring of Latin to me, although Cole and Faltynski were certain that the sergeant had actually forgotten the real words. Our tutor for the 1945 refresher course really did seem

314

to know Japanese and was more intent on teaching it to us than our reluctant sergeant had been.

Teki ni kofuku suru—pronounced "tekinoo coughkoo suh-rew," he told us—means "submit, surrender." *Tewatasu*, pronounced "teewatuh-sue," means "hand over your weapon" or "give up your weapon." *Ryote ageru*, pronounced "rye-oh-tu-ah-ger-oo," means "raise both hands." There were a few other expressions, but for our purposes in accepting the surrender of Japanese units around Tokyo Bay, these, our instructor assured us, would suffice.

After this instruction session, we wandered about yelling Japanese phrases at each other until our imprecise repetition converted the terms to "up your sursu" and "riot now ah gon screw you." Finally, Colonel Maxim threatened to have our ship converted to a prison hulk in which we could plan to spend the years 1945 to 1950. Subdued, we became more serious until we were at last able to pronounce the surrender terms with an accuracy of perhaps 60 percent. Linguistically armed for the great day of the Japanese surrender, we cleaned and loaded our weapons one last time, after being cautioned maybe twenty times over not to put a round in the firing chamber and not, under any circumstances, to have an accidental discharge, or we would immediately be keel-hauled and then drawn and quartered. A single chance shot might, it was generally believed, scare MacArthur all the way back to Brisbane and delay the whole surrender ceremony for weeks.

We landed in Japan on 27 August. To be sure that the Japanese really intended to surrender, the 4th Marines hit the beach all around Tokyo Bay and sent squads in every direction to secure or destroy the cannon the Japanese had emplaced there and to make certain that the gun crews had adopted the correct attitude of submission. People like MacArthur and Nimitz did not want any stray 14-inch shells coming their way from a shore battery whose crew had not received from their emperor the magic word *desist*.

Intelligence had reported that we could expect to find a few Japanese gun emplacements on the east side of Tokyo Bay, an assessment based, of course, on the usual flyboy underestimate. In fact, we had advanced less than two hundred yards inland from the beach before encountering the first big gun, a 5-inch cannon in a bunker with walls of reinforced concrete three feet thick. It was typical of those that Marine outfits knocked out on Guam, Saipan, Iwo, and Okinawa, with the loss of many men.

As we approached, we had the strange feeling that Japanese machine guns would begin firing on us at any moment. Instead, the ten men of the 5-inch-gun crew and the supporting machine gunners and riflemen stood at attention in front of their bunker. Overhead, a large, white flag waved in the morning breeze. The whole of F Company gathered round and watched the Japanese gun captain come forward and hand over his samurai sword. Captain McNail accepted it without a word and detailed a couple of men to herd the Japanese to a collection point back at the beach.

The company moved on, spreading out now into a thin skirmish line across a thousand-yard front. We entered a pine forest and began encountering gun emplacements hidden throughout the trees. It soon became obvious that to secure all the guns and accept the surrender of each gun crew, the company would have to be split into fire groups of no more than three or four men. In that pine forest, the Japs had an unbelievable number of guns emplaced and skillfully hidden—anything from 40-millimeter anti-aircraft rifles to huge 12-inch naval cannon.

During a short break, Top-sergeant Brushmore came panting up to the 3d Platoon. "Holy Jesus!" he exclaimed. "Compared to what this death trap would have been, Okinawa was a two-month vacation. We've already secured thirty-eight gun emplacements and over a hundred cannon. If we'd made a combat landing here, we never would have made it to the beach."

Brushmore was closely followed by Red Salleng, who had returned to the outfit the day we left Guam. Red pointed to a grove of pines two hundred yards ahead. A white flag flew above the trees. It was about the size of a bed sheet. "Moe, take two men and check that out!"

"Two men?" I said. "Hell, Red, there might be a company of Japs there. I better take the whole squad."

"We can't spare a squad, goddammit! Too many Jap guns. Too many of the bastards trying to surrender. Now take your men and get your ass over there!"

I beckoned to a couple of young Marines who had joined us a day or two before we'd left Guam. They looked about fifteen. I didn't even know their names.

"You two," Salleng was sizing them up. He didn't know their names either. "Are your rifles loaded?"

"Yes, sir!" They were a chorus.

"Unload them," said Salleng. "We're too far along toward peace to have any accidental discharges." He turned to me. "Moe, how about your BAR?"

"I've never had an accidental discharge, and I ain't going to have one today. I'm not going to unload this BAR either. There might be some crazy Japs out there."

"Keep the safety on and the bolt forward then," said Red.

"That's the way I got it, Red." I held the BAR up so he could see for himself. "I'm sure not planning to start another war."

"Go then. Get the hell gone!" he ordered. As we trotted off we could hear him sending three more men off in another direction.

The gun emplacement so cleverly hidden in the pines was a big one—four 9-inch cannon, their long barrels tilted off toward the center of Tokyo Bay. As we came up to the emplacement out of a cluster of low trees, we saw lined up at the gun platform under the white flag a platoon-size contingent of Japs, all in white, a single blue-clad figure standing a few paces in front of them. Seeing us, he swung to face his men and uttered a single command. They snapped to a rigid attention. Then, doing a flawless about-face, he saluted us, bowed, and came forward. Two paces from me he stopped, bowed again, straightened, uttered a few words in Japanese, and handed me a key. Then, bowing more deeply than before, he stepped back and came smartly to attention.

317

It was the first day I had ever seen any Japanese soldiers who were not shooting or running or screaming or dying or lying dead. I examined the key while thirty-six Japanese and two young Marines watched me and waited. It was a large key, not fancy, well worn through the brass plating to the base metal below. It appeared to be of a type used to unlock a large padlock or to fit the keyhole of a very substantial door. What was its significance? What was it intended to unlock?

I looked up at the man who had surrendered it to me. Solemn and inscrutable, he remained stiffly at attention. I turned to my two young companions. They were puzzled, too. Nobody knew what to do next. We stared at the Japanese soldiers; they stared back.

I switched my BAR to my left hand and with my right, I waved the key in front of their leader and shrugged. He bowed once more and smiled, revealing a double row of gold crowns.

"He better not get too close to Blackie and his pliers," one of the young Marines muttered. They both snickered. They had already heard of Blackie's tendency to go for the gold.

"Knock it off!" I said, without thinking. "You'll get this guy so confused he won't know his ass from his gold." It was about time, I realized suddenly, for me to secede from the Corps. I was beginning to sound like a damned top-sergeant.

The Japanese leader was bowing again, and the thirty-five men lined up on the gun platform were still at attention, still solemn. I supposed it would be appropriate to say "Surrender!" in Japanese, but I could not remember the right expression. Time was passing while I pondered, everyone waiting breathlessly. Frustrated and uncertain, I made a slight motion with my Browning automatic. Thirty-five pairs of hands shot toward the sky.

Again I waved the key in front of the gold-toothed one. His arms were still at his sides. I waved the key once more, pointed to my head, and shook it from side to side.

"Ah!" he said suddenly in a cross between a cough and a hiss. Half turning, he pointed toward a building in the open area beyond the gun platform. Now we were beginning to get somewhere. I handed over the key and waved for him to precede me. As I followed, I realized that the gun crew, all thirty-five of them, were still standing stiffly, arms held high. I made a down gesture with the BAR. As one man, they went to their knees, heads bowed, looks of dismay on their countenances as if they expected immediate execution.

"For Christ's sake!" I said. Behind me I heard my two young privates laughing. "Knock it off, you dumb bastards!" I shouted. I looked again at the thirty-five Japs on their knees. They were sweating, although the morning sun was not yet providing much heat. "Oh, for Christ's sake, stay there then," I said and hurried off after my gold-toothed friend. He was several yards ahead, halting at the door to the building he had pointed out to me. It was maybe thirty by twenty feet, of rough boards, and had a metal roof painted green to blend with the surrounding trees. Inserting the key into a large padlock, he popped it open and pushed the door inward. Inside, stacked neatly along one wall, were the rifles and Nambus of the gun crew. Everywhere else in the building, piled to the rafters, were row upon row of the huge shells for the 9-inch guns themselves.

"Ah," I said to my gold-toothed friend. "Mucho boom-boom."

There were rapid footsteps behind me. It was one of the interpreters who had been assigned to the company. "What the hell are all those guys doing down on their knees out there?" he asked.

"I waved my BAR at them and down they went," I said. "They expect us to shoot them. Get the hell on out there and tell them to relax." I pointed to my Japanese guide. "Take him with you and tell him to quit bowing." The interpreter said a few Japanese words and the two of them hustled off to get the gun crew up off their knees. A few minutes later, when I joined the group, they were standing around smiling and chattering like kids on a holiday. One of them, bolder than the others, looked at me and rattled off some Nipponese.

"He wants to know if they can smoke," the interpreter said.

"It's OK, I guess," I said. "Hell, the war's over."

A half dozen Seabees came up and dismantled the breech mechanisms on the guns.

"There's a shed full of small arms and 9-inch shells back there," I said, pointing to the building.

"OK," one of them said. "We'll take care of them. You and your Jap buddies can take off for Tokyo."

We lined up the Japanese in a loose formation, marched them back to a collection point, and handed them over to the MPs.

Once we had secured the big Japanese guns, we were ferried across Tokyo Bay to the naval base at Yokosuka. We moved into the barracks the Japanese had vacated. After we had set up our cots and tossed our few belongings on them, we stood around waiting for orders. Captain McNail soon brought them: we were free to wander around the base but not to go into the inhabited areas nearby. We were not to have any contact with Japanese civilians.

Although a few of our men were already entertaining ideas about seductive geisha girls, most had no thought of associating with an enemy we had come to despise. When we were dismissed, we scattered in every direction to explore the area and to hunt for souvenirs. The harbor was filled with smashed up Japanese battleships, cruisers, and destroyers. But one battleship, older and smaller than the others, rested in concrete moorings along a nearby dock. The ship was virtually undamaged; it still flew, in a last gesture of defiance, a very large Japanese flag. About ten of us rushed aboard and headed toward that flag: it would be a priceless souvenir.

Werden was already on board. He had been there, he told us, since a few hours before. He had found the flag in what he supposed was the admiral's cabin; for the fun of it, he had run it up to scare hell out of all the rear echelon bastards like MacArthur and the British and Russian sons of bitches signing the peace treaty on the battleship *Missouri*. Apparently, in all the panoply aboard the *Missouri*, no one had aimed a pair of binoculars in the direction of Yokosuka. No one had noticed that the banner of the rising sun still flew above the flagship that, we assumed, Admiral Togo had captained and on which a young ensign named Yamamoto had served during the Russo-Japanese war.

"It's about time to pull it down," Werden said. "It's time to lower it before some damned officers show up and try to run off with it."

Slowly, respectfully, he hauled it down, untied it from its lines, and spread it on the polished deck. It was a very large flag, perhaps ten by fifteen feet of the purest silk with bright crimson streamers against a snow-white background. We had fought a war despising everything that flag represented, but we stood there looking down at it in a strange, silent appreciation.

"What're you going to do with it, Bill?" I asked.

"I'm going to put it back where I found it," he said. "Back in the admiral's cabin." He produced a key. "I'm going to lock it back in its drawer so no one can steal it away."

We were amazed. "You must have got more concussion on Okinawa than any of us knew about, Bill," someone said. "That flag is worth a fortune."

By now Werden was down on one knee, carefully folding the flag.

"It's worth more than a fortune," said Corella. "Some dogface or swab jockey would give you a truckload of whiskey for it."

Werden had finished folding the flag. We followed him into the admiral's cabin and watched as he stowed it away, locked the small compartment that held it, and headed back onto the main deck. One by one, we followed. On the main deck, Werden halted, looking out across the placid waters of Tokyo Bay. "I've killed a hundred Japs," he said. "I've killed more than that. If I had my way we'd kill every bastard on these islands, plow the damned place with bulldozers, and spread salt. But this old ship is history. We'll leave the flag."

One hour later the Navy threw a cordon of armed swab jockeys around the old ship. From that moment it was off limits to all but the mighty.

Next day while our battalion settled once more into a routine of exercise, drill, and guard duty, the Scouts and Snipers were sent off on a special detail. It was obviously some kind of hurry-up job because we saw them, fully armed, loading into a fast new destroyer that pulled out in a rush as soon as the last man was on board. Several of us who had hurried to the dock to see them off spotted Bill Werden waving and calling something that sounded like bomb, or maybe Guam.

The destroyer had no more than faded into the distance when word came that all survivors of the original 4th Raiders were to report to Colonel Maxim on the double. As I hurried off toward the colonel's office, I was joined by Reardon, Red Salleng, and Corella.

We caught up with Top-sergeant Brushmore. "What's the scoop, Top?" Red asked him.

"How the hell would I know," said Brushmore. "I ain't the colonel's confessor."

As soon as Colonel Maxim was sure our group had arrived, he ordered Major Bank to make a head count. There were, Bank reported, 48 men left out of the original 1,000.

"Any bastard that ain't here, answer up!" shouted Colonel Maxim. There was the usual appreciative laughter. "Here's the word!" said Colonel Maxim, grinning. "You people are going home. You got the points according to the latest regulation put out by Fleet Marine Force."

We let go with a loud, spontaneous cheer.

"Knock it off!" the colonel bellowed. "Hell, you bastards just got here. I don't mean to Japan. I mean to the Pacific. Hell, some of you ain't even been in for a four-year hitch." Everyone was grinning at him. "And knock off those damned self-satisfied smirks," he ordered. "Maybe I can get the damned regulation changed. Anyway you got two weeks to get your asses ready. So get the hell out of here and get started!"

We had turned and started away when the colonel suddenly shouted "Halt! Goddammit, I said halt!" We halted, turned. "I got one more thing to say," he said, looking as if the next words were coming hard. "You bastards did a good job." We stood there silently for a moment, no one saying anything, savoring the words. "Now you can get your asses out of my sight!" Maxim shouted.

Right after roll call next morning Captain McNail called me into his office. Top-sergeant Brushmore was there, grinning. "Moe," said McNail, "we have been informed by the United States Army that you are away without leave from one of their hospitals." He looked at the paper he held. "I believe it's the hospital on Saipan. They say they want you back so they can finish doing a vulcanizing job on your arm, after which they plan to lock you up for the rest of your natural life. What say you to all this?"

Coached by Top-sergeant Brushmore, I had already rehearsed my lines. "I'm throwing myself on the mercy of the Marine Corps," I said.

"All right," said McNail, "I hereby fine you a dollar and sentence you to carry Top-sergeant Brushmore's tommy gun when he makes the rounds of the barracks tonight to check on all the drunks. To make the burden of a one dollar payment more tolerable, the Marine Corps is presenting you with a carton of Lucky Strike cigarettes."

"Moe doesn't smoke, Captain," Brushmore said.

"All right, cigarettes rescinded. Give him a bottle of that putrid Jap sake or maybe that barrel of wood alcohol we liberated yesterday."

I accepted the sake. Next day McNail summoned me once more. "You're getting to be a damned nuisance around here, Moe," he said. "Now we get word that the Navy wants to have you horsewhipped for insubordinating a female nurse lieutenant. I've never heard of it. How did you manage it?"

"I attacked her ego," I said.

"Does that mean you plead guilty?"

"Yes, guilty!" I said. "I throw myself on the mercy of the Marine Corps."

"Guilty as charged," said McNail. "That will be a fine of one dollar. Pay the company clerk and get a receipt. I'm afraid we don't have any sake for you today, Moe. How about three bottles of 3.2 beer?"

I accepted.

"You're a free man," said McNail. "Free to get the hell out of here and take the next available transport to San Diego unless you want to reenlist for another four years. Although I still don't have the schedule for the next war, we do have some new BARs coming soon, or maybe you'd like to be assigned to flamethrowers."

Two weeks later we caught a transport bound for Guam, where we went ashore to a transient camp and waited for a ship headed for San Diego. The wait was not unpleasant. We had no duties. Reveille was at 7:00 a.m., followed by roll call, after which we lounged around and went our way. About the only order we received was to keep our rifles handy and someone on watch at night in each tent. There were still plenty of Jap stragglers in the hills and jungles of Guam—desperate, forsaken men who either had not received word of Japan's surrender or had decided to go on fighting their own war. A Marine unit was said to be out hunting them down; once in a while, we did hear the sound of distant gunfire, especially at night.

The third day on Guam, as I waited in the sunset beer line to buy a couple of cans of green Pabst Blue Ribbon, someone bumped into me rather forcefully. I whirled. There stood Bill Werden. "Watch that temper, Moe! Get you into a lot of trouble." He gave me a mock salute.

"You caught up with us," I said.

"No, you caught up with us," Bill said. "We've been here a month." He waved toward the line snaking along behind us, and I saw a half dozen other veterans from Scouts and Snipers.

"You've been here waiting for a ship for a month?" I said.

"We've been hunting Japs here for a month," Werden corrected. "The Army is building a big airstrip on the north end of the island. When some Jap stragglers started shooting at them, the damned flyboys began hollering for help. General Vandegrift or some other son of a bitch volunteered the Marine Corps for the job. Guess who

324

got the detail? The war has been over a month and we're still killing Japs. They act like they want to be killed; but there are a few mean ones like the bastards we ran into on Okinawa. We've had two killed and seven wounded. They got Braswell yesterday."

"Dead?" Braswell was one of the old timers.

"Dead! His BAR jammed and a Jap got off the first shot."

"Goddamn!" I said. "Why don't the chicken Army fight its own war?"

"That's what Captain Certin's been asking. We're supposed to be relieved in four or five days."

We got our beer and stood there sipping and talking a few minutes. Some of the other guys from Scouts and Snipers gathered near us, their voices muted and bitter. Werden emptied his second bottle. "Well, good luck, Moe," he said. "We're heading out on another kill mission at three in the morning. See you in the States."

"Hang loose, Bill," I said. "I'll see you in San Diego."

Two days later our ship arrived, and we lucky ones were on the way home. I never really expected to see Bill Werden again.

The Furtive Patah

There were no national homecoming celebrations for the Marines who fought the Pacific War, nor did we expect any. We had our home folks to welcome us and the battalions of pretty young women brimming with health and enthusiasm. And we had the G.I. Bill, the best method a nation has ever devised to tell its returning warriors "Well done!"

Taking immediate advantage of it, I was already enrolled at Saint Ambrose, a small Iowa college, by January of 1946. A Marine Corps buddy, Elmer Mapes, had enrolled the same day, and for two years we shared a room on campus. Our instructors were excellent, the chow was ten times as good as Move-the-Line Sledd's, our bunks had springs and mattresses, and beer was available only two blocks away.

One April day in 1946, I was wrestling with some problems in trig at my desk in our room. Suddenly I felt a rough object pulled across my throat. "You're a dead man, Moe!"

Bill Werden acted as if he were really pleased to see me; he seized my hand and shook it and actually patted me on the back. "We had some mean times together, Moe," he said, as if explaining why he had taken such an uncharacteristic liberty.

"But thank the Lord we never had to bring God out of reserve for the invasion of Japan," I said.

Werden laughed. "You remembered. The night we got the little boy. Anyway it's good to know He's still there in reserve if we ever really need Him."

"Are you still in the Corps, Bill?" I said. "Maybe teaching boot-camp clowns how to cut with a K-bar?"

Werden sat down on the edge of my desk. "I've got a job that pays better than the Corps. And nobody blows reveille, either."

"Holding up small California banks, I bet."

"Same old Moe," Werden said. "Smart, cynical bastard. No, I quit that job. Too much strain on the girls in the cages."

"What's your racket, then?"

He considered the question a few seconds. "I guess some folks would call me a special messenger. I get called in when people have a hard time settling their troubles. Right now I'm on my way to Chicago. I have to deliver a message to a couple of guys. Then I go on to Joliet for a meeting with a gentleman there. I'm four days ahead of schedule. Thought I'd drop off here and go to college with you scholars."

"Sure," I said. "We can find you an extra room in the dorm. I'm taking four courses. You'll like the logic class best—arguments, debate, confrontations, and a professor who was once a light heavyweight boxer."

"No need for the extra room," Werden said. "I'll bunk right here on the floor."

Werden was traveling light—just a single canvas bag not much larger than a briefcase. "I've got something here you'll remember," he said. He reached into the bag and pulled out his old special pistol, silencer and all.

"How come they let you keep that?" I said.

"Sent it back as a war souvenir," he said. "I kept the K-bar too, the stiletto the Raiders gave me, my tommy gun, and a dozen grenades. Once Captain Certin signed the permit, I boxed every-thing up and mailed it to General Delivery, La Jolla. When I got back to the States I picked it up at the post office. I still got about ten pounds of nitro too. Never can tell when these things will come in handy."

He had probably told me a little more than he would have ordinarily, but he knew it didn't matter. I had never repeated to anyone anything that Werden had told me in confidence.

Three days after Bill Werden boarded a Greyhound for Chicago, the newspapers there published several stories describing the abrupt demise of a fashionable denizen of the Loop who had, in his youth, been in the bump and run business for some suburban extortionists. After fifteen years he had repented, apologized to the world and underworld, and begun making his living by bribing certain Chicago judges, jurors, council members, and precinct committeemen.

He and a companion had been found in the Chicago River, each shot once in the head with what experts later announced was a .38-caliber pistol. The Chicago police rejoiced and assigned the investigation to a veteran detective and union steward who had never solved a case.

In Joliet, two days later, a well-known Chicago gangster expired, a missile from a considerable distance having caught him directly between the eyes. After a cursory study, the coroner announced that a .38-caliber pistol had probably done the job.

On the evening of the same day the gangster was killed, as Elmer Mapes and I sat enjoying a beer or three in a neighborhood bar, Bill Werden, lugging his canvas bag, sauntered in. He tossed the bag on the table, slid into the booth, and ordered two beers and two large, lean steaks. The Chicago assignment had gone very well, he told us, and he had had to spend only a couple of hours in Joliet that morning. "I thought I'd come by and waste the weekend with you two guys," he said. "Then I'm heading for St. Louis and back to the Coast."

A few days after Werden left for St. Louis, the papers announced a series of mishaps in that city. A drug dealer took a ten-story tumble from his suite in a downtown hotel; a thug was found in a St. Louis alley with his throat cut; and a gambling kingpin was stiffened by a deep stab wound in the lower abdomen. The coroner said that the wound had been inflicted with an unusual weapon, perhaps a large, long, and not very sharp screwdriver.

Although the St. Louis police had no witnesses, they were searching without enthusiasm for an extremely powerful man. "A man about as strong as the strongest gorilla in the woods," a police spokesman said, "and maybe twice as big as a defensive tackle for the Chicago Bears."

A few days later came a card from Bill Werden postmarked Las Vegas. His work in St. Louis had gone very well, he wrote; so well that he probably wouldn't be back in the Midwest for several months. Meantime, he wanted to thank us for letting him sleep on the floor of our room.

As the years went by, I would see and hear much more of Bill Werden. And he was not the only ex-Raider who was keeping in touch. In the year after the war's end I heard several times from Faltynski who, after being discharged from the Marines, had gone right back to his old job at Studebaker in South Bend. In one of his letters, Faltynski mentioned that he had run across Cole, who was bouncing around northern Indiana trying to organize a non-profit bingo league. When marriage in 1947 seemed like a good idea, I sent Faltynski an invitation and enclosed one for Cole.

As my wife of ten minutes and I walked up the aisle that morning, there they were, Faltynski and Cole and their own young wives, standing wide-eyed about three-fourths of the way back. They had driven the 240 miles from South Bend during the night and had arrived in time for the wedding. They seemed amazed at the sight of my pert, pretty, strawberry blonde bride, with all her curvy charms showing or suggested in spite of the long wedding gown.

At the reception, Faltynski went around bumming cigarettes and making friends. Cole spent his time scandalizing my new mother-in-law with apocryphal stories about Los Angeles "B-girls" and light-hearted New Zealand women. When he saw he had convinced her that I had been the Marine Corps' most determined libertine, he moved on to tell all my male relatives, in-laws, and

329

other friends that I had been wounded in the back on several occasions because every time I saw a Jap, including one peddling pornographic pictures in Yokosuka, I had run away.

Cole was in fact so busy spreading this kind of negative propaganda at our wedding reception that in all the excitement and action of that day, I was never able to corner him long enough to inquire about the furtive patah. During the post-war years, I considered from time to time the possibility of calling Cole to ask him about the furtive patah. Each time I discarded the idea, hoping first to discover its identity myself.

The furtive patah? What was it? A shy denizen of the deep forest, an apparition, a reluctant spirit? Finally I cornered the furtive patah in a remarkable place: the *United States Government Printing Office Style Manual*. There in the section on Hebrew was the patah lurking at the bottom of the second page.

> *The furtive patah*
> All vowels [in Hebrew] are pronounced as if they follow the consonant to which they are ascribed, with the exception of the final ה̣, which is pronounced not *ha*, but *ah*. This patah is termed "furtive patah."

I was so pleased with my discovery that I called Faltynski. He was even more elated than I. At the next Raider reunion, we agreed, we would put the question to Cole and relish his impromptu response. But for one reason or another, Cole didn't attend the next reunion, nor the one after that. And before we got the opportunity we were seeking, it was too late.

One summer day, Faltynski called from South Bend to tell me that Cole was in the intensive care ward of a hospital in La Porte. Several months before, he had begun complaining about headaches. The doctors diagnosed a brain tumor and operated. When Faltynski arrived at the hospital, Cole was in a deep coma and not expected to live. By the time I reached La Porte, my old friend was dead and the funeral already arranged for the next day.

At the funeral, Faltynski cried and Father Redmond, who had come all the way from California, cried, and a rabbi sitting next to Mel Blum and me seemed tearful. And as I sat there and the funeral moved on, I realized that now I would never again be able to ask my old friend about the furtive patah or anything else. And I began to feel tears in my eyes. I had to get my mind on some other subject or I would soon be weeping like Faltynski. I would, I decided as the eulogy began, construct a poem about the furtive patah. Beginning was easy.

> A furtive patah cast its spell
> On all the tribes of Israel.

The eulogist was addressing Cole's family, assuring them that a mild, devoted man like Bernard Cole would surely be warmly welcomed in that place where heroes go. I scarcely heard the words. My poem was creating itself.

> A furtive patah cast its spell
> On all the tribes of Israel.
> And in a game that patahs play,
> Stole every vowel sound away.

Perhaps one-fifth of my mind was still absorbing an occasional sentence from the oration—that Bernard Cole had been a man of character, which was true. He had been a character, all right. That Bernard Cole had been a good Marine, which was true. That Bernard Cole had been loyal to his friends, which was true, except when he was improvising some complex plan to confound us.

The tears were beginning to form again. I closed my mind to the eulogy and went back to the furtive patah, moving the words here and there until the rhymes arrived and the larger pattern of a third couplet emerged.

> Now that explains why Heaven's word
> At first in consonants was heard.

The speaker droned on, but my mind had focused successfully on the doings of the patah. The next couplet practically popped into existence.

331

> Until a Greek or Roman band
> Brought vowels to the Holy Land.

I was in full sail now, the earnest accolades fading to a background murmur.

> And told the world of Joseph's flight,
> Of Moses' law, Jehovah's might.
> And spread the Gospel wide and far,
> From Innisfree to Jamnagar.

The eulogy was over, the service now proceeding to the funeral's end. I had time to create a last quick stanza.

> Yet still the patah's spell abides
> Wherever Orthodox resides.
> There where the consonants abound,
> One often hears the furtive sound
> —of *patah*.

I got no further. The service ended, we went to the cemetery, heard the volley from the rifles, listened to the mournful notes of taps, and then we went away.

There was not much time for sadness in those days, the years rolling rapidly by as all of us ex-servicemen ran hard to catch up with those who had stayed at home. During one of those catch-up years, as the strawberry blonde and I were returning from a trip to the Far East, our flight from Manila made an unscheduled stop at Guam. Equipment trouble, the pilot announced. There would be a six-hour layover. We immediately left the plane and rented a car for a quick tour of Guam.

Leaving the airport, we turned right on Marine Drive toward Andersen Air Force Base at the north end of the island, then crossed the island to the east side and made a short stop where the Japanese had erected a monument to their soldiers who had died on Guam. Afterward we drove south to Pago Bay past the site of the 4th Marines' old camp. At Talofofo we stopped for a while, and I showed my wife the approximate spot where we had shot the Jap soldiers who had held the villagers in bondage. Leaving Talofofo, we drove south to the end of the island and turned north up the west side.

As we approached the village of Agat and the spot where the 4th Marines had come ashore on that July morning in 1944, I began to feel an increasing tension. It became a tightening anxiety as the highway came down from the hills and, a mile or so south of Agat, swung westward close to the sea. There from the highway I saw it, the spot where our amphibious tractors had churned up from the sea to a ripped and torn shore. The huge chunks of coral that had defeated our tractors were gone now, flattened, apparently, by heavy equipment, time, and the tide. But it was the place. There was no doubt of that. I parked the car just off the highway, and my wife and I walked the short distance to the shore. After snapping a few photos with her small camera, my wife went silently off to the car.

Alone on that quiet beach looking off in the direction from which we Marines had come so violently so long ago, I recalled not the amphibious tractor tilting precariously on the shattered coral, not the blast of cannon and mortars, not the crackle of rifle fire or the steady hammer of machine guns, but all the young men who had died that day and on the days of fierce battle that followed. I thought too of the friends I had lost in the jungle islands below the equator and of those who were killed later far to the north during the deadly struggles on Iwo and Okinawa. Those of us who had fought here thirty-four years before and all those other young men who had battled the Japanese from Guadalcanal to the very borders of Japan had been, almost all of us, amateurs who had learned a warrior's lesson in a hard and bitter school. We had learned and persevered, and we had won that right kind of war against a brave and relentless foe.

I heard a soft call. "Honey, time to go."

Slowly, silently, we drove north on Marine Drive, pulled in to the airport, turned in the car and key, and checked in for the long ride home.

The **Naval Institute Press** is the book-publishing arm of the U.S. Naval Institute, a private, nonprofit society for sea service professionals and others who share an interest in naval and maritime affairs. Established in 1873 at the U.S. Naval Academy in Annapolis, Maryland, where its offices remain, today the Naval Institute has more than 100,000 members worldwide.

Members of the Naval Institute receive the influential monthly magazine *Proceedings* and discounts on fine nautical prints and on ship and aircraft photos. They also have access to the transcripts of the Institute's Oral History Program and get discounted admission to any of the Institute-sponsored seminars offered around the country.

The Naval Institute also publishes *Naval History* magazine. This colorful quarterly is filled with entertaining and thought-provoking articles, first-person reminiscences, and dramatic art and photography. Members receive a discount on *Naval History* subscriptions.

The Naval Institute's book-publishing program, begun in 1898 with basic guides to naval practices, has broadened its scope in recent years to include books of more general interest. Now the Naval Institute Press publishes more than sixty titles each year, ranging from how-to books on boating and navigation to battle histories, biographies, ship and aircraft guides, and novels. Institute members receive discounts on the Press's nearly 400 books in print.

For a free catalog describing Naval Institute Press books currently available, and for further information about subscribing to Naval History magazine or about joining the U.S. Naval Institute, please write to:

Membership & Communications Department
U.S. Naval Institute
118 Maryland Avenue
Annapolis, Maryland 21402-5035

Or call, toll-free, (800) 233-USNI.

THE NAVAL INSTITUTE PRESS
THE RIGHT KIND OF WAR

Designed by Pamela Lewis Schnitter

Set in New Baskerville and Birch
by BG Composition
Baltimore, Maryland

Printed on 50-lb. antique
and bound in Holliston Kingston Natural and DSI Papan Raven
Homespun
by The Maple-Vail Book Manufacturing Group
York, Pennsylvania